THE LOST WORLDS OF 2001

Other books by the author

THE LOST WORLDS
OF 2001
Arthur C. Clarke

SIDGWICK & JACKSON LONDON

First published in Great Britain in 1972 by
Sidgwick and Jackson Limited
Copyright © 1972 by Arthur C. Clarke
'The Sentinel' copyright © by Arthur C. Clarke

Reprinted November 1972
Reprinted June 1973
A new edition December 1976
Reissued in this new edition September 1978
Reprinted March 1980
Originally published in the United States of America
by the New American Library Inc. in 1972

Printed in Great Britain by
Love & Malcomson Ltd.,
Brighton Road, Redhill, Surrey
for Sidgwick and Jackson Limited
1 Tavistock Chambers, Bloomsbury Way
London WC1A 2SG.

ISBN 0 283 98611 5

To Scott, who conceived this book,
and
Stanley, who inspired it

"Sorry to interrupt the festivities, but we have a problem."
(HAL 9000, during Frank Poole's birthday party)

"Houston, we've had a problem."
(Jack Swigert, shortly after playing the Zarathustra theme to his TV audience, aboard Apollo 13 Command Module Odyssey)

CONTENTS

FOREWORD

Behind every man now alive stand thirty ghosts, for that is the ratio by which the dead outnumber the living. Since the dawn of time, roughly a hundred billion human beings have walked the planet Earth.

So began the novel *2001: A Space Odyssey* when it was published in July 1968. But the first version, four years earlier, had started like this. . . .

1

VIEW FROM THE YEAR 2000

Between the first and last decades of the twentieth century lay a gulf greater than the wildest imagination could have conceived. It was the gulf between gunpowder and nuclear bomb, between messages tapped in Morse and global television from the sky, between Queen Victoria, Empress of India, and Kwame Chaka, Supreme President of the African Federation. But above all, it was the gulf between the first hundred-foot flight at Kitty Hawk, and the first billion-mile mission to the moons of Jupiter. All of these things, ages apart in terms of culture, lay within the span of that one incredible century.

The thunder of doom had barely ceased to roll above Eniwetok Atoll when the first Sputnik rose beeping into the sky. Across the constellations moved stars that no astronomers had seen before, and as the ancient dust of the Sea of Rains received the first emissary from Earth, the long loneliness of the Moon was ended forever.

Barely a moment later, as the universe counts time, Man followed his messengers into space. Project Apollo, dominating the '70's like a bloodless war, was to pass into history, with all its triumphs and tragedies. After that, nothing would ever again be the same. When men raised their eyes to the Moon, they would know that their comrades were looking down at them. And they would remember that there were some whom Earth could never reclaim, as it had gathered back all their ancestors since the beginning of time. These were the voyagers who had failed to reach their goals, but had won instead the immortality of space, and were beyond change or decay.

Before the '70's had ended, the first permanent colony had been established on the Moon. The cost of space travel had been slashed tenfold, and would be cut tenfold again with coming of nuclear power. The brief age of the rocket dinosaurs, each capable of but a single flight, was drawing to its close. Instead of the thousand-ton boosters whose bones now littered the Atlantic deeps, men were building far more efficient aerospace planes—giant rocket aircraft which could climb up to orbit with their cargoes, then return to Earth for another mission. Commercial space flight had not yet been achieved, but it was on the horizon.

Only a few percent of the Moon's millions of square miles had been thoroughly explored, and the detailed examination of its vast wilderness might take centuries yet. But no one believed that it held any more surprises; it was hostile but familiar territory, and the home of more than a thousand men. The real frontier was far away, in the cold night beyond the path of Mars, the searing day inside the orbit of Venus.

Herald of the dawn, star of evening, Venus had been the first bitter disappointment of the space age. Even after Mariner II had reported the furnace heat of the eternally hidden surface, there were some who had hoped that the instruments might be wrong. But now, too many probes had been lost in the howling hell of the Cytherean atmosphere for any optimism to remain. Venus was dead; perhaps one day men would bring her to life, but that would be in the far, far future, with the aid of technologies yet unborn.

There remained Mars, source of so much mystery and romance, perhaps the only other home of life in the Solar System. After heartbreaking failures, a TV scanner was landed on the planet, and the whole world peered from forty million miles away, through a single mobile eye rolling jerkily across the desolation of the misnamed Lake of the Sun.

No one who saw will ever forget that first encounter between Martian and machine. Undramatic, absolutely silent, it was one of the great moments of history. Advancing slowly on its broad balloon tires, its vision turret rotating continuously, the exploring robot moved with mindless purpose over a dry, dusty plain. It was on its own, beyond aid or advice from Earth. The scenes its makers were watching were already four minutes in the past: any orders they might send, though racing at the speed of light, could not reach Mars until as many in the future.

The plain was covered with large, spherical boulders, and the robot was rolling straight toward one. Its builders were not worried: the machine's obstacle-detecting skirt would warn it before there was danger of collision, and it would automatically turn off at a right angle. That was the theory: what happened was somewhat different.

Before the robot could reach it, the boulder moved. It heaved itself off the ground on a myriad stumpy legs, crawled slowly out of the track of the advancing explorer, and settled down again. As it plunged forward unaware of the consternation it was causing on Earth and Mars, the robot disturbed two more of the boulders: then it was through them, and encountered no others until, ten hours later, it became trapped in a canyon and continued to radio back maddeningly repetitious views of bare rock until its batteries failed.

But it had done its work; it had detected life on Mars— life, moreover, of a fairly advanced form Whether animal, vegetable, or neither, was a question that would not be answered for years—until the first expedition reached the planet in the mid-80's.

The early explorers knew that they would find life: they could only hope that they would find intelligence. But Mars has as much land area as Earth—for though it is a small world, it has no seas. Even to map the planet adequately would take decades; to learn all its secrets would be the work of centuries.

The main Martian life-forms—the "roving stones" browsing on the mineral deserts, the leechlike predators that hunted them in the desperate battle for existence, the yet fiercer parasites that preyed on *them*—showed only the dimmest flickers of intelligence. Nor was there any sign that these were the degenerate survivors of superior creatures· Mars, it appeared certain had never been the home of Mind. Yet there were still many who hoped that, somewhere in the endless crimson deserts, or beneath the frozen poles, or sealed in the eroded hills, there might yet be found the relics of civilizations that had flourished when the giant reptiles ruled the Earth. It was a romantic dream, and it would be slow to die.

Beyond Mars, there were greater worlds, and mightier problems. Enigmatic Jupiter, with a thousand times the bulk of Earth, teased the minds of men with its mysteries. Perhaps there was life far beneath those turbulent clouds of ammonia and methane, thriving in the hot darkness at pressures unmatched in the deepest terrestrial seas. If so, it would be as unreachable as another universe; for no ship yet imagined could fight its way down through that immense gravitational field, or withstand the forces that were raging in the Jovian atmosphere. Some robot probes had been launched on that fearful journey; none had survived.

One day, perhaps in the early years of the new century, there would be manned expeditions to the moons of Jupiter—to Io, Europa, Ganymede and Callisto, the beloved of the father of the gods, large enough to be called planets in their own right. But there was so much to do nearer home, with the buildup of the lunar colony and the establishment of a bridgehead on Mars, that the outer worlds must wait. Though there would be robot fly-by missions to all the giant planets, and even out into the comet-haunted darkness beyond Pluto, no men would travel on these lonely flights.

As for voyaging outside the Solar System, to the still-undiscovered planets of other stars, few scientists believed that it would ever be possible. At the best, interstellar travel was certainly a dream of the very distant future, of no practical concern during the first few centuries of space flight.

That was a very sensible, very reasonable prediction, repeated over and over again in the writings of the '70's and '80's. For who could possibly have guessed—

2

SON OF DR. STRANGELOVE

Who could, indeed?

Those words were written five years before the first men reached the Moon: now, ironically enough, it seems that, far from "dominating the '70's," Project Apollo has been dominated by them; it has shrunk pitifully from the original plan of ten lunar missions. But if we survive our present Time of Troubles, history will restore the correct perspective. An age may come when Project Apollo is the only thing by which most men remember the United States—or even the world of their ancestors, the distant planet Earth.

Yet when Stanley Kubrick wrote to me in the spring of 1964, saying that he wanted to make the "proverbial good science-fiction movie," the lunar landing still seemed, psychologically, a dream of the far future. Intellectually, we knew that it was inevitable; emotionally, we could not really believe it—as indeed, some foolish people do not believe it even now.

To put early 1964 in perspective: it was eleven months since an American astronaut (Gordon Cooper—Mercury 9) had been in space; the first two-man Gemini flight (Grissom and Young) would not take place for another year; and argument was still raging about the nature of the lunar surface, owing to the heartbreaking failure of Ranger VI's TV cameras fifteen minutes before impact.

Though there was great activity behind the scenes, and NASA was spending the entire budget of our movie (over $10,000,000) every *day,* space exploration seemed to be marking time. But the portents were clear; I often reminded Stanley—and myself—that the film would still be on its first run when men were actually walking on the

Moon. This turned out to be a considerable understatement; the Toronto release, for example, spanned Apollos 11, 12 *and* 13. . . .

Our main problem, therefore, was creating a story which would not be made obsolete—or even worse, ridiculous—by the events of the next few years. We had to outguess the future; one way of doing that was to be so far ahead of the present that there was no danger of facts overtaking us. On the other hand, if we got *too* far ahead there would be a grave risk of losing contact with our audience. Though MGM's motto has long been *Ars gratia artis*, it is no great secret that movie companies exist to make money. We had to aim for an audience of about a hundred million—give or take a million, as General Turgidson would say.

Even before I left Ceylon to join Stanley in April 1964, I had run through my published stories in search of a suitable starting point for a space epic. Almost at once, I settled upon a very short piece called The Sentinel, *written during the 1948 Christmas holiday for a BBC competition. (It wasn't placed, and I'd like to know what did win.) It is a story of the pioneering days of lunar exploration (1980+?); though it has been widely anthologized, and appears in my own collections* Expedition to Earth *and* The Nine Billion Names of God, *it is such an essential introduction to* 2001 *that I would like to repeat it here. Over, then, to* The Sentinel. . . .

3

THE SENTINEL

The next time you see the full moon high in the south, look carefully at its right-hand edge and let your eye travel upward along the curve of the disk. Round about two o'clock you will notice a small, dark oval: anyone with normal eyesight can find it quite easily. It is the great walled plain, one of the finest on the Moon, known as the Mare Crisium—the Sea of Crises. Three hundred miles in diameter, and almost completely surrounded by a ring of magnificent mountains, it had never been explored until we entered it in the late summer of 1996.

Our expedition was a large one. We had two heavy freighters which had flown our supplies and equipment from the main lunar base in the Mare Serenitatis, five hundred miles away. There were also three small rockets which were intended for short-range transport over regions which our surface vehicles couldn't cross. Luckily, most of the Mare Crisium is very flat. There are none of the great crevasses so common and so dangerous elsewhere, and very few craters or mountains of any size. As far as we could tell, our powerful caterpillar tractors would have no difficulty in taking us wherever we wished to go.

I was geologist—or selenologist, if you want to be pedantic—in charge of the group exploring the southern region of the Mare. We had crossed a hundred miles of it in a week, skirting the foothills of the mountains along the shore of what was once the ancient sea, some thousand million years before. When life was beginning on Earth, it was already dying here. The waters were retreating down the flanks of those stupendous cliffs, retreating into the empty heart of the Moon. Over the land which we were

19

crossing, the tideless ocean had once been half a mile deep, and now the only trace of moisture was the hoar-frost one could sometimes find in caves which the searing sunlight never penetrated.

We had begun our journey early in the slow lunar dawn, and still had almost a week of Earth time before nightfall. Half a dozen times a day we would leave our vehicle and go outside in the space suits to hunt for interesting minerals, or to place markers for the guidance of future travelers. It was an uneventful routine. There is nothing hazardous or even particularly exciting about lunar exploration. We could live comfortably for a month in our pressurized tractors, and if we ran into trouble we could always radio for help and sit tight until one of the spaceships came to our rescue.

I said just now that there was nothing exciting about lunar exploration, but of course that isn't true. One could never grow tired of those incredible mountains, so much more rugged than the gentle hills of Earth. We never knew, as we rounded the capes and promontories of that vanished sea, what new splendors would be revealed to us. The whole southern curve of the Mare Crisium is a vast delta where a score of rivers once found their way into the ocean, fed perhaps by the torrential rains that must have lashed the mountains in the brief volcanic age when the Moon was young. Each of these ancient valleys was an invitation, challenging us to climb into the unknown uplands beyond. But we had a hundred miles still to cover, and could only look longingly at the heights which others must scale.

We kept Earth time aboard the tractor, and precisely at 2200 hours the final radio message would be sent out to Base and we would close down for the day. Outside, the rocks would still be burning beneath the almost vertical sun, but to us it was night until we awoke again eight hours later. Then one of us would prepare breakfast, there would be a great buzzing of electric razors, and someone would switch on the short-wave radio from Earth. Indeed, when the smell of frying sausages began to fill the cabin, it was sometimes hard to believe that we were not back on our own world—everything was so normal and homely, apart from the feeling of decreased weight and the unnatural slowness with which objects fell.

It was my turn to prepare breakfast in the corner of the main cabin that served as a galley. I can remember that moment quite vividly after all these years, for the radio had just played one of my favorite melodies, the old Welsh air "David of the White Rock." Our driver was already outside in his space suit, inspecting our caterpillar treads. My assistant, Louis Garnett, was up forward in the control position, making some belated entries in yesterday's log.

As I stood by the frying pan waiting, like any terrestrial housewife, for the sausages to brown, I let my gaze wander idly over the mountain walls which covered the whole of the southern horizon, marching out of sight to east and west below the curve of the moon. They seemed only a mile or two from the tractor, but I knew that the nearest was twenty miles away. On the Moon, of course, there is no loss of detail with distance—none of that almost imperceptible haziness which softens and sometimes transfigures all far-off things on Earth.

Those mountains were ten thousand feet high, and they climbed steeply out of the plain as if ages ago some subterranean eruption had smashed them skyward through the molten crust. The base of even the nearest was hidden from sight by the steeply curving surface of the plain, for the Moon is a very little world, and from where I was standing the horizon was only two miles away.

I lifted my eyes toward the peaks which no man had ever climbed—the peaks which, before the coming of terrestrial life, had watched the retreating oceans sink sullenly into their graves, taking with them the hope and the morning promise of a world. The sunlight was beating against those ramparts with a glare that hurt the eyes, yet only a little way above them the stars were shining steadily in a sky blacker than a winter midnight on Earth.

I was turning away when my eye caught a metallic glitter high on the ridge of a great promontory thrusting out into the sea thirty miles to the west. It was a dimensionless point of light, as if a star had been clawed from the sky by one of those cruel peaks, and I imagined that some smooth rock surface was catching the sunlight and heliographing it straight into my eyes. Such things were not uncommon. When the moon is in her second quarter, observers on Earth can sometimes see the great ranges in the Oceanus Procellarum burning with a blue-white iridescence as the sunlight flashes from their slopes and leaps again from world to world. But I was curious to know what kind of rock could be shining so brightly up there, and I climbed into the observation turret and swung our four-inch telescope round to the west.

I could see just enough to tantalize me. Clear and sharp in the field of vision, the mountain peaks seemed only half a mile away, but whatever was catching the sunlight was still too small to be resolved. Yet it seemed to have an elusive symmetry, and the summit upon which it rested was curiously flat. I stared for a long time at that glittering enigma, straining my eyes into space, until presently a smell of burning from the galley told me that our breakfast sausages had made their quarter-million-mile journey in vain.

All that morning we argued our way across the Mare Crisium while the western mountains reared higher in the sky. Even when we were out prospecting in the space suits, the discussion would continue over the radio. It was absolutely certain, my companions argued, that there had never been any form of intelligent life on the Moon. The only living things that had ever existed there were a few primitive plants and their slightly less degenerate ancestors. I knew that as well as anyone, but there are times when a scientist must not be afraid to make a fool of himself.

"Listen," I said at last, "I'm going up there, if only for my own peace of mind. That mountain's less than twelve thousand feet high—that's only two thousand under Earth gravity—and I can make the trip in twenty hours at the outside. I've always wanted to go up into those hills, anyway, and this gives me an excellent excuse."

"If you don't break your neck," said Garnett, "you'll be the laughing stock of the expedition when we get back to Base. That mountain will probably be called Wilson's Folly from now on."

"I won't break my neck," I said firmly. "Who was the first man to climb Pico and Helicon?"

"But weren't you rather younger in those days?" asked Louis gently.

"That," I said with great dignity, "is as good a reason as any for going."

We went to bed early that night, after driving the tractor to within half a mile of the promontory. Garnett was coming with me in the morning; he was a good climber, and had often been with me on such exploits before. Our driver was only too glad to be left in charge of the machine.

At first sight, those cliffs seemed completely unscalable,

but to anyone with a good head for heights, climbing is easy on a world where all weights are only a sixth of their normal value. The real danger in lunar mountaineering lies in overconfidence; a six-hundred-foot drop on the moon can kill you just as thoroughly as a hundred-foot fall on Earth.

We made our first halt on a wide ledge about four thousand feet above the plain. Climbing had not been very difficult, but my limbs were stiff with the unaccustomed effort, and I was glad of the rest. We could still see the tractor as a tiny metal insect far down at the foot of the cliff, and we reported our progress to the driver before starting on the next ascent.

Inside our suits it was comfortably cool, for the refrigeration units were fighting the fierce sun and carrying away the body heat of our exertions. We seldom spoke to each other, except to pass climbing instructions and to discuss our best plan of ascent. I do not know what Garnett was thinking; probably that this was the craziest wild-goose chase he had ever embarked upon. I more than half agreed with him, but the joy of climbing, the knowledge that no man had ever gone this way before and the exhilaration of the steadily widening landscape gave me all the reward I needed.

I don't think I was particularly excited when I saw in front of us the wall of rock I had first inspected through the telescope from thirty miles away. It would level off about fifty feet above our heads, and there on the plateau would be the thing that had lured me over these barren wastes. It was, almost certainly, nothing more than a boulder splintered ages ago by a falling meteor, and with its cleavage planes still fresh and bright in this incorruptible, unchanging silence.

There were no handholds on the rock face, and we had to use a grapnel. My tired arms seemed to gain new strength as I swung the three-pronged metal anchor round my head and sent it sailing up toward the stars. The first time, it broke loose and came falling slowly back when we pulled the rope. On the third attempt, the prongs gripped firmly and our combined weights could not shift it.

Garnett looked at me anxiously. I could tell that he wanted to go first, but I smiled back at him through the glass of my helmet and shook my head. Slowly, taking my time, I began the final ascent.

Even with my space suit, I weighed only forty pounds here, so I pulled myself up hand over hand without

bothering to use my feet. At the rim I paused and waved
to my companion: then I scrambled over the edge and
stood upright, staring ahead of me.

You must understand that until this very moment I had
been almost completely convinced that there could be
nothing strange or unusual for me to find here. Almost,
but not quite; it was that haunting doubt that had driven
me forward Well, it was a doubt no longer, but the
haunting had scarcely begun.

I was standing on a plateau perhaps a hundred feet
across. It had once been smooth—too smooth to be natural—but falling meteors had pitted and scored its surface
through immeasurable eons. It had been leveled to support
a glittering roughly pyramidal structure, twice as high as
a man, that was set in the rock like a gigantic, many-
faceted jewel.

Probably no emotion at all filled my mind in those first
few seconds Then I felt a great lifting of my heart, and a
strange, inexpressible joy. For I loved the Moon, and now
I knew that the creeping moss of Aristarchus and Eratosthenes was not the only life she had brought forth in her
youth. The old discredited dream of the first explorers
was true. There had, after all, been a lunar civilization—
and I was the first to find it. That I had come perhaps a
hundred million years too late did not distress me; it was
enough to have come at all.

My mind was beginning to function normally, to analyze and to ask questions. Was this a building, a shrine—
or something for which my language had no name? If a
building. then why was it erected in so uniquely inaccessible a spot? I wondered if it might be a temple, and I
could picture the adepts of some strange priesthood calling
on their gods to preserve them as the life of the Moon
ebbed with the dying oceans—and calling on their gods in
vain.

I took a dozen steps forward to examine the thing more
closely, but some sense of caution kept me from going too
near. I knew a little archaeology, and tried to guess the
cultural level of the civilization that must have smoothed
this mountain and raised the glittering mirror surfaces that
still dazzled my eyes.

The Egyptians could have done it, I thought, if their
workmen had possessed whatever strange materials these
far more ancient architects had used. Because of the
thing's smallness, it did not occur to me that I might be
looking at the handiwork of a race more advanced than

my own. The idea that the moon had possessed intelligence at all was still almost too tremendous to grasp, and my pride would not let me take the final, humiliating plunge.

And then I noticed something that set the scalp crawling at the back of my neck—something so trivial and so innocent that many would never have noticed it at all. I have said that the plateau was scarred by meteors; it was also coated inches deep with the cosmic dust that is always filtering down upon the surface of any world where there are no winds to disturb it. Yet the dust and the meteor scratches ended quite abruptly in a wide circle enclosing the little pyramid, as though an invisible wall was protecting it from the ravages of time and the slow but ceaseless bombardment from space.

There was someone shouting in my earphones, and I realized that Garnett had been calling me for some time. I walked unsteadily to the edge of the cliff and signaled him to join me, not trusting myself to speak. Then I went back toward that circle in the dust. I picked up a fragment of splintered rock and tossed it gently toward the shining enigma If the pebble had vanished at that invisible barrier I should not have been surprised, but it seemed to hit a smooth, hemispherical surface and slide gently to the ground.

I knew then that I was looking at nothing that could be matched in the antiquity of my own race. This was not a building but a machine, protecting itself with forces that had challenged Eternity. Those forces, whatever they might be, were still operating, and perhaps I had already come too close. I thought of all the radiations man had trapped and tamed in the past century. For all I knew, I might be as irrevocably doomed as if I had stepped into the deadly, silent aura of an unshielded atomic pile.

I remember turning then toward Garnett, who had joined me and was now standing motionless at my side. He seemed quite oblivious to me, so I did not disturb him but walked to the edge of the cliff in an effort to marshal my thoughts. There below me lay the Mare Crisium—Sea of Crises, indeed—strange and weird to most men, but reassuringly familiar to me. I lifted my eyes toward the crescent Earth, lying in her cradle of stars, and I wondered what her clouds had covered when these unknown builders had finished their work. Was it the steaming jungle of the Carboniferous, the bleak shoreline over which the first amphibians must crawl to conquer the land—or, earlier still, the long loneliness before the coming of life?

Do not ask me why I did not guess the truth sooner—the truth that seems so obvious now. In the first excitement of my discovery, I had assumed without question that this crystalline apparition had been built by some race belonging to the Moon's remote past, but suddenly, and with overwhelming force, the belief came to me that it was as alien to the Moon as I myself.

In twenty years we had found no trace of life but a few degenerate plants. No lunar civilization, whatever its doom, could have left but a single token of its existence.

I looked at the shining pyramid again, and the more remote it seemed from anything that had to do with the Moon. And suddenly I felt myself shaking with a foolish, hysterical laughter, brought on by excitement and overexertion: for I had imagined that the little pyramid was speaking to me and was saying: "Sorry, I'm a stranger here myself."

It has taken us twenty years to crack that invisible shield and to reach the machine inside those crystal walls. What we could not understand, we broke at last with the savage might of atomic power, and now I have seen the fragments of the lovely, glittering thing I found up there on the mountain.

They are meaningless. The mechanisms—if indeed they are mechanisms—of the pyramid belong to a technology that lies far beyond our horizon, perhaps to the technology of paraphysical forces.

The mystery haunts us all the more now that the other planets have been reached and we know that only Earth has ever been the home of intelligent life in our Solar System. Nor could any lost civilization of our own world have built that machine, for the thickness of the meteoric dust on the plateau has enabled us to measure its age. It was set there upon its mountain before life had emerged from the seas of Earth.

When our world was half its present age, *something* from the stars swept through the Solar System, left this token of its passage, and went again upon its way. Until we destroyed it, that machine was still fulfilling the purpose of its builders; and as to that purpose, here is my guess.

Nearly a hundred thousand million stars are turning in the circle of the Milky Way, and long ago other races on the worlds of other suns must have scaled and passed the heights that we have reached. Think of such civilizations, far back in time against the fading afterglow of Creation, masters of a universe so young that life as yet had come to only a handful of worlds. Theirs would have been a loneliness we cannot imagine, the loneliness of gods looking out across infinity and finding none to share their thoughts.

They must have searched the star clusters as we have searched the planets. Everywhere there would be worlds, but they would be empty or peopled with crawling mindless things. Such was our own Earth, the smoke of the great volcanoes still staining the skies, when that first ship of the peoples of the dawn came sliding in from the abyss beyond Pluto. It passed the frozen outer worlds, knowing that life could play no part in their destinies. It came to rest among the inner planets, warming themselves around the fire of the sun and waiting for their stories to begin.

Those wanderers must have looked on Earth, circling safely in the narrow zone between fire and ice, and must have guessed that it was the favorite of the sun's children. Here, in the distant future, would be intelligence; but there were countless stars before them still, and they might never come this way again.

So they left a sentinel, one of millions they have scattered throughout the Universe, watching over all worlds with the promise of life. It was a beacon that down the ages has been patiently signaling the fact that no one had discovered it.

Perhaps you understand now why that crystal pyramid was set upon the Moon instead of on the Earth. Its builders were not concerned with races still struggling up from savagery. They would be interested in our civilization only if we proved our fitness to survive—by crossing space and so escaping from the Earth, our cradle. That is the challenge that all intelligent races must meet, sooner or later. It is a double challenge, for it depends in turn upon the conquest of atomic energy and the last choice between life and death.

Once we had passed that crisis, it was only a matter of time before we found the pyramid and forced it open. Now its signals have ceased, and those whose duty it is will be turning their minds upon Earth. Perhaps they wish to help our infant civilization. But they must be very, very old, and the old are often insanely jealous of the young.

I can never look now at the Milky Way without wondering from which of those banked clouds of stars the emissaries are coming. If you will pardon so commonplace a simile, we have set off the fire alarm and have nothing to do but to wait.

I do not think we will have to wait for long.

4

CHRISTMAS, SHEPPERTON

When I met Stanley Kubrick for the first time, in Trader Vic's on April 22, 1964, he had already absorbed an immense amount of science fact and science fiction, and was in some danger of believing in flying saucers; I felt I had arrived just in time to save him from this gruesome fate. Even from the beginning, he had a very clear idea of his ultimate goal, and was searching for the best way to approach it. He wanted to make a movie about Man's relation to the universe—something which had never been attempted, still less achieved, in the history of motion pictures.* Of course, there had been innumerable "space" movies, most of them trash. Even the few that had been made with some skill and accuracy had been rather simpleminded, concerned more with the schoolboy excitement of space flight than its profound implications to society, philosophy, and religion.

Stanley was fully aware of this, and he was determined to create a work of art which would arouse the emotions of wonder, awe . . . even, if appropriate, terror. How he set about it I have described elsewhere (see "Son of Dr. Strangelove: or How I Learned to Stop Worrying and love Stanley Kubrick"—reprinted in *Report on Planet Three*, Harper & Row). His success has been recorded or disputed in millions of spoken and written words, a fair sampling of which will be found in Jerry Agel's entertaining book *The Making of Kubrick's 2001* (New American

---

*I once accused my friends in MGM's publicity department of having a special labor-saving key on their typewriters which, when pressed, automatically began to print out: "Never, in the history of motion pictures . . . ."

Library). I am concerned here, however, not with the movie but with the novel, regarded as an independent and self-contained work—even though it was created specifically as the basis for the movie.

This, of course, is the reverse of the usual state of affairs. Most movies are adapted from already existing novels, preferably ones which have proved to be best sellers and so have a built-in box-office guarantee. (Good examples are *Gone with the Wind* and *Doctor Zhivago*.) Other movies are based on screenplays specifically written for them, and no novel version (or even—ugh!— "novelization") ever exists. All of Chaplin's films, *Citizen Kane*, and *Lawrence of Arabia* are in this category. They were conceived purely as movies from start to finish; the only thing that exists on paper is the screenplay and the subsequent shooting script.*

Some directors of genius have even managed to dispense with these. Though it seems incredible, David Wark Griffiths is supposed to have carried *Intolerance* entirely in his head. I think that Stanley would like to have done the same with *2001,* and would hesitate to say that, for him, it was theoretically impossible. But it was certainly impossible in practice—if only for the reason that he had to have a fairly complete treatment to show his backers. Banks and movie companies require more than a few notes on scraps of paper before they will disgorge their cherished millions.

Now a screenplay is not a work of art, though its production requires considerable skill. It bears somewhat the same relationship to a movie as the musical score does to a symphonic performance. There are people who can read a musical score and "hear" the symphony—but no two directors will see the same images when they read a movie script. The two-dimensional patterns of colored light involved are far more complex than the one-dimensional thread of sound—which can, in principle, be completely described on paper. A movie can never be pinned down in such a way, though the scriptwriter has to attempt this impossible feat. Unless the writer *is* the director, everything has to be specified in boring detail; no wonder that screenplays are almost as tedious to read as to

* The screenplay gives the dialogue, action, scenes, etc. in the order in which they will actually appear on the screen. But it would be absurd to film them in this order, so the shooting script groups together all the scenes involving the same locations, sets and actors.

write. John Fowles has put it very well: "Any novelist who has written scripts knows the appalling restrictions—obligatory detailing of the unnecessary—the cinema imposes. Writing a novel is like swimming in the sea: writing a film script is thrashing through treacle." ("Is the Novel Dead?"—*Books*, Autumn 1970).

Though I was only dimly aware of this in 1964, Stanley knew it very well. It was his suggestion that, before embarking on the drudgery of the script, we let our imaginations soar freely by developing the story in the form of a complete novel. Of course, to do this we would have to generate far more background than could ever be used in the final film. That wouldn't matter. Every good novelist "knows" much more than he writes down: every film maker should be aware of a larger universe than his script.

In theory, therefore, the novel would be written (with an eye on the screen) and the script would be derived from this. In practice, the result was far more complex; toward the end, both novel and screenplay were being written simultaneously, with feedback in both directions. Some parts of the novel had their final revisions after we had seen the rushes based on the screenplay based on earlier versions of the novel . . . and so on.

After a couple of years of this, I felt that when the novel finally appeared it should be "by Arthur Clarke and Stanley Kubrick; based on the screenplay by Stanley Kubrick and Arthur Clarke"—whereas the movie should have the credits reversed. This still seems the nearest approximation to the complicated truth.

After various false starts and twelve-hour talkathons, by early May 1964 Stanley agreed that "The Sentinel" would provide good story material. But our first concept—and it is hard now for me to focus on such an idea, though it would have been perfectly viable—involved working up to the discovery of an extraterrestrial artifact as the *climax*, not the beginning, of the story. Before that, we would have a series of incidents or adventures devoted to the exploration of the Moon and Planets. For this Mark I version, our private title (never of course intended for public use) was "How the Solar System Was Won."

So once more I went back to my stockpile of short stories, to find material which would fit into this pattern. I returned with five: "Breaking Strain" (from *Expedition to Earth*); "Out of the Cradle, Endlessly Orbiting . . .", "Who's There?", "Into the Comet", and "Before Eden" (all from *Tales of Ten Worlds*). On May 28, 1964, I sold the lot to Stanley and signed an agreement to work on the projected movie. Our initial schedule was hilariously optimistic: writing script, 12 weeks; discussing it, 2 weeks; revising, 4 weeks; fixing deal, 4 weeks; visuals, art, 20 weeks; shooting, 20 weeks; cutting, editing, 20 weeks—a total of 82 weeks. Allowing another 12 weeks before release, this added up to 92, or the better part of two years. I was very depressed by this staggering period of time, since I was (as always) in a hurry to get back to Ceylon; it was just as well that neither of us could have guessed the project's ultimate duration—*four* years. . . .

The rest of 1964 was spent brainstorming. As we developed new ideas, so the original conception slowly changed. "The Sentinel" became the opening, not the finale; and one by one, the other five short stories were discarded. A year later, deciding (not necessarily in this order) that (a) it wasn't fair to Stanley to make him pay for something he didn't need and (b) these stories might make a pretty good movie someday, I bought them back from him. . . .

The announced title of the project, when Stanley gave his intentions to the press, was *Journey Beyond the Stars*. I never liked this, because there had been far too many science-fictional journeys and voyages. (Indeed, the inner-space epic *Fantastic Voyage*, featuring Raquel Welch and a supporting cast of ten thousand blood corpuscles, was also going into production about this time.) Other titles which we ran up and failed to salute were *Universe*, *Tunnel to the Stars*, and *Planetfall*. It was not until eleven months after we started—April 1965—that Stanley selected *2001: A Space Odyssey*. As far as I can recall, it was entirely his idea.

Despite the unrelenting pressure of work (a mere twelve hours was practically a day off) I kept a detailed log of the whole operation. Though I do not wish to get bogged down in minutiae of interest only to fanatical Kubrickologists, perhaps these extracts may convey the flavor of those early days:—

May 28, 1964. Suggested to Stanley that "they" might be machines who regard organic life as a hideous disease. Stanley thinks this is cute and feels we've got something.

May 31. One hilarious idea we *won't* use. Seventeen aliens—featureless black pyramids—riding in open cars down Fifth Avenue, surrounded by Irish cops.

June 20. Finished the opening chapter, "View from the Year 2000," and started on the robot sequence.

July 1. Last day working at Time/Life completing *Man and Space*. Checked into new suite, 1008, at the Hotel Chelsea.

July 2-8. Averaging one or two thousand words a day. Stanley reads first five chapters and says "We've got a best seller here."

July 9. Spent much of afternoon teaching Stanley how to use the slide rule—he's fascinated.

July 11. Joined Stanley to discuss plot development, but spent almost all the time arguing about Cantor's Theory of Transfinite Groups. Stanley tries to refute the "part equals the whole" paradox by arguing that a perfect square is not necessarily identical with the integer of the same value. I decide that he is a latent mathematical genius.

July 12. Now have everything—except the plot.

July 13. Got to work again on the novel and made good progress despite the distraction of the Republican Convention.

July 26. Stanley's birthday. Went to the Village and found a card showing the Earth coming apart at the seams and bearing the inscription: "How can you have a Happy Birthday when the whole world may blow up any minute?"

July 28. Stanley: "What we want is a smashing theme of mythic grandeur."

August 1. Ranger VII impacts on moon. Stay up late to watch the first TV closeups. Stanley starts to worry about the forthcoming Mars probes. Suppose they show something that shoots down our story line? [Later, he approached Lloyd's of London to see if he could insure himself against this eventuality.]

August 6. Stanley suggests that we make the computer female and call her Athena.

August 17. We've also got the name of our hero at last—Alex Bowman. Hurrah!

August 19. Writing all day. Two thousand words exploring Jupiter's satellites. Dull work.

September 7. Stanley quite happy: "We're in fantastic shape." He has made up a 100-item questionnaire about our astronauts, e.g. do they sleep in their pajamas, what do they eat for breakfast, etc.

September 8. Upset stomach last night. Dreamed I was a robot, being rebuilt. In a great burst of energy managed to redo two chapters. Took them to Stanley, who was very pleased and cooked me a fine steak, remarking: "Joe Levine doesn't do this for *his* writers."

September 26. Stanley gave me Joseph Campbell's analysis of the myth *The Hero with a Thousand Faces* to study. Very stimulating.

September 29. Dreamed that shooting had started. Lots of actors standing around, but I still didn't know the story line.

October 2. Finished reading Robert Ardrey's *African Genesis*. Came across a striking paragraph which might even provide a title for the movie: "Why did not the human line become extinct in the depths of the Pliocene? . . . we know that but for a gift from the stars, but for the accidental collision of ray and gene, intelligence would have perished on some forgotten African field." True, Ardrey is talking about cosmic-ray mutations, but the phrase "A gift from the stars" is strikingly applicable to our present plot line.

October 6. Have got an idea which I think is crucial. The people we meet on the other star system are humans who were collected from Earth a hundred thousand years ago, and hence are virtually identical with us.

October 8. Thinking of plot all morning, but after a long walk in the sun we ended up on the East River watching the boats. We dumped all our far-fetched ideas—now we're settling for a Galactic Peace Corps and no blood and thunder.

October 17. Stanley has invented the wild idea of slightly fag robots who create a Victorian environment to put our heroes at their ease.

November 20. Went to Natural History Museum to see Dr. Harry Shapiro, head of Anthropology, who took a poor view of Ardrey. Then had a session with Stan, arguing about early man's vegetarian versus carnivorous tendencies. Stan wants our visitors to turn Man into a carnivore; I argued that he always was. Back at the Chelsea, phoned Ike Asimov to discuss the biochemistry of turning vegetarians into carnivores.

November 21. Read Leakey's *Adam's Ancestors*. Getting rather desperate now, but after six hours' discussion Stan had a rather amusing idea. Our E. T.'s arrive on Earth and teach commando tactics to our pacifistic ancestors so that they can survive and flourish. We had an entertaining time knocking this one around, but I don't think it's viable.

November 22. Called Stan and said I didn't think *any* of our flashback ideas were any good. He slowly talked me out of this mood, and I was feeling more cheerful when I suddenly said: "What if our E. T.'s are stranded on Earth and need the ape-men to help them?" This idea (probably not original, but what the hell) opened up whole new areas of plot which we are both exploring.

November 23. Stanley distracted by numerous consultations with his broker, and wants my advice on buying COMSAT.

December 10. Stanley calls after screening H. G. Wells' *Things to Come,* and says he'll *never* see another movie I recommend.

December 21. Much of afternoon spent by Stanley planning his Academy Award campaign for *Dr. Strangelove.* I get back to the Chelsea to find a note from Allen Ginsberg asking me to join him and William Burroughs at the bar downstairs. Do so thankfully in search of inspiration.

December 24. Slowly tinkered with the final pages, so I can have them as a Christmas present for Stanley.

December 25. Stanley delighted with the last chapters, and convinced that we've extended the range of science fiction. He's astonished and delighted because Bosley Crowther of the New York *Times* has placed *Dr. S* on the "Ten Best Films" list, after attacking it ferociously all year. I christen Bosley "The Critic Who Came In from the Cold."

From these notes, it would appear that by Christmas 1964, the novel was essentially complete, and that thereafter it would be a fairly straightforward matter to develop the screenplay. We were, indeed, under that delusion—at least, *I* was. In reality, all that we had was merely a rough draft of the first two-thirds of the book, stopping at the most exciting point. We had managed to get Bowman into the Star Gate, but didn't know what would happen next, except in the most general way. Nevertheless, the existing manuscript, together with his own salesmanship, allowed

Stanley to set up the deal with MGM and Cinerama, and "Journey Beyond the Stars" was announced with a flourish of trumpets.

Through the spring of 1965, we continued to revise and extend the novel, and threw away—again and yet again—whole sections which we had once imagined to be final and complete. All this time, Stanley was also hiring staff, checking designs, negotiating with actors and technicians, and coping with the millions of other problems which arise in the production of even the most straightforward movie. The rush of events became far too hectic to enter more than a small fraction of them in my log, and few of them (luckily) concerned me directly. My primary job was still polishing the novel, though I was constantly involved in technical discussions with the artists and production staff. (Sometimes with disastrous results; see entry for November 10, below.)

February 9, 1965. Caught Dali on TV, painting in a Fifth Avenue store window to promote *Fantastic Voyage*. Reported this to Stanley, who replied: "Don't worry—we've already reserved a window for you."

March 8. Fighting hard to stop Stan from bringing Dr. Poole back from the dead. I'm afraid his obsession with immortality has overcome his artistic instincts.

April 6. To COMSAT Headquarters, Washington, for launch of first commercial communications satellite, "Early Bird." Introduced to Vice-President Humphrey, who is also Chairman of the Space Council, and told him we were spending ten million dollars to publicize space. Added that one character in the movie would be the Chairman of the Space Council . . . thirty years from now. "Oh," said H. H. H. at once, "I still intend to be chairman then."

April 12. Much excitement when Stanley phones to say that the Russians claim to have detected radio signals from space. Rang Walter Sullivan at the New York *Times* and got the real story—merely fluctuations in Quasar CTA 102.

April 14. Reception at Harcourt, Brace and World. Those present included Bill Jovanovich (president), Jeremy Bernstein (*New Yorker* Magazine), Dennis Flanagan (*Scientific American*), Dr. Robert Jastrow (Goddard Space Center), Stanley and Christiane Kubrick, Al Rosenfeld (Science Editor, *Life*), Sylvester (Pat) Weaver, Scott Meredith and many other friends. There was a general belief that the party was to celebrate Harcourt's publication of *Journey Beyond the Stars*, but I explained that this was not definite, and depended upon the size of the mortgage they could raise on the building.

April 19. Went up to the office with about three thousand words Stanley hasn't read. The place is really humming now—about ten people working there, including two production staff from England. The walls are getting covered with impressive pictures and I already feel quite a minor cog in the works.

Some psychotic who insists that Stanley *must* hire him has been sitting on a park bench outside the office for a couple of weeks, and occasionally comes to the building. In self-defense, Stan has secreted a large hunting knife in his briefcase.

May 1. Found that a fire had broken out on the third floor of the Chelsea. Waited anxiously in the lobby while the firemen dealt with it . . . visions of the only complete copy of the MS going up in smoke. . . .

May 2. Completed the "Universe" chapter—will soon have all Part Three ready for typing, hurrah. . . . Stan phoned to say he liked the "Floating Island" sequence. Strange and encouraging how much of the material I thought I'd abandoned fits in perfectly after all.

May 3. Finished first draft of the runaway antenna sequence.

May 25. Now Stanley wants to incorporate the Devil theme from *Childhood's End*. . . .

June 7. Bad book review in *Tribune*—says I should stick to science exposition and am an amateur at fiction.

Late June. Read Victor Lyndon's production notes; they left me completely overwhelmed. Glad that's not *my* job. One scene calls for four trained warthogs.

On that note, more or less, I returned to Ceylon after an absence of over a year, and subsequently rejoined Stanley at the MGM studios at Boreham Wood, fifteen miles north of London, in August. His empire had now expanded vastly, the art department was in full swing, and impressive sets were being constructed. My time was now equally divided between the apparently never-ending chore of developing ideas with Stanley, polishing the novel, and almost daily consultations at the studio.

August 25. Suddenly realized how the novel *should* end, with Bowman standing beside the alien ship.

September 25. Visitors from NASA—Dr. George Mueller, Associate Administrator, and "Deke" Slayton (Director of Flight Crew Operations). Gave them the Grand Tour—they were quite impressed. George made several useful suggestions and asked wistfully if he could have the model of *Discovery* for his office when we'd finished with it. Deke was later reported to have said: "Stanley, I'm afraid you've been conned by a used capsule salesman." An improbable story—I suspect the fine Italian hand of Roger Caras, Stanley's vice-president i/c promotion.

October 1. Stanley phoned with *another* ending. I find I left *his* treatment at his house last night—unconscious rejection?

October 3. Stanley on phone, worried about ending . . . gave him my latest ideas, and one of them suddenly clicked—Bowman will regress to infancy, and we'll see him at the end as a baby in orbit. Stanley called again later, still very enthusiastic. Hope this isn't a false optimism: I feel cautiously encouraged myself.

October 5. Back to brood over the novel. Suddenly (I think!) found a logical reason why Bowman should appear at the end as a baby. It's his image of himself at this stage of his development. And perhaps the Cosmic Consciousness has a sense of humor. Phoned these ideas to Stan, who wasn't too impressed, but I'm happy now.

October 15. Stan has decided to kill off *all* the crew of *Discovery* and leave Bowman only. Drastic, but it seems right. After all, Odysseus was the sole survivor. . . .

October 17. For the first time, saw Stan reduced to helpless hysterics as we developed comic ideas. There will be *no one* in the hibernacula—all the trainees chickened out, but the mission had to go ahead regardless.

October 19. Collected by studio car, and spent all day working (or trying to work) with Stan. Despite usual crowds of people getting at him, long phone calls to Hollywood, and a "work-to-rule" the unions called, got a lot done and solved (*again!*) our main plot problems.

October 26. Had a discussion with Stanley over his latest idea—that *Discovery* should be nuclear-pulse-driven. Read a recently declassified report on this and was quite impressed—but the design staff rather upset.

November 10. Accompanied Stan and the design staff into the Earth-orbit ship and happened to remark that the cockpit looked like a Chinese restaurant. Stan said that killed it instantly for him and called for revisions. Must keep away from the Art Department for a few days.

November 16. Long session with Stanley discussing script. Several good ideas, but I rather wish we didn't have any more.

November 18. Feeling rather stale—went into London and saw Carol Reed's film about Michelangelo, *The Agony and the Ecstasy*. One line particularly struck me—the use of the phrase "God made Man in His own image." This, after all, is the theme of our movie.

November 30. To the Oxford and Cambridge Club with Roger Caras and Fred Ordway (Technical Adviser) to meet Dr. Louis Leakey and his son Richard. Dr. Leakey is just as I imagined him—full of enthusiasm and ideas. He thinks that Man now goes back at least four to five million years. He also confided to me that he'd written a play—a fantasy about primitive man which he thought would make a fine movie. It's about a group of anthropologists who are sent back into the past by a witch doctor. I said (breaking all my rules) that I'd be glad to see the MS—which is true.

December 16. My 48th birthday—and Somerset Maugham dies. Trying to make something of this (last of the competition?).

December 25. Christmas Day, ha-ha! Hacked my way to Jupiter—slow but steady going.

December 26. Working all day. Stan phoned to thank me for the presents and sent a driver to collect what I'd written. He called later to say that he didn't think much of the dialogue. I agreed.

That Christmas of 1965 we were really under the gun, and no one had a holiday. Stanley was up against an unbreakable deadline. The enormous set of the TMA 1 excavation, containing the monolith found on the Moon, had been constructed at the Shepperton Studios, in South West London—and it had to be torn down by the first week of the New Year, so that another production could move in. Stanley had only a week to do all his shooting, for the second crucial encounter between Man and Monolith.

It was not until several years later that I remembered another association between Shepperton and space. If you

turn to H. G. Wells' masterpiece *The War of the Worlds*
you will discover Chapter 12:—"What I saw of the Destruction of Weybridge and Shepperton." This first of all
descriptions of armored warfare is still quite terrifying to
read:

> The decapitated colossus reeled like a drunken giant;
> but it did not fall over. It recovered its balance by a
> miracle, and, no longer heeding its steps and with the
> camera that fired the Heat-Ray now rigidly upheld, it
> reeled swiftly upon Shepperton. The living intelligence,
> the Martian within the hood, was slain and splashed to the
> four winds of heaven, and the thing was now but a mere
> intricate device of metal whirling to destruction. It drove
> along in a straight line, incapable of guidance. It struck
> the tower of Shepperton Church, smashing it down as
> the impact of a battering ram might have done, swerved
> aside, blundered on, and collapsed with tremendous force
> into the river out of my sight.
> A violent explosion shook the air, and a spout of water,
> steam, mud and shattered metal shot far up into the sky.
> As the camera of the Heat-Ray hit the water, the latter
> had immediately flashed into steam. In another moment
> a huge wave, like a muddy tidal bore but almost scald-
> ingly hot, came sweeping round the bend. . . .

Of course, now we have the heat ray, and we can do a
lot better than Wells' feeble Martians with a small tactical
atomic bomb. Still, it's not at all bad—for 1898. . . .

5

MONOLITHS AND MANUSCRIPTS

I still have the call sheet for that first day's work at Shepperton on a freezing December 29, 1965. For sentimental reasons—and because it is surely of interest even to the benighted inhabitants of that limbo once called (by one of Hollywood's lady dragons) the "non-celluloid world"—I would like to reproduce it here. There are few better ways of conveying the behind-the-scenes work that went into every frame of the movie.

My diary records that first day in some detail:

December 29, 1965. The TMA 1 set is huge—the stage is the second largest in Europe, and very impressive. A 150 x 50 x 20-foot hole, with equipment scattered around it. (E.g. neat little electric-powered excavators, bulldozers, etc. which could *really* work on the Moon!) About a hundred technicians were milling around. I spent some time with Stanley, reworking the script—in fact we continued through lunch together. I also met the actors, and felt quite the proper expert when they started asking me astronomical questions. I stayed until 4 p.m.—no actual shooting by then, but they were getting near it. The spacesuits, back-packs, etc. are beautifully done, and TMA 1 is quite impressive—though someone had smeared the black finish and Stanley went on a rampage when I pointed it out to him.

The jet-black slab of the monolith was, of course, an extraordinarily difficult object to light and photograph—and the scene would certainly have been wrecked if naked fingerprints had appeared on the ebon surface, even *before*

FIRST DAY OF SHOOTING

HAWK FILMS LTD   AMENDED

CALL SHEET   No. 4 (a)

PRODUCTION "2001: A Space Odyssey"   DATE   Wednesday
29th December '65

UNIT CALL 8:30 A.M.   Where Working: Shepperton—STAGE H.
TMA-1 EXCAVATION SITE

ARTISTE	CHARACTER	PORTABLE DRESSING ROOM	Make-up	Ready on set
WILLIAM SYLVESTER	FLOYD	3 (OH29)	7:45	9:00
ROBERT BEATTY	HALVORSEN	6 (OH46)	8:00	9:00
SEAN SULLIVAN	MICHAELS	10 (OH24)	8:00	9:00
BURNELL TUCKER	PHOTOGRAPHER	2 (OH25)	7:45	9:00
JOHN SWINDELL	1ST TECHNICIAN	1 (OH25)	7:30	9:00
JOHN CLIFFORD	2ND TECHNICIAN	1 (OH25)	7:30	9:00
STANDINS:				
JOHN FRANCIS	for Mr. Sullivan		8:00	8:30
EDDIE MILBURN	for Mr. Beatty		8:00	8:30
GERRY JUDGE	for Mr. Sylvester		8:00	8:30
BRIAN CHUTER	for Mr. Tucker		8:00	8:30
TOM SHEPPARD	for Mr. Swindell		8:00	8:30
ROBIN DAWSON-WHISKER	for Mr. Clifford		8:00	8:30

SOUND

(1) P. A. System required from 8:30 a.m.
(2) 2 Loud hailers required from 8:30 a.m.

WARDROBE

(1) Coveralls for all Artistes.
(2) White overalls and crash helmets for Standins.
(3) Floyd's suit for Sc. C150.

42

PRACTICAL ELECTRICIANS

(1) Heating on Stage H, portable dressing rooms, huts and offices from 7:30 a.m.
(2) On no account should the heating in the Camera Room be switched off over the Christmas period.

CATERING

(1) Breaks in the Tea Hut at 10:00 a.m. and 3:30 p.m. please.
(2) Urns of Bovril and Coffee to be ready for collection at 8:30 a.m. and a constant refill supply to be available please.

PROPS

(1) As per script to include Photographer's camera and equipment.
(2) Please collect the Bovril and Coffee from the Canteen at 8:00 a.m. and thereafter maintain the supply.
(3) Provide litter bins and large ashtrays for set.
(4) Standby with repeat air bottles for space suits.

N.B. TO ALL CONCERNED:

(1) In an effort to keep the Stage reasonably warm at all times, will members of the Unit please ensure that the Stage doors are kept shut. If it becomes necessary at any time to open the doors, please advise the Assistant Director.
(2) Please keep the set free of litter and use the bins provided.

SCENE NUMBERS:

B42 B38 B44 B46
TV MONITOR MATERIAL FOR SC. NOS. B45 & C151
STANDBY SC. C150

STANDBY SET:

INT. FLOYD'S RECORDED BRIEFING: SC. NO. C150—STAGE K

WILLIAM SYLVESTER	FLOYD	From above.

TRANSPORT:	Camera, Sound, Prop and Wardrobe vehicles as arranged by departments. Unit Coach will leave M-G-M Studios at 7:05 a.m. sharp.	
LUNCH:	12:45—1:45 p.m.	DEREK CRACKNELL
RUSHES:	THEATRE 4—12:45 p.m.	ASSISTANT DIRECTOR

it had been touched by the gloved hands of the astronauts. (Five years later, in the Smithsonian, I was able to flex my own fingers inside the very glove which had first made contact with the surface of the Moon.)

The famous monolith, which has caused so much controversy and bafflement, was itself the end product of a considerable evolution. In the beginning, the alien artifact had been a black tetrahedron—the simplest and most fundamental of all regular solids, formed of four equal triangles. It was a shape which inspired all sorts of philosophical and scientific speculations (Kepler's cosmography, the carbon atom, Buckminster Fuller's geodesic structures . . .), and the art department constructed models of various sizes which were set in African and lunar landscapes. But somehow, they never looked right, and there was also the danger that they would arouse wholly irrelevant associations with the pyramids.

For a while, Stanley considered using a transparent cube, but it proved impossible to make one of the required size. So he settled on the rectangular shape, and obtained a three-ton block of lucite—the largest ever cast. Unfortunately, that also looked unconvincing, so it was banished to a corner of the studio and a completely black slab of the same dimensions was substituted. I frantically followed—and occasionally anticipated—all these changes on my typewriter, but must admit that I had a considerably easier job than the Props Department.

Despite such problems as birds (or were they bats?) invading the gigantic stage and flying across the lunar landscape, Stanley completed shooting before the one-week deadline. The monolith was carefully wrapped in cotton wool, and stored in a safe place until it would be needed again—a year or so later, for the confrontation in the final hotel-room sequence. The unit went back to the Borehamwood studios, and I continued to beat out my brains. . . .

January 7, 1966. Realized last night that the Star Gate had to be Iapetus with its six-to-one brightness ratio. Got off a memo to Stan about that.

January 8. Record day—three thousand words, including some of the most exciting in the book. I got quite scared when the computer started going nuts, being alone in the house with my electric typewriter. . . .

January 14. Completed the Inferno chapter and have got Bowman into the hotel room. Now to get him out of it.

January 16. Long talk with Stan and managed to resolve most of the outstanding plot points. Got straight to work and by the time I staggered to bed stupefied had at last almost completed the first draft of the final sequence. Now I really feel the end's in sight—but I've felt *that* twice before.

January 17. About midday got a first draft of the last chapters completed. Have had a headache ever since and my brain's still spinning around. Too exhausted to feel much pleasure—only relief. Trying to unwind all day; luckily I'm off to the studio tomorrow, which will be a break.

January 18. Lord Snowdon on the set, shooting Stanley from all angles for *Life*.

January 19. Stanley phoned to say that he was very happy with the last chapters and feels that the story is now "rock-hard." Delighted, I tried to pin him down at once to agree that the existing version could be typed and sent off to our agent.

February 2. Spent all day with Stan—developed a few new ideas but of course there are endless interruptions, e.g. Gary Lockwood and Keir Dullea with makeup tests (we want them to look thirty-five-ish). I have a sore throat and incipient cold, so Stan kept me at arm's length.

February 4. Saw a screening of a demonstration film in which Stan has spliced together a few scenes to give the studio heads some idea of what's going on. He'd used Mendelssohn's *Midsummer Night's Dream* for the weightless scenes, and Vaughan Williams' *Antarctica Symphony* for the lunar sequence and the Star Gate special effects, with stunning results. I reeled out convinced that we have a masterpiece on our hands—if Stan can keep it up.

A few days after this, I escaped to Ceylon. But not for long:

March 15. Cable from Stan asking for "three minutes of poetic Clarkian narration" about HAL's breakdown. Got it off to him by express in the afternoon. [It was never used. . . .] Also started on the $(last)^n$ revision, and made good progress.

March 20. Worked hard on the novel all day, and by 9 p.m. had completed the messy final draft (what, again!).

April 2. Inserted a couple of hundred final (?) words into the MS, and tucked it away. As far as I'm concerned, it's finished.

Alas, it wasn't. A couple of days later I flew from Ceylon to Lawrence, Kansas, for the centennial celebrations of the University of Kansas. I cabled Stanley to say that I was heading back to London to make final arrangements for the publication of the novel. He replied "Don't bother—it's not ready yet." I retorted that I was coming anyway, and did:

April 19. First full day back at studio—saw shooting in the centrifuge. A portentous spectacle, accompanied by terrifying noises and popping lamp bulbs. Stanley came in during a shooting break and himself raised the subject of publication date. On being challenged, he swore that he didn't want to hold up the novel until release of the movie. He explained that general release would not be until late in 1967 or even 1968. Even if the first showing is in April 1967 [It was actually April 1968] it will be running only in a few Cinerama houses, which will give us some more breathing space.

April 23. Drove with Roger Caras and Mike Wilson to an excellent private zoo near Nuneaton, which had all the big apes. Mike had a very hard time filming the chimps, who kept dashing around and throwing themselves at the camera. I was a bit nervous of the baby gorilla, as it was inclined to nibble with most impressive teeth. . . . An enjoyable day, and I hope it's given me some ideas about Moon-Watcher and Co.

May 29. Soviet Air Attaché visited set. He looked at all the little instruction plaques on the spaceship panels and said, with a straight face, "You realize, of course, that these should all be in Russian."

At the end of May I flew back to the United States to assist with general promotion on the movie, and did my best to placate the anxious executives of MGM when they asked, "What *is* Stanley up to?" I also paid my first visit to Cape Kennedy, in a very small VIP guided tour conducted by James Webb, the NASA Administrator, to watch the launch of Gemini IX. Like every visitor, I was overwhelmed by the Vehicle Assembly Building and that land-going ship, the 3,000-ton crawler-transporter, with its maximum speed (unloaded) of two miles an hour. I recall watching Representative George Miller, Chairman of the House Committee on Astronautics, as he tried out the controls of the crawler—and warning him not to exceed the speed limit, because Chief Justice Warren was standing right behind him.

Unfortunately, the Atlas-Agena target vehicle, with which Gemini IX was supposed to rendezvous, failed to go into orbit, and so the manned launch was canceled. I admired Administrator Webb's resilience as he took this in his stride and promptly turned to Congressman Miller with the remark, "I'm afraid I'll have to go back to your committee for more money."

The next month, I was once again in London, still trying to convince Stanley that the novel was finished and the MS could go out to market. During one of my more frantic arguments, he remarked, "Things are never as bad as they seem," but I was in no mood to agree.

Stanley's attitude was that he wanted to do some more work on the manuscript, and simply didn't have time because of the overwhelming pressure at the studio. (It *was* overwhelming, and I was continually awed by Stanley's ability to cope with a dozen simultaneous and interlocking crises, any one of which could cost half a million dollars. No wonder he is fascinated by Napoleon. . . .) But I maintained that *I* was the writer and he should rely on my judgment; what would he say if I wanted to edit the film?

In the end we decided on a compromise—Stanley's. He would attempt during odd moments in the bathroom, or while being ferried home in his Rolls-Royce at the maximum permitted speed of 30 m.p.h., to note down the improvements he wanted me to make. On this basis, Scott Meredith was finally able to draw up an excellent contract with Delacorte Press.

Stanley was as good as his word. I still have a nine-page memorandum of thirty-seven paragraphs, dated June 18, 1966, containing some very acute, and occasionally acerbic, observations:

1. Can you use the word "veldt" in a drought-stricken area?
6. Where do you find bees in a drought-stricken area? What do the bees live on?
9. Do leopards growl?
11. Can a leopard carry a man?

14. Since the book will be coming out before the picture [sic!] I don't see why we shouldn't put something in the book that would be preferable if it were achievable in the film. I wish the block had been crystal-clear but it was impossible to make. I would like to have the block black in the novel.

15. I don't think the verb "twittering" seems right. We must decide how these fellows talk.

19. This reference sounds a little bit like a scene from *Bambi*.

22. The literal description of these tests seems completely wrong to me. It takes away all the magic.

24. This scene has always seemed unreal to me and somewhat inconceivable. They will be saved from starvation but they will never become gorged, sleek, glossy-pelted, and content. This has barely happened in 1966. I think that one day the cube should disappear and that Moon-Watcher and his boys passing a large elephant's skeleton which they have seen many times before on the way to forage are suddenly drawn to these bones and begin moving them and swinging them, and that this whole scene is given some magical enchantment both in the writing and then ultimately in the filming, and that from this scene they approach the grazing animals which they usually share fodder with and kill one, etc.

27. I don't understand the meaning of this.

33. I prefer the previous version. . . . The expression "moons waxed and waned" seems terribly cliché. The expression "toothless thirty-year-olds died" also is a bit awful.

37. I think this is a very bad chapter and should not be in the book. It is pedantic, undramatic and destroys the beautiful transition from man-ape to 2001.

Lest these extracts give a false impression, I should also add that the memorandum contained several highly flattering comments which modesty has forced me to omit. In fact, Stanley sometimes overdid this. He would build up my morale (which often needed it) by unstinted praise of some piece of writing I'd just produced; then, in the course of the next few days, he would find more and more flaws until the whole thing was slowly whittled away. This was all part of his ceaseless search for perfection, which often provoked me to remind him of the aphorism, "No work of art is ever finished; it is only abandoned."

I am afraid I was prepared to abandon ship before he was; but I admired him for his tenacity, even when I wished it was not focused upon me.

Matters came to a climax in the summer of 1966, and I find this pathetic entry in my log:

> July 19. Almost all memory of the weeks of work at the Hotel Chelsea seems to have been obliterated, and there are versions of the book that I can hardly remember. I've lost count (fortunately) of the revisions and blind alleys. It's all rather depressing—I only hope the ultimate result is worth it.

The reason for this gloom was understandable. Stanley had refused to sign the contract—after Delacorte had set the book in type and taken an impressive two-page advertisement in *Publisher's Weekly*. He still argued that he wasn't satisfied with the manuscript and wanted to do some more work on it. I considered writing to Dr. Leakey to get the name of a good witchdoctor, and Scott Meredith bought some pins and wax. Delacorte and Co., fighting back corporate tears, broke up the type. I have always felt extremely grateful to them for their forbearance in this difficult matter, and am happy to have given them a modest best seller in *Time Probe*.

It was just as well that no one dreamed that another two years would pass before the book was finally published, by New American Library in the summer of 1968 —months after the release of the movie. In the long run, everything came out all right—exactly as Stanley had predicted.

But I can think of easier ways of earning a living.

6

THE DAWN OF MAN

During November 1950 I wrote a short story about a meeting in the remote past between visitors from space and a primitive ape-man. An editor at Ballantine Books gave it the ingenious title "Expedition to Earth" when it was published in the book of that name, but I prefer "Encounter in the Dawn." However, when Harcourt, Brace and World brought out my own selection of favorites, *The Nine Billion Names of God*, it was mysteriously changed to "Encounter at Dawn." There the matter rests at present.

Though "Encounter" was not one of the half-dozen stories originally purchased by Stanley, it greatly influenced my thinking during the early stages of our enterprise. At that time—and indeed until very much later—we assumed that we would actually show some type of extraterrestrial entity, probably not too far from the human pattern. Even this presented frightful problems of make-up and credibility.

The make-up problems could be solved—as Stuart Freeborn later showed with his brilliant work on the ape-men. (To my fury, at the 1969 Academy Awards a special Oscar was presented for make-up—to *Planet of the Apes*! I wondered, as loudly as possible, whether the judges had passed over *2001* because they thought we used *real* apes.) The problem of credibility might be much greater, for there was danger that the result might look like yet another monster movie. After a great deal of experimenting the whole issue was sidestepped, both in the movie and the novel, and there is no doubt that this was the correct solution.

But before we arrived at it, it seemed reasonable to

show an actual meeting between ape-men and aliens, and to give far more details of that encounter in the Pleistocene, three million years ago. The chapters that follow were our first straightforward attempt to show how ape-men *might* be trained, with patience, to improve their way of life.

It was part of Stanley's genius that he spotted what was missing in this approach. It was too simpleminded; worse than that, it lacked the magic he was seeking, as he explained in item 24 of his memorandum, quoted earlier.

In the novel, we were finally able to get the effect we wanted by cutting out the details and introducing the super-teaching machine, the monolith—which, even more important, provided the essential linking theme between the different sections of the story. In the film, Stanley was able to produce a far more intense emotional effect by the brilliant use of slow-motion photography, extreme close-ups, and Richard Strauss's *Zarathustra*. That frozen moment at the beginning of history, when Moon-Watcher, foreshadowing Cain, first picks up the bone and studies it thoughtfully, before waving it to and fro with mounting excitement, never fails to bring tears to my eyes.

And it hit me hardest of all when I was sitting behind U Thant and Dr. Ralph Bunche in the Dag Hammarskjold Theater, watching a screening which we had arranged at the Secretary General's request. *This*, I suddenly realized, is where all the trouble started—and this very building is where we are trying to stop it. Simultaneously, I was struck by the astonishing parallel between the shape of the monolith and the UN Headquarters itself; there seemed something quite uncanny about the coincidence. If it is one. . . .

The skull-smashing sequence was the only scene *not* filmed in the studio; it was shot in a field, a couple of hundred yards away—the only time Stanley went on location. A small platform had been set up, and Moon-Watcher (Dan Richter) was sitting on this, surrounded by bones. Cars and buses were going by at the end of the field, but as this was a low-angle shot against the sky they didn't get in the way—though Stanley did have to pause for an occasional airplane.

The shot was repeated so many times, and Dan smashed so many bones, that I was afraid we were going to run out of wart-hog (or tapir) skulls. But eventually Stanley was satisfied, and as we walked back to the studio he began to throw bones up in the air. At first I thought this was sheer *joi de vivre*, but then he started to film them with a hand-held camera—no easy task. Once or twice, one of the large, swiftly descending bones nearly impacted on Stanley as he peered through the viewfinder; if luck had been against us the whole project might have ended then. To misquote Ardrey (page 34), "That intelligence would have perished on some forgotten Elstree field."

When he had finished filming the bones whirling against the sky, Stanley resumed the walk back to the studio; but now he had got hold of a broom, and started tossing *that* up into the air. Once again, I assumed this exercise was pure fun; and perhaps it was. But that was the genesis of the longest flash-forward in the history of movies—three million years, from bone club to artificial satellite, in a twenty-fourth of a second.

[At one time we had intended not a flash-forward but a flash*back;* I had quite forgotten this, until I noticed that the four chapters that follow were originally numbered 35 to 38. It seems more logical, and certainly less confusing, to reproduce them here, so giving this book the same structure as the novel—and the movie.]

7

FIRST ENCOUNTER

The glaciers had retreated now, and the shapes of the continents were much as Man would know them, when he made his first maps three millions years hence. There were, of course, minor differences; the British Isles still formed part of Europe, and the causeway between Asia and America had not yet crumbled into the islands of the Bering Strait. And the Mediterranean valley was still unflooded; the Pillars of Hercules would stand fast for ages yet, before the ocean broke through and the false, sweet legend of Atlantis was born.

And just what creatures will this world hold? asked Clindar as he looked down upon the turning globe. The great ship had come through the Star Gate only a few hours before, and the excitement of planetfall was still upon all its crew. Every world was a new challenge, a new problem, with its endless possibilities of life and death—and its hope of companionship in this still achingly empty universe.

In the five centuries since he had left Eos, Clindar had walked on thirty worlds, and devoted at least ten years of his life to each. On two he had suffered minor deaths, but this was one of the inevitable hazards of exploration. He expected to die many times again before he returned to his native world, now a thousand light-years away in normal space. As long as his body was not totally destroyed, the doctors could always repair it.

Apart from their unusual height—more than seven feet—the creatures looking down upon the world of the Pliocene were strikingly human; far more human, indeed, than anything that yet walked on the planet below. Only if one examined them in detail was it obvious that they belonged to an entirely different evolutionary tree; Nature had rung the changes once again on one of her favorite designs.

There are millions of two-armed, upright hined races in the universe. Thousands of them, on a dark night or in a thick fog might be mistaken for human beings. But there are only a few hundred species who could mingle undetected in the society of man—and none at all that could pass even the most superficial medical examination.

With a little plastic surgery, Clindar could have passed as a man. He was hairless, and there were no nails on his six fingers and toes; these stigmata of the primitive jungle his race had lost eons ago. Despite his size, he moved swiftly, with a jerky, almost avian walk and rhythm. He thought and spoke more quickly than any man would ever do, and his normal body temperature was almost 105 degrees. His skeleton and his biochemistry were utterly inhuman, and any cannibals foolish enough to feast upon his flesh would surely die. Yet despite all this, one would have to search a million worlds to find a closer approximation to a man.

And, like Man, he and his companions were insatiably inquisitive. Now that they had the power to explore the universe, they would enjoy it to the full.

The maps, the photographic surveys, the spectrochemical analyses, were all completed. After a year in orbit, it was time to land. Like a stick of bombs ten glittering spheres were ejected from the thousand-foot-long mother ship, and fell toward the cloud-wrapped globe below.

They drifted apart, spread themselves out along the equator, and settled gently on mountain, plain, and swamp. Clindar and his two companions floated for miles across the jungles before they saw a good landing place; then the sphere extended its three telescopic legs and came to rest as delicately as a falling soap bubble, upon the land that would one day be named Africa.

For a moment no one spoke; each wanted to savor this moment in silence. The three of them, as was usually the case on such expeditions, were all members of the same mating group, so neither their bodies nor their minds held any secrets from each other. This was their fifth landing together, and silence united them more closely than any words.

At last, Clindar touched the control panel, and into the

cabin came the sounds of the new world. For a long time they listened to the voices of the forest, to the sighing of the wind through the strange trees and grasses, to the cries of animals killing or being killed—and a changeless background of muted thunder, the roar of the great waterfall two miles away. One day they would know every thread in this tapestry of sound; but now it was full of menace, and woke forgotten fears. For all their wisdom and sophistication, they felt like children facing the unknown terrors of the night; and their hearts ached for home.

The familiar routines of the landing procedure soon turned them back into calm, professional explorer-scientists. First the little collection robots were sent rolling in all directions, to gather leaves and grasses and, with luck, any small animals slow-moving enough to be caught. All the samples they brought back were examined in the scoutship's sealed and automatic lab, so that there was no danger of contamination. The biochemical patterns were swiftly evaluated—it was rare to find a wholly novel one, especially on an oxygen-carbon world like this—and the information flashed up to the hovering mother ship, twenty thousand miles away. There seemed to be no virulently hostile microorganisms here, but life was of such infinite complexity that one could never be sure. Planets could produce deadly surprises, generations after they had been declared completely safe.

No large animals came near the ship during the hours of daylight—which was not surprising, for it stood in several acres of open ground where the only cover was a few low bushes. But at dusk, the picture changed, and the land became alive as the shadows lengthened and deepened into night.

To the watchers on the ship, darkness was no handicap. Through the infrared periscope they could see the world around them as if it were still daylight; they could follow the shy herbivores on their way to the waterholes, and could study the tactics of the great predators who hunted them. There were still tigers in this land, with twin sabers jutting from their jaws; but in another million years they would be gone, and Africa would belong to the lion.

It was slow, sometimes exasperating, but always fascinating work—making a census of a world one could not touch. Several times Clindar moved the ship a few miles to change the vantagepoint, and to make sure that the animals and plants formed a representative sample. And in the second week, they found the hominids.

It was the din through the long-distance microphones that drew attention to them. As Clindar swung the periscope in the direction of the uproar, he found that his view of the disturbance was partly blocked by trees, but he could see enough to make it unnecessary to move the ship.

About half a mile away, in a small clearing near the bank of an almost dried-up river, a leopard had made a kill. It was crouched over some unfortunate victim who had presumably been drinking at the water's edge, and was snarling angrily at a hostile chorus from the surrounding trees. There were dark, shadow animals of fair size moving through the branches of those trees, and it was some time before Clindar could get a good view of one. But suddenly, as he tracked through the foliage, he came upon a clear line of sight—and looked straight into a hairy caricature of his own face.

The creature was screaming with rage as it danced up and down on the tree limb, directing its fury at the leopard. On other branches, its companions were doing the same, and though they could not harm the killer they were obviously annoying it, for presently the big cat started to move away, dragging the bloody carcass of its victim by the leg. As the body rolled over, Clindar found himself once again looking into the distorting mirror of time.

He had seen the reconstructions of his own ancestors, five or ten million years ago; the mask now stiffening into a grimace of death might have belonged to any one of them. There was the same low, ridged forehead, close-set eyes, muscular but chinless jaw, protruding teeth. It was not the first time he had met this pattern, for variations of it were common on many worlds, yet it always filled him with wonder, and with a sense of kinship that spanned the evolutionary gulfs.

The leopard and its victim vanished from view; the chorus of fear and anger died away. Clindar watched, and waited.

Slowly and cautiously, the hominids came down from the trees, in which they did not seem to be completely at home. They walked on all fours, but from time to time reared up on their hind limbs and took several steps in an upright position. Abruptly, as if they had spotted the leopard again, they all fled in panic, away from the river and the trees. As they ran, they became true bipeds, covering considerable distances without their forelimbs touching the ground.

Clindar followed them with some difficulty, and at first thought he had lost them. Then he spotted their brown figures swarming up the almost vertical face of a sandstone cliff, heading for a cave some fifty feet from the ground. It was a well-chosen refuge, for the entrance was too high to be reached by the great cats. Such a choice of dwelling place might be instinctive, but it might also indicate the dawn of intelligence. These creatures, Clindar told himself with mounting excitement, would certainly merit watching.

Through long but fascinating hours at the periscope, he grew to know them all, and to learn the pattern of their behavior. There were only ten of them—four males, three females, three infants—and physically they were unimpressive specimens, living always on the edge of hunger. Most of their food was obtained by foraging among grasses and shrubs, but they were not exclusively vegetarian. They ate meat whenever they could get it, which was seldom, for they were inefficient hunters. About the only animals that fell prey to them were tortoises, small rodents, and occasional fish that they could catch in the shallows of the river.

Because they did not possess the simplest tools, they could not even take proper advantage of such rare and accidental windfalls as a mired elephant, or an antelope that had broken its leg. The meat would rot before they could tear it all out with their teeth: and they could not fight off the big carnivores that would be attracted to such a feast.

It was a wonder that they had survived, and their future did not look promising. Clindar was not in the least surprised when one of the infants died, apparently of starvation, and the little body was thrown out of the cave for the hyenas to carry away. These creatures had not yet learned the useful accomplishment of burying their dead, lest they lead wild animals to the living.

But Clindar, with the experience of many worlds behind him, knew that appearances could be deceptive. These unprepossessing near-apes had one great advantage over all the other creatures of their planet. They were still unspecialized: they had not yet become trapped in any evolutionary *cul-de-sac*. Almost every animal could beat them in some respect—in strength, or speed, or hearing, or natural armament. There was no single skill in which the hominids excelled, but they could do everything after a fashion. Where the other animals had become virtuosos, they had specialized in a universal mediocrity—and there-in, a million years hence, might lie their salvation. Having failed to adapt themselves to their environment, they might yet one day change it to suit their own desires.

Other humanoid races, times without number, had tak-en a different road. Clindar had seen, either with his own eyes or through the records of other explorers, those who had chosen to specialize—though the choice, of course, was never a conscious one. He had seen near-men who could run like the wind, swim like fish, hunt in the dark with sonar or infrared senses; on one world of exception-ally low gravity he had even encountered men who could fly. Most of these specialists had been extremely success-ful; so successful that they had had no need to develop more than a rudimentary intelligence.

And therefore they were doomed, though they might flourish for a million years. Sooner or later, the environ-ment to which they were so perfectly adapted would change, and they could not change with it. They were too far from the crucial fork in the evolutionary road ever to retrace their steps.

On this world, the choice remained; the irrevocable decision between brain and body had not yet been made. The future was still in the balance. Here, on this tropical plain, the balance might be tipped—in favor of intelli-gence.

8

MOON-WATCHER

It was surprising how quickly all the animals grew accustomed to the ship; because it did nothing, and merely stood motionless on its tripod of legs, they soon came to regard it as part of the landscape. In the heat of noon, lions would shelter beneath it, and sometimes elephants and dinotheria would rub their thick hides against the landing gear. Clindar preferred to choose a moment when none of the larger or more dangerous beasts were around when he made his first exit.

From the underbelly of the ship a transparent, cylindrical tube ten feet in diameter lowered itself until it had reached ground level; down this, in an equally transparent cage, rode Clindar and his equipment. The curving walls slid open, and he stepped out onto the new world.

He was insulated from it, as completely as if he were still inside the ship, but the flexible suit that surrounded him from head to foot was only a minor inconvenience. He had full freedom of movement, for there was no external vacuum to make the suit stiff and rigid. Indeed, he could even breathe the surrounding atmosphere—after it had been scrubbed and filtered and purified by the small processing pack on his chest. The air of this planet might carry lethal organisms, but it was not poisonous.

He walked slowly away from the ship, feeling his balance in this alien gravity and accustoming himself to the weight of his equipment. Besides the usual communication and recording gear, he was carrying nets, small boxes for specimens, a geologist's hammer, a compact explosive-powered drill, and a coil of thin but immensely strong rope. And though he had no offensive weapons, he had some extremely effective defensive ones.

The land through which he was walking seemed absolutely barren of animal life, but he knew that this was an illusion. Thousands of eyes were watching him from trees and grass and undergrowth, and as he moved slowly along one of the trails which the herbivores had beaten to the waterhole, he was also conscious that the normal patterns of sound had changed. The creatures of this world knew that something strange had come into their lives; there was a hushed expectancy about the land—a subdued excitement that communicated itself to Clindar. He did not anticipate trouble, or danger; but if it came, he was ready for it.

He had already chosen his vantagepoint, a large rock about a hundred yards from the watering place where the hominid had been killed. Near the summit was a cave formed by two boulders resting against each other; it would provide just the shelter and concealment he needed. Such a desirable residence was not, of course, empty; it contained several large, indignant, and undoubtedly poisonous snakes. He ignored them, since they could not harm him through the tough yet almost invisible envelope of his suit.

He set up his cameras and his directional microphones, reported back to the ship, and waited.

For the first few days he merely observed without interference. He learned the order in which the various animals came to the water, until he could predict their arrival with fair accuracy. Above all, he studied the little group of hominids, until he knew them as individuals and had christened them all with appropriate private names. There was Greypate, the oldest and most aggressive, who dominated all the others. There were Crookback and One-Hand and Broken-Fang, but the most interesting was the young adult that Clindar had called Moon-Watcher, because he had once spotted him at dusk, standing on a low rock and staring motionless into the face of the rising moon. The posture itself was unusual, for the hominids seldom stood erect for more than a few seconds at a time, but even more striking was the suggestion of conscious thought and wonder. Perhaps this was an illusion; yet Clindar doubted if any other inhabitant of this world ever stopped to stare at the moon. Nor was it, in this environment, a very sensible thing to do. Clindar was strangely relieved when the creature started to trot back toward its cave, away from the unsleeping perils of the night.

His first attempt to collect specimens was not a success. A small antelope, with graceful, corkscrew horns, had apparently become detached from the herd and was wandering along the trail to the waterhole in a rather distracted manner. Clindar got it in the sight of his narcotic gun, aimed carefully at the fleshy part of the flank, and squeezed the trigger. With barely a sound, the dart whispered to its target.

The antelope started, though no more violently than if a mosquito had bitten it. For a moment there was no other reaction—but the biochemists had done their work well. The animal walked three or four paces, and then collapsed in a heap.

Clindar hurried out of the cave to collect his victim. He was halfway down the sloping rockface when there was a flash of yellow, and almost before he had realized what had happened, the antelope was gone. A passing leopard had outsmarted an intelligence that could span the Galaxy.

Some hunters would have cursed; Clindar merely laughed and went back to his cave. Two hours later, he shot Moon-Watcher.

He reached the fallen hominid only seconds after the flying dart. Beneath its hairy pelt the body was well-muscled but undernourished; he had no difficulty at all in lifting it and carrying it back to the ship, where a thorough examination could be made.

Moon-Watcher was still unconscious, but breathing steadily, when the elevator took him up into the ship. He slept peacefully in the sealed test chamber for many hours, while scores of instruments measured his reactions and beams of radiation scanned the interior of his body as if it had been made of glass. His head was shaved, with considerable difficulty, for the hair was a matted and well-populated tangle and electrodes were attached to his scalp. In the mother ship, thousands of miles above the earth, the great computers probed and analyzed the patterns of cerebral activity, so much simpler than their own; and presently they delivered their verdict.

When it was all finished, Clindar carried Moon-Watcher back to the elevator and down to ground level. He left him still unconscious, propped up against one of the landing legs, and guarded him from the ship until he had come to his senses. He would have done the same with any other animal; centuries of traveling through the empty wastes of the universe had given him an intense reverence for life in all its forms. Though he never hesitated to kill when it was necessary, he always did so with reluctance.

Presently Moon-Watcher stirred drowsily, scratched his newly bared scalp with obvious astonishment, and staggered to his feet. He proceeded for a few yards in a wavering line, then became aware of the ship looming above him, and stopped to examine it. Perhaps he thought it was some peculiar kind of rock, for he showed no signs of alarm. After a few minutes, now much steadier, he set off briskly in the direction of his cave, and soon disappeared from view.

When the intelligence profiles and brain-capacity assessments came down from the mother ship, Clindar brooded over them for a long time, discussed them with his colleagues, and asked the computers far overhead for their extrapolations into the future. There was potential here— several billion brain cells, as yet only loosely interconnected. Whether that potential could ever be realized depended on time and luck. Time could not be hurried; but luck was not altogether beyond the power of intelligent control.

Here was a situation common in the history of stellar exploration, though it was new to Clindar himself. Often the ships of his people had arrived at a world where some creature was at the watershed between instinct and conscious thought, and in the early days there had been much debate about the appropriate action. Some argued that it was better to stand aside and to leave the ultimate decision to chance and nature; but when this was done, the result was almost always the same. The universe was as indifferent to intelligence as it was to life; left to themselves, the dawning minds had less than one chance in a hundred of survival. Most of them achieved no more than a tragic consciousness of their own doom, before they were swept into oblivion.

In these circumstances, the choice was clear—though not all races would have been sufficiently unselfish to make it. When an emerging species could be helped, aid was given. But too much assistance could also be fatal, and it was necessary to aim for a minimum of interference, lest the rising culture become no more than a distorted echo of an alien society.

For in the long run a species, like an individual, had to stand on its own feet, and find its own destiny. Clindar was very well aware of this, as he studied the hominids and prepared to play God.

There had been a heavy rainstorm, and the world around him was tantalizingly fresh and sparkling beyond the impermeable barrier of his suit. On such a morning, it seemed a crime to kill, nor was there any exoneration in the knowledge that thousands of hidden deaths were occurring every minute in this shining land.

The hunter from the stars stood at the edge of the savannah, choosing his victim. Out to the horizon he could see uncountable numbers of gazelles and antelopes and wildebeest and zebras—or creatures whose descendants would one day bear these names—browsing on the sea of grass. He raised his weapon to his shoulder, aimed through it like a telescope, and pressed the firing stud. There was a flicker of light, barely visible in the fierce glare of the African sun, and a young gazelle dropped so swiftly and silently that none of its companions took the slightest notice. Even when Clindar walked out to collect the body—unmarked except for the charred hole above the heart—they trotted only a few yards away and regarded him with only mild alarm.

He threw the gazelle over his shoulder and set off at a brisk walk toward the cave of the hominids. Before he had gone three hundred yards he realized, with some amusement, that he was being stalked by a saber-toothed tiger that had emerged from the undergrowth at the edge of the plain.

He put down the gazelle and turned to face the great cat. When it saw that he was aware of it, the tiger growled softly and opened its jaws in a terrifying display of fangs. At the same moment, it quickened its pace.

Clindar also wasted no time. He threw a switch on his suit, and at once the air was rent by a hideous, undulating howl as of a thousand souls in torment. Out on the plain, the flocks of herbivores began to stampede, and even above the cacophony of the siren he could hear the drumming of their hooves like a distant thunder.

The tiger reared up on its haunches, slashing viciously at the empty air in its surprise. Then it dropped back to the ground and, to Clindar's utter astonishment, continued its advance. It was very brave, or very stupid, or very hungry. In any event, it was very dangerous.

Clindar whipped his projector into the firing position,

and barely had time to defocus it before the tiger charged. This time there was no visible flash, for the beam fanned out over too wide an area to produce its characteristic scintillation. But when the tiger reached the ground it was already blind, for it had stared into the light of a hundred suns. Clindar had no difficulty in avoiding it as it staggered away, shaking its massive head from side to side in confusion.

It would be at least an hour before the magnificent beast's sight returned to normal; as it tottered away, Clindar hoped that it would not injure itself by crashing into any obstacles.

There were no more interruptions in his morning walk, and presently, not even winded by his exertions, he arrived at the cliff face where the hominids lived. Keeping in full view, and making as much noise as possible, he placed his offering immediately beneath the opening of the cave. Then he moved back a hundred yards, sat down, and waited with the patience of a being who had already seen a thousand birthdays and could, if he wished, see endless thousands more.

There must, he knew, be many eyes watching him from the darkness of the cave, and behind those eyes would be dim brains in which fear and hunger strove together. It would be rare indeed for the hominids to encounter such a windfall as this, for the gazelles could outrun them easily and they had not yet invented any of the arts of the hunter.

It was a full hour before the oldest of the males appeared in the shadows of the opening, started outside for a few seconds, and then disappeared again into the gloom. Nothing else happened for another hour or so; then Clindar's friend Moon-Watcher emerged, looked around nervously, and started to descend the face of the cliff. He scuttled across to the dead gazelle, which was now surrounded by a cloud of buzzing flies, and paused here for a moment, obviously torn with agonizing indecision.

Clindar could read the creature's mind with the utmost ease. Shall I feast here, it was saying to itself, and risk being eaten myself—or shall I carry this banquet back to the safety of the cave—where I will have to share it with the others?

Moon-Watcher solved his excruciating problem by a compromise. He buried his fangs in the neck of the gazelle, and with great difficulty, tore out a hunk of bloody meat. Then he threw the corpse over his shoulder and swarmed up the rockface with quite astonishing speed.

Lesson one was over; feeling very satisfied, Clindar went back to the ship. He did not expect that the hominids would leave the cave again that day.

Seven gazelles and two antelopes later, he had made considerable progress. When he left his present at the foot of the cliff, the whole family would emerge and quarrel over it. Their table manners left much to be desired, but they were beginning to take him for granted. Though he sat in full view, a strange and utterly alien figure in his shimmering protective envelope, they appeared quite unafraid of him. Every day he had moved a little closer, until now he sat within fifty feet of the dining place.

Before the hominids became completely dependent upon him, and forgot how to fend for themselves, he would take the next step.

9

GIFT FROM THE STARS

Jupiter was a brilliant star, almost vertically above him, as Clindar walked through the sleeping bush an hour before dawn. Up there, half a billion miles away, was the entrance of the Star Gate, and the road across the light-years that led to his infinitely more distant home. It was a road with many branches, most of them still unexplored and leading to destinations which were perhaps unimaginable. Down a few of those byways were the lonely civilizations scattered so sparsely throughout this arm of the galactic spiral. One day this world might be among them; but that time could not come for at least a million years.

The hominids never left their cave during the hours of darkness, but Clindar could hear them barking and quarreling sleepily as they prepared to meet the new day. He placed his bribe—a young boar—at the foot of the cliff, where they were bound to pass. This time, however, he did not withdraw. He sat down only a few feet away from the sacrifice, and waited.

The stars faded from the sky, Jupiter last of all. Presently the rays of the rising sun began to gild the face of the cliff, moving slowly downward until they shone straight into the cave. Then, from the interior, came a sudden excited chattering, and the high-pitched "Eek-Eek" which Clindar had grown to recognize as an alarm signal. The hominids had spotted him.

He could see their hairy figures milling around in the entrance, undecided what to do next. If they did not pluck up enough courage to come down in a reasonable time, Clindar would leave. But he would take the boar with him, and hope that they would draw the conclusion that food and friendship were inseparably linked.

To his pleased surprise, he did not have long to wait. Moving slowly but steadily, Moon-Watcher was descending the face of the cliff. He got to within twenty feet of ground level and then paused to survey the situation. Presumably he still felt quite confident that he was safe, and in ordinary circumstances he would have been right. Only a nimble ape, and not one of the great cats, would be able to scale this almost vertical rock.

Clindar pulled a knife from his equipment belt, and, with rather more energy than skill, started to disjoint the boar. It must, he thought, look like magic to Moon-Watcher to see how swiftly the tough meat came apart; he was performing in a few seconds acts which took the hominids many minutes of tearing and biting. When he had detached a foreleg, he held it out to his fascinated spectator.

He was patient, and Moon-Watcher was hungry, but the result was not inevitable. For many minutes the creature hovered hesitantly on the face of the cliff, descending a few feet, then hastily scrambling upward again. At last it made its decision, and gathered all its courage together. Still prepared for instant flight, Moon-Watcher dropped from the face of the cliff and started to sidle towards Clindar, approaching him in a cautious, crab-wise manner. Every few steps he stood upright for a second, grimacing and showing his teeth. He was obviously trying to demonstrate that he could defend himself if the need arose.

It took him several minutes, with numerous retreats and hesitations, to cross the last few feet. While he was doing this, Clindar pretended to chew avidly at the leg of boar, holding it out invitingly from time to time.

Abruptly, it was snatched from his hand, and in seconds Moon-Watcher was halfway up the cliff, carrying his prize between his teeth. Patiently, Clindar started to slice away at the carcass once more, waiting for the next move. It came within the hour, when Moon-Watcher returned for a second helping. This time, Graypate and Broken Fang followed him part of the way down the cliff face, anxious to see how it was done.

So the experiment in primitive diplomacy continued, day after day—sometimes in the morning before the hominids had left their cave, sometimes in the evening as they returned from the day's foraging. By the end of a week, Clindar had become accepted as an honorary member of the tribe. They were completely unafraid of him, and would squat in a circle watching his actions from a few feet away. Some of the infants would scamper over and touch him, until scolded by their mothers; but the adults still avoided direct contact. They were inquisitive, but not yet friendly.

To Clindar it was a weird, almost unreal existence, this daily switching between two worlds a million years apart. While his colleagues were probing the planet with the most advanced instruments of their science, he was mentally identifying himself with creatures who had barely reached the dawn of reason. He had to see through their eyes, remember the limitations of their clumsy fingers, imagine the slow processes of their brains when they were confronted with something new. Fortunately, there was the experience of others to guide him; when he was aboard the scoutship, he would search the records of the past, learning what earlier expeditions had done, on other worlds. He could profit from their successes, and avoid their mistakes.

Because speech still lay a million years in the future, the only way to instruct these creatures was by example. And because his people excelled in anything they turned their minds to, Clindar was soon the most efficient hunter on the planet. He was surprised, and a little disturbed, to find how much he enjoyed it. The ancient instincts had not wholly died, even though it had been a hundred thousand generations since they had last been given rein.

His favorite weapon was the thighbone of one of the larger antelopes; with its knobbly end, it formed a perfect natural club, much superior to any branch that could be wrenched off a tree. With a single well-placed blow it could kill animals up to the size of the hominids themselves, and it could drive off creatures that were far larger. Clindar was anxious to prove this, and had thought of staging a demonstration. As it turned out, his wish was granted without any deliberate planning.

The horde—it could not yet be granted the name of tribe—had now completely identified him with food, and the males were ready to follow him wherever he went. Even those females who were not burdened with infants would sometimes stop gathering leaves and fruit to accompany him, in the hope of profiting from his success.

They found the dead zebra only a few hundred yards from the scoutship, surrounded by the hyenas that had run it down. There were six of the mangy, unprepossessing scavengers worrying the carcass; confident that nothing smaller than a lion could disturb them, they continued

their feasting as Clindar approached. Behind his back he
could hear his pupils chattering nervously as they kept
their distance.

The hyenas looked at Clindar warily, snarling and holding their ground, as he came nearer. He was the first
biped they had ever seen—indeed, the only biped in all
this world—but his strangeness did not alarm them. They
were certain that they could protect their spoils.

A second later, they were not so sure. Clindar advanced
on them like a whirlwind, a club in each hand—for he
was completely ambidextrous—and started raining blows
on the startled beasts. Too astonished to fight back, they
fled, yelping hideously; then one of them regained his
courage, spun around, and launched himself straight at
Clindar's head.

That was good; it must not seem too easy, or the
hominids would put too great a faith in these primitive
weapons, and get themselves into disastrous situations.
They must learn that a club would not make them invinci-
ble, and that the outcome of a fight would still depend on
their own skill and strength.

Nevertheless, Clindar cheated; it was not really a fair
demonstration, though it served its purpose admirably. He
was far more powerful and better coordinated than these
clumsy ape-men, and in an emergency he could move with
a speed which very few animals on this world could
match. Moreover, he was completely protected by the
flexible yet incredibly tough film that insulated him from
the microscopic killers that teemed in air and soil. The
hyena did not really have a chance.

Clindar had already moved aside as it went hurtling by
him, drifting past in slow motion to his accelerated senses.
He caught it one terrific blow with the club as it sailed
by—misjudging his strength, because the bone splintered
and snapped and he was left holding the stump in his
hand. But it did not matter; the hyena was dead before it
reached the ground. The others, who had turned to watch
the fight and were prowling hopefully in the near distance,
did not wait for a further demonstration.

During the fight, the hominids had also kept their
distance, but at least they had not been scared away. Now
they approached with a kind of nervous eagerness, their
attention equally divided between Clindar and his victim.

Moon-Watcher, always in the forefront, reached him
first. He edged over to the slain hyena, put out a cautious
paw, touched the body, and quickly withdrew. Twice he

repeated this, until he was convinced that the animal was really dead. Then his jaw dropped in a comical expression of astonishment, and he stared at Clindar as if he could not believe his eyes.

Clindar held out the second, unbroken club in his right hand, and waited. This was the moment; no better one would ever come. If Moon-Watcher had not learned the lesson now, he would never do so.

The hominid came slowly toward him, then squatted down only five feet away; he had never approached so closely before. Holding his head slightly on one side in an attitude of intense concentration, he stared at the bone held rigidly in Clindar's hand. Then he reached out a paw and touched the crude club.

His fingers grasped the end, and tugged gently at it. Clindar held firm for a moment, then released his grip.

Moon-Watcher drew the bone away from him, looked at it intently, then began to sniff and nibble at it. A spasm of disappointment shot through Clindar's mind; the lesson was already forgotten. This was just another morsel of food—not a key to the future, a tool that could lead to the mastery of this world, and of many others.

Then Moon-Watcher suddenly remembered. He jumped to his feet, and began to dance around waving the club in his right paw. As long as he kept moving, he could rear almost upright; only when he stood still did he have to use his free forelimb as a support. He had already begun to make the awesome and irrevocable transition from quadruped to biped.

The little dance lasted about five seconds; then Moon-Watcher shot off on a tangent. He raced toward the dead hyena in such a frenzy of excitement that his companions, who had already started to quarrel over the feast, scattered in fright.

Awkwardly, but with an energy that made up for his lack of skill, Moon-Watcher began to pound the carcass with his club, while the others looked on with awed astonishment. Clindar alone understood what was happening, and knew that this world had come to a turning point in time. To the most promising of its creatures, he had given the first tool; and the history of yet another race had begun.

10

FAREWELL TO EARTH

During the next five years, as the scoutships drifted far and wide over the face of the planet gathering thousands of specimens and millions of items of information, Clindar revisited the hominids many times. He never went hunting with them again; they had learned that lesson with astonishing—indeed, with ominous—speed, and all the males now knew how to use clubs when the need arose. Instead, he had tried to introduce other tools, of which the most important were stone knives and hammers.

These small hand tools, crude though they might appear at first sight, represented a gigantic leap forward in technology. They multiplied the efficiency—and therefore the chance of survival—of their users many times. With a properly shaped flint one could dig up tough roots and hack off succulent branches which would otherwise be exhausting and laborious to collect. And a small, round pebble that fitted the hand nicely could split bones to get at the marrow, or crack animal skulls to reach the tenderest and most well-protected of all meat.

One day, if all went well, the hominids would not only use tools—they would *make* them; and they would make them of metal and of plastic and, in the end, of pure fields of force. But how they would use those tools—whether for good or for evil—was beyond prediction, and to be revealed only by the passing of the ages.

They had been given their initial impetus, and that was all that one could, or should, do for a species at this level of intelligence; the rest was up to them. The outcome might yet be disastrous, as it had often been in the past. Failures could not be avoided, but they could be expunged; if one world was lost, there were many others.

For Clindar's race, driven by impulses long buried in their own infancy, were gardeners in the field of stars. They sowed, and often they reaped. But sometimes they had to weed.

For the last time, Clindar stood on the African plain, brooding over his experiment with destiny. Above him loomed the globe of the scoutship, already throbbing with the energies that would soon carry him up to the lonely heights of space. And on his shoulder, completely unafraid, sat one of the little ape-children, searching hopefully for lice and salt crystals in the folds of his outer clothing. Clindar had long since been able to discard his protective envelope; he was now immune to the micro-fauna of this world, and carried nothing in his own body that could destroy the life around him.

A few yards away, the mother hominid was plucking berries; she had ignored her child completely, as if quite confident that it was in safe hands. She could never guess, thought Clindar, how much this little creature's chances of survival had improved. The tribe had prospered, thanks to the tools and weapons he had given it; no longer was it starving and defenseless. Even the big cats had begun to avoid these animals whose forelimbs, though they had no claws, could inflict such stinging pain.

A series of musical notes sounded from the communicator at Clindar's waist; his friends were growing impatient. He could not blame them; all these years they had remained insulated from this world, while he took the risks— and the rewards. Their turn would come later, on other planets, while he watched the instruments and recorders from the safety of the ship. Where was Moon-Watcher? Not far away, he was sure. He gave the three piercing whistles that the hominid had learned to recognize as his signal, and waited.

A few minutes later, there was a rustling in the undergrowth, and Moon-Watcher emerged, carrying a small gazelle over his shoulder. He grimaced and chittered with pleasure at the sight of his friend, and started to lope toward him with the awkward but swift three-limbed gait he employed when one of his forepaws was holding something.

In the last five years Moon-Watcher had matured and aged a good deal, and was now nearing the—doubtless violent—end of his short life. But he was in good condition, with only a few bald patches on his chest and thighs, and he was well fed. He had lost his left ear in a fight with a hyena a few months ago, and that in itself was a sign of progress. None of his ancestors would have dreamed of competing with the snarling scavengers of the plains.

Still carrying the infant on his shoulder, Clindar moved out from the shadow of the ship to meet his friend. Perhaps the baby was Moon-Watcher's; there was no way of telling, for mating among the hominids was completely promiscuous and stable family relations were still ages in the future. The infants were indiscriminately mothered by all the females, and cuffed out of the way by all the males.

This open place would do well enough. Clindar reached out his hand toward Moon-Watcher, and waited. In the early days the hominid had avoided all contact, especially when he was carrying food, but now he was no longer in the least shy. Trustingly, he held out his free hand toward Clindar, and for the last time they touched across the gulfs that sundered them.

Clindar tugged the hairy paw upward, so that Moon-Watcher stood teetering on his hindlegs, in the position his remote descendants must one day assume if they were ever to free their hands and their minds. He turned his face toward the ship, and gave the slight twist of the head that signified "now." The brief affirmative tone came from his communicator almost at once, and he let Moon-Watcher's hand drop back to the ground.

Ages after the little hominid's bones had dissolved into dust, this recording of their farewell would still exist, to be recalled whenever Clindar pleased. He would add others to it, in the years and the millennia that lay ahead, until the time came—if it ever did—when at last he was tired of the Universe, and of immortality.

Silent as rising smoke, the bubble of the scoutship lifted from the African plain and dwindled into the sky. Moon-Watcher never saw it go; the gazelle he had killed now engaged his full attention. Soon he would forget his visitor—but not the gifts he had brought from the stars.

And his descendants would use them, with ever-increasing skill, until it was time for the next meeting.

There was one small but important matter still to be arranged, and the ship landed briefly on the Moon to do it.

In the lunar midnight, the cold rocks split and scattered as the traction fields tore into them, digging the cavity that would protect the Sentinel from all foreseeable accidents of time and space. The black tetrahedron was set upon its supporting apron, and then sealed off from the light of the sun and the light of the earth. The broken rock was poured back into place; in a few thousand years, the incessant rain of meteor dust would have hidden the scar completely.

But the buried machine's magnetic signal would shout its presence to the empty sky, and any intelligence that came this way could not fail to observe it. If, ages hence, Moon-Watcher's descendants attained the freedom of space, they must pause here on the way to the stars; and those who had set them on the road would know that they were coming, and would prepare to welcome them.

Or it might be that a culture would arise on this planet, flourish briefly in the innocent belief that the universe revolved around it, and then sink back once more into the dim twilight of preconscious thought, rejoining the animal kingdom from which it had emerged. Such civilizations were too numerous to be counted, far less examined, in this galaxy of a hundred billion worlds. Though they might contain many marvels and hold much of interest, yet one had to pass them by. Indeed, few lasted long enough for a second visit; they were ephemeral flashes of intelligence, flickering like fireflies in the cosmic night.

But once a species had begun to move out from its native world, and had become aware of the universe around it, it was worthy of attention. Only a space-faring culture could truly transcend its environment, and join others in giving a purpose to creation. Therefore such cultures had to be detected and cherished, when they merited it; which was not always the case. The sentinel-beacons that now kept hopeful watch upon more than a million planets sometimes brought bad news as well as good.

As the ship lifted from the heart of Tycho, Clindar caught one last glimpse of the blue-green globe hanging motionless in the lunar sky. Africa was turned toward him, warming itself in the rays of the hidden sun. He wished he could have stayed longer—a hundred years, at least—but new worlds were calling, far down the unimaginable convolutions of the Star Gate.

It was unlikely that he would ever know the outcome of the chain reaction he had started here; the chances were that it would die out in a few generations, and leave no trace. In these early stages disease or changing climate or accident could so easily wipe out the glimmering, predawn intelligence, before it was strong enough to protect itself against the blind forces of the Universe.

For if the stars and the galaxies had the least concern for mind, or the slightest awareness of its presence, that was yet to be proved.

11

THE BIRTH OF HAL

The movie *2001* has often been criticised as lacking human interest, and having no real characters—except HAL. In leaping straight from the Pleistocene into space, Stanley Kubrick bypassed all the problems that would have been involved in developing the personal backgrounds of the astronauts, the political and cultural impact produced by the discovery of the monolith, and the general details of life at the beginning of the next century. We could have written a whole book about that; in fact, we did. . . .

And when we had done so, we realized that it was irrelevant to the main theme of the movie. To have developed all this background material—besides adding a couple of hours to the running time and several millions to the cost—would have thrown the whole story out of focus. So the novel contains only a few pages set on Earth, 2001 AD, while the film ignores the subject completely, and jumps straight into space.

One of the problems facing any science-fiction writer who is aiming for the general public is how much to explain, and how much to take for granted. He must try not to leave his readers baffled, but at the same time must avoid those disguised lectures which are all too typical of the *genre* ("Now tell me, Professor. . . ."). At one time, Stanley hoped to get around this problem—as far as the movie was concerned—by opening with a short documentary-type prelude, in which noted scientists and philosophers would establish the credibility of our theme. With this idea in mind, he sent Roger Caras around the world, to interview, on film, more than twenty authorities on space, computers, anthropology—even religion. They included the astronomers Harlow Shapley, Sir Bernard Lovell, Fred Whipple, Frank Drake; Dr. Margaret Mead (who was a space bug long before Sputnik) and the great Russian scientist A. I. Oparin, the first man to point out (in the 1920's) a plausible way in which life could arise from the simple chemicals of the primitive Earth.

These interviews, many of them quite fascinating, were never used—a fact which understandably upset some of the distinguished and busy men involved. (Transcripts of several interviews may be found in Jerry Agel's *The Making of Kubrick's 2001.*) But as it turned out, to have incorporated them in the film would have been aesthetically impossible; it also proved to be unnecessary. We did not have to educate the public, as the headlong rush of astronautical events did it for us.

While the film was in production, the first space rendezvous (Gemini VI and VII) took place. Luna IX landed in the Ocean of Storms and gave us our first close-ups of the lunar surface from a distance of a few inches. (Too late to help the Art Department—all *our* lunar scenes had already been shot—but fortunately our educated guesses had been pretty close to the reality.) Most astonishing and unexpected of all—the discovery of the first apparently artificial radio sources in outer space was announced just a month before the movie was premiered. (April 1968). We now believe that the so-called "pulsars" are natural objects (neutron stars), but it was interesting to see how ready the public and the scientists were to consider seriously the "Little Green Men" hypothesis.

And at the end of that same year, Apollo 8 looped round the Moon, and half the human race heard that unforgettable Christmas message from another world. It was just as well, therefore, that Stanley had thrown his audience straight into space, without wasting time on preliminaries. A cautious, pedestrian approach would have resulted in instant obsolescence.

Nevertheless, I was quite sorry to lose many of the Earthbound sequences, which established the background for the expedition to Jupiter (or Saturn, as we later decided in the novel version). They included several items of—I hope—painless exposition, such as the attempt in the chapter entitled "Universe" to describe a film giving the scale of the cosmos. I have since encountered two films (one by Charles Eames) made on precisely these lines.

The section that follows also reveals the early evolution of HAL (or Socrates, or Athena, as he/she was christened in earlier versions). It will be seen that in the course of writing, HAL lost mobility but gained enormously in intelligence.

And while I am on this subject, I would like to demolish one annoying and persistent myth, which started soon after the movie was released. As is clearly stated in the novel (Chapter 16), HAL stands for *H*euristically programmed *AL*gorithmic computer. (No, I'm not going to explain that, except to say that it gets the best of both worlds in computer design.) However, about once a week some character spots the fact that HAL is one letter ahead of IBM, and promptly assumes that Stanley and I were taking a crack at that estimable institution.

As it happened, IBM had given us a good deal of help, so we were quite embarrassed by this, and would have changed the name had we spotted the coincidence. For coincidence it is, even if the odds are twenty-six cubed, or 17,576 to 1. (Just checked by HAL Jr., the beautiful 9100A calculator that my friends at Hewlett-Packard gave me at Christmas 1969.)

The following seven chapters contain only part of the Earthbound background material that Stanley and I developed; I have omitted thousands of words of description and characterization which are no longer of interest. (There is no record that I ever answered Stanley's question: "Do they sleep in their pajamas?") What is left, however, is still relevant, and will be for a long time to come—until the first encounter with aliens actually takes place.

It will be noticed that in this first version we decided not to keep the purpose of the mission a secret; in reality, I very much doubt whether this could be done, for the length of time we assumed in the film. And on rereading, after all these years, the last chapter—"Midnight, Washington"—I have suddenly remembered that just four years after those words were written, I received an invitation to a White House dinner in honor of the first men who would fly around the Moon, that coming Christmas. But I was already on my way to Ceylon, and so missed the opportunity to wish good luck to Borman, Anders, and Lovell.

I have never quite forgiven Bill Anders for resisting the temptation, which he later admitted had passed through his mind, of radioing back to Earth the discovery of a large, black monolith on the Far Side of the Moon. . . .

12

MAN AND ROBOT

"Bruno," asked the robot, "What is life?"

Dr. Bruno Forster, director of the Division of Mobile Adaptive Machines, carefully removed his pipe in the interests of better communication. Socrates still misunderstood about two percent of spoken words; with that pipe, the figure went up to five.

"Sub-program three three zero," he said carefully. "What is the purpose of the universe? Don't bother your pretty little head with such problems. End three three zero."

Socrates was silent, thinking this over. Sometime later in the day, if he understood his orders, he would repeat the message to whichever of the lab staff had initiated that sequence.

It was a joke, of course. By trying out such tricks, one often discovered unexpected possibilities, and unforeseen limitations, in Autonomous Mobile Explorer 5—usually known as Socrates or, alternatively, "That damn pile of junk." But to Forster, it was also something more than a joke; and his staff knew it.

One day, he was sure, there would be robots that would ask such questions—spontaneously, without prompting. And a little later, there would be robots that could answer them.

"Sub-program two five one," Bruno enunciated carefully. "Correction, recognition matrix for Senator Floyd. Erase height five feet eleven; insert height six feet one."

That should cover it, unless some other practical joker had been at the robot's memory. There had been one occasion when Socrates had welcomed a party of directors' wives with a passionate plea for a twenty-hour week and holidays with pay, and had ended by throwing accusations of brutality at his designer, whom he had repeatedly referred to as Dr. Bruno Frankenstein. It had been most convincing; some of the ladies were still looking suspiciously at Bruno when they left.

The door opened. Stepping lightly, gracefully, Socrates moved to meet the delegation.

"Good morning, Senator Floyd; welcome to General Robotics Division of Adaptive Machines. My name is Socrates; I would like to show you some of our latest work."

The senator and his colleagues were clearly impressed; they had seen photographs of Socrates and his predecessors, but nothing quite prepared one for the steel and crystal grace of the moving, talking reality. Though the robot was roughly the size and shape of a man, there were few of those disquieting echoes of the human body which make the metal monsters of horror movies either ludicrous or repulsive. Socrates possessed an inherent mechanical beauty that had to be accepted on its own terms.

The legs, rising from wide circular pads, were intricate assemblies of sliding shock absorbers, universal joints, and tensioning springs, held in a light framework of metal bars. They flexed and yielded at each step with a fascinating rhythm, as if they possessed a life of their own.

Above the hips—it was impossible to avoid *some* anthropomorphic terms—Socrates' body was a plain cylinder, covered with access hatches for his racks of electronic gear. His arms were slimmer and more delicate versions of the legs; the right one ended in a simple, three-fingered hand, capable of complete and continuous rotation, while the left terminated in a sort of multipurpose tool combining, among other useful elements, a corkscrew and beer-can opener. Socrates seemed well equipped for most emergencies.

The upper part of his body was crowned not by a head, but by an open framework carrying an assorted collection of sensors. A single TV camera gave all-round vision, through four wide-angled lenses aimed at each point of the compass. Unlike a man, Socrates needed no flexible neck; he could see in every direction simultaneously.

"I am designed," he explained, as he walked with a curious rocking motion toward the Medical Section, "for all types of space operation, and can function independently or under central control. I have enough built-in intelligence to deal with ordinary obstacles, and to evaluate simple emergency situations. My current assignment is supervisor on Project Morpheus."

"He's got *your* accent," said Representative Joseph Wilkins to Bruno, rather suspiciously.

"That's correct," the engineer answered, "but it's not a recording. Though my voice was the mode, he generates the words himself. The grammar and construction are all on his own—and sometimes they're better than mine."

"And just how intelligent is he?"

"It's impossible to make a direct comparison. In some ways, he's no more intelligent than a bright monkey. But he can learn almost without limit, and he'll never get tired or bored. That's why we'll be able to use him as a back-up for human crews, on really long space missions."

"Ah yes, this Morpheus idea. I'm interested, but it gives me the creeps."

"Well, here it is. Now you can judge for yourself."

The robot had led the party into a large, bare room dominated by a full-scale mockup of a space capsule. A cylinder twenty feet long and ten feet high, with an airlock at one end, it was surrounded by pumps, electronic gear, recording equipment, and TV monitors. There were no windows, but the whole of the interior could be watched on a series of TV screens. One pair of these showed somewhat disquieting pictures—closeups of two unconscious men. Their eyes were closed, metal caps were fitted over their shaven heads, electrodes and pick-up devices were attached to their bodies, and they did not even appear to be breathing.

"Our sleeping beauties," said Bruno to Representative Wilkins. (And why, he wondered to himself with some annoyance, did he always lower his voice? Even if they were awake, they certainly couldn't hear him.) "Whitehead on the left, Kaminski on the right."

"How long now?" asked Wilkins, whispering in return.

"One hundred and forty-two days—but Socrates will tell you all about it."

The robot paused at the airlock entrance, and glanced around, uncannily like a human speaker sizing up an audience. *That,* thought Bruno, was not a programmed reaction; Socrates had either copied it or invented it himself. He was always doing things like this, as his learning circuits worked through their almost infinite number of permutations. Sometimes the reaction was wholly inappropriate, and had to be blanked out; sometimes it was an amusing idiosyncrasy, like the apparently pointless little dance Socrates often performed when reactivated after a long shutdown; and occasionally it was useful. The robot's education was proceeding continuously, and so was that of its makers.

"This," began Socrates, "is Project Morpheus. Here we have two astronauts who, by a combination of drugs and electronarcosis, can be kept in a state of hibernation for prolonged periods. Their food and oxygen intake is thus cut ninety percent, greatly simplifying the supply problem. Equally important, this technique almost eliminates the psychological stresses produced when a group of men spend many months in confined quarters."

"What does *he* know about psychological stresses?" murmured Wilkins.

"You'd be surprised," Bruno answered glumly, thinking of several near-human tantrums that Socrates had thrown in the early days of his development.

"This technique," continued the robot, "is being developed for possible missions to the outer planets, which would involve very long flight times. During such flights, a robot like myself could run the ship and attend to the crew. It would automatically awaken them at the end of the journey, or if any emergency developed. If you will watch through the monitors, I will perform my daily check."

Socrates walked to the airlock entrance, and there conducted a ritual which clearly fascinated all the congressmen. With his trifurcated right hand, he twisted off the multi-purpose tool at the end of his left arm, and replaced it by a more normal, five-fingered hand that was virtually a large, padded paw. The operation was as quick as changing the lens on a camera; with it, Socrates had switched from general handyman to nurse.

The robot walked into the airlock, and a moment later appeared on the TV monitors that showed the inside of the capsule. He moved slowly down the central aisle, plugging a test probe into various instrument panels as he walked past them. His movements were swift and certain, like a trained human who knew his job perfectly.

He came to the sleeping men, leaned over them, and very gently checked the adjustment of their helmets and the location of their biosensors. There was something at once sinister and touching about this encounter between quasi-conscious machine and wholly unconscious humans; all the spectators showed their involuntary tenseness. Even Bruno, who had watched this a hundred times before, felt apprehension mingle with his pride as chief designer and project engineer.

As Socrates, satisfied that all was well, straightened up and started to walk back toward the airlock, Representative McBurney of New York breathed a sigh of relief, and spoke for most of his colleagues when he said: "I don't think I'd care to go to sleep for a few months, with only a robot nursemaid to look after me. Are you sure it's safe?"

Bruno had hoped that someone would ask that.

"We've taken all imaginable precautions," he answered. "Every movement that Socrates makes is monitored from outside. If anything goes wrong, we'll push the stop button—but no one has had to do that yet. And let me show you something."

He walked to a microphone set in the wall of the capsule, threw a switch, and ordered: "Socrates—check operating mode."

At once the robot's voice boomed from a speaker.

"I am on independent mode."

Bruno turned to the visitors.

"That means he's operating on his own, not under external command. He's not a slave, but an individual. Now please watch this."

He breathed a silent prayer, then ordered: "Switch all oxygen systems off—repeat, *off*."

Socrates stood for a moment in an attitude of paralyzed indecision, making no attempt to move. Then, after a pause that probably lasted only a second but seemed much longer, he answered: "Order rejected. Law-one violation."

Bruno gave a sigh of relief; the circuits weren't foolproof yet, and he had been taking a chance.

"Continue independent program," he said. Then he flashed a smile of satisfaction at the congressmen. "You see—he's well trained. He knew that cutting off the oxygen would endanger his charges, and that would violate the First Law of Robotics."

"The First Law?"

"Yes—we have them pinned up somewhere—ah, over there."

A large and rather grimy notice, obviously the work of an amateur artist, was hanging from the wall of the lab. Printed on it were the following words:

THE LAWS OF ROBOTICS

(1) A robot may not injure a human being, or through inaction, allow a human being to come to harm.

(2) A robot must obey the orders given it by human beings, except where such orders would conflict with
the First Law.

(3) A robot must protect its own existence as long as
such protection does not conflict with the First and
Second Laws.

                                    ISAAC ASIMOV (1920-   )

Against each law was a little sketch. The First Law
showed a diabolical metal monster cleaving a startled
human in two with a battleaxe, while uttering the words:
"Dr. Frankenstein, I presume." The second law was illustrated by a weeping lady robot, carrying a smaller replica
of herself, obediently trudging out into the snow as directed by an irate Bruno Forster. And the third sketch
showed an obviously insane and partly dismantled robot in
the act of committing suicide with screwdriver and monkey
wrench.

When the congressmen had finished laughing at these,
Bruno explained: "We haven't got as far as the Third Law
yet, and there may even be times when it's hard to decide
if an act violates Laws One or Two. Obviously, a robot
policeman would have to have different instructions from
a robot nurse. But on the whole, these rules are a pretty
sound guide."

"Isaac Asimov?" said Representative McBurney, "Didn't
he give evidence to our committee, a couple of years
ago?"

"I'll say he did—he was the lively old boy who wanted
to build a high-pressure chemistry lab to study the life
reactions that might take place on the giant planets. He
got fifteen million out of us by the time he'd finished."

As they walked back to the capsule, Representative
Wilkins waved toward it and said: "I'm still not completely convinced that this sort of thing is *really* necessary."

"It's not, at the moment," Bruno agreed. "But all our
space journeys so far have been very short. Mars and
Venus are only a few months away and as for the moon—
why, you practically trip over it before you've started!
Beyond Mars, though, the Solar System gets so much
bigger. The journey to Jupiter takes at least a year, one
way—which is why they're still arguing about sending men
there. *This*—" he gestured toward the space capsule—"is
how we may be able to get Project Jupiter off the ground.
Hibernation will open up all the planets to manned exploration. And it may do much more than that, ultimately."

"What do you mean?" asked Senator Floyd, rather sharply.

"The stars, of course," answered Bruno, warming up to one of his favorite subjects. "We've found no intelligent life on the other planets of our own sun, so we'll have to look farther afield. How exciting it will be, to meet creatures wiser than us, yet perhaps using wholly different thought processes! We believe *our* systems of logic—and the ones we build into robots like Socrates—are universal, but we can't be sure. The answers to that, and to a lot of other questions, lie out in the stars."

"But most of the scientists who've been up before our committee," said Floyd, "believe that flight to the stars will always be impossible, because of the enormous distances. They say that any trip, with propulsion systems that we can imagine, will take thousands of years."

"What if it does?" answered Bruno. "The solution's right here. We're not sure if simple hibernation stops the ageing process, but we're fairly certain that deep-freezing does—and there are groups working on that, at Bethesda and San Antonio. I can imagine a ship starting on a ten-thousand-year voyage, with robots like Socrates in charge until the time comes to thaw out the crew."

Senator Floyd seemed to be thinking this over; he appeared to have forgotten the demonstration that had been so carefully arranged for his benefit. For the first time Bruno realized that the Senator, whom he knew rather well, had been very preoccupied during his visit to the lab; he was not his usual inquisitive self. Or he had not been until this moment; now something seemed to have triggered him off.

"Let me get this straight," he continued. "You think that flight to the stars—not just to the planets—is possible, and that robots could be built that would operate for thousands of years?"

"Certainly."

"What about—millions of years?"

That's a damned odd question, thought Bruno; what the devil is the old boy driving at?

"I certainly wouldn't guarantee a million-year robot with our present materials and technologies," he answered cautiously. "But I can imagine a virtually immortal automaton, if its thinking circuits were properly encapsulated. A crystal—a diamond, for example—lasts a long, long time; and we've already started building memories into crystals."

"This is all very fascinating," interrupted Representative McBurney of New York, "but I'm not a robot, and it's past lunchtime." He pointed to Socrates, who had now emerged from the capsule and, his programmed demonstration completed, stood waiting further orders. "*He* may be satisfied with a few minutes plugged into a wall socket, but I want something more substantial."

"Eating food," said Bruno with a grin, "is a terribly inefficient and messy way of acquiring energy. Some of my friends in Biotechnology are trying to bypass it."

"Thanks for warning us—that's one project we won't support. I prefer the human body the way it is; and while we're on the subject, we do have another fundamental advantage over robots."

"And what's that?"

"*We* can be manufactured by unskilled labor."

Bruno dutifully joined in the laughter, though he had heard that particular joke a hundred times before and was just a little tired of it. Besides, what did it prove?

To Bruno, as to many of his colleagues, the machines with which he was working were a new species, free from the limitations, taints, and stresses of organic evolution. They were still primitive, but they would learn. Already they could handle problems of a complexity far beyond the scope of the human brain. Soon they would be designing their own successors, striving for goals which *Homo sapiens* might never comprehend.

Yes, it was true that—for a while—men would be able to outbreed robots; but far more important was the fact that one day robots would outthink men.

When that day came, Bruno hoped that they would still be on good terms with their creators.

13

FROM THE OCEAN,
FROM THE STARS

Four thousand miles above the surface of Mars, experimental spacecraft Polaris 1-XE rested at the end of her maiden voyage. Her delicate, spindle-shaped body with its great radiating surfaces and ring of low-thrust ion engines would be torn to pieces by air resistance if she ever entered an atmosphere. She was a creature of deep space, and had been built in orbit around Earth; now she was as near to any world as she would ever be, suspended by a network of flimsy cables between two jagged peaks of Phobos, the inner satellite of Mars. On this fifteen-mile-diameter ball of rock, the ship weighed only a few hundred pounds; for all practical purposes she and her crew were still in free orbit. Gravity here was little more than a thousandth of Earth's.

To David Bowman, now that his responsibility for the voyage was over, the spectacle of the red planet was a never-failing source of wonder. The glittering frost of the South Polar Cap, the brown and chocolate and green of the *maria*, the infinitely varied rosy hues of the deserts, the movements of the occasional dust storms across the temperate zones—these were sights of which he never tired. Every seven hours the gigantic disk of the planet waned and waxed from full to new and back again; even when the dark side of Mars was turned toward them, it still dominated the sky, for it seemed as if a vast circular hole was moving across the stars, swallowing them up one by one.

David Bowman, biophysicist and cybernetics expert, still found it hard to believe that he was really floating here on one of the offshore islands of Mars—the planet that had dominated his youth. He had been born in Flagstaff, Arizona, where David Bowman Sr. had spent most of his working life at the Lowell Observatory, center of Martian research since long before the dawn of the space age. It seemed only a few years ago that they had both been present at the observatory's centenary celebrations in 1994.

Percival Lowell, Bowman often thought, was really a man of the Renaissance, born out of his time. Diplomat, orientalist, author, brilliant mathematician, and superb observer, Lowell had focused the attention of the scientific world upon Mars and its "canals" in the early 1900's. Though most of his conclusions were now known to be erroneous, he was one of the patron saints of Solar System studies, and had kept interest in the planets alive during the decades of neglect.

The splendid 24-inch refractor through which he had stared at Mars for countless hours was still in use. Now, a hundred years later, the largest settlement on that planet bore his name—and a man whose father had known Lowell's own colleagues would soon be walking on the world to which the great astronomer had devoted his life.

The older Bowman had hoped that his son would step into his place, but though the boy was fascinated by the stars and spent many nights at the observatory, his real interests lay in the behavior of living creatures. Inevitably, that had led him into cybernetics, and the shifting no-man's-land between the world of robots and the animal kingdom. He had helped to design the circuits and control mechanisms that made this ship almost a living entity, with a central nervous system, a computer brain, and sense organs that could reach out into space for a million miles around.

How strange that, after he had turned aside from astronomy, his work should have brought him out here to Mars! When the docking had been completed, he had radioed his father: JUST LANDED SAFELY PHOBOS. NATIVES FRIENDLY. HOPE YOU CAN SEE ME THROUGH 24 INCHER. DAVID.

Less than half an hour later had come the reply: SORRY FLAGSTAFF CLOUDY WILL TRY TOMORROW LOVE FROM ALL DAD.

And what, David Bowman asked himself, would old Percival Lowell have thought of *that*?

Now something else was coming through from Earth,

most brilliant of all the stars in the Martian sky. The printer in the communications rack of the tiny satellite-base—manned only when a ship was arriving or departing from orbit—gave the faint chime that indicated the end of the message. Bowman floated across to the rack, holding onto the guide rope with his right hand, and tore off the rectangle of paper.

He read the few lines of type several times before he could really believe them. Then he began to swear, rather competently, in English and Navajo.

He had traveled fifty million miles, and at this moment was no further from Mars than New York from London. In a few hours, he should have been taking the shuttle down to Port Lowell.

But now he was not going to Mars at all; there would be no time for that. For some incredible reason, Earth was calling homeward the latest and swiftest of all its ships.

Peter Whitehead received his orders on the shore of the Sea of Fire, where a monstrous sun hung forever bisected by the horizon.* He had been sent to Mercury to install and supervise the life-support system for the first manned base on the planet, in the narrow temperate zone at the edge of the Night Land. A few years hence, this would be the starting point for expeditions into the furnace of the day side, where metal could melt at the eternal noon. But before that time came, a foothold had to be secured on Mercury, and the silver-plated domes of Prime Base nestled in a small valley where the deadly sunlight would never shine. That light lay forever in a band of incandescence upon the peaks two thousand feet above the settlement, moving up and down slightly as the weeks passed and the planet rocked through its annual librations. The reflected glare from the mountains could do no harm; in the valley it provided a kind of perpetual moonlight, with only a trace of the murderous heat.

Whitehead was not sorry to leave. He had done his job, and unless one was a geophysicist or a devoted solar observ-

---

*While these words were being written, radio observers were discovering—to the embarrassed amazement of the astronomers—that Mercury does *not* keep the same face always turned toward the sun. This wiped out a whole category of science-fiction stories overnight, but makes very little difference to surface conditions on the planet.

er, Mercury's peculiar charms soon waned. When he got back to Earth, he decided, he would like to take a vacation in Antarctica. But he suspected—correctly—that he was not going to have a holiday for quite some time.

Slightly closer to Earth, Victor Kaminski was in orbit a thousand miles about the dazzling white cloudscape of Venus. In the three months that he had been here, aboard Cytherean Station One, those clouds had never broken, and had shown only the most fugitive changes of color and shading. They were as eternal as the day—and the night—of Mercury; probably the sun's rays had not reached the surface of Venus since life began on Earth.

Nor had any men yet descended through those clouds, into the heat and darkness and pressure of the planet's hidden lands. But there were many instruments down there, sending up their reports to the space station, scanning and probing their hostile surroundings with radar, sound waves, neutron beams, and the other tools of planetary exploration. As information accumulated, so the personality of Earth's nearest neighbor slowly emerged; it was fascinating to see old mysteries resolved, and new ones loom up on the frontiers of knowledge. What, for example, could possibly cause that steady, continuous roaring at 125 North, 52 West? It sounded like a waterfall—but there could be no waterfalls on a world where the temperature was far above that of superheated steam. Microphones had pinpointed the source to within five kilometers, yet so far no probes had managed to locate it.

This was only one of the problems that made life exciting for Victor Kaminski, astronomer and planetologist. Venus was a strange, unfriendly world, yet he had fallen in love with her. (He never thought of the planet as anything but feminine.) And now, to his anger and disappointment, Earth was calling him back.

He did not know it yet, but he was after far bigger game.

Two miles from the Queensland coast, the hydroskimmer *Bombora* (Mario Lombini Pty., Coolangatta—Motor Repairs) gently rose and fell in the waters of the Great Barrier Reef. The three Lombini brothers, and the one Lombini sister, watched skeptically while their guest made the final adjustments to his new invention.

The object that William Hunter was kneeling beside looked, at first glance, like a perfectly normal surfboard, painted a brilliant yellow. However, the curved leading edge was broken by a series of narrow slots, so that from the front it resembled an overgrown mouth-organ. There were two larger slots at the rear, on either side of the stabilizing fin.

Hunter turned a wide-bladed screwdriver, and a flush-mounted panel opened in the underside of the board. The hollow interior held two slim gas cylinders and some neatly laid-out plumbing, as well as a few control wires and a tiny pressure gauge. After turning a valve and checking the gauge, he carefully replaced the panel.

"Stand back!" he warned, gripping the recessed hand-holds. There was a sudden high-pitched shriek of gas, and the board jerked like a living creature.

"Seems lively enough," said the satisfied inventor. "See if you can catch me."

He lowered the board into the water, lay flat upon it, and squeezed the throttle.

The smooth plastic shook and bucked beneath him; the oily, blue-green water slid by with satisfying swiftness inches beneath his nose. Leaving a wide, creamy wake, he took off in the general direction of New Zealand. He was too busy controlling the board to look back, but he knew that *Bombora* would be following on her cushion of air.

A great wave was humping up ahead; over or through? That was the problem, and Hunter usually made the wrong decision. He aimed the nose of the board slightly downward, took a deep breath, and squeezed the throttle controls.

A curving green wall rose above his head, and he slipped effortlessly through its surface into the roaring underwater world. For a few seconds the wave tugged him landward; then he was beyond its power and an instant later emerged, shaking the water from his eyes, on the other side.

He looked round for *Bombora*, but there was no time to locate her, for here came another wave, its wind-ripped crest hissing like a giant snake. Again he dived into the luminous green underworld, feeding the tiny hydrojets a three-second jolt of power.

He had almost lost count of the waves that had gone storming by when suddenly he was in quiet water, rising and falling on a gentle swell. Swinging the board around, he looked back toward the coast—and swallowed hard when he saw the huge, humped shoulders of the moving, liquid hills that now separated him from solid land. Where was *Bombora*?

Then he saw that the skimmer had used her speed to take a longer but smoother route out to sea, and had avoided the line of surf. He also saw that Mario was signaling to him—perhaps warning him not to attempt to shoot those waves. If the Aussies were nervous, *he* was certainly going to take no chances; he relaxed on the board, and waited.

Bombora came whistling up to him in a cloud of spray; and then, with a sinking heart, he saw that Mario was holding out the telephone.

"Call from Washington," said the senior Lombini, as he cut the engines and *Bombora* settled down on her floats. "I told them you weren't here, but it was no good."

He handed over the cordless receiver, and Hunter, still bobbing up and down on the board, heard the peremptory voice from the other side of the world. He answered dully: "Yes, sir—I'll be there at once," and then gave the instrument back to Mario.

Being the number one propulsion specialist of the Space Agency had its disadvantages. His holiday was over almost before it had begun, and the Lombini brothers would have to finish the development and marketing of the Squid. Worse still, his trip out to the Great Barrier Reef with Helena was also off, and he'd have to cancel their reservation on Heron Island.

Perhaps it was just as well; combining business with pleasure was seldom a very good idea. But that, he knew, was only sour grapes.

Twenty-two thousand miles above the earth, aboard Intelsat VIII, Jack Kimball had been rather more fortunate. It was not too easy to find privacy aboard the great floating raft which now handled most of the communications traffic of the Pacific area, but he and Irene Martinson had managed it, with most satisfactory results.

The ribald speculations which had grown with the Space Age were not altogether ill-founded. In the total absence of weight, some of the more exuberant fantasies of Indian temple art had moved into the realm of practical politics; one did not have to be an athlete to surpass anything that the ingenious sculptors of the great Konarak Temple at Puri had been able to contrive. And it was an interesting fact—which the psychologists had not overlooked—that reproductions of such art were rather popular in all the larger, permanently inhabited space stations.

There were those who argued that sex in zero gee was tantalizing, and not wholly satisfying. One school of thought insisted on at least a third of a gravity—which meant that its advocates would be happy on Mars, but permanently discontented on the Moon. As Kimball filed away his memories for future reference, he decided that those who felt this way had too many inhibitions, or too little ingenuity. Neither charge applied to him.

When they were both presentable again, he unlocked the door of the spacesuit storage locker. As he did so, Irene started giggling.

"Just suppose," she said, "that there'd been an emergency and everyone came rushing in here for suits."

"Well," grinned Jack, "we should have had a head start. When are you off duty again?"

Before she could reply, the corridor speaker cleared its throat and said firmly: "Dr. Kimball—please report to Control."

"Oh no!" gasped Irene. "You don't suppose they had a mike in there?!"

"If there is," said Kimball ominously, "*we're* not the ones in trouble. I have to authorize all circuit changes, and I'm damned if I ever said anything about mikes in suit lockers."

He realized, a little belatedly, that Irene might have a different point of view. Before she could express it, he kissed her firmly, said, "Give me a couple of minutes to get clear," and dived through the door.

Two hours later, just as he was about to reenter atmosphere, he suddenly realized that he had forgotten to say goodbye. Oh well, he would have to phone from Washington.

There were fewer complications that way.

Dr. Kelvin Poole was a hundred feet down, in the Cornell Underwater Lab off Bimini, when he received his orders. Like all aerospace physiologists, he was fascinated by the problems of submarine existence, but he had a particular reason for returning to the sea. His specialty was the study of sleep and the rhythms which seemed to control the activities of all living creatures. In the open sea, and at depths where the sunlight never penetrated,

those rhythms were disturbed; it even appeared that some
fish never slept at all, and Kelvin Poole wanted to know
how they managed this remarkable feat.

He was supposed to be working, but the view from the
window was not only distractingly beautiful—it was hyp-
notically restful. The water was so clear that he could see
almost two hundred feet, and at a guess his field of view
contained ten thousand fish of fifty different species—as
well as several dozen varieties of coral. At this depth,
though the sunlight was still brilliant, it had lost all its red
and orange hues; the world of the reef was tinged a
mellow bluish-green, very soothing to the eyes. It looked
incredibly peaceful—an underwater Eden that knew nothing of sin or death.

Nor was that wholly an illusion, now that the sun was
still high. From time to time a barracuda or a shark
would go patrolling past, without creating the slightest
concern or alarm among its myriads of potential victims.
During all the daylight hours while he had been staring
out of the window of the biology lab, Poole had never
once seen one fish attack or eat another. Only at dawn
and sunset was the truce suspended, and the reef became
the scene of a thousand brief and deadly battles.

He was watching one of the submarine scooters returning to the garage fifty feet away, towing plankton nets and
recording gear behind it, when the telephone rang.
Switching off the centrifuge that was rather noisily separating some protein samples, he picked up the receiver
and answered, "Poole here."

He listened carefully for a minute, sometimes nodding
his head in agreement, occasionally pursing his lips in
disapproval.

"Of course," he said at last. "It's perfectly practical—
you've read my report. There's an element of risk—but
I'm still fit, and I've done it seven—no, eight—times. But
why the rush? . . . Well, if *that's* the way it is . . . Yes, of
course, I can fly to Washington in an hour, if you have a
jet here—but there's one big snag."

He looked at the roof overhead, and contemplated the
hundred feet of water above the metal shell of the lab. On
dry land, he could walk that distance in twenty seconds—
but he had been down here, living at a pressure of four
atmospheres, for almost a month.

This was going to be rather hard to explain. No one
had ever found a safe way of accelerating the decompres-
sion process; Poole had seen the "bends" just once in his

life, and he had a hearty respect for this dreaded divers' sickness. He had no intention of turning his bloodstream into soda water, or even risking a single bubble of compressed air in some inconvenient artery.

One could not argue with the laws of physics; Washington would simply have to accept the rather surprising facts.

It was going to take him just as long to ascend through that mere hundred feet of water above his head, as it would to come homeward from the Moon.

14

WITH OPEN HANDS

At first, there was some criticism of the risks being taken, but this slowly faded with the passage of time. The world began to appreciate the skill and care that were being poured into the mission, and to realize that this was no desperate, do-or-die stunt. At every opportunity, the astronauts themselves expressed full confidence in success; and they were the ones whose opinions really mattered.

Moreover, the ominous, silent presence of TMA-1 was now beginning to affect all mankind. The initial excitement had worn off, to be replaced by an undercurrent of anxious apprehension, and a determination to discover the truth as soon as was humanly possible. Until the meaning of that black pyramid was known, the whole world was in a state of uncertainty, unable to make any longrange plans.

For two diametrically opposite reasons, those involved in such vast international engineering projects as the Sahara Irrigation Scheme, the Gibraltar Dam, and the Sargasso Sea Farms now felt unable to commit themselves to the billions of dollars and decades of work required. It would obviously be foolish to plow vast resources into such enterprises, if there were hostile forces out there in space which might suddenly undo the toil of ages.

The second argument was more subtle, but in its way just as enervating. The creatures who had built TMA-1 were clearly far more advanced than mankind; suppose they were prepared to share their knowledge? To struggle ahead without their aid might be like building dams and roads with bare hands—while they had the equivalent of bulldozers and earthmovers.

Mankind was becoming slowly paralyzed by ignorance,

and there were some who clamored for an all-out assault on TMA-1 itself with every weapon of scientific research. These appeals had been resisted; whatever secrets the pyramid held would probably be destroyed in the attempt to reach them. Moreover, it might have ways of defending itself—and there was the still more disturbing possibility that its makers, if not far away, would be annoyed by any action that damaged their property.

The stock market was particularly affected. It first took a mild dip, then rose again on the hunch that space issues would lead a general upward surge. "After all," an analyst wrote, "this could open up vast new markets for some industries." But no one was at all certain of what "they" might want to buy, or what "they" might use to buy it with.

One bright fellow negotiated a deal with several of the leading motion-picture distribution companies to buy the extraterrestrial rights to their entire library of back films— excluding the Moon, which had already been annexed by MGM.

Very privately, heads of government were deeply concerned about the possible threat such an incredibly advanced society might represent. No one could give a completely plausible reason why they might be hostile, but it was a possibility which could not be ignored.

A high-level, top-secret, military commission was set up by the major powers to study the possibilities of global defense. It would be unwise, they felt, to believe our weapons systems would mean a great deal against a culture at least three million years older, but a nuclear explosion might be annoying enough to deter a hostile but insufficiently motivated alien society. "We have absolute supremacy over a wasp's nest," one general explained, "but unless we have a damned good reason, we'll leave it alone."

Though this was mildly reassuring, most pessimists felt the problem would not be that "they" were invulnerable to a nuclear explosion—but that our delivery systems might be like Brazilian headhunters trying to spear low-flying supersonic aircraft.

The optimists refused to believe that an advanced extraterrestrial society would behave in a hostile manner. They felt that the fantastic knowledge of three million years must bring an equivalent advance in ethics and morality— or else, it was argued, any society would eventually destroy itself.

In countless subtle ways, that silent pyramid was leaving its mark upon the world. It had long been predicted that only an external threat could really unite mankind; this prediction now appeared to be coming true. Behind the scenes, statesmen were already at work, trying to end the national rivalries that had been in existence so long, and of which few could remember the origin. There was even a chance that the concept of world government, that battered dream of the idealists, would soon become reality, though for reasons that were hardly idealistic.

And as far as the mission was concerned, one vital matter of policy had already been decided—even though there were some who considered that it was taking good manners beyond the point of common sense.

The human race, until it knew what it was up against, would be well behaved. Whatever preparations might be made back on Earth, no weapons of any kind would be carried to Jupiter.

Man's emissaries would go into the unknown with open hands.

15

UNIVERSE

"But this is absurd," protested Victor Kaminski. "I'm not a bloody film star."

"Agreed," said Jules Manning, the Space Agency's Director of Public Affairs. "But you *are* the best-known astronomer in the world. If you do the commentary, we'll multiply the audience many times over. And the major networks will rush to carry it—especially as it won't cost them anything."

"I'm not even a particularly good astronomer—only a particularly healthy one, unaddicted to cannibalism, homosexuality, postnasal drip, and similar habits Not Wanted on Voyage. Or so the psychologists tell me."

"Seriously, Victor—you'll be doing the whole project a great service, and it won't take much of your time. Once you've read the script, the whole job can be done in an afternoon."

"I don't have any afternoons. Is it really all that important?"

"We think so. The last survey was rather depressing. Even now, twenty-three percent of the public thinks that the Sun is nearer than the Moon, that there are only a few thousand stars, and that they're not very big anyway. You can strike a major blow for education, and for astronomy, if you'll go along with this."

"I'll make a deal—I'll speak the introduction. But I'm damned if I'll deliver the whole commercial—you'll have to get one of your tame actors for that. Agreed?"

"Agreed," said Manning promptly. He knew that half a loaf was better than no loaf at all. And, with a little patience and persuasion, he might yet get the other half as well.

MAN IS THE MEASURE OF ALL THINGS, burned the slogan on the screen; then, superimposed on the lettering, appeared da Vinci's famous drawing of the standing human figure inscribed in a circle.

"If this statement is indeed true, and not vanity," began the commentator, "we can use man as a yardstick to measure the universe. Of course, he is a very short yardstick; so let us multiply him a thousandfold. . . ."

The camera zoomed away; the figure dwindled until it was barely visible. Then it reproduced itself hundreds of times, to form a dotted line—one side of an empty square.

"Here is our man—our yardstick—one thousand times repeated. That square is a mile* on a side. Now we'll keep on changing scale—a thousandfold each time—until we have reached the edge of the known universe. And because we'll have to make quite a few jumps, let us write down the scale factor as a reminder."

The number 1000 appeared on the bottom of the screen. Then the square began to shrink, the digits blurred swiftly—and a new square appeared, with the number 1,000,000 beneath it. This 1000-mile-on-a side square was superimposed on the eastern seaboard of the United States; the original one-mile square was still just visible, marked by an arrow.

"Now we jump again, another thousand times. . . ."

The number 1,000,000,000 came up, and in the million-mile-wide square on the screen appeared Earth and Moon, looking quite small.

"Now we are out into astronomical space, and we are dealing with numbers that are already too large for comprehension. We need a more convenient measure, and we can get it by using the fastest thing in the universe—light itself. . . .

"A beam of light could go round our entire globe seven times in a single second. . . ."

Here a glowing spot appeared beside the Earth, and blurred into a circle as it orbited the globe once every seventh of a second.

"And it takes just over a second to reach the Moon. . . ."

The spot broke away from its orbit, and sailed across to the tiny disk of the Moon, taking 1 1/4 seconds for the trip.

*Hopefully, by *2001* even the U.K. and the U.S. will have joined the civilized world and adopted the metric system.

"Now our next thousand-to-one jump—the fourth since we started with that man, back on Earth. . . ."

Here were all the planets out to Jupiter—the whole inner Solar System: Sun, Mercury, Venus, Earth, Mars, and Jupiter itself.

"On this scale, the planets are too small to be seen; we can only show their orbits. The picture is a billion miles on a side; light or radio waves would cross it in just over an hour. It shows the volume of space we have begun to explore; by our standards, it is enormous. All the men who have ever lived, laid end to end, would span about one tenth of it. But by the standards of the Universe, it is nothing. Here comes jump number five. . . ."

The square shrank again; the number 1,000,000,000,-000,000 flickered on to the screen. In the center of the new square, there was just one shining point—the Sun.

"The planets, of course, have vanished completely. But notice this—for the first time, nothing new has entered the picture. Even this huge jump has not taken us to the very nearest of the stars.

"If we wish to see them, we must jump again. . . ."

1,000,000,000,000,000,000 flashed up; now the new square was dotted with dozens of tiny points of light.

"At last we enter the realm of the stars. There are a few hundred of them in this picture, which light takes 150 years to cross—the light which, remember, went from Earth to Moon in little more than a second. Of these stars, our own Sun is a perfectly average specimen. And because it is so average—so normal—we believe that many of the other stars are accompanied by similar planets, though they are too distant for our telescopes to show them. More than that—we also feel certain that many of those planets must have life.

"On this scale, the stars—our neighboring suns—appear scattered at random. But when we make the next, and seventh, thousandfold jump, we see that they form a pattern. . . ."

Up came the number 1,000,000,000,000,000,000,000, and now even the individual stars had vanished. There was only a great spiral of glowing mist, almost filling the outlines of the square.

"This is the Galaxy—the slowly turning city of stars of which our Sun is a modest suburbanite—somewhere about here."

An arrow pointed to a region two-thirds of the way out from the center of the spiral.

"It takes light a hundred thousand years to cross this immense whirlpool of suns—this island universe. And it is turning so slowly that it has made only a dozen revolutions since life began on Earth.

"Call this the Home Galaxy, if you wish. The stars you see in the night sky are merely the local residents—most of them very close at hand. The more distant ones form the glowing background we call the Milky Way.

"And how many stars, how many suns, would you guess that the whole Galaxy contains? If you said a few million, you would be hopelessly in error. A few billion would be better; there are, in fact, about a *hundred* billion stars in the Galaxy. Every one of those a sun—thirty of them to every man, woman, and child now alive!

"We will return to our own Galaxy again—after we have seen the still greater background of which it is a tiny part. So once more we multiply our scale a thousand times. . . .

"Yes, it looks like a field of stars. But it is not: each of those tiny smudges of light is a whole galaxy—*this* one might be ours. Our splendid star-city of a hundred billion suns, now reduced to a faint star itself! It would take light a hundred and fifty million years to cross this picture; this is how far we have gone in eight jumps. each of a thousand times, from the man we started with. . . .

"But now—at last!—we are coming to the end of the line. For if we make one more jump, we run out of space itself. . . ."

In the center of the screen, filling only a small fraction of the square frame that had surrounded each of the earlier pictures, was a globe of light. Its edges were slightly diffuse, fading away into the nothingness around it.

"This may be all of Creation—the Universe of Galaxies. Beyond this region, our most powerful telescopes cannot penetrate; indeed, there may be *no* beyond. For out at the cosmic horizon, at the ultimate limits of our vision, the galaxies themselves are disappearing from our sight, as if falling over the edge of space. What happens here we do not know: it may well be something which our minds can never grasp.

"So let us return from these far reaches, back to our Home Galaxy, with its hundred billion suns. . . ."

The shining globe of the Cosmic All expanded at a dizzying speed. Presently its uniform glow broke up into tiny grains of light; these too expanded and drove apart.

The screen was once more full of little whirlpools and spirals—some tangled in clusters, some alone. One of them grew and grew until it spanned the sky, and its raveled edges condensed into knots of stars.

"Our home galaxy, again, with its hundred billion suns," repeated the commentator, "most of them are little suns, like our own—too small to be visible on this scale. All those you see here are giants; ours is only a dwarf, despite its overwhelming importance to us.

"And of those hundred billion suns, large and small— how many shine upon worlds that carry life? Perhaps most of them, for matter has the same properties throughout the universe. We know that life arose independently on Earth and Mars; we believe that it arises automatically on all worlds that are not too hot or cold, that have the common elements of oxygen and carbon and hydrogen, and that are bathed by sunlight for a few billion years.

"Yet even if life is common, intelligence may be rare; in the long story of Earth, it has evolved only once. Nevertheless, there may be millions of advanced cultures scattered throughout the Galaxy—but they will be separated by gulfs that light itself takes years to span."

Two arrows appeared, aimed at stars so close together in the sparsely populated outer arms of the Galaxy that they seemed to be neighbors.

"If *this* was our Sun, and we sent a radio signal to a planet circling this nearby one, it would take a thousand years for the reply. . . . Or, to put it in another way, we might expect an answer now, if the message left our world around the birth of Christ. . . . And this would be a conversation with one of the closest of our galactic neighbors!

"Yet even if it takes thousands of years to travel from star to star, a really advanced race might attempt the feat. It could send robot ships exploring for it—as Man has already sent his robots ahead of him to explore the Moon and planets."

There were shots of ungainly space probes—some familiar, others obviously imaginary—drifting across the stars, peering down at passing worlds with their television eyes.

"Or they might build huge space arks—mobile planetoids which could travel between the stars for centuries, while generation after generation lived and died upon them. . . .

"Or they might hibernate, or be frozen in the changeless

sleep of suspended animation, to be awakened by robots when their age-long journey neared its end. . . .

"Even these are not the only possibilities. A very advanced race might be able to build ships that could attain almost the speed of light. According to Einstein, no material object can travel faster than this; it is the natural, built-in speed limit of our universe. However, as we approach this speed, time itself appears to slow down. A space traveler might fly to a distant star in what, *to him*, appeared to be only a few months—or even a few hours.

"*But only to him*. When he returned from his destination, he would find that years or centuries had passed, that all his friends were dead, and, perhaps, that his very civilization had vanished. That would be the price of stellar exploration—trading Time for Space, with no possibility of refund. Yet the price might be attractive, to creatures whose lives are much longer than ours.

"Finally—perhaps Einstein's theory, like so many theories in the past, does not tell the whole truth. There may be subtle ways of circumventing it, and so exceeding the speed of light. Perhaps there are roads through the universe which we have not yet discovered—shortcuts through higher dimensions. 'Wormholes in Space,' some mathematicians have called them; one might step through such a hole—and reappear instantaneously, a thousand light-years away.

"But even if this is true—and most scientists think it pure fantasy—the exploration of the universe will still require unimaginable ages. There are more suns in the whole of space than there are grains of sand on all the shores of Earth; and on any one of those grains, there may be civilizations that will make us look like primitive, ignorant savages.

"What will we say to the peoples of such worlds, when at last we meet? And *what will they say to us?*"

"Thank you, Victor," said Manning when the screen blanked out and the red light in the dubbing room went off. "I knew you'd do it. Don't worry about the fluffs—we'll fix them. Anyway—what did you think of it?"

"Not bad—not bad. But I wish you hadn't put in that nonsense at the end."

"Eh? What nonsense?"

"Higher dimensions, wormholes in space, and all that

rubbish. That's not science; it's not even good science fiction. It's pure fantasy."

"Well, that's exactly what the script said."

"Then why bring it in? Whose bright idea was it?"

"One Dr. Heywood Floyd's, if you want to know. I suggest you take it up with him."

Kaminski really meant it, but somehow the matter slipped his mind. There was so much work to do, so much to learn, that it was months before he thought of it again.

And then it was far, far too late.

16

ANCESTRAL VOICES

The ape-man stood on a low, rocky hill, grasping a point-ed stone and looking out across a dusty African plain. Overhead, the sky was cloudless, and a hot sun baked the yellowing grass of the savannah and the stunted trees which provided the only shade. In the middle distance, a small herd of gazelles was browsing, watched intently by a saber-toothed tiger crouching in the scrub.

There were more ape-men—about a dozen of them—scattered over the crown of the little hill. Propped up against a large boulder, one female was nursing her baby; not far away, two juveniles were quarreling over a hunk of meat—all that was left of some small dismembered animal. One bent and gray-haired male was trying to suck the marrow from a cracked bone; another was curled up asleep; two females were grooming each other for lice; and yet another male was hunting through a pile of dried bones in search of future weapons.

"It's a beautiful model," said Bowman at last, when he and his two companions had looked their fill.

"Thank you," answered the curator of Anthropology. "It's as accurate as humanly possible—several years of work went into it."

Dr. Anna Brailsford was a striking, dark-haired woman in her early forties, who seemed much too vivacious to have devoted her life to fossils. Though she was a famous explorer and veteran of many expeditions, she had lost none of her femininity; it was hard to believe that she was one of the world's leading authorities on early Man.

"So these," said Phillip Goode, Bowman's understudy, "are the characters the pyramid-makers would have met, if they landed on Earth three million years ago?"

"Not necessarily. It depends on the thoroughness of their investigation. *Australopithecus* was probably not very common; he might easily have been overlooked among the elephants and giraffes and other more conspicuous animals. In fact, he wasn't even the most impressive of the primates. To a casual visitor, he might have seemed just another ape."

It was rather difficult, thought Bowman, to take so detached a view. His great-to-the-hundred-thousandth grandfather was not a very prepossessing sight, but there was a wistful sadness about the hairy, no-longer-quite-animal face staring at him through the glass of the diorama. He was not ashamed to admit kinship with his remote ancestor across the unimaginable ages that sundered them. "I rather doubt," he said dryly, "that creatures landing on Earth back in the Pleistocene would have been casual visitors. And this is one of the things we wanted to discuss with you—their motivations."

"Well, I can only tell you how *I'd* behave, in the same circumstances. I'd note that Earth was teeming with advanced life forms, but that none of them had developed high intelligence. However, I'd probably guess—I might even be able to predict, with the knowledge I'd undoubtedly have—that intelligence would arise in a few million years.

"So I'd leave behind some intelligence monitors—or, better still, civilization detectors. I might put some of them on Earth, though I'd realize that they would probably be destroyed or buried before they had a chance to operate. But the Moon would be an ideal spot for such a device—especially if I was only interested in civilizations that had reached the space-faring stage. Any culture still planet-bound might be too primitive to concern me."

"So you're in favor of the fire-alarm theory, as we call it, to explain TMA-1?"

"Yes—it seems very plausible. But perhaps it's *too* plausible. Human motivations vary so much that any attempt to analyze wholly alien behavior must be pure guesswork."

"But guesswork is all we have to go on for the present. We're trying to think of every possibility that may arise, when and if we do catch up with the creatures who built TMA-1."

Bowman pointed to the frozen tableau of his ancestors.

"Look how far we've progressed since then! Yet after that same three million years, where will the pyramid-makers be? I don't mind admitting it—the thought sometimes scares me."

"It scares me. But remember, progress is never uniform; even after three million years, they may not be incomprehensibly far ahead of us. Perhaps there's a plateau for intelligence that can't be exceeded. They may already have reached it when they visited the Moon. After all, it has yet to be proved that intelligence has real survival value."

"I can't accept that!" protested Bowman. "Surely, our intelligence has made us what we are—the most successful animals on the planet!"

"As an anthropologist, I'm naturally biased in favor of Man. From the short-term point of view, intelligence has undoubtedly been an advantage. But what about geological time—and how do you define a 'successful' species? My friend the curator of reptiles keeps reminding me that the dinosaurs flourished for more than a hundred million years. And their I.Q.'s were distinctly minimal."

"Well, where are they now? I don't see any around today."

"True—but you can't call a hundred-million-year reign a failure; it's a thousand times as long as *Homo sapiens* has existed. There may be an optimum level of intelligence, and perhaps we've already exceeded it. Our brains may be too big—dooming us as Triceratops was doomed by his armor. He overspecialized in horns and spikes and plates; we overspecialized in cerebral cortex. The end result may be the same."

"So you believe that as soon as a species reaches more than a certain level of intelligence, it is heading for extinction?"

"I don't state it as a fact; I'm merely pointing out the possibilities. There's no reason to assume that the universe has the slightest interest in intelligence—or even in life. Both may be random, accidental by-products of its operations, like the beautiful patterns on a butterfly's wing. The insect would fly just as well without them; our species might survive as long as—oh, the sharks, which haven't changed much in a couple of hundred million years—if we were a little *less* clever. Look at the daily newspapers, and the history of the whole twentieth century."

Dr. Brailsford smiled at her obviously disapproving audience.

"No—I'm not a pessimist," she said, answering their unspoken accusation. "Just a realist, who knows that only a tiny fraction of the species that have lived on this planet have any descendants today. And because I am a realist, perhaps I understand the importance of your project better than you do."

"Go on, please."

"The creatures who built the pyramid—how far ahead of us would you say they were from the technical viewpoint?"

"Probably no more than a hundred years, at our present rate of progress."

"Exactly. Now suppose that they are still in existence, even if they've made little progress during the three million years since they visited the Moon. Don't you see—this will be the first definite proof that intelligence *does* have real survival value. That will be very reassuring."

"Quite frankly, doctor," said Goode, "I don't need any reassurance. Even if intelligence has limited survival value, it has a good deal of comfort value. I wouldn't change places with *them*." He jerked his thumb toward the tableau of ape-men.

The anthropologist joined in the laughter; then she became serious again.

"There's another possibility, though—and that's cultural shock. If they are too advanced, and we come into contact with them, we may not be able to survive the impact psychologically. As Jung put it, half a century ago, we might find all our aspirations so outmoded as to leave us completely paralyzed. He used a rather striking phrase— we might find ourselves 'without dreams.' Like the Atlanteans, you know—Herodotus said that they never dreamed. I always thought that made them peculiarly inhuman—and pitiable."

"I don't believe in cultural shock," said Hunter. "After all, we *expect* to meet a very advanced society. It wouldn't be such an overwhelming surprise to us as—well, as it would be to *him,* if he was suddenly dumped here in Manhattan."

"I think you are too—optimistic," answered Dr. Brailsford; Bowman guessed that she had been tempted to use the word "naive." "On our planet, societies only a few generations apart culturally have proved to be incompatible."

"Perhaps our Pleistocene astronauts were aware of the danger—perhaps that's why they've left us alone, all these years."

"Have they?" said the anthropologist. "I wonder. If

you'd like to come to my office now, I've something to
show you."

They walked out of the Leakey Memorial Exhibit,
through the great, cathedral-like halls of the museum.
From time to time Bowman was recognized by other
visitors, and several eager youngsters rushed up for his
autograph. Goode and Hunter were not asked for theirs,
but they were accustomed to this; Goode was fond of
quoting, a little ironically, Milton's line "They also serve
who only stand and wait."

Bowman's relationship with his two understudies was,
on the whole, excellent—which was not surprising, for
their intellectual and psychological profiles had been
matched with great care. They were colleagues, not com-
petitors, and they were often able to act as his alter egos,
reporting back to him after missions and trips which he
was too busy to make. Of course, each hoped that *he*
would be the one finally selected, but they served Bowman
loyally and with the minimum of friction. They had had
disagreements, but never a serious quarrel—and so it had
been with the other five trios. The psychologists had done
their work well; but by this time, they had had plenty of
practice.

Every time he entered a place like the Natural History
Museum, Bowman was overwhelmed by the infinite vari-
ety of life produced by evolution on a single world, this
one planet Earth. As he walked past the great displays
with their panoramas of scenes from other times and
other continents, he realized again the sheer foolishness of
the question he was so often asked about the builders of
the pyramid: "What do you think they *looked* like?"

Even if one were given every relevant fact about
Earth's climate, geography, atmosphere, and chemical
composition, who could have predicted the elephant, the
whale, the giraffe, the giant squid, the duck-billed
platypus—or Man himself? How infinitely more impossible
it was, therefore, to make sensible guesses about the
inhabitants of a totally unknown, and perhaps quite alien,
planet! Yet it was equally impossible to stop trying. . . .

Dr. Brailsford's office was that of any museum curator—
piled high with books, reports, journals from other institu-
tions, exhibits being packed and unpacked, and hundreds
of small drawers which covered two whole walls. On her
desk were several skulls; she picked up one and said:
"Here is the gentleman we have been talking about: not
much of a forehead yet, but he's taken the first steps

toward us. And I *mean* first steps; even today, none of the other anthropoids are good walkers."

She placed the skull reverently back into its bed of cotton wool, then began ruffling through the folders, drawings, maps, and photographs on her crowded desk. Presently she dug out a large book,* opened it at a marker, and handed it over to her visitors.

"My god!" said Hunter. "What the devil is that?"

"That" was a line drawing of a looming, roughly anthropomorphic figure, shown from the waist up. The head appeared to be covered by some kind of helmet, in the center of which was a large, Cyclopean eye. Another, smaller eye was tucked away in one corner of the helmet; there were no other features, and by no possible distortion or artistic license could it be converted into a human face.

"Thought-provoking, isn't it? It's a Paleolithic cave painting, found in the Sahara half a century ago—back in 1959. And it made such an impression on the discoverers that, believe it or not, they christened it the 'Great Martian God.'"

"How old is it?"

"About ten thousand years. Not very old compared with your TMA-1—but ancient enough by human standards."

There was a long and profound silence while the three astronauts studied the painting. Then Hunter asked: "Do you *really* think it's a record of a meeting with extraterrestrials?"

"Frankly, no. It's probably a medicine man or witch doctor wearing some peculiar hairdress. I should have mentioned that it's extremely large—about eighteen feet high—so the artist obviously considered it quite important."

"Or it was something that made a big impression on him. I guess a spacesuit back in the Stone Age would create a sensation."

"Not necessarily; you should see a New Guinea devil-dancer in full regalia. But I think we can draw a lesson from this; just suppose it *was* a visitor from space, wearing some kind of protective suit. Granted that, I think you'll agree that the Stone Age artist did a fine job of recording something utterly incomprehensible, and beyond the farthest limits of his own culture. Could you do as well, if you encountered a supercivilization?"

*The Search For the Tassili Frescoes, Henri Lhote (Dutton, 1959).

"Perhaps not—but at least we have cameras."

"Even in photographs, you can only recognize things you already know. The shapes and colors of a really advanced civilization might be so strange that we might go mad trying to interpret them. Its time scale, too, might be incompatible with ours—faster, for example. Suppose you put *Australopithecus* in a car and drove him at high speed down Broadway one night. What sense would he make of it?"

"I see your point," said Bowman. "So what should we do, if we ever find ourselves in a similar situation?"

"I would say—try to become a passive recorder of events, and not attempt to understand anything. Take as many photographs as possible. And, of course, hope that the entities you meet are patient, and aware of your limitations."

"And if they are not?"

"Then I am afraid you will survive just about as long as *Australopithecus* would—if he got out of the car and tried to cross Broadway against the lights."

17

THE QUESTION

The weeks of preflight checkout in orbit went smoothly and uneventfully, as they were supposed to do. There was only one moment of drama and emotion: the christening of the ship.

Officially, most spacecraft have only numbers. Unofficially, they all have names, as ships have since the beginning of time. This one, the astronauts decided, would be called *Discovery*, after the most famous of polar-exploration ships. It seemed appropriate, for they were going into regions far colder than the South Pole, and the discovery of facts was the sole purpose of their mission.

But how does one christen a spaceship, in orbit two hundred miles above the earth? The traditional champagne bottle was obviously out of the question, and the distinguished ladies who were expected to wield it would balk at carrying out the ceremony while floating around in spacesuits. Some kind of compromise was necessary.

Almost eighteen times a day, the ship passed directly above every point on the equator. The largest city beneath its path was Nairobi, and here, at night, the christening took place.

The lights of the city were extinguished, and all eyes were turned to the sky, when the world's First Lady made a brief speech of dedication and, at the calculated moment, said, "I christen you *Discovery*." Then, with all eyes upon her as she stood regal and resplendent in her tribal robes, the Secretary-General pressed a switch.

Directly overhead, a dazzling star burst into life—the billion-candlepower flare that was drenching both Space Station One and *Discovery* with its brilliance. It moved slowly from west to east while the whole world watched—

114

both from the ground, and through cameras on the station. The fastest vessel built by man had been christened by the swiftest of all entities, light itself.

Other much more important events in the program were less publicized; and there was one that took place in complete secrecy.

Weeks ago, the final team selection had been made, and the twelve back-ups had swallowed their disappointment. It had been short-lived, for they knew that their time would come; already they were looking ahead to the rescue mission—the Second Jupiter Expedition—which would require them all. Yet, even now, at this late moment, there was a chance that some of them might leave with *Discovery*. . . .

The Space Center's large and lavishly equipped operating room contained only three men, and one of those was not conscious of his surroundings. But the figure lying prone on the table was neither sleeping nor anesthetized, for its eyes were open. They were staring blankly at infinity, seeing nothing of the spotless white room and its two other occupants.

Lester Chapman, Project Manager of the Jupiter Mission, looked anxiously at the Chief Medical Officer.

"Are you ready?" he asked, his voice in an unnecessarily low whisper.

Dr. Giroux swept his eyes across the gauges of the electrohypnosis generator, felt the flaccid wrist of his subject, and nodded his head. Chapman wet his lips and leaned over the table.

"David—do you hear me?"

"Yes." The answer was immediate, yet toneless and lacking all emotion.

"Do you recognize my voice?"

"I do. You are Lester Chapman."

"Good. Now listen very carefully. I am going to ask you a question, and you will answer it. Then you will forget both the question and the answer. Do you understand?"

Again that dead, zombie-like reply.

"I understand. I will answer your question. Then I will forget it."

Chapman paused, stalling for time. So much depended on this—not millions, but *billions* of dollars—that he was almost afraid to continue. This was the final test, known only to a handful of men. Least of all was it known to the astronauts, for its usefulness would be totally destroyed if they were aware of it.

"Go on," said Giroux encouragingly, making a minute adjustment to the controls of the generator.

"This is the question, David. You have completed your training. In a few hours you go aboard the ship for the trial countdown. But there is still time to change your mind.

"You know the risks. You know that you will be gone from Earth for at least five years. You know that you may never come back.

"If you have any mental reservations—any fears which you cannot handle—you can withdraw now. No one will ever know the reason. We will have a medical cover story to protect you. Think carefully. Do you *really* want to go?"

The silence in the operating room stretched on and on. What thoughts, wondered Chapman with desperate anxiety, were forming in that brain hovering on the borders of sleep, in the no man's land of hypnosis? Bowman's training had cost a fortune, and though he could be replaced even now by either of his back-ups, such a move would be certain to create emotional strains and disturbances. It would be a bad start to the mission.

And, of course, there was even the remote possibility that *both* back-ups would take the same escape route. But that was something that did not bear thinking about. . . .

At last Bowman spoke. For the first time there seemed a trace of emotion in his voice, as if he had long ago made up his mind, and would not be deflected or diverted by any external force.

"I . . . am . . . going . . . to . . . Jupiter," he said.

And so, each after his fashion, presently answered Whitehead and Poole and Kimball and Hunter and Kaminski. And not one of them ever knew that he had been asked.

18

MIDNIGHT, WASHINGTON

The reception at the Little White House, as the Vice-President's mansion was invariably called, was one of the events of the season. There was much heart-burning because invitations were restricted to those associated with the project; but if this had not been done, most of official Washington would have been there. Moreover, everyone wanted to keep this as small and intimate as possible; it would be the last time all six astronauts would be gathered together on Earth, and the last opportunity for many of their friends to say farewell to them.

No one mentioned this, but everybody was aware of it. So this was no ordinary reception; there was a curious emotional atmosphere—not one of sadness or foreboding, but rather of excitement and exaltation.

"Look at them!" said Anita Andersen as she and Floyd orbited together across the dance floor. "What do you suppose they're really thinking?" She nodded her head toward the little group around the Vice-President and Mrs. Kelly; their hosts were talking to Bowman, Kaminski, Whitehead, and Poole.

"I can probably tell you," Floyd said. "By this time, I know as much about them as any of the psychologists. But why are you interested?"

His curiosity was genuine, quite unaffected by any taint of jealousy or sexual rivalry. (Besides, who could be jealous of six men about to leave Earth for years, perhaps forever?)

"It's hard for a woman to understand," Anita murmured above the background of the music, as they swirled round the little island of trees in the center of the dance floor. "Leaving all this behind, going off into space, not knowing what they're going to find, or even if they'll come back. . . ."

"I thought there was Viking blood in your veins," Floyd chided gently.

"I was always sorry for their women; they must have spent half their lives wondering if they were widows."

"At least we've avoided that problem here. There will be some unhappy girl friends, but that's all." He lowered his voice. "Here comes one of them."

Jack Kimball swirled by, his arms around a rather plump, vivacious blonde. As they were swept away by the other dancers, the girl suddenly began to laugh at something her consort had said.

"She certainly doesn't sound unhappy," commented Anita.

"Excellent. I shouldn't tell tales, but Jack has quite a reputation. Perhaps she realized that she couldn't hold on to him, and is making the best of a bad job."

"Bowman's the one who fascinates me; I've heard such conflicting stories about him. Is he really unpopular?"

"It depends on the point of view. He's a perfectionist. He can't stand people who aren't fit, or machines that won't work—and that makes life tough for his associates. Incidentally, he also seems to be lucky—he's never been involved in an accident. Maybe he's earned his luck; either way, we want to share it."

"But his crewmates?" persisted Anita. "Do *they* like him?"

"They like him; otherwise, he wouldn't be there. He has that indefinable quality we call leadership—people will trust his decisions, and feel confident that he's made the correct ones. And ninety-nine percent of the time, he has. We can only hope he'll keep up that batting average, when he gets out to Jupiter."

"The one I really like," confided Anita, "is Dr. Poole. There's something warm and friendly about him—not that the others are unfriendly, of course."

"Everyone feels the same way about Kelvin. He *cares* for people—but sometimes I wonder if he cares enough for himself."

"What do you mean by that?"

"It's hard to express, and I may be seeing things that aren't there. Probably I can't understand the medical viewpoint—to an astronomer, physiology is so damn *messy*. But sometimes I think that Kelvin takes too many risks with himself. He's had several narrow escapes; he was nearly drowned—twice—testing artificial lungs. He's always breathing peculiar atmospheres, riding centrifuges, trying out medical gadgets. And I've lost count of the number of times he's hibernated."

"You make him sound just a little peculiar. I'm surprised he passed the psychological tests."

Floyd laughed.

"He helped to set most of them, and you know what a tight labor union the doctors have. But I don't mean that Kelvin is psychotic. I suspect he's just an unusually dedicated medical researcher, who finds that he's his own best guinea pig. Hello, Paul."

As Hunter and his companion swept past, Anita commented, "She's stunning. "Who is she?"

"Australian friend of Paul's—he has some business in Queensland."

"So it seems."

"Darling—are we going to dance or talk? I'm running out of gas."

"Mrs. Kelly seems to be signaling to us—let's break off when we reach her."

A few seconds later, a little breathless, they came to a halt at the Vice-President's group. Bowman and Poole had now disappeared, but Kaminsky and Whitehead were talking animatedly with the Kellys.

"Hello, Miss Andersen," said the Vice-President. "I hope you don't mind us interrupting for a moment."

There was the very faintest of underlining to the "Miss"; the Kellys were very old-fashioned, and like the rest of Washington knew perfectly well that Floyd and his lady were not particularly interested in matrimony. But they liked Anita, even if they did not altogether approve of her.

"Mr. Whitehead was telling us about your Council's report on extraterrestrial life forms, Haywood. He says you've worked out the design of a perfectly efficient creature. Is that really true?"

"I was referring," Whitehead said hastily, "to that last Rand Corporation study. But I don't think the Vice-President altogether believed me."

Everyone laughed at this, for Whitehead's hobby had been well publicized. Though he was one of the world's experts on life-support systems, and had once, by miracles of improvisation, kept a team of six men alive on Mars for a week when they had lost their oxygen reserve, he was also extraordinarily imaginative and could have earned a good living as a professional writer. That he had published some excellent science fiction under the pseudonym "Paul Black" was an open secret, and he had been responsible for negotiating the serialization, book, film, and TV rights for the mission. It often seemed that he spent most of his time in the old Life building; there were rumors that he had been observed in the picket lines protesting the demolition of that venerable antique.

It took Floyd several seconds to recall the details of the study; he must have read—or at any rate skimmed—at least a thousand reports in the last couple of years, and they tended to blur together. The Space Agency was always issuing contracts to universities, research organizations, and industrial firms for astronautical studies. Sometimes the result was a thick volume of graphs or equations, and sometimes it was what one acute congressional critic had called "high-priced science fiction."

"As I remember," he said, collecting his thoughts rapidly, "the biologists asked themselves the question, 'If we had no preconceived ideas, and were starting with a blank sheet of paper—how would we design an intelligent organism?' "

"I'm not much of an artist," Floyd apologized, after he had managed to borrow paper and pencil, "but the general conclusion was something like this."

He sketched quickly, and when he had finished Mr. Kelly said, "Ugh!"

"Well," chuckled Floyd, "beauty lies in the eye of the beholder. And talking of eyes, there would be four of them, to provide all-round vision. They have to be at the highest part of the body, for good visibility—so."

He had drawn an egg-shaped torso surmounted by a small, conical head that was fused into it with no trace of a neck. Roughly sketched arms and legs were affixed at the usual places.

"Getting rid of the neck removes a fundamental weakness; we only need it because our eyes have a limited field of view, and we have to turn our heads to compensate."

"Why not a fifth eye on top, for upward vision?" asked Kaminski, in a tone of voice which showed what *he* thought of the whole concept.

"Too vulnerable to falling objects. As it is, the four eyes would be recessed, and the head would probably be covered with a hard protective layer. For the brain would be somewhere in this general region—you want the shortest possible nerve connections to the eyes, because they are the most important sense organs."

"Can you be sure of that?"

"No—but it seems probable. Light is the fastest, longest-ranging carrier of information. Any sentient creature would surely take advantage of it. On our planet, eyes have evolved quite independently, over and over again, in completely separate species, and the end results have been almost identical."

"I agree," said Whitehead. "Look at the eye of an octopus—it's uncannily human. Yet we aren't even remote cousins."

"But where's the thing's nose and mouth?" asked Mrs. Kelly.

"Ah," said Floyd mischievously, "that was one of the most interesting conclusions of the study. It pointed out the utter absurdity of our present arrangements. Fancy combining gullet and windpipe in one tube and *then* running that through the narrow flexible column of the neck! It's a marvel we don't all choke to death every time we eat or drink, since food and air go down the same way."

Mrs. Kelly, who had been sipping at a highball, rather hastily put it down on the buffet table behind her.

"The oxygen and food intakes should be quite independent, and in the logical places. *Here.*"

Floyd sketched in what appeared to be, from their position, two oversized nipples.

"The nostrils," he explained. "Where you want them—beside the lungs. There would be at least two, well apart for safety."

"And the mouth?"

"Obviously—at the front door of the stomach. Here."

The ellipse that Floyd sketched was too big to be a navel, though it was in the right place, and he quickly destroyed any lingering resemblance by insetting it with teeth.

"As a matter of fact," he added, "I doubt if a really advanced creature would have teeth. We're rapidly losing ours, and it's much too primitive to waste energy grinding and tearing tissues when we have machines that will do the job more efficiently."

At this point, the Vice-President unobtrusively abandoned the canapé he had been nibbling with relish.

"No," continued Floyd remorselessly. "Their food intake would probably be entirely liquid, and their whole digestive apparatus far more efficient and compact than our primitive plumbing."

"I'm much too terrified to ask," said Vice-President Kelly, "how they would reproduce. But I'm relieved to see that you've given them two arms and legs, just like us."

"Well, from an engineering viewpoint it is quite hard to make a major improvement here. Too many limbs get in each other's way; tentacles aren't much good for precision work, though they might be a useful extra. Even five fingers seems about the optimum number; I suspect that hands will look very much the same throughout the universe—even if nothing else does."

"And *I* suspect," said Kaminski, "that the people who designed our friend here failed to think far enough ahead. What's the purpose of food and oxygen? Why, merely combustion, to produce energy—at a miserable few per cent efficiency. This is what our really advanced extraterrestrial will look like. May I?"

He took the pen and pad from Floyd, and rapidly shaded the egg-shaped body until the air and food intakes were no longer visible. Then, at waist level, he sketched in an electric power point—and ran a long cable to a socket a few feet away.

There was general laughter, in which Kaminski did not join, though his eyes twinkled.

"The cyborg—the electromechanical organism. And even he-it is only a stepping stone to the next stage—the purely electronic intelligence, with no flesh-and-blood body at all. The robot, if you like—though I prefer to call it the autonomous computer."

"And what would *that* look like?" asked the Vice-President.

Before Kaminski could answer, Whitehead annexed his sketchpad and started to draw swiftly.

"It could look just like one of our present computers," he said. "On the other hand—it could be this."

He handed the pad to Mr. Kelly. It showed a simple, unadorned tetrahedron.

"I see—TMA-1 itself."

"Exactly, sir. There may be no pyramid-builders—there may only be pyramids. *They* may be our super-intelligences."

"That would be disappointing," said the Vice-President. "I don't know what I expect you to find out on Jupiter, but I hope it's more exciting than that."

"*I* don't," interjected Mrs. Kelly. Then she began to laugh.

After a while she pulled herself together, obviously with an effort.

"I've just had the most hilarious idea," she said. "Suppose you're right, and they send back an ambassador. Can you imagine that welcoming parade down Fifth Avenue— and the President sharing his Cadillac with a large, black pyramid?"

The Vice-President began to grin, and very quickly the grin spread right across his face. He made no comment, but everyone remembered the stories of his occasional disagreements with the Chief Executive.

It was quite obvious that he could imagine that parade; and that, on the whole, he rather liked the idea.

It was a glorious night; there had been rain earlier in the day, and the freshly washed sky was unusually dark. Bowman had never seen so many stars above Washington; and now, soon after midnight, the brightest of them all was rising in the east.

"Look, Mr. Vice-President," he said, as they took their final leave. "Our target—eight months from now."

They all stood in thoughtful silence, wholly forgetting the other guests, not even hearing the soft background of music from the band inside the house. Around them was the sleeping city, dominated by the floodlit bubble of the Capitol dome. And over that ghostly white hemisphere, Jupiter was rising.

19

MISSION TO JUPITER

Like everything else in *2001*, the good ship *Discovery*
passed through many transformations before it reached its
final shape. Obviously, it could not be a conventional,
chemically propelled vehicle, and there was little doubt
that it would have to be nuclear-powered for the mission
we envisaged. But how should the power be applied?
There were several alternatives—electric thrusters using
charged particles (the ion drive); jets of extremely hot gas
(plasma) controlled by magnetic fields; or streams of
hydrogen expanding through nozzles after they had been
heated in a nuclear reactor. All these ideas have been
tested on the ground, or in actual spaceflight; all are
known to work.

The final decision was made on the basis of aesthetics
rather than technology; we wanted *Discovery* to look
strange yet plausible, futuristic but not fantastic. Eventually we settled on the plasma drive, though I must confess
that there was a little cheating. Any nuclear-powered vehicle must have large radiating surfaces to get rid of the
excess heat generated by the reactors—but this would
make *Discovery* look somewhat odd. Our audiences already had enough to puzzle about; we didn't want them to
spend half the picture wondering why spaceships should
have wings. So the radiators came off.

There was also a digression—to the great alarm, as
already mentioned, of the Art Department—into a totally
different form of propulsion. During the late 1950's,
American scientists had been studying an extraordinary
concept ("Project Orion") which was theoretically capable of lifting payloads of thousands of tons directly into
space at high efficiency. It is still the only known method

of doing this, but for rather obvious reasons it has not made much progress.

Project Orion is a nuclear-pulse system—a kind of atomic analog of the wartime V-2 or buzz-bomb. Small (kiloton) fission bombs would be exploded, at the rate of one every few seconds, fairly close to a massive pusher-plate which would absorb the impulse from the explosion; even in the vacuum of space, the debris from such a mini-bomb can produce quite a kick.

The plate would be attached to the spacecraft by a shock-absorbing system that would smooth out the pulses, so that the intrepid passengers would have a steady, one-gravity ride—unless the engine started to knock.

Although Project Orion sounds slightly unbelievable, extensive theoretical studies, and some tests using conventional explosives, showed that it would certainly work—and it would be many times cheaper than any other method of space propulsion. It might even be cheaper, per passenger seat, than conventional air transport—*if* one was thinking in terms of million-ton vehicles. But the whole project was grounded by the Nuclear Test Ban Treaty, and in any case it will be quite a long time before NASA, or anybody else, is thinking on such a grandiose scale. Still, it is nice to know that the possibility exists, in case the need ever arises for a lunar equivalent of the Berlin Airlift. . . .

When we started work on *2001*, some of the Orion documents had just been declassified, and were passed on to us by scientists indignant about the demise of the project. It seemed an exciting idea to show a nuclear-pulse system in action, and a number of design studies were made of it; but after a week or so Stanley decided that putt-putting away from Earth at the rate of twenty atom bombs per minute was just a little too comic. Moreover—recalling the finale of *Dr. Strangelove*—it might seem to a good many people that he had started to live up to his own title and had really learned to Love the Bomb. So he dropped Orion, and the only trace of it that survives in both movie and novel is the name.

As has already been indicated by the frantic entries in my log, the story line took a couple of years of hard labor to pin down. We had the beginning and (approximately) the end; it was the center portion which refused to stay in one place. I sometimes felt that we were wrestling with a powerful and uncooperative snake, anchored at both ends.

Discovery's crew kept altering in names and numbers, but what caused us the most excruciating problems were the accident in mid-voyage, and the precise nature of HAL's insubordination. We knew that faulty communication would be the heart of the trouble (as of most troubles), and wanted therefore to break the radio link with Earth, in such a manner that it could not be easily repaired. One way of doing this was to immobilize the ship's main directional antenna—or even to lose it. This appeared to be rather difficult, but as the extracts that follow will demonstrate, we succeeded. Here will also be found, casually thrown away in a few lines, the germ of the final confrontation between Bowman and HAL.

The Star Gate—that transdimensional shortcut across space and time which leads to another universe—also passed through many metamorphoses. Originally, we placed it on the innermost moon of Jupiter; I felt that such a device might somehow require the gravitational field of a giant planet to anchor it. And at that time we had not brutally killed off all but one of our astronauts, so we let the survivors do some exploring of this anomaly in space, before venturing into it. All these preliminaries were greatly shortened in the final version of the book— and eliminated altogether in the movie.

We also wavered uncertainly between Jupiter and Saturn as *Discovery*'s target planet. In the novel, we greedily chose both, using the "slingshot effect" of Jupiter's gravitational field to boost the spaceship on to Saturn. This is the principle behind the Grand Tour concept, whereby *all* the outer planets, from Jupiter to Pluto, may be surveyed during the late '70's and the '80's by space probes which we can launch with rockets that already exist. The line-up of the planets which makes this possible will begin in 1976 and will last about four years. If we miss the opportunity, an equally good one will not arise again for almost two centuries. However, if one is only going to Saturn, Jupiter can give major assistance for a year or two in every decade.

Stanley and his special-effects team spent a great deal of time working on Saturn before it was decided to stick to Jupiter. There can be little doubt that Saturn, with its glorious system of rings, is the most spectacular of all the planets, and personally I was rather sorry when we abandoned it. But the more accurately we reproduced this extraordinary world, the less believable it seemed.

One of the reasons why I was drawn to Saturn (and

still stuck with it in the novel version) is that its ninth
moon, Iapetus, is one of the most mysterious bodies in the
Solar System; it is six times brighter at one end of its orbit
than at the other. After studying the light curves, I decided that it must have a brilliant oval patch on one
hemisphere, and cunningly worked this into the narrative.
I was therefore delighted when Drs. Cook and Franklin of
the Smithsonian Institution Astrophysical Obervatory sent
me their paper "An Explanation of the Light Curve of
Iapetus," which contains the unusual reference: "Our picture of the current state of Iapetus has, to some extent,
been anticipated on rather different grounds by Clarke
(1968). We are, however, unable to substantiate his claim
that the center of the bright region contains a curious
dark structure."

Throughout the novel, I used the name "Japetus" instead of "Iapetus," and this has been queried in some
quarters. (Jerry Agel even wondered if I was attempting a
pun.) Only recently have I discovered why I used this
spelling; I undoubtedly caught it from my old friend Willy
Ley. In the beautiful volume *The Conquest of Space*,
which he produced with Chesley Bonestell in 1949, he
used the "J" form throughout.

I presume this is the German rendering of the Greek;
alas, I can no longer query "Villy" on this point. After
preaching the cause of space travel for more than forty
years, he died just a month before the flight of Apollo 11.
Now he has his own crater, near Wiener and Von Neu-
mann, on the far side of the Moon.

*The fifteen chapters that follow—20 to 34—
developed alternative versions of the accident, the nature
of the Star Gate, and the mode of entry into it. Because it
usually takes a long time to see the obvious, we went to a
great deal of trouble to save some of Bowman's companions, and even to maneuver the entire spaceship, with its
slightly depleted crew, into the universe beyond the Star
Gate. I cannot recall how long it was before we realized
that Bowman alone need survive.*

*We should have taken a hint from Melville, who placed
at the opening of his brief Epilogue the line from Job:
"And I only am escaped alone to tell thee."*

20

FLIGHT PAY

The six members of the crew made their departures from Earth as quietly as possible, on separate and unannounced flights—some from the Kennedy Spaceport, some from the Baikonur Cosmodrome. They had all said goodbye to their families and friends, and had given countless interviews. They wanted no publicity during their last moments on Earth, and most of them managed to avoid it.

The actual launch date was still a week ahead. They would need all that amount of time to become accustomed to working and living as a team aboard *Discovery* under actual flight conditions—conditions which could never be completely simulated on Earth. The "Orbital Shakedown" could be carried out safely yet realistically, with Space Station One hovering only a few miles away, ready to provide immediate help in case of emergency.

That preflight week was also essential for medical reasons. As Dr. Poole expressed it, with concise accuracy, "It gives us a chance to share our germs." The ship would be rigorously quarantined; its inhabitants would catch no diseases from outside, and if they developed any allergies to each other, something could still be done about it.

There were countless little problems, but no major ones—at least, of a technical nature. However, Bowman was distracted from more important matters by one annoying piece of bureaucratic ineptitude.

From the earliest days, the financial rewards of astronauts had always been the subject of controversy. Everyone agreed that they should be paid well—but how well?

After a long series of policy changes in which both the

Space Agency and the individual astronauts had come in for much criticism, general rules had been worked out to everyone's satisfaction. On this mission, where every man except Dr. Poole was an Astronaut, First Class, all crew members would receive the standard basic pay for that grade, which worked out at $34,945 per annum. By special arrangement with the Federal Health Insurance Agency, which had somehow got into the act, Dr. Poole's salary was supposed to be made up to that of his colleagues. For reasons that no one even attempted to understand, he actually received $35,105.

However—and this was where the trouble started—that was only the *basic* pay. On this mission there would be a flight bonus of $25,000 a year, as well as a substantial lump sum on return and provision for dependents in case of death or disablement. Bowman was just okaying the final payroll statements in the Administration Office of Space Station One when he noticed, quite by chance, that the flight bonus would not commence until the moment of injection into the transfer orbit to Jupiter.

The amount involved was only about $500 a man, but Bowman was quite sure that on earlier missions the full bonus had been paid from the beginning of the final checkout period in Earth orbit, when the full crew was assembled under captain's orders and the ship was in all respects operational—even though the flight had not actually begun. So he sent back a memorandum to Accounts, quoting precedents.

There is a type of civil servant (fortunately not as common as the critics sometimes maintain) who refuses to admit a mistake. Such a one appeared to be at the other end of the line. He refused to budge, and so did Bowman. So while the captain of the multi-billion-dollar *Discovery* was taking over command of his ship, he was conducting an increasingly astringent debate with an anonymous Washington bureaucrat for a $500 bonus. They were still shooting radio memos at each other when the voyage began.

21

DISCOVERY

To the sightseers, cameramen, and commentators aboard Space Station One, it was hard to tell that the ship was actually moving. There was, of course, none of the thunder and fury of a takeoff from earth as *Discovery* pulled out of her parking orbit; the only sign of acceleration was the unbearable, blue-white radiance of the plasma jets, blasting out their streams of ionized gas at hundreds of miles a second.

Even aboard the ship, the only sound produced by the drive units was a faint, far-off hissing, and their thrust was so low that weight was almost negligible. But they could maintain that thrust for hour after hour, as they spewed out their jets of star-stuff, hotter than the face of the sun. When they finally closed down, *Discovery* would be hurtling starward at almost thirty miles a second.

There was little for Bowman and Kaminski—acting as co-pilot—to do except to monitor all systems, and to be prepared to make decisions if a situation arose outside the computer's experience or programming. But Athena was working perfectly, measuring the ship's mounting speed and checking it second by second with the radars back on earth. From time to time she made minute corrections, utterly imperceptible to the men aboard, to bring *Discovery* back onto the precomputed path.

Less than an hour after departure, she announced the uneventful passing of the voyage's first milestone. The announcement was for the benefit of the waiting earth, for the crew knew it already from their instruments; nevertheless, that cool, soprano voice filled them with many conflicting emotions:

130

"We have now attained escape velocity. I repeat: We have now attained escape velocity."

Here, already receding behind them, was what had once seemed the ultimate goal of rocket engineering. Whatever happened now, Earth could never call them back. Though power might fail in the next second, theirs would still be the freedom of space, to circle the sun forever on an independent planetary orbit.

There were still hours of acceleration ahead, but this was the psychological break-off point. Even though the cloud-girdled globe of Earth still filled the sky, she had lost them. Her backward-tugging gravity could now merely reduce their speed; it was no longer able to cancel and reverse it.

No man, however many times he went into space, could fail to react to this moment. His feelings depended on what he had left behind; for most, it was an instant of ineffable sadness, like the last sight of home to a seafarer who knows he will never return. For this was a parting that no men had ever experienced before this generation—a parting from the world more final than any earlier death, for Earth could not even reclaim their bones.

Soon afterward, the first booster unit was discarded. The acceleration ebbed to zero as the last precious drops of propellant were drained from the tank, and *Discovery* floated inert against the stars. Then the explosive bolts separated cleanly, and there was a gentle nudge as small solid rockets eased the two stages apart.

It was strange to see another manmade object hanging there in space, where a moment ago there had been only Earth, Sun, and stars. As the jets began to thrust again, the booster slowly dwindled astern; it seemed to be falling back to earth, but that of course was an illusion. It was now a satellite of the Sun, never to return to the world that had built it.

Three hours later, for the first time in the history of mapped flight, *Discovery* passed another milestone.

"We have now attained solar escape," said Athena. "I repeat: we have now attained solar escape velocity."

At their control panels, Bowman and Kaminski looked at each other with a mingling of pride and awe. Now they had not merely escaped from Earth; they had loosened the grip of the Sun itself. Unless they slowed themselves deliberately, they could now go sailing out past all the planets—gradually losing speed, but never falling back into the Solar System. In a few years they would pass the orbit of Pluto and go drifting onward, slowly but inevitably, toward the stars. It might take them a million years to reach the very nearest; but they would get there.

And still the speed mounted, minute by minute, through eight full hours of gentle acceleration. Earth was now a brilliant, waning crescent three hundred thousand miles sunward; though it was still a mere stone's throw away, astronomically speaking, it already seemed more distant than Jupiter. To *Discovery*'s crew, it lay in their past, and they might never return to it. Jupiter lay in their future— and nothing, except the incredibly rare chance of a direct collision with a large meteorite or an asteroid, could prevent them from reaching it. For the ship was easing itself, with exquisite precision, into the final orbit.

"One minute from injection," said Athena. "Cutting main drive in ten seconds."

Far away, the barely audible hissing of the jets died into silence. With their passing went also the last sensation of weight, except for occasional ghostly pats and nudges as the low-powered vernier jets made infinitesimal adjustments to the orbit. Soon even these were finished; and Athena announced: "On course for Jupiter. Estimated transit time two hundred nineteen days five hours."

22

THE LONG SLEEP

Every day the Sun was two million miles farther away, and the Earth was no more than the most brilliant of the stars. *Discovery* was hurtling effortlessly out into the night, her drive units quiescent, but all her other systems functioning at full efficiency.

This was the final shakedown period, when the crew would acquire the skills that could never be learned on Earth, or even in free orbit. One by one they cross-checked each other's performances, studied all that was known or suspected about their still-distant goal, and reacted to simulated disasters.

Of these, the most feared were fire and meteorites. Even more than a ship of the sea, a ship of space is vulnerable to fire. It contains great stores of concentrated energy—chemical, mechanical, electrical, nuclear—any of which may be accidentally unleashed. Every other day, at unexpected times, Bowman would hold a fire-control exercise, and all the heat-sensing alarms were tested with almost fanatical regularity.

As for meteorites, one could only hope for the best and put one's faith in statistics. Complete safety was impossible; every day, many thousands of dust particles would bombard the ship, but the vast majority would be so tiny that the mark they made on the outer skin could be seen only through a microscope. The few that did penetrate would be stopped by the inner hull.

If everything went completely according to plan, there would be no need for even a single member of the crew to stay out of hibernation until Jupiter was reached; Athena could attend to all the running of the ship. On a seven-month voyage, however, the unexpected was bound to happen; hence it was wise to have a man available at a moment's notice.

And any man, no matter how stable and well balanced, needed a back-up at least as badly as did Athena. Otherwise, the sense of isolation might overpower him, and he would move into that realm of inhuman detachment that had, in the early days of astronautics, caused so many accidents.

The psychologists disliked the term "break-off," because it gave the impression of abruptness; but the name had stuck. The first men to fly alone in high-altitude balloons, and the pioneer explorers of the underwater world, had experienced the phenomenon as long ago as the 1950's. It was a sense of remoteness, and of total separation from everyday life, which was not in the least unpleasant. Indeed, it could be positively exhilarating—and that was its greatest danger; for in extreme cases, it could lead to delusions of omnipotence. Divers had been known to swim from deep bases without their breathing gear; astronauts had ignored the plain warnings of their instruments. Some had escaped the consequences of their rashness; many had not.

The cause of break-off was usually sensory deprivation; robbed of the normal flow of messages from all its inputs, the ever-active brain started to build its own world, which seldom coincided with reality. The cure was simple; if a man was kept busy on assigned tasks, and was in continual communication with his colleagues, he was in little danger.

So Bowman had to have a deputy, and the obvious choice was Peter.

Whitehead sometimes called himself "Engineer in charge of everything else." Another of Whitehead's favorite sayings was that every problem had a technical solution—it was just a matter of choosing the best. His genius for trouble-shooting was probably another aspect of his high-powered imagination, for he seemed able to identify himself with recalcitrant machinery. There were some who claimed that he had paranormal powers, for whereas most engineers had to kick their black boxes when they misbehaved, Whitehead merely had to glare at them.

On the tenth day, at last satisfied that the ship was running flawlessly, Bowman called a final crew conference. Anyone looking at the six men gathered on the control deck could have divided them at once into two categories. Bowman and Whitehead were in good physical shape, whereas the other four were sleek and plump. There had been many jokes about condemned men eating hearty breakfasts, and cattle being fattened for the slaughter. But the low-residue, high-calorie diet was an essential preparation for the long sleep; some fuel was necessary, even at the low metabolic level of hibernation. When they awoke in little over half a year, most of this fat would be gone.

And so would Earth, that brilliant star now dominating the sky. The next time the four sleepers opened their eyes, their home planet would be lost against the glare of the Sun; and Jupiter would be lord of the heavens.

It was a solemn moment, this parting of the ways; no one felt like making any of the usual wisecracks, for all knew that they might not meet again. And the men who were about to hibernate, though they had been through this before, and thoroughly understood its necessity, were reluctant to go. Any one of them would have changed places with Bowman or Whitehead.

"This is for the record," said Bowman, a little self-consciously, glancing out of the corner of his eye at the TV camera which surveyed the Control Center, and which continually reported the situation to Earth. At this close range it was still operating in real time; out at Jupiter, it would be sending only one frame a second—but that was quite adequate for monitoring purposes.

"All the scheduled checkouts have been completed; there have been no unexpected problems. We are now at Day 10, which is the time planned for hibernation to commence. It is my opinion that we should continue according to program. If any of you disagree, please say so now."

There was a rather restless silence. Everyone seemed waiting for someone else to speak, but no one did. And no one knew that Dr. Poole, who had secret orders of his own, was carefully watching both Bowman and Whitehead for any signs of disturbance. He was satisfied by what he saw.

"Very well," continued Bowman. "You all know what to do. As soon as you're ready, please call Doc."

It was all very crisp and impersonal and businesslike, but the individual goodbyes would not take place under the gaze of the TV camera. One by one, Kimball and Hunter and Kaminski and Poole drifted back to their cabins in the carousel, and put their few belongings in order. And presently each one spoke privately over a radio circuit to Earth, and for the only time on the voyage the ship's recorders were shut off, while verbal farewells were transmitted. To most of them this was an ordeal they would have preferred to avoid, and they were secretly glad that there could be no direct reply. By this time, the round-trip radio delay was over two minutes, and a conversation with Earth was impossible.

At the last moment, Poole made the final tests of the men he would soon be following into sleep. To each, Bowman delivered appropriate versions of the same rather forced jest: "You lucky bastard! Pete and I will be working like dogs for seven months, while you take it easy." Then the electronarcosis currents started to pulse, and *Discovery*'s operational crew diminished to five, to four, to three. . . .

"That's it," said Dr. Poole. "All sleeping like babies." He looked at Bowman with a serious, thoughtful expression; they were alone together, while Whitehead stood watch on the control deck. "How do you feel?" he asked.

"A little tired, but very glad it's gone so smoothly. Don't worry about us, Kel. The first time we cut our fingers, or feel colds coming on, we'll wake you up."

Poole chuckled. "You make me feel like an old-time country doctor, wondering whether the telephone will let him have an undisturbed night. O.K.—do your stuff."

Bowman adjusted the biosensor straps around Poole's chest and right arm, checked the head bands carefully, and triggered the high-pressure hypodermic. There was a brief hiss as the drugs were forced into Poole's bloodstream.

"Happy dreams, Doc," said Bowman.

"Be seeing you," answered Poole. He started counting: "One . . . Two . . . Three. . . ." but got no further.

For a moment, Bowman stood looking at his sleeping friend, half envious of his freedom from responsibility. Then, with quite unnecessary quietness, he tiptoed away and went to join Whitehead at Control.

He found his shipmate staring, with undisguised fascination, at the four little panels on the situation display board marked KAMINSKI, KIMBALL, POOLE, HUNTER. Each showed a small constellation of green lights, indicating that all was well.

And on each was a tiny screen, across which three sets of lines traced leisurely rhythms, so hypnotic that Bowman also found it hard to tear away his eyes. One line showed repiration, another pulse, another EEG.

But the panels marked BOWMAN and WHITEHEAD were blank and lifeless. Their time would come a year from now, out at the orbit of Jupiter.

23

RUNAWAY

To Bowman, the first intimation of trouble was a quiet voice saying over the open radio circuit: "Dave—I'm having control problems." Whitehead sounded slightly annoyed, but not in the least alarmed.

Before Bowman could answer, he saw the pod emerge from the shadow of the ship, only twenty feet beneath the main observation window. It was under full power, heading roughly along the line of *Discovery*'s orbit.

"What's the trouble?" he called. For a few seconds there was no answer, and the pod was already a hundred feet away before Whitehead replied.

"Throttle jammed at full thrust," he said, quite calmly. "I'm building up a little distance before I try anything."

That made sense; a runaway pod needed plenty of space to maneuver. And there was still no cause for real worry; Bowman was quite sure that Whitehead would soon fix the trouble, as he had always done in the past.

The seconds ticked slowly by; the pod was still gaining speed—and now it was so far away that it was barely recognizable. Though Whitehead would have no difficulty in homing on the ship from a distance of many miles, he had better not leave matters until too late, for his main drive would empty the propellant tanks in a very few minutes.

The pod was now a tiny spot, its distance impossible to judge by the eye. Bowman locked the navigation radar on it, and was surprised to find that it was still only two miles away. But, far more serious, it was already traveling at a hundred and ninety miles an hour.

"Peter!" cried Bowman. "What the hell's happening? Can't you fix it?"

For the first time, there was a note of alarm in White-head's voice.

"Controls won't respond," he said. "I'm pulling the main fuse to cut off power. Call you back."

A second later, his radio went dead. While waiting, Bowman searched for the pod with a telescope, and found it quickly enough. With a sinking heart, he saw the little cloud of mist flaring from the rocket nozzle, and knew that the capsule was still accelerating.

Whitehead was back on the air almost at once.

"No use," he said abruptly. "Trying to turn with auxil-iaries."

It was a tricky manuever, but the obvious next step. Even if he could not turn off the main drive, he should be able to spin the pod around so that he reversed the direction in which it was building up its uncontrollable velocity. Then the runaway would eventually be brought to rest; and presently it would start coming back again.

Tense and pale, with a dreadful feeling of helplessness, Bowman stared through the telescope. In its field of view, the pod seemed only a few feet away, and he could see every detail of its construction. Then, to his enormous relief, little spurts appeared from the attitude-control noz-zles, and the capsule began to turn slowly on its axis.

The treacherous main drive swung out of sight, still firing; next he had a broadside view—then he was looking straight into the bay window at the seated figure of his friend. He could have seen Whitehead's expression, if it had not been for the glare of reflected sunlight on the transparent panels.

"You've done it!" he cried. "Thank God!"

The capsule was still racing away at over two hundred miles an hour—but at least it was now losing speed, no longer gaining it, as its jet acted as a brake.

"Looks like it," said Whitehead, his voice showing his immense relief. "I knew Betty wouldn't let me down, if I treated her properly."

Though it seemed ages, it was less than a minute before Bowman could tell, even without the aid of radar, that Whitehead was on the way back. Presently the capsule began to grow in the field of the telescope—slowly at first—then rapidly—then *too* rapidly.

"Still can't cut the damn thing," said Whitehead. "Hate to waste all this fuel, but I'll just have to swing to and fro until I run out of gas."

It seemed to Bowman that the capsule was now heading

straight toward the ship; they were out of the frying pan and into the fire. The risk of losing Whitehead had now been replaced by an even more serious danger.

"Watch your track," he called anxiously. "I think you're on a collision course."

"I know," said Whitehead breathlessly. "Trying to flip her around again."

He was too late. For one hideous moment, the capsule seemed to be heading straight for the observation windows of the Control Deck. Then, barely in time, the steering jets opened up, and the runaway vehicle skimmed above the curving hull of the ship and behind Bowman's field of view.

"Sorry about that," said Whitehead. "Give you a wider berth next—"

The sound of the crash came simultaneously over the radio and through the fabric of the ship. Bowman half rose from his seat,, waiting for the alarms to go and for the damage signals to start flashing. But nothing happened; it must have been a glancing impact—no real harm done. To *Discovery*, at least; but what about the capsule?

"Peter!" he called. "Are you all right? Do you read me?"

There was no reply. Bowman turned the gain of the radio full up, and listened intently. The carrier wave was still coming in, but that proved very little. He had hoped to hear the sound of Whitehead's breathing, even if he had been knocked unconscious. If the capsule had been cracked, of course, there would be no breathing—and no sound, except for the muffled roar of the jet drive, as loud as ever through the metal framework of the runaway.

That roar was still audible over the radio, but there was nothing else. Bowman called again, and again; Whitehead did not reply. At the same time, he swiftly ran through the pictures on the rear-view monitors, and after a quick search located the capsule a few hundred yards away.

To his great relief, it appeared intact—but it was still under power. Whether he was dead or alive, it was carrying Whitehead inexorably away from the ship; and there was nothing whatsoever he could do about it.

"Peter!" he called. "Peter! Can you hear me?"

Still no answer—only that maddening jet roar. It seemed to last forever; and then, suddenly, it stopped. The capsule had at last used up its fuel.

Once more, Bowman strained to detect the sound of breathing over the hiss of the carrier wave. The micro-

,phone was only a few inches from Whitehead's mouth; if the space pod still contained air, he should hear *something*. . . .

He did, and with a sigh of relief he resumed his own breathing. First there were some soft bangings, then a mumbled exclamation like a drunken man talking in his sleep. That was followed by a short blast of well-organized profanity; Whitehead was wholly conscious again.

"Hello, Dave," he said, even before Bowman could call him. "I'm O.K. now—just a bruise on my forehead—no other damage. Will you get a fix?"

A quick glance at the radar showed Bowman that the capsule was still less than five miles away. That was a perfectly trivial distance—but it was increasing rapidly. For despite its periods of braking, the pod was now racing away from *Discovery* at three hundred and sixty miles an hour.

Every minute it would incease its distance by six miles—and so on, hour after hour, day after day. But before long, of course, this would be of no practical interest to Peter Whitehead.

Bowman reported the facts; then he asked quickly: "What's your oxygen reserve, Pete?"

"About . . . five hours."

"Only *five!*"

"Yes. It was a single-tank job—so I thought."

Bowman did not say what had flashed through his mind, but he was sure that it had already occurred to Whitehead. No matter how much oxygen the pod carried, it might make no difference now.

For several seconds there was no sound over the radio circuit; then Whitehead said, with a kind of resigned sadness: "Well, I guess that's it, Dave."

"I'm damned if it is. I'm coming out to catch you. Hold on."

There was another pause, before Whitehead replied: "You can't do that—not enough safety time, anyhow. You know you can't leave the ship."

"I bloody well can; Athena can handle things. I'm coming."

"Let's not fool ourselves. What was that velocity vector?"

"Five hundred thirty feet a second."

"Give that sum to Athena, if you like. I know the answer already."

So, in his heart, did Bowman. If he risked abandoning the ship and his four sleeping companions, he could eventually catch up with Whitehead. But then they would both be several hundred miles from *Discovery*—*and still moving away from her at that deadly five hundred thirty feet a second.* The rescue pod would first have to cancel that speed, and not until then could it start on the return journey. With that extra payload, it could never make it home.

Nevertheless, Bowman fed the figures to Athena. The answer came back instantly: IMPOSSIBLE.

Just for a moment, before his years of training asserted themselves, he was overcome by a sense of blind rage, and wanted to hammer his fists against the cold display panels of the computer. But that would be no help to Whitehead or to himself. It was impossible to argue with the laws of mathematics, and stupid to feel anger at them. If one chose to live by the implacable equations of the Universe, then when the time came one must also die by them.

But he refused to admit defeat; men did not give up as easily as this. He remembered Whitehead's own favorite saying: "Every problem has a technical solution." There *must* be a solution for this problem, if only he could think of it.

The situation was so absurd, so utterly ironic. Here he was in a ship that could cross half a billion miles of space and travel at thousands of miles an hour—and he could not save a friend drifting slowly to his death a mere ten miles away. If he returned to Earth, who would ever understand his terrible dilemma? Always there would be the unspoken question: "But surely you could have done *something?*"

But this was no TV space opera, where the hero conjured some brilliant answer out of his hat. This was a problem for which there was no solution.

"Dave," said the loudspeaker suddenly. "Can the ship do anything?"

Though Whitehead was not a propulsion expert, he certainly knew better than this. The very fact that he had asked such a question indicated some loss of self-control, but Bowman could hardly blame him. A desperate man would clutch at any straw.

"I'm sorry, Peter," he answered gently and patiently. "You know the main reactor has been shut down and the thrusters have all been mothballed. It takes over a day to test them and run them up."

And even then, he might have added, it would not have helped. The ship's acceleration was so low that it could never overtake the pod before the five hours were up.

That was going to be the longest five hours in Bowman's life.

24

FIRST MAN TO JUPITER

And then while Bowman was still considering his next move, Whitehead asked an extraordinary question.

"Dave," he said, in a curiously flat voice, "Are there any asteroids close to us?"

"Not according to the Ephemeris. Why?"

"Unless I'm crazy, there's something else out here—only a few miles away."

Bowman's first reaction was one of surprised disappointment. He had not expected Peter to start cracking up so soon, but perhaps that blow on the head had produced aftereffects. Not for a moment did he credit the report; space was so inconceivably empty that a close passage by any other object was almost a mathematical impossibility. Whitehead could only be suffering from hallucinations; it would be best to humor him.

But that thought had already occurred to Whitehead himself.

"No—I'm not seeing things," he said, almost as if he was reading Bowman's mind. "There it is again—it's flashing every ten or fifteen seconds. And it's definitely moving against the star background—it can't be more than five or ten miles away."

"Can you give me a bearing?"

Bowman still did not believe a word of it, but he started the wide-scan radar—and almost at once his jaw dropped in astonishment.

There was Whitehead's echo, now at twenty-two miles. But thirty degrees away from it, at considerably less range, was a far larger one.

"Christ!" he exclaimed, "you're right! And it's bloody enormous. Let me get a scope on it."

As he fed the radar coordinates to the telescope, and waited for the instrument to swing to the right quarter of the sky, his mind was a tumult of conflicting emotions. Perhaps they were *both* hallucinating; looked at dispassionately, that was the likeliest explanation.

And then, just for a few comforting seconds, a naive wish-fulfillment fantasy flashed through his mind. They were not alone; there was another ship out here, arriving to rescue Whitehead in the nick of time. . . . It could not, of course, be a ship from Earth; it could only be—

The star images stabilized. There in the center of the field was, without any question, something large and obviously artificial, glittering metallically as it turned slowly in the sun. With fingers that trembled slightly, Bowman zoomed up the magnification.

Then the fantasy dissolved, and for the first time he realized the full extent of the disaster that had overwhelmed the expedition. He knew now why none of the alarms had sounded when Whitehead's capsule had collided with the ship. In missing the hull, it had hit a target that was almost equally vital.

Receding there behind them, still spinning with the force of the impact, was the entire long-range antenna complex. The big forty-foot-diameter parabola, the smaller dishes clustered around it, the gear designed to aim their radio beams across half a billion miles of space—all were drifting slowly back toward the sun.

The runaway capsule that had doomed Peter Whitehead had also destroyed their only link with Earth.

"Funny thing," said Whitehead, as he passed the six-hundred-mile mark, "but there are no messages I want to send, anyhow. I made all my goodbyes back on Earth; I'm glad I don't have to go through that again." He paused, then added; "There was a girl, but she told me she wouldn't be waiting. Just as well."

There was a curious detachment and lack of interest in Whitehead's voice. Already, it seemed, he was drifting away from the human race in spirit as well as in body. Perhaps the defensive mechanisms of the mind were quietly coming into play, extinguishing the fires of emotion, as the engineer of a sinking ship will close down his boilers lest they cause a last-minute explosion.

Presently he said: "I wish I could see Earth; a pity it's lost in the sun. But Jupiter looks beautiful; it seems so close already. I hope you make it—I hope you find what you're looking for."

"We'll do our best," answered Bowman, swallowing hard. "Don't worry about that." He wondered if White-head realized that he had said "you," not "we." Conscious-ly or unconsciously, he had already removed himself from the roll call of the expedition.

The leaden minutes ticked slowly away, while Bowman waited with mingled grief and frustration. If Whitehead wished to be left to his own thoughts, so be it; he was not going to engage him in light chatter at moments such as this.

The radio circuit to the capsule was still heartbreakingly clear; there was no sense of distance or separation. Over such a trivial span of miles, the low-power transmitter in the Control Center was perfectly adequate. Though it was designed for communication with space pods working in the immediate vicinity of the ship, it had more than enough range for this task.

Then Whitehead said, quite unexpectedly: "There's one thing I'd like you to do for me, Dave."

"Of course."

"Play some music—something cheerful."

"What would you like?"

"The *Pastoral*, I think. Yes, that would do nicely."

Midway between Mars and Jupiter, two tiny, and slowly separating, bubbles of warmth and light began to rever-berate to the sounds of spring. When the symphony had run its course and ebbed into silence, the pod was more than a thousand miles away.

It was still quite clearly recognizable in the telescope, though its finer details could no longer be seen. Every day, it would draw eight thousand miles further ahead of *Discovery*, and though its future position could be predict-ed to the end of time, it would soon be lost against the background of the stars.

"Dave," said Whitehead suddenly, "can you still hear me?" His voice sounded more animated—less remote and detached. It was as if he had made some decision, and was no longer drifting helplessly.

"I read you loud and clear."

"There's a job I still have to do. I want to find what went wrong. It won't make any difference now—but it may help someone else."

That thought had already passed through Bowman's mind, but he wanted the suggestion to come from Whitehead. He felt an absurd impulse to say "Be careful!" and managed to fight it down.

"What do you think happened?" he asked instead.

"I was in shadow for thirty minutes on that last job, and I noticed it was getting very cold; the heater system must have gone on the blink. Nothing really serious—but perhaps the cold cracked one of the pipelines. I guess there was a leak; some propellant may have got out, and then frozen on the controls. I still don't see how it was possible, but it's the only theory that makes sense. Anyway, I'm going out to check it. I have thirty minutes of air in this suit. I'll call you back as soon as I've depressurized the capsule."

"I'll be listening out," said Bowman. He found it very hard to say anything—even to make the simplest responses. The feeling of utter helplessness and inadequacy still overwhelmed him; the sense of loneliness would come later.

He knew exactly what Whitehead was attempting to do. When he had depressurized the capsule, he would open the hatch and work his way, hand over hand, around to the propulsion unit at the rear. It would not be hard for him to take off the protective covers, and perhaps he could see what had gone wrong. It was not very likely, but it was worth trying. And certainly it was better than waiting passively for the end.

One minute—two minutes—went by. Surely he had made the trip by now!

"Peter—have you found anything?" Bowman called at last.

There was no answer. He called again, and again.

Then he began to wonder. Perhaps something had gone wrong—but if so, was it really an accident this time?

Once more he called out into the unreverberant silence, but already he was certain that he would never know the answer.

There were times when the greatest heroism consisted

of dying quietly, without making a fuss. This Peter Whitehead had done; no one could ask for more.

And two months from now, a million miles ahead of his
comrades, he would be the first of all men to reach
Jupiter.

25

THE SMELL OF DEATH

Hours ago, Bowman knew very well, he should have awakened his back-up. But while Whitehead was still alive, he had not the heart to do so; it would have been too final an admission of hopelessness. Now he would delay it no longer, for his own peace of mind as much as for the safety of the ship. He felt a desperate need to hear a human voice again; never before had he realized so clearly that man was a social animal, and could not long survive in isolation. And no man before, since the beginning of history, had known such isolation as this.

Bowman made his way slowly through the silent passageways; somehow the ship already seemed empty, like a deserted house. He drifted down the axis of the carousel, and when he was gripped by its centrifugal field the sudden return of weight almost made him collapse. Though he wanted to lie down and rest, if he gave way to this impulse he did not know when he would wake again. He was the ship's only human guardian now; he could not sleep while he was still on duty.

Luckily, the revival procedure was automatic; there was nothing he had to do, no stages where he could make an error through tiredness. Once he had given Athena her orders, she would carry them out with superhuman infallibility.

In Kelvin Poole's room all was cold and silent, as it had been for the last five months. The biosensor display was normal; respiration, body temperature, blood pressure, heartbeat were all inside the safety limits. And according to Athena, who alone could interpret it, the EEG was also satisfactory for a hibernating man.

Bowman broke the seal on the REVIVAL switch, pressed

the button, and waited. First, the electronarcosis current would be switched off. There was no apparent physical change in the sleeping man, but at once the dancing waves of the EEG display increased in amplitude and became more complex. Slowly, and perhaps reluctantly, the brain of Kelvin Poole was turning back from the world of dreams.

Two minutes later, Athena triggered the hypodermic strapped to Poole's forearm; Bowman could hear the tiny hiss as high-pressure gas forced the stimulants through the skin. Now he should see the first reaction; normally it came in about thirty seconds.

He was not worried when nothing happened for well over a minute. Then Poole's eyelids started to flutter, and he gave a slow yawn. His diaphragm began to heave with normal respiration, and he rolled his head slightly to the side.

A minute later, he opened his eyes, and stared vacantly through Bowman, like a newborn baby still unable to focus upon the external world. But presently awareness came into his gaze, and his lips began to move. It was impossible to hear what he was saying, if indeed he had enunciated any words at all.

"Take it easy, Kel," said Bowman. "Everything's O.K." He only wished that this were true.

Again Poole's lips moved, and now his voice was just audible as a faint sibilation, producing no intelligible sounds. At the same moment, Athena spoke.

"Poole cardiogram abnormal. Recommend injection H.6."

Bowman grabbed the hypodermic from the emergency medical kit. He fired it into Poole's arm, then anticipating the worst, broke out the autorespiration mask and its attached oxygen cylinder.

But the shot seemed to be working. Poole was obviously quite conscious, though his chest was heaving erratically. He looked straight at Bowman, and his lips began to move again. At last he spoke—only two words, laden with sadness and regret, banishing all hope with their finality.

"Goodbye, Dave."

Bowman's paralysis lasted little more than a second: it was broken when Athena's calm, impersonal voice announced:

"All systems of Poole now No-Go. It will be necessary to replace him with a spare unit."

"Shut up, damn you!" yelled Bowman, as he clamped

the mask over Poole's face and switched on the oxygen. The gas began to pulse through the plastic tubes, the noise it made sounding like a horrible parody of human breathing. Though he knew that it was no use, he continued until the oxygen was exhausted, and all the biosensor displays showed flat, featureless lines.

Kelvin Poole lay calm and quiet again; it was impossible to tell that he was no longer in hibernation. But to David Bowman, commander of the only ship beyond the orbit of Mars, it seemed that the gently circulating air around him already carried the smell of Death.

26

ALONE

Bowman did not remember leaving Poole's spinning tomb in the carousel, but now he was back on the Control Deck, looking out at the unchanging stars. He was in a state of shock, going about his business like a machine, and hardly aware of any emotion. Though he felt unutterably tired, it seemed that he could carry on forever, as sleepless as Athena, while there was still work to be done and decisions to be made.

Tragedy had snowballed into disaster; what had now happened could be far more serious than the loss of Whitehead. Poole's death might be another accident, or a piece of sheer bad luck that would never occur again. But if something was fundamentally wrong with the revival process, his sleeping shipmates were already doomed. And he with them; for he could not handle *Discovery* alone, when the time came to steer her into her final orbit.

This was not a situation anyone had been pessimistic enough to imagine; no procedure had been laid down to deal with it. When some utterly unexpected problem arose, his orders were to consult with Earth, if time permitted. He had the time; no one had ever dreamed that he would lack the ability. For if any part of the radio equipment failed, it could always be repaired or replaced; the only item that had not been duplicated, because of its size and weight, was the antenna assembly. Who would have imagined that anything could ever demolish that system, short of wrecking the ship itself? It was not, in the jargon of the designers, a credible accident; but it had occurred.

The loss of the antenna had not only made it impossible to obtain medical advice from Earth; it had endangered the whole purpose of the mission. Whatever they might discover when they reached Jupiter, they would have no way of reporting it home.

There was one slim chance of saving the situation. The antenna was not many miles distant and traveling away from the ship at a relatively low speed. He might be able to retrieve it and effect temporary repairs; even if he could not do so, perhaps Kimball and the others would succeed—as long as he recaptured the lost equipment before it was forever out of reach.

He took careful measurements of speed and velocity with the ship's radar, then made estimates of the mass that was now drifting away into space. He fed the information into Athena, set up the problem, and watched the answer flash on the display before he could even lift his finger from the keys.

Yes, a fully fueled and provisioned pod could do it, if he acted now and if everything went smoothly. But time was fast running out; the chance of success diminished with every passing minute. If he did not leave within the next few hours, the operation would be impossible.

Like most space missions, it involved subtle trade-offs between time and speed and payload, and the answer was not at all obvious. Merely to get to the drifting antenna was easy enough; the pod could make the round trip in four or five hours—*if* it had nothing else to do. But Bowman had to hold in reserve a substantial portion of his total fuel for the task of slowing down the runaway equipment, and then turning it back toward the ship. This drastically reduced the overall performance of his little vehicle, by limiting the speed it could obtain. The outward trip would take five hours, the return run another five—and the capsule carried oxygen for only twelve hours.

Two hours to grapple the antenna and reverse its velocity; that seemed an adequate margin of time, though he would have preferred more. He was well aware of the risks, but they were not so great that a reasonable man would be deterred by them. Whitehead's mishap would not occur again in a million hours of operational time; the worst dangers were those of carelessness, for space was pitilessly unforgiving of mistakes. And though he would be leaving the ship without a human watcher at the controls, Athena could handle the situation. If he did not come back, in a few hours she would awaken the next man. He was not endangering his sleeping colleagues; indeed, he was increasing their chances of life, and of completing the mission successfully.

When he had satisfied himself that there was no flaw in his logic, he entered his decision in the log. Then, swiftly but conscientiously, he made his preparations to leave the ship. He was not going alone, for he had a second task to perform.

He had also to consign Kelvin Poole to the deeps of space.

Space capsule *Alice* hung in the airlock, holding her somber cargo in her mechanical arms like a robot Pietá. Bowman had checked and double-checked her systems: he was ready to go.

"Mary Sarah Alice," he ordered Athena. "Pumping sequence start."

"Mary Sarah Alice," Athena should have echoed. "Pumping sequence start." But she did nothing of the sort.

Her immediate response was a sound that Bowman had never heard before, except during practice runs. It was a high-pitched PING-PING-PING, completely distinctive and quite unmistakable. He knew exactly what it meant, but in case he had forgotten, Athena reminded him.

"Order violates Directive Fifteen," she said. "Please cancel or amend."

Bowman cursed silently. It was no good arguing with Athena; she had her instructions—her built-in laws—and she would obey them. This was something he should have remembered, and the error was alarming, though understandable in the circumstances. He was very tired and under a great strain; what else might he also have forgotten?

He could not leave the ship, if there was no deputy commander to take over from him. Athena knew the present state of affairs; it was no use trying to fool her. She would not let him go—and, without her cooperation, he could not even open the airlocks.

It was a maddening situation, and illustrated perfectly the lack of initiative shown by even the most advanced computers. He had spent almost an hour with Athena analyzing this mission, and not once had she reminded him that he could not carry it out. . . .

The captain of the *Discovery* was a stubborn man, particularly when he was frustrated. He looked at his chronometer; there was still plenty of time. Then, angry at

Athena and at himself, yet coolly determined on his plan of action, he climbed out of the capsule, shucked off his spacesuit, and returned to the Control Deck.

The laws governing Athena's behavior were not inviolable; like any computer, she could be reprogrammed. But this was a skilled job, and it took time. When Bowman had consulted the logic diagrams, decided which steps could be cut out, checked that he had not introduced undesired side-reactions, run the new program through several times, and corrected a number of trivial mistakes, he had wasted more than an hour. Yet this was one operation that certainly could not be hurried; if the revised program was faulty, Athena might let him out of the ship—but she might not allow him to return.

Before he left the Control Center, he checked the position of the drifting antenna once more, both visually and by radar. It was now considerably further away, and when he recomputed the mission he was alarmed to find that he would have only about an hour of working time when he caught up with the runaway hardware. But that should be sufficient; all he had to do was to make contact with the antenna and push it gently back toward the ship. It seemed a straightforward enough operation, and he did not anticipate any difficulty.

There were no protests from Athena, and no further delays in the airlock. At his command, the door swung open into space.

Like a tiny, complex toy, surrounded by stars and the distant glow of the Milky Way, *Discovery* hung in space between Mars and Jupiter. She seemed absolutely motionless, not even rotating; but in reality she was still leaving the Sun at almost a million miles a day. The tiny, shrunken Sun, whose pale rays had long lost the power of bringing warmth.

One might have watched the ship for hours, even for days, and seen no sign of life. Yet now a black circle had appeared in the hull, as a door swung out into nothingness. From that circle slowly emerged the glittering, ungainly shape of a space capsule. Bowman and Poole were leaving *Discovery*.

With great difficulty, Bowman had sealed Poole into his suit, for he did not wish to see the transformation which the body of an unprotected man undergoes in a vacuum. It was an extremely expensive coffin, this armor that had been built to guard him in life. But it was of no use to anyone else; it had been tailored to fit Poole, and now would perform this last service for him.

He set the timer for a five-second burst, and punched the firing key. With a faint hiss, the jet burst into life; he felt the momentary surge of weight as the pod's seat pressed against him with its fifth-of-a-gee accleration. Then it was over—but he was moving away from *Discovery* at twenty miles an hour.

For one horrible instant, it seemed that the metal hands of the space pod had become entangled in the harness of the suit, but he managed to get them loose. Then the body was floating beside him, no longer in contact, but still sharing his speed as they both drifted away from the ship.

And now Kelvin Poole was following the road along which Peter Whitehead had already traveled. Both of them, in strange and literal truth, were on their way to the stars. For they were moving fast enough to escape from the Solar System; though they would sweep past Jupiter, even its giant gravity could never capture them. They would sail onward through the silence, passing the orbits of the outer planets one by one; and only then would their journey really begin—a journey that would never end, and might outlast Earth itself.

It was well that David Bowman had other work to do; he had no time for sorrow or regret. With great care, he aimed the pod toward its goal, now more than five hundred miles away, and signaled for the calculated twenty-five seconds of firing time.

He was only a quarter of a mile away, but moving at over a hundred miles an hour, when the period of powered flight ended. *Discovery* already looked too small and remote for comfort; she would soon grow smaller still. About a thousand feet from the ship, a just-identifiable package was hanging in space, apparently motionless. But Bowman knew that it was traveling steadily outward, and that when he returned Kelvin Poole would no longer be in sight. Now there was nothing he could do, except sit and wait for five hours while *Alice* coasted to her destination.

After a few minutes, he had to look hard to find *Discovery*; she was a rather dull star, easily lost against her more brilliant companions. Before the voyage was half completed, he could no longer see her with the unaided eye, and he was glad that he had programmed Athena to send him a regular situation report, running through the main instrument readings over and over again. That calm voice quoting temperatures and pressures and radiation levels was an assurance of normalcy and stability in the little world from which he had temporarily exiled himself. He might have chosen music, but had decided against it: it would have reminded him too closely of Whitehead's last moments.

When *Discovery* was no longer visible, he tried to concentrate on his destination; though the drifting antenna was easy enough to locate by the capsule's radar, and he knew the exact moment when he would intercept it, he nevertheless felt a surge of relief when he saw one star becoming brighter in the sky ahead. Soon he could make out the details of the structure—and then, quite suddenly, it was time to decelerate, with another twenty-five-second burst of power.

He brought the pod almost to rest while it was still a hundred yards from the antenna, for he dared not risk damaging it by his jet blast. As he drifted slowly toward it, he studied its condition, and planned his line of attack.

The six delicate, curving rods of metal that formed the main elements of the parabolic dish were shaped like the ribs of an umbrella, and were almost as fragile. They were covered by a fine, metallic net, that looked quite beautiful as it sparkled in the sun like a giant spider's web. Around the rim of the parabola smaller antennas sprouted; some of them had snapped off and hung dangling in space. One of the main ribs had also been broken, but on the whole there was surprisingly little damage.

At the center of the big dish was the universal-joint mechanism which could aim it with fractional-degree accuracy to any quarter of the sky; about ten feet of supporting mast, snapped cleanly, and trailing wires and cables, was attached to this. The initial impact had started the system pinwheeling, at the rate of about two revolutions a minute, and Bowman realized that he would have to kill this spin before he could attempt any towing.

At close quarters, this whirling umbrella was uncomfortably impressive, and he was not sure how to tackle it. Bowman had done very little work in space itself, and was not skilled in extravehicular operations—for no man could become an expert in all astronautical techniques. In theory, he could carry out any maneuver with his control jets, and even perform such remarkable feats as tying knots with the mechanical fingers of the remote manipulator, or "waldoes." But that was theory; he lacked the practice, and as he slowly drifted up toward the rotating mass of wires and spars he began to realize that he might have bitten off more than he could chew. To make matters worse, he was now desperately tired.

He brought *Alice* completely to rest about fifty feet from the antenna, braking the pod with a gentle puff from the retros, and considered his next move. If he tried to grab this slowly turning buzz saw, it would donate some of its momentum to him, and he would start to spin with it. True, he could de-spin it with his side jets—but this was exactly the sort of situation in which even a skilled space-construction worker could become hopelessly disoriented.

First he thought of lassoing the thing with his safety line, but then he realized that this would only make matters worse—the antenna would simply wind him in until he collided with it. The impact would be negligible, but he might be in grave danger if the pod became entangled in this spinning mass, and he could not extricate himself again.

Time was steadily running out, but he dared not hurry. He had to think calmly and clearly, tired though he was. In principle, the answer to his problem in dynamics was quite straightforward; it was rather like docking at a spinning space station. If he approached along the axis of rotation, and matched the antenna's spin before he made contact with it, the impact would be as gentle and as harmless as a kiss. He could then clutch the main spars of the antenna with his waldoes, and now that it was firmly attached to the pod, could start to kill the spin. When that had been done he could begin his cosmic bulldozer act, cancel the outward velocity of all this priceless wreckage, and head it back toward home.

But this was not a neatly symmetrical structure like a space station, with a clearly defined axis about which it was turning. It was a huge, shallow dish, badly warped at one side, with some heavy equipment dangling from its center—the whole thing tumbling over and over in space. He maneuvered slowly around it, keeping his distance and trying to locate the spin axis.

Before long, he was hopelessly confused. His mind became full of a slowly rotating montage of curved rods and wires and glittering metallic mesh, through which the stars appeared and disappeared, until he could not be sure what was turning and what was stationary. If he ignored the background of the universe and concentrated on the antenna, there would be no problem; but the universe was not easy to ignore.

Even if he had been in good condition, not exhausted and depressed, he might have succumbed sooner or later. No one is wholly immune to space sickness, however experienced he may be, if the circumstances are right. And in this case, the circumstances were perfect.

The attack hit suddenly, without warning. The stars and the antenna blurred, and Bowman had an overwhelming conviction that he was spinning rapidly in space. He gritted his teeth together as that cold, clammy sensation—never forgotten once it had been experienced—swept over his body. With all the strength of will he could muster, he tried to regain control of his rebellious entrails.

The first urgent task was to close his eyes, and shut out the vision of that spinning chaos—shut it out mentally as well as physically. This was a great help; after a few minutes he felt that he had averted an immediate catastrophe. Presently he dared to look at his instrument panel—that, after all, was one fixed thing in his universe, and he tried to concentrate his attention upon it.

Slowly the dials and numbers came back into focus, and presently he began to feel a little better. The queasy sensation in the pit of his stomach ebbed away, but he dared not risk a relapse by looking out of the window. He was still coming back to normal when Athena suddenly reminded him of the inexorable passage of time.

"Fifteen minutes to return sequence," she called, from the now far-distant and steadily receding ship.

Only fifteen minutes! It was incredible. Bowman glanced at his watch to confirm the fact, but he did not really doubt that Athena was telling the truth.

He must make the effort now, or not at all. It was inconceivable to have come all this way, and to be frustrated by a brief spasm of bodily weakness. Slowly, he raised his eyes from the instrument board and stared out the window.

Let's see, he told himself firmly. That point just in front of the servo-motor seems to be almost stationary. If I move in and grab it there . . .

He fed a gentle burst to the rear jet, and *Alice* drifted toward the turning saucer. At the same time, he flexed the pod's mechanical arms, opening and closing the claws so that they would be ready to grip as soon as the opportunity arose.

He made contact; the claws snapped shut. After that, things began to happen rather quickly.

There was a twisting sensation, as the antenna tried to

impart its spin to the pod. Then, almost like some wilful, living creature—a bucking bronco that did not wish to be ridden—it started to flip over, changing its direction of rotation completely.

Bowman knew at once what had happened, but that did not help him in the least. The diabolical thing was like a gyroscope that had started to precess, because torque had been applied to it. It was tumbling in space, and he was tumbling with it.

In a few seconds it would take up a new, stable mode of rotation, turning more slowly now because of his parasitic mass. But in those few seconds, he would be completely incapacitated.

He released the claws; the antenna gave him a final, gentle swipe and *Alice* broke away, turning over and over with the spin she had acquired in the transaction. Bowman just managed to find the EMERGENCY DESPIN button; then he had to fight his own private battle again.

He felt and heard the brief stabbing of the jets as the pod's gyros and autopilot, unaffected by visceral confusion, straightened things out. After that there was a long silence, broken only by Athena's emotionless voice saying: "Ten minutes to return sequence. Repeat, ten minutes to return sequence." But still he did not open his eyes.

Not until Athena had called: "Five minutes to return sequence. Repeat, five minutes to return sequence" did he risk a look at the external world again. The stars were reassuringly motionless; he glanced very quickly at the antenna—so quickly that he had no time to grasp its current antics. He merely noted, with satisfaction, that it was a good hundred feet away.

He knew when he was beaten, and was too tired even to feel much sense of disappointment. Slowly he turned *Alice* toward the now invisible star of the ship, and checked and rechecked the direction in which she was aimed, and fed just less than half his remaining fuel to the motor. Then, as soon as he was well on his homeward journey, he ordered Athena: "Wake me up in three hours," and made her repeat back her instructions.

That was all he knew until he saw the ship again, still a hundred miles away. It began to grow minute by minute, from a star to a tiny world; and presently he could see the open airlock.

One loneliness was almost over; another was about to begin.

☆

[In this version, Bowman managed to revive the three remaining sleepers, Kaminski, Hunter and Kimball. *Discovery* made rendezvous with Jupiter, and went into orbit round the giant planet.]

27

JOVEDAY

The parking orbit in which the ship now moved was a million-mile-long ellipse, coming to within only fifty thousand miles of Jupiter and then swinging out to the orbit of Callisto. *Discovery* could retrace it forever, if she pleased, making one complete circuit every seven days until the end of time. Sooner or later she would pass within a few thousand miles of each of the inner moons, and could survey them all in detail. And though she would be unable to land on any of them, she still carried enough fuel to make any orbit changes that would improve opportunities for observation.

That seven-day period was very convenient. The first turn around Jupiter had been on a Sunday morning, by the Earth calendar; they would skim past Jupiter, therefore, every Sunday for the whole of the mission. By Wednesday evening they would be out at their far point, the orbit of Callisto, and then the fall back to Jupiter would begin again. It was not surprising that Sunday was soon informally christened "Joveday."

On the very first Monday, on the outward leg of their first orbit, *Discovery* passed within thirty thousand miles of the satellite Europa. There would be closer approaches later, but this was a good opportunity for the crew to practice with their battery of instruments. They had to learn to make the most of the precious moments when the worlds they had come so far to study grew from points to disks and then to swiftly passing globes.

A group of telescopic cameras mounted in a kind of gun turret outside the Control Deck produced images which could be inspected on monitors inside the ship; then

162

they were stored in a solid-state memory unit which could hold several million high-quality pictures. After a fly-by had been completed, these could be played back and examined at leisure under the different degrees of magnification.

There were also several spectrometers, operating from the short ultraviolet out into the far infrared. These should give clues to the chemical composition of the worlds that were being examined, but their records could be fully interpreted only by the experts back on Earth.

The infrared scanner, on the other hand, provided information of immediate value, which could be understood at a glance. It reproduced a "heat map" of the body at which it was pointed, and so would reveal at once any sources of thermal energy. Originally developed for military purposes, it could spot a power plant even if it was buried under a thousand feet of ice. Since any conceivable civilization or technology—or indeed any living creature—must produce heat, the infrared scanner was one of the most promising instruments at *Discovery*'s command.

The most spectacular, and controversial, instrument that the ship carried was a laser spectrograph, which had been developed especially for the mission, despite the protests of a large section of the scientific community. One critic had said sarcastically, "Why not drop an atom bomb and photograph the debris?"

The idea behind the instrument was very simple. An extremely powerful laser beam was focused through a system of mirrors, on to a target which might be an asteroid or satellite a few hundred miles away. In a fraction of a second, the object receiving the laser pulse was heated to incandescence, producing its characteristic spectrum. The optical system that sent out the beam caught the returning flash of light, which was then photographed and analyzed. And so it was possible to find the composition of a cold, dark, and inaccessible body that might be racing past at thousands of miles an hour.

It was immediately pointed out that to be probed by a laser beam, even though the damage was restricted to an area only a few inches across, might be regarded as an unfriendly act. So Bowman had been directed to use the instrument only if he was satisfied, beyond all reasonable doubt, that he was not aiming it at an inhabited body.

He had rather mixed feelings about the device. Although he approved of the expedition's "no weapons" policy, he could easily imagine circumstances when the laser spectrograph's nonscientific applications might be more than useful. It was reassuring to know that they were not completely defenseless.

28

JUPITER V

Moving more and more slowly as she approached the far point of her ellipse, *Discovery* soared past the orbits of Ganymede and Callisto—but they were out of range on the other side of Jupiter. The ship began to fall back, cutting again across their orbits, as well as those of Europa and Io. She was about to make her first approach to the closest and in some ways oddest of all the satellites, tiny Jupiter V.

Only seventy thousand miles above the turbulent Jovian cloudscape, and completing each orbit in less than twelve hours, Jupiter V is the nearest thing to a natural synchronous satellite in the whole Solar System. For as Jupiter revolves in about ten hours, V stands almost still in its sky, drifting very slowly indeed from east to west.

It was not easy to observe Jupiter V. The tiny moonlet, only a hundred miles in diameter, was so close to Jupiter that it spent much of its time eclipsed in the planet's enormous cone of shadow. And even when it was in the sunlight, it moved so rapidly that it was hard to find and to keep in the field of view.

The fly-by on the morning of that second Joveday was not very favorable; the satellite was twenty thousand miles away, and visible only for about ten minutes. There was time for nothing more than a quick look through the telescopes, while the cameras snapped a few hundred shots of the rapidly vanishing little world.

The detailed examination of the photos would take several hours; after a while the endless repetition of impact craters, fractured rocks, and occasional patches of frozen gas produced something close to boredom. But no one could tear himself away from the screen; and at last, after more than half the stored images had been scanned, patience was rewarded.

The crucial sequence had been taken with a telephoto lens, just as Jupiter V was emerging from shadow. At one moment there was a black screen; then, magically, a thin crescent suddenly materialized, as the little moon came out of eclipse.

Kimball was the first to spot the curious oval patch near the terminator. He froze the picture, and zoomed in for full magnification. As he did so, there were simultaneous gasps from all his colleagues.

Part of the side facing Jupiter had been sheared off flat, as if by a cosmic bulldozer, leaving a perfectly circular plateau several miles across. At its center was a clear-cut, sharply defined rectangle, about five times as long as it was wide, and pitch-black. At first glance it seemed to be a solid object; then they realized that they were staring into shadow; this was an enormous hole or slot, wide enough to engulf *Discovery*, and extending deep into the heart of Jupiter V. It was at least a quarter of a mile in length, and perhaps a hundred yards wide.

Time and geology could play some odd tricks with a world; but this was not one of them.

It was an unusually quiet and subdued group that gathered in the artificial gravity of the carousel for the luxury of coffee that could actually be drunk from cups, not squirted from plastic bulbs.

The wonder and the excitement of the discovery had already passed, to be replaced by more somber feelings. What until now had been only a possibility—and, to tell the truth, rather a remote one—had suddenly become an awesome reality. That pyramid on the Moon had been astonishing, but it was only a tiny thing. *This* was something altogether different—a whole world with a slice carved off, just as one may behead an egg with a knife.

"We're up against a technology," said Bowman soberly, "that makes us look like children building sandcastles on the beach."

"Well," answered Kaminski, "we suspected that from the beginning. Now the big question is—are they still here?"

Jupiter V looked utterly lifeless, but an entire civilization could exist, miles below the surface, at the bottom of that rectangular chasm. The creatures who put TMA-1 on the Moon, three million years ago, could still be going about their mysterious business.

Perhaps they had already observed *Discovery*, and knew all about this mission. They might be totally uninterested in the primitive spacecraft orbiting at their threshold; or they might be biding their time.

29

FINAL ORBIT

This was the situation classified in the mission profile as "Evidence of intelligent life—no sign of activity," and the response had been outlined in detail. They would do nothing for ten days except transmit the prime numbers 1 ... 2 ... 3 ... 5 ... 7 ... 11 ... 13 ... 17, at intervals of two minutes, over a broad band of the radio spectrum. Luckily, the loss of the main antenna complex did not affect this operation; the low-powered equipment on the Control Deck was quite adequate for such short-range work.

They called, and they listened on all possible frequencies; but there was no reply. Though this could indicate many things, it began to seem more and more likely that the tiny moonlet was abandoned. It was hard to believe that it could ever have been anything except a temporary encampment for an expedition—from Jupiter itself, or from the stars?

While they were waiting and watching, and continuing to survey the other four moons whenever the opportunity arose, Bowman prepared for the next step. If it was physically possible, *Discovery* would make a rendezvous with Jupiter V.

Kaminski spent hours considering approach orbits; Athena spent seconds computing them. The maneuver was a very difficult one, for though Jupiter V's own gravity was negligible, the satellite was trapped deep in Jupiter's enormous gravitational field. *Discovery* would have to make a speed change of over twenty thousand miles an hour to match orbits and achieve a rendezvous.

It could just be done—and, ironically, only the earlier disasters made it possible. The ship was more than a ton lighter than expected at this stage of the mission, for it had lost two crew members, a spacepod, and the antenna complex. That was enough to make the difference between a maneuver that was barely feasible, and one which had a good safety margin.

Once *Discovery* had entered the parking orbit around Jupiter V, she could never leave it; her propellant reserves would be completely exhausted. And though the recovery ship would hardly expect to find her here, it would soon spot her radio beacon and her flashing strobe lights. Nuclear batteries would power them for twenty years; their detectable range was only about a million miles, but that was ample.

As soon as he was sure of the calculations, Bowman wasted no more time. The ten days were up: Jupiter V was still silent. The mission profile said: "Proceed with caution—in the event of hostility, withdraw."

That was excellent advice—except that retreat would be impossible. Once they had used their final reserves, they would be wholly committed.

After more than fifty orbits of Jupiter V, they had mapped and inspected its entire surface, most of which was covered with an icy rime of frozen ammonia. There was no sign of life, no hint of any activity. A search for radio emissions or electrical interference was fruitless; the little moon appeared to be completely dead. The theory that it was some kind of abandoned base, perhaps even a deserted city-world that ages ago had come here from some other solar system, slowly gained ground. Hunter was its chief advocate; when asked where he thought the hypothetical star-people had gone, he answered: "*I* think they were our ancestors." He was more than half serious about this, and refused to budge in the face of all the anthropological and geological evidence that could be thrown at him.

On the fourth day they dropped two of the ship's soft-landing probes—one on Kimball's Plain, the other at its antipodes. The radioed reports were inconclusive: the seismographs could detect no tremors—the sensitive geophones, not a whisper of internal sound. As far as the instruments could tell, Jupiter V was a dead lump of rock.

After two more days of waiting to see if anything had emerged to investigate the probes, Bowman made his decision. The others had been expecting it; from time to time, each had quietly hinted to Bowman that *he* should be the one to make the first reconnaissance.

In the carousel lounge, which had once seemed so small but was now, alas, larger than they required, he outlined the plan.

"We have only two pods," Bowman began, "and I'm going to commit them both: I think it will be safer that way. If one gets in trouble, the other will be there to help.

"Two pods will go down to the surface; one will stay on the brink of the chasm and the other will go in for a distance of not more than a thousand meters—less, if there's the slightest sign of danger. I'll take the forward one; Jack will be my Number Two."

At this, there were groans from Kaminski and Hunter; Bowman smiled and shook his head firmly.

"You have to stay behind and run the ship. If we don't come back, there's absolutely nothing you can do to help us. Your job is to watch, record what happens, and see that Earth gets the story—even if it's five years from now."

He listened patiently while Hunter and Kaminski pressed their superior claims, but he had already made up his mind. They were all equally qualified, but Kimball had discovered this place, and it now bore his name. It was only fair that he should be first to set foot on it.

Within an hour, the airlocks opened and the two little pods jetted themselves slowly out into space. After a few seconds of careful braking, they had checked their orbital speed, and *Discovery* was pulling away from them at her regular two hundred miles an hour. They were falling free, in the weak gravity field of Jupiter V. Their ten-thousand-foot drop here was equivalent to a fall of less than a hundred feet on earth; they could wait until they were quite close to the surface before attempting to brake.

After a one-minute hover at a thousand feet, Bowman gave the signal for the final descent. There were no landing problems on this utterly flat plain, and he had decided to come down within a hundred yards of the pit. A last burst of power canceled the space pod's five or six pounds of weight, and he hovered for a second to give Kimball the privilege of landing first. Then he touched down on Jupiter V with scarcely a bump.

He glanced out of the port, saw that Kimball was O.K., and called the ship.

"Bowman to *Discovery*. Landed on Jupiter V. Can you read me?"

The answer, as he had expected, was already fading. In the few minutes of their descent, the ship's orbit had taken it down to the horizon, and was dropping below the edge of the satellite.

"*Discovery* to Bowman. Message received but signal strength fading. Good luck. Will listen out and call you in ninety minutes."

"Roger."

Discovery was gone—not yet twenty miles away, but out of reach. It was true that she would be back again, by the inexorable laws of celestial mechanics, in just one and a half hours as she came up over the opposite horizon of this tiny world. That knowledge was some help, but not as much as they would have liked, to a pair of lonely men faced with a three-million-year-old enigma.

Jetting the pod twenty feet off the surface, Bowman aimed toward the opening of the pit. As he approached that dark, gaping cavity, he suddenly remembered a childhood impression. When he was about ten years old, his father had taken him to the Grand Canyon, and the shock of first seeing that stupendous wound on the face of the earth had left a permanent imprint on his mind. The rectangular cleft toward which he was now drifting was tiny by comparison—but in this setting, on this desolate world, with the ominous half-moon of Jupiter hanging forever fixed in the inky sky—it seemed as awe-inspiring as the Grand Canyon. More so, indeed, for it was far deeper, and he could not guess what it concealed.

He brought the pod to rest a few feet from the brink, and surveyed the smooth, polished walls converging into the depth. The far walls were brilliant in the light of the sun, which ended abruptly in a slashing line of shadow about four hundred feet down. The feebler light of Jupiter, shining straight into the cleft, seemed to lose its power at a distance which Bowman could not even guess. Their was no sign of a bottom; the pit was like a classical exercise in perspective, all its parallel lines meeting at infinity. He tied the small, portable light which hooked onto the side of his space pod to his safety line, and let it fall the full length of the thousand meters. It took three minutes of uncannily slow-motion descent for the line to become taut; then the lamp was a bright star far down against the face of the shadowed wall. It had encountered no obstacles, provoked no reaction. Jupiter V had maintained its usual indifference.

Bowman suddenly decided that he had been cautious long enough. Not only were they running out of time, but there was only limited fuel for the pods. They had to make every minute count.

"I'm going in," he told Kimball. "I won't go further than the end of your safety line. Haul me out when I give the signal—or if I don't answer when you call me."

He could have made a free fall and come back on the jets, but there was no need to waste precious fuel. Kimball could reel him back without difficulty, for the safety line would have an apparent weight of only about five pounds at its end.

"Keep talking all the way, skipper," said Kimball. "It's kinda lonely up here."

Bowman was perfectly willing to comply. No matter how accustomed one became to low gravity, the ingrained responses of a million terrestrial ancestors died hard. He had to keep reminding himself that this pit in which he was dangling was *not* a miles-deep shaft on earth, down which he could go crashing to destruction if the slim thread of the safety line snapped. Though there might be danger here, it was not from gravity, and he must ignore the insistent warnings of his instincts.

"I must be two hundred feet down now," he said to Kimball. "Keep lowering me at the same rate—there's nothing to see yet, but I'll get a better view as soon as I'm out of the sunlight. Radiation count still negligible. There goes the sun—now I'm in the shadow, but there's still plenty of light from Jupiter. Still no sign of a bottom—this thing must be at least five miles deep—I feel like an ant crawling down a chimney—HELLO . . . !"

His voice trailed off in sudden excitement.

"What is it? Do you see something?" Kimball demanded.

"Yes—I think so. Now I'm out of the glare, my eyes are getting more sensitive. There's a light down there—a very dim one—a hell of a long way off. Just a minute while I unship the telescope."

There were sounds of heavy breathing and metallic clankings from Bowman's pod, now almost half a mile below the surface of Jupiter V. From the lip of the shaft, where his own tiny private spacecraft was balanced as far over the brink as he dared risk it, Kimball could see the other pod only as a little group of red and white identification lights. He waited, with mounting excitement and impatience, as Bowman took his time with the telescope.

Then, coming from far below via the speaker of the radio link, came three simple words that chilled him to the bone.

"Oh my God . . ." said David Bowman, very quietly in a tone that conveyed no fear or alarm—only utter, incredulous, surprise.

"What is it?!"

He heard Bowman draw a deep breath, then answer in a voice that he would not have recognized, yet was completely under control.

"You won't believe this, Jack. That light down there—I wasn't mistaken. I've got the telescope on it—the image is perfectly clear. I can see the bottom end of the shaft. *And it's full of stars.*"

30

THE IMPOSSIBLE STARS

"Say it again, Dave," said Kimball. "I didn't hear you clearly."

"I said it's full of stars."

"Do I read you correctly—stars?"

"Yes—thousands of them. It's like looking at the Milky Way."

"Listen, Dave—I'm going to haul you up and have a look myself—okay?"

To Kimball's surprise, Bowman agreed at once to this change of plan. Usually it was very difficult to divert the skipper from any procedure he had decided upon: he was fond of quoting Napoleon's "Order plus counterorder equals disorder." But now, he seemed not only willing but anxious to change places.

The line came up effortlessly; Bowman was obviously using the jets to help. When the pod floated up over the edge of the slot, Kimball peered into the bay-window, and was relieved to see his friend smile back, though in a slightly dazed manner.

"Sure you're okay?" he asked.

Bowman nodded.

"Sure," he said. "Go down and look yourself."

As the flawlessly smooth walls drifted by him, unbroken by any markings, unscarred by age, Kimball could not help recalling Alice's fall down the rabbit hole. It was an uncomfortable memory, for that strange descent had led to an underworld where magic reigned, and the normal laws of nature were overthrown. For the first time, he began to wonder if this might be happening here.

From the very beginning, they had known that they were dealing with a science greater than man's. But they had not doubted—they *dared* not doubt—that it was a science that they could ultimately understand. As the light below grew in size and brilliance, Kimball felt the first, appalling intimations that this might not be true.

It was a thought to hold at arm's length, especially in surroundings such as these. He was coming to the end of the line, and was already far below the last reflected rays of the sun. It required an act of physical courage to put the binoculars to his eyes, and to stare steadfastly at the tunnel's glowing end.

Bowman was right! He could have been looking at the Milky Way. The field of the instrument was full of stars—thousands of them, shining in the black core of this tiny, frozen world.

Some facts are so incredible that they are believed at once, for no one could possibly have imagined them. Kimball never doubted the message of his eyes, and did not try to understand it. For the moment, he would merely record what he saw.

Almost at once, he noticed that the stars were moving. They were drifting out of the field on the left, while new ones appeared from the right. It was as if he was looking down a shaft drilled clear through Jupiter V, and observing the effects of its rotation as it turned on its axis every ten hours.

But this, of course, was impossible. They had mapped and surveyed the entire area of the satellite, deliberately searching for any other entrance, and had found nothing but unbroken rock and ammonia ice. Kimball was quite certain that there was no window at the antipodes through which stars could shine.

And then, rather belatedly—he was, after all, a communications engineer and not an astronomer—he noticed something that totally demolished this theory. Those stars were drifting to his left; if the movement had been due to Jupiter V's spin, it should have been in a direction almost at right angles. So the rotation of the little moon had nothing whatsoever to do with it. . . .

That was quite enough for one man, on one visit.

"I'm coming up," he called Bowman. "We'd better talk this over with Vic—maybe he has an explanation."

When he had rejoined Bowman on the surface of the satellite, it seemed to him that the once incredible sight of Jupiter spanning the sky was as familiar and reassuring as a quiet country landscape back on Earth. Jupiter they understood—or where it still held mysteries, they were not such that sapped the mind. But the thing beneath their feet defied all reason and all logic.

They waited, lost in their own thoughts and saying nothing, merely listening for the first sound of *Discovery*'s beacon as she came up over the horizon. Luckily for their peace of mind, she was exactly on time; still without a word, they jetted themselves up toward her and, ten minutes later, were jockeying themselves through the air-lock.

Astronauts are somewhat addicted to harmless practical jokes; it is one of their ways of asserting superiority over the Universe, which has no sense of humor. Kaminski and Hunter might, for a moment, have thought that the others were pulling their legs, but their doubts lasted no more than seconds.

Two orbits later, they went down themselves, taking cameras with long-focus lenses to record the star-patterns at the bottom of the shaft. Within minutes, Kaminski had an additional piece of information. He timed the movement of the stars across the opening, and calculated that it took fifteen hours for a complete revolution—as against Jupiter V's ten. It seemed that, by some magic of space or time, they were looking out into a strange universe through a window in the surface of a world that turned upon its axis once in every fifteen hours.

Kaminski was almost half a mile down the shaft when, with shocking abruptness, the window looked upon a different scene.

31

SOMETHING IS SERIOUSLY
WRONG WITH SPACE

Hunter, up on the surface, heard and recorded every word.

"I'll try a long exposure with the thousand-millimeter lens," Kaminski began. "I hate to confess it, but this is the first time I've ever done any astronomical photography. ... Hello!"

"What's happening?"

"The end of the slot's getting lighter. Yes, there's no doubt of it. There's a very faint glow along one side. You know, it looks like—my God—*that's* what it is!!"

"What, for heaven's sake?!"

"Sunrise! Sunrise! Leave me alone—I want to watch."

There were maddening minutes of silence, during which Hunter could hear only Kaminski's heavy breathing and, occasionally, the sound of instruments and controls being operated. Then, at long last, the astronomer spoke again, his voice full of wonder.

"It's a sun, all right. And it's enormous—it's completely filling the view. If I could see it all at once, it would look as big as Jupiter.

"And it's not a G-zero type like our sun. It's very dull and red—I don't even need dark filters on the telescope. Must be a red giant, like Antares. That's an idea—maybe it *is* Antares. Ah, here comes a sunspot—looks pretty small, but it could be as big as our whole sun. ..."

His voice trailed off into silence and again Hunter possessed himself in patience until at last Kaminski said: "Still no change—that sun's still blocking the view. It'll take hours to move out of the way. Let's get back to the

H

ship—I want to study these photos. And I'd like to try an experiment, if I can talk Dave into it."

"What sort of experiment?"

"We still have most of our instrumented probes. This is the place to use them."

When they returned to the ship, Bowman was at first reluctant. If anything was dropped down the shaft, he pointed out, even this low gravity could give it a terminal speed of over a hundred miles an hour. There was no telling what damage it might do—or what reactions it might produce.

Kaminski finally settled the argument by pointing out that the designers of this place would certainly have protected their handiwork against such trivial accidents. Every few centuries, a large meteor must plunge into the chasm at a far higher speed than any falling probe could attain.

Once the project had been agreed upon, Kimball acted as bombardier. Since the orbiting *Discovery* could track the probe only during the few seconds while it was passing directly over the slot, space capsule *Alice* was fitted with receiving gear. Kimball dropped the probe at the exact center of the chasm, then flew to the edge and waited on the brink, *Alice*'s receiving antenna jutting out over the abyss.

At first the probe fell with the lethargic slowness to be expected in Jupiter V's gravity field. Its instruments recorded a very slight temperature rise, but nothing else of importance. There was no radioactivity, no magnetic field.

And then, five miles down, it began to accelerate. Its signals started to drop rapidly in pitch, indicating a Doppler effect of astonishing magnitude. Kimball had to continually retune the receiver in order to keep track of the signals, and the radar started to indicate impossible ranges and velocities. In a few seconds, the probe was two hundred miles away—which, taken at face value, meant that it had gone right through Jupiter V and out the other side. Thereafter, it became more and more difficult to detect, and swiftly passed beyond the tuning range of the receiver. On the last contact, it had descended *nine thousand and fifty miles down a hole which under no circumstances could be more than a hundred miles deep*—the diameter of the tiny moon.

The radar was working perfectly; Kimball checked it with the utmost care as soon as he got back to the ship. The trouble must lie in Jupiter V—and Hunter neatly summed up what everybody was now beginning to suspect.

"I'm afraid," he said, "that there's something seriously wrong with space."

"A long time ago," said Kaminski, "I came across a remark that I've never forgotten—though I can't remember who made it. 'Any sufficiently advanced technology is indistinguishable from magic.' That's what we're up against here. Our lasers and mesotrons and nuclear reactors and neutrino telescopes would have seemed pure magic to the best scientists of the nineteenth century. But they could have understood how they worked—more or less—if we were around to explain the theory to them."

"I'd be glad to settle without the theory," remarked Kimball, "if I could even understand what this thing *is*—or what it's supposed to do."

"It seems to me," said Bowman, "that there are two possibilities—both just about equally impossible. The first is that Jupiter V is hollow—and there's some kind of micro-universe down there. A whole galaxy a hundred miles across."

"But the probes went thousands of miles, according to the radar readings."

"There could be some kind of distortion. Suppose the probes got smaller and smaller as they went in. Then they might seem to be thousands of miles away, when they were still really quite close."

"And *that*," said Kaminski, "reminds me of another quotation—one of Niels Bohr's. 'Your theory is crazy—but not crazy enough to be true.' "

"You have a crazier one?" asked Hunter.

"Yes, I do. I think the stars—and that sun down there—are part of our own universe, but we're seeing them through some new direction of space."

"I suppose you mean the fourth dimension."

"I doubt if it's anything as simple as *that*. But it probably does involve higher dimensions of some kind. Perhaps non-Euclidean ones."

"I get the idea. If you went down that hole, you'd come out hundreds or thousands of light-years away. But how long would the journey *really* be?"

"How long is the journey from New York to Washington? Two hundred miles if you fly south. But twenty-four thousand if you go in the other direction, over the North Pole. Both directions are equally real."

"I seem to remember," said Bowman, "that back on Earth you once told me that shortcuts through space-time were scientific nonsense—pure fantasy."

"Did I?" replied Kaminski, unabashed. "Well, I've changed my mind. Though I reserve the right to change it back again, if a better theory comes along."

"I'm a simpleminded engineer," said Hunter rather aggressively. "I see a hole going into Jupiter V, and not coming out anywhere. But you tell me that it *does* come out. How?"

Everyone waited hopefully for Kaminski to answer. For a moment he hemmed and hawed; then he suddenly brightened.

"I can only explain by means of analogy. Suppose you were a Flatlander, an inhabitant of a two-dimensional world like a sheet of paper—unable to move above or below it. If I drew a circle in your flat world, but left a small gap in it, you would say that the gap was the only way into the circle. Right?"

"Right."

"If anyone went into the circle, they could only come out the same way?"

"So that's what you're driving at. The circle could be a cross-section of a tube passing through Flatland. If I was clever enough to crawl *up* the tube, by moving into the third dimension, I would leave my flat universe altogether."

"Exactly. But the tube might bend back into Flatland again, and you could come out somewhere else. To your friends, it would seem that you'd traveled from A to B without crossing the space between. You'd have disappeared down one hole and emerged from a totally different one, maybe thousands of miles away."

"But what advantage would that be? Surely the straight line in Flatland itself would still be the shortest distance between A and B."

"Not necessarily. It depends what you mean by a straight line. Flatland might really be wrinkled, though the Flatlanders wouldn't be able to detect it. I'm not a topologist, but I can see how there might be lines that were straighter than straight, if some of them went through other dimensions."

"We can argue this until kingdom come," said Hunter. "But supposing it's true—what shall we do about it?"

"There's not much we can do. Even if we had an unlimited fuel and oxygen supply, it might be suicide to go into that thing. Though it may be a shortcut, it could be a damn long one. Suppose it comes out somewhere a thousand light-years away—that won't help us, if the trip takes a century. We wouldn't appreciate saving nine hundred years."

That was perfectly true; and there might be other dangers, as inconceivable to the mind of man as this anomaly in space itself. *Discovery* had come to the end of her travels; she must remain here in an eternal orbit, just a few miles from a mystery that she could never approach.

Like Moses looking into the promised land, they must stare at marvels beyond their reach.

32

BALL GAME

After a while they began to call it the Star Gate; no one was quite sure who coined the name. And because the human mind can accept anything, however strange, its mystery soon ceased to haunt them. One day, perhaps, they would understand how the stars were shining down there at the bottom of that chasm; the night sky, reflected in a pool of still water, might have seemed just as great a mystery to early man.

They still had twenty days of operating time before they would have to go into hibernation, and there was enough fuel for the pods to make five more trips down to the surface. Bowman allowed three visits, at intervals of a week, and then left the pods in their airlocks, fully provisioned, ready for any future emergency that might arise.

The descents taught them little more than they already knew. They watched the regular transit of those strange stars and the giant red sun, drifting with clockwork precision across the distant end of the Star Gate—still in a direction, and at a speed, that had nothing to do with the spin of Jupiter V itself.

Kaminski brooded for hours over his photographs, trying to identify the star patterns with the aid of the maps stored in Athena's memory. His total failure neither disappointed nor surprised him. If indeed he was looking out through a window onto some remote part of the Galaxy, there was no hope of recognizing the view. One of those faint stars might even be the Sun; he could never identify it. From a few score light-years away, Type G-zeroes are as indistinguishable as peas in a pod.

The three remaining instrumented probes were dropped at intervals of a week—the last one, just before hibernation was due to commence. Each performed in an identical manner, dwindling away into impossible distances before its signals were lost. The record depth—in this hundred-mile-diameter world!—was eleven thousand miles. . . .

After that, they had done everything that was humanly possible; their stores were almost exhausted, and it was time to sleep. In one sense, their mission had been a success; they had discovered what they had been sent to find—even if they did not know what it was. But in another, the expedition had failed, since they could not report their findings to Earth. All Kimball's attempts to re-establish communications with jury-rigged antennas and overloaded output circuits had been successful. The daily messages and news reports continued to come in, and were at once encouraging and frustrating. It was good for their morale to know that Earth, and their friends, had not forgotten them, and that the preparations for their return were going ahead at the highest priority. But it was maddening not to be able to reply, and to be the custodians of a secret that would rock human society to its foundations.

And it was also unsettling to hear the messages that continued to arrive for Poole and Whitehead, and to see the faces of their friends and relatives as they sent greetings to men who had been dead for months. It was a constant reminder of their own uncertain future, now that it was time for their hibernation to begin.

There were better places to have slept, but they had little choice in the matter. They could only hope that Jupiter V would continue to treat them with complete indifference, as they circled it every ninety minutes until, three or four or five years from now, the recovery expedition arrived.

During the last days they checked every detail of the ship, closed down all unnecessary equipment, and tried to anticipate everything that could possibly go wrong. The shadow of Poole's death often lay heavy on their minds, but they never mentioned it. Whether it had been due to a random failure, or a loss of tolerance, there was nothing that could be done. They had no alternative but to proceed as planned.

One by one, their work completed, they made their goodbyes and went to rest, until at last only the captain was left. To Bowman, all this had a haunting familiarity; once before he had cracked the same jokes, made the same—he hoped—temporary farewells, and had been left alone in the sleeping ship.

He would wait two days before he followed the others. One would be long enough to check that everything was running smoothly; the second would be his own—to share with the last game of the World Series.

Curiously enough, while on Earth, he had never been an avid baseball fan, but like all the members of the crew he had acquired a passionate interest in the sport programs relaying from Earth. One day more or less made no difference to Bowman now, and he was anxious to see if the New York Yankees would make a comeback after their long years in the doldrums. He doubted it; the Mets seemed more impregnable than ever.

And so, in the now deserted Control Center, David Bowman took his leave of the strangest sky that any man had ever seen. Half of it was filled with the steeply curving, ammonia-spattered landscape of Jupiter V; most of the rest was occupied by Jupiter itself. A huge, waning crescent, it was shrinking almost visibly as the ship rushed into its shadow; the distant Sun would soon be eclipsed behind it. And when, thought Bowman, shall I see the sun again?

The solar glare had already swallowed up the evening star called Earth. But though he could not see the world of men, its voice was still echoing through the ship, and on the Control Center monitor screen was a spectacle that would doubtless have baffled many quite intelligent extraterrestrial races.

One entity, holding a stubby rod in both hands, confronted another carrying a small spherical object. They both stood on a flat, triangular area of ground, while grouped around them in frozen, expectant postures, were some dozen other individuals. And at a greater distance, thousands more sat motionless on concentric tiers of seats.

The creature holding the sphere started to whirl its grasping limb around with ever-increasing violence. Suddenly, so swiftly that the eye could hardly follow its motion, the sphere escaped from its resting place and hurtled toward the entity with the rod. The creature was obviously in grave danger—but the projectile missed the intended target, and went racing past it.

There was a brief flurry of activity; then the sphere was returned to the original holder. The ordeal, it seemed, was to continue. . . .

This time, however, the victim was able to defend

himself more effectively. Puny though his protective shield was, by luck or skill he managed to intercept the hurtling projectile—and even to send it soaring back over the head of his tormentor. Then, while his enemies were distracted, he started to spring for safety. . . .

But Bowman never saw Malczinsky finish his home run. At that moment the alert and sleepless Athena, still watching over the ship, sounded the collision alarm.

The image from Earth was wiped off screen, as if it had never existed, to be replaced by the impersonal rings and spokes of the radar display. Bowman read their message in a second—and felt a sense of freezing loneliness that he had not known even when he had sent Kelvin Poole to follow Peter Whitehead to the stars.

Once more he was the only master of the ship, with none to help or advise him, in a moment of crisis. And this was a crisis indeed; for twenty miles ahead, directly in his line of flight, something was rising out of the Star Gate.

33

LAST MESSAGE

A moment later, Bowman switched to the high-definition display, and had a second surprise. The object was quite small—only about six feet long. Far too large to be a meteor, yet far too small to be a spaceship. He did not know whether to be disappointed, or relieved.

He locked the optical telescope onto the radar, and peered eagerly through the eyepiece. There it was, glinting in the sunlight—obviously metallic, obviously artificial. And then he cried out in astonishment; for the thing soaring out of the abyss was one of *Discovery*'s own space probes, dropped into Jupiter V days or weeks ago.

He switched on the radio and searched the telemetry band. The signal came in at once, loud and clear. All these probes had short-lived power supplies, so that they should not clutter up the spectrum when they had done their work—but this one was still radiating. A quick check of the frequency confirmed what he had already guessed.

This was the very last probe they had dropped into the Star Gate. It had vanished into that abyss, eleven thousand miles "down," while apparently moving faster than any manmade object in history. Yet now it had returned, still in perfect working order—only two days later.

It was moving quite slowly, rising up towards the face of Jupiter. And presently it vanished from sight against that looming disk; but he could still hear it, chirping briskly as it settled into an orbit that might or might not be stable —but which, he was quite certain, could only be the result of intelligent planning.

This could never have happened by chance, or by the

operation of natural laws. The Star Gate had returned their gift; it must have done so deliberately.

Someone or something knew that they were here.

"This is David Bowman, recording for log. The ship is in perfect order and I am now scheduled to join Kaminski and Hunter and Kimball in hibernation.

"I am not going to do so. Instead, I am taking one of the pods, which is fully provisioned and fueled, and am descending into the Star Gate.

"I am completely aware of the risks, but I consider them acceptable. The safe return of our probe, after only two days, is proof that an object can pass unharmed through the Star Gate in a short period of time. I have enough oxygen for at least the one-way trip, and am prepared to take my chances at the other end.

"It seems to me that this is an invitation—even a sign of friendliness. I'm prepared to accept it as such. If I am wrong—well, I won't be the first explorer to make such a mistake.

"Bill, Vic, and Jack—if I don't see you again, good luck, and I hope you make it back to Earth. This is Dave, signing off."

34

THE WORLDS OF THE STAR GATE

A writer who sets out to describe a civilization superior to his own is obviously attempting the impossible. A glance at the science fiction of fifty—or even twenty—years ago shows how futile it is to peer even a little way into the mists of time, and when dealing merely with the world of men.

Longer-range anticipations are clearly even less likely to be successful; imagine what sort of forecast one of the Pilgrim Fathers could have made of the United States in the year 1970! Practically nothing in his picture would have had any resemblance to the reality—which, in fact, would have been virtually incomprehensible to him.

But Stanley Kubrick and I were attempting, at the climax of our Odyssey, something even more outrageous. We had to describe—*and to show on the screen*—the activities and environments, and perhaps the physical nature, of creatures millions of years ahead of man. This was, by definition, impossible. One might as well expect Moon-Watcher to give a lucid description of David Bowman and his society.

Obviously, the problem had to be approached indirectly. Even if we showed any extraterrestrial creatures and their habitats, they would have to be fairly near us on the evolutionary scale—say, not more than a couple of centuries ahead. They could hardly be the three-million-year-old entities who were the powers behind the Black Monolith and the Star Gate.

But we certainly had to show *something*, though there were moments of despair when I feared we had painted ourselves into a corner from which there was no possible escape—except perhaps a "Lady or the Tiger" ending where we said goodbye to our hero just as he entered the Star Gate. That would have been the lazy way out, and would have started people queuing at the box office to get their money back. (As Jerry Agel has recorded, at least one person did just this—a Mrs. Patricia Attard of Denver, Colorado. If the manager of the handsome Cooper Cinerama did oblige, I shall be happy to reimburse him.)

Our ultimate solution now seems to me the only possible one, but before arriving at it we spent months imagining strange worlds and cities and creatures, in the hope of finding something that would produce the right shock of recognition. All this material was abandoned, but I would not say that any of it was unnecessary. It contained the alternatives that had to be eliminated, and therefore first had to be created.

Some of these Lost Worlds of the Star Gate are in the pages that follow. In working on them, I was greatly helped by two simple precepts. The first is due to Miss Mary Poppins: "I never explain anything."

The other is Clarke's Third* Law: "Any sufficiently advanced technology is indistinguishable from magic."

Stanley once claimed if anything could be written, he could film it. I am prepared to believe him—if he was given unlimited time and budget. However, as we were eventually a year and four million dollars over estimate, it was just as well that the problem of creating explicit super-civilizations was by-passed. There are things that are better left to the imagination—which is why so many 'horror' movies collapse when some pathetic papier-mâché monster is finally revealed.

Stanley avoided this danger by creating the famous "psychedelic" sequence—or, as MGM eventually called it, "the ultimate trip." I am assured, by experts, that this is best appreciated under the influence of various chemicals, but do not intend to check this personally. It was certainly not conceived that way, at least as far as Stanley and I were concerned, though I would not presume to speak for all the members of the art and special-effects departments.

I raise this subject because some interested parties have

*Oh, very well. The First: "When a distinguished but elderly scientist says that something is possible, he is almost certainly right. When he says it is impossible, he is very probably wrong." (*Profiles of the Future*)

The Second: "The only way of finding the limits of the possible is by going beyond them into the impossible."

I decided that if three laws were good enough for Newton, they were good enough for me.

tried to claim *2001* for their own. Once, at a science-fiction convention, an unknown admirer thrust a packet into my hand; on opening it turned out to contain some powder and an anonymous note of thanks, assuring me that this was the "best stuff." (I promptly flushed it down the toilet.) Now, I do not know enough about drugs to have very strong views on the matter, and am only mildly in favour of the death penalty even for tobacco peddling, but it seems to me that "consciousness-expanding" chemicals do exactly the opposite. What they *really* expand are uncriticalness ("Crazy, man!") and general euphoria, which may be fine for personal relationships but is the death of real art ... except possibly in restricted areas of music and poetry.

This recalls to mind Coleridge's "Kubla Khan," written under the influence of opium and interrupted by the persistent and thrice-accursed "Person from Porlock"—which incidentally, is a charming little village just four miles from my birthplace. At one time I started composing a parody of "Kubla Khan," which started promisingly enough:

> For MGM did Kubrick, Stan
> A stately astrodome decree,
> Where Art, the s.f. writer, ran
> Through plots incredible to man
> In search of solvency. . . .
> So twice five miles of Elstree ground
> With sets and props were girdled round . . .

Unfortunately, or perhaps not, inspiration evaporated at this point, and I was never able to work in:

> A savage place! as eerie and enchanted
> As ere beneath a flickering arc was haunted
> By child-star wailing for her demon mother . . .

still less get as far as the projected ending:

> For months meandering with a mazy motion
> Through stacks of scripts the desperate writer ran
> Then reached that plot incredible to man
> And sank, enSCUBA'd in the Indian Ocean.
> And midst the tumult Kubrick heard from far
> Accountants' voices, prophesying war!

The three "Worlds of the Star Gate" that follow are, to some extent, mutually incompatible with each other and with the final novel *and* movie versions. (There were still others—now forgotten or absorbed.) In the first, not only the surviving astronauts but *Discovery* itself encountered the immortal alien who had walked on earth, three million years ago.

The flying island that is the background of that meeting owes a little to Swift, more to René Magritte, and most of all to the Singhalese king Kassapa I (circa 473-491 A.D.) In the very heart of Ceylon, on an overhanging rock five hundred feet above the surrounding plain, Kassapa built a palace which is one of the archeological (and artistic) wonders of the world. When you walk among the windy ruins of Sigiriya, it is easy to believe that you are actually airborne, high above the miles of jungle spread out on every side. Sigiriya is, indeed, uncannily like a Ceylonese Xanadu—complete with pleasure gardens and dusky damsels.

35

REUNION

Of the Clindar who had walked on Earth, in another dawn, three million years ago, not a single atom now remained; yet though the body had been worn away and rebuilt times beyond number, it was no more than a temporary garment for the questing intelligence that it housed. It had been remodeled into many strange forms, for unusual missions, but always it had reverted to the basic humanoid design.

As for the memories and emotions of those three million years, spent on more than a thousand worlds, not even the most efficient storage system could hold them all in one brain. But they were available at a moment's notice, filed away in the immense memory vault that ringed the planet. Whenever he wished, Clindar could relive any portion of his past, in total recall. He could look again upon a flower or an insect that had fleetingly caught his eye ten thousand years before, hear the voice of creatures that had been extinct for ages, smell the winds of worlds that had long since perished in the funeral pyres of their own suns. Nothing was lost to him—if he wished to recall it.

So when the signal had come in, and while the golden ship was being prepared for its journey, he had gone to the Palace of the Past and let his ancient memories flow back into his brain. Now it seemed that only yesterday— not three million years ago—he had hunted with the ape-men and shown Moon-Watcher how to find the stones that could be used as knives and clubs.

"They are awake," said a quiet voice in the depths of his brain. "They are moving around inside their ship."

That was good; at least they were alive. The robot's

first report had indicated a ship of the dead, and it had been some time before the truth was realized. They were going to have a surprise, thought Clindar, when they woke so far from home, and he hoped they would appreciate it. There were few things that an immortal welcomed and valued more greatly than surprise; when there was none left in the universe, it would be time to die.

He walked slowly across the varying landscape of his little world, savoring this moment—for each of these encounters was unique, and each contributed something new to the pattern and the purpose of his life. Though he was alone upon this floating rock, unknown myriads of others were looking through his eyes and sharing his sensations, and myriads more would do so in the ages yet to come. Most of them would approximately share his shape, for this was a meeting that chiefly concerned those intelligences that could be called humanoid. But there would be not a few much stranger creatures watching, and many of them were his friends. To all these multiformed spectators he flashed a wry greeting—an infinitely complex and subtle variation on the universal jest that could be crudely expressed in the words, "I know all humanoids look the same—but *I* shall be the one on the right."

This sky-rock was not Clindar's only home, but it was the one he loved the best, for it was full of memories that needed no revival in the Palace of the Past. He had shared it thirty thousand years ago with a mating group long since dispersed through the Galaxy, and the radiance of those days still lingered, like the soft caress of the eternal dawn.

And because it was far from the shattering impact of the great centers of civilization, it was a perfect place to greet and reassure startled or nervous visitors. They were awed, but not overwhelmed; puzzled, but not alarmed. Seeing only Clindar, they were unaware of the forces and potentialities focused within him; they would know of these things when the time was ripe, or not at all.

The upper surface of the great rock was divided into three levels, with the villa at the highest end, and the flat apron of the landing stage at the lowest. Between them, and occupying more than half the total area, were the lawns and pools and courtyards and groves of trees among which Clindar had scattered the souvenirs of a thousand worlds and a hundred civilizations. The labor force to maintain all this skyborne beauty in immaculate condition was nowhere in sight; the simple animals and the more

complex machines that supervised them had been ordered
to remain in concealment until the meeting was over. The
Eater of Grass and the Trimmer of Trees, utterly harmless though they were, could cause great terror to other
beings who met them without adequate preparation. The
only animals now visible on the surface of the rock were
two brightly colored creatures, for all the world like flying
carpets, that flapped around and around Clindar emitting
a faint, musical hum. Presently he waved them away, and
they undulated out of sight into the trees.

Clindar never hurried, except when it was absolutely
essential, for haste was a sign of immaturity—and mortal-
ity. He paused for a long time beside the pool at the heart
of his world, staring into the liquid mirror which reflected
the sky above, and echoed the ocean far below. He was
rather proud of that little lake, for it was the result of an
experiment that had taken several thousand years to complete. Six varieties of fish from six different planets shared
it, and looked at each other hungrily, but had learned
from bitter experience that their biochemistries were highly incompatible.

He was still staring into the pool when he saw the
reflection of the golden ship pass across it, as it settled
down toward the landing stage at the far end of the rock.
Raising his eyes, he watched while the ship came to rest in
midair, dematerialized its center section, and extruded the
cargo it had carried across the light-years.

The shining artifact of metal and plastic descending at
the barely visible focus of the traction field seemed no
cruder than most first-generation spacecraft. It touched
the surface of the rock, the field supporting it flickered
off, and the golden ship departed—to be ready again in a
hundred years, or a thousand, as the case might be.

The first ship from Earth had arrived. Why, he won-
dred, had they taken so long?

Clindar stood in full view at the top of the wide
stairway leading down to the landing place. It was hard,
he thought, to imagine a greater contrast than that between the two ships lying there. The newcomer was huge
and clumsy, covered with crude pieces of equipment that
seemed to have been bolted on as an afterthought. His
own vehicle, resting a hundred feet away, was only a
fraction of the size, and its slim, fluted projectile shape

was the very embodiment of speed and power. Even in repose, it seemed about to hurl itself into stars.

The visitors could not fail to observe it, and to wonder in vain at the powers that drove it through the sky. To any inquisitive spacefarers, it was at once a challenge—and a bait.

They had seen him. Through the windows of their ship, they were pointing and gesturing; very vividly, Clindar could imagine their surprise. They had come all this way—by now they must realize that they were in another solar system—and would be expecting to meet the fantastic creatures of an alien evolution. Something as apparently human as himself might be the very last thing they would anticipate.

Well, they would have their full of strangeness in due course, if their minds could face it. There was a preview here, in the line of cyclopean heads flanking the stairway. Though no two were alike, all were approximately human, and all were based upon reality. Some had no eyes, some had four; some had mouths or nostrils, some did not; some had wide-band radiation sensors, others were blind except to ordinary light. There had been a time when many had seemed ugly and even repellent to Clindar, but now they were all so perfectly familiar to him that he sometimes found it hard to recall which had once seemed hideous. After a thousand worlds, nothing alien was inhuman to him.

He began to walk slowly down the steps, past the graven heads of his still and silent friends. The figures framed in the window of the ship were equally motionless, staring towards him. They could not guess how many thousands of times they were outnumbered, and how many eyes were looking through his.

He reached the foot of the stairway, and began to move across the multihued tapestry of the wire-moss that covered the landing stage. With every step, little shock waves of color went rippling out over the sensitive living carpet, mingling and merging in complex interference patterns that slowly faded out into the distance.

Clindar walked through the dancing wave patterns created by his own footsteps, until he was within forty feet of the ship; now its occupants could see him as clearly as he could see them. He stopped, and held out his hands in the gesture which, throughout the universe, proclaimed: "I have no weapons—I come in friendship." Then he waited.

He did not think he would have to wait for long—probably a few hours, certainly no more than a few days. They would be excited and inquisitive, and though they would be cautious, they would be intelligent enough to realize that they were completely in his power. If he wished to harm them, the flimsy walls of their vehicle could give no protection whatsoever.

Already—so soon!—one of them had disappeared from the window, heading into the interior of the ship. The others continued to watch, while adjusting controls and speaking into instruments. They had some kind of recording device focused upon him; he could not remember a single race that had omitted to do this.

A door was opening in the side of the ship. Clumsy and awkward in its protective suit, a figure was standing in the entrance, clutching a large, flat package. Doubtless these creatures knew that they could breathe the atmosphere, but they would also be aware of the dangers of contamination. They were proceeding with care, and Clindar approved.

The figure stepped down onto the moss, and was momentarily distracted by the beauty of the shock waves that went flowing out from its feet. Then it looked up at Clindar, and held the package toward him. After a moment's hesitation, it started to walk.

Slowly, cautiously, the hominid was coming toward him, leaving the shelter of its metal cave. Clindar remained motionless, relaxed yet observant, remembering many meetings, on many worlds.

Now only a few feet away, the creature came to rest and slowly stretched out one opened hand. So this, thought Clindar, is how they greet each other; the gesture was a common one among bipeds, and he had met it often before. He stretched out his own hand in return.

Slim, nailless fingers closed around flexible glove, meeting across the light-years and the ages. Eyes locked together, as if the minds they mirrored would bypass the medium of speech. Then the hominid dropped its gaze, and handed the package to Clindar.

It consisted of dozens of very thin sheets of some light, stiff material, covered with illustrations and drawings. The first was a simple astronomical diagram, obviously of the planetary system from which the creature came. Arrows pointed prominently to the third planet outwards from the sun.

Clindar turned the page. There, beautifully executed in

an apparently three-dimensional color technique, were views of a globe as seen from space; and he recognized the continents at once.

He pointed to himself, then to the heart of Africa. Was the visitor startled? It was impossible to judge the reactions of another hominid until one had grown to know him intimately; the expression of even such basic emotions as fear or hostility was almost entirely arbitrary, differing from species to species.

Almost forgetting his visitor for the moment, Clindar stared at that familiar blunt triangle, whose shape had changed so little in a mere three million years. But everything in that triangle—all the beasts and plants that he had once known, and probably the climate and the detailed topography of the land—would have changed almost beyond recognition.

As *these* creatures were changed from the starveling savages who were their ancestors. Who could have dreamed that the children of Moon-Watcher would have climbed so far? Though he had watched this happen so many times before, it always seemed a miracle.

Some races were incredibly ignorant of their own past; Clindar wondered if they had any conception of the journey they had made from cave to spaceship. It was certain that they could not guess at the journey that still lay ahead.

They had made their first stumbling steps toward the stars—but the freedom of space was only a symbol, and not always an accurate one, of a certain level of understanding. There were many peoples who had stood thus upon the threshold of the universe, only to be destroyed by the sight of treasures too great for their self-control, and mysteries too deep for their minds. Some had survived, at the cost of turning their backs upon the stars, and encapsulating themselves behind barriers of ignorance in their own private worlds. Others had been so shattered in spirit that they had lost the will to live, and their planets had reverted to the mindless beasts.

For there were some gifts too heavy to be born; and for many races, those included the gift of truth, and the gift of time. As he turned the leaves of the book which he had been handed, pausing to look at diagrams and photographs crammed with visual information, Clindar wondered if these newcomers were ready to face the infinite promise of either time or truth.

The garnered art and knowledge of a thousand worlds

would be showered upon them, if they wished to receive it. Stored in the memory banks of this very planet were the answers to the questions that had haunted them, as well as the cures of all illnesses, the solutions to all problems of materials and power and distribution—problems that Clindar's race had solved so long ago that they now found it hard to believe that they had ever existed.

They could be shown the mastery of their minds and bodies, so that they could achieve the full expression of their powers, not spend heir lives like ineffectual ghosts trapped in a marvelous machine beyond their skill to operate. They could break the domination of pain, so that it became a sentinel and not a tyrant, sending messages which the rational mind could accept or ignore as it pleased.

Above all, they could choose to die only when they wished; they would be shown the many paths that led beyond the grave, and the price that must be paid for immortality in all its forms. A vista of infinite time would open up before them, with all its terror and promise. Some minds could face this, some could not; here was the dividing line between those who would inherit the universe, and those who were only quick-witted animals. There was no way of telling into which category any race would fall, until it came to its moment of truth—the moment which this race was now, in total ignorance, so swiftly approaching.

Now, for better or worse, they must leave behind the toys and the illusions of their childhood. Because they would look into the minds and survey the histories of a myriad races, they would discover that they were not unique—that they were indeed low on the ladder of cosmic achievement. And if, like many primitive societies, their culture still believed in gods and spirits, they must abandon these fantasies and face the awesome truths. It would not be for centuries yet, but one day they too might look across the fifty thousand light-years to the core of the Galaxy, glimpse the titanic forces flickering there among the most ancient of the stars—and marvel at the mentalities that must control them.

Meanwhile, there was work to be done; and a world was waiting to meet his guests.

The rock began to move, rotating on its axis so that the shining rainbow of the rings marched around its sky. With steadily increasing speed, the aerial island was driving toward the waterfall that spanned the entire horizon, and the twin towers that flanked it dropped below the edge of the world.

Now the sky ahead was a sheet of veined and mottled whiteness, drifting down forever from the stars. In shocking silence, the island crashed into the wall of cloud, and the golden sunlight faded to a rose-tinged dusk.

The darkness deepened into night, but in that night the island now glowed faintly with a pale luminescence from the sensitive moss and the trees. Beyond that glow nothing was visible, except tendrils of mist and vapor flickering past at an unguessable speed. The rock might have been moving through the chaos that existed before Creation, or crossing the ill-marked frontier between life and death.

At last, the mist began to thin; hazy patterns of light were shimmering in the sky ahead. And suddenly, the rock was through the wall of cloud.

Below it still was that endless sea, lit softly by the pearly white radiance pouring down from the crystal rainbows beyond the sky. Scattered across the ocean in countless thousands, from wave level up to the uttermost heights of the stratosphere, were airbone islands of all possible shapes and sizes and designs. Some were brilliantly illuminated, others mere silhouettes against the sky; the majority were motionless, but some were moving with swift purpose like liners catching the midnight tide from some great harbor, the buoys and beacons flashing around them. It was as if a whole galaxy had been captured and brought down to earth; and at its upper edges it merged imperceptibly into the glowing dust of the Milky Way.

After three million years in the wilderness, the children of the apes had reached the first encampment of the Star-Born.

[*In the version that follows—Chapters 36 to 39— only Bowman survived to pass through the Star Gate. Stanley Kubrick and I were still groping toward the ending which we felt must exist—just as a sculptor, it is said, chips down through the stone toward the figure concealed within.*]

36

ABYSS

Now his eyes were drawn to the planet that began to fill the sky ahead; and for the first time he realized that it was entirely covered with sea. On the sunlit hemisphere turned toward him, there were no continents, nor even any islands. There was only a smooth and featureless expanse of ocean.

It was a most peculiar ocean—straw-yellow in some areas, ruby-red over what Bowman assumed were the great deeps. At the center of the disk, almost immediately beneath him, something metallic glittered in the sunlight.

And now for the first time, the effects of atmosphere became noticeable. A barely visible ovoid appeared to have formed around the capsule, and behind it trailed a flickering wake of radiation. Bowman could not be sure, but for a moment he thought he could hear the shriek of tortured air: one thing was certain—he was still being protected by the forces that had drawn him to the stars. This vehicle was designed only for the vacuum of space, and a wind of a few score miles an hour could tear it to pieces. But there was no wind against the fragile metal shell; the incandescent furies of reentry were held at bay by an invisible shield.

The metallic glitter grew and took shape before his eyes. He could see now that it consisted of a group of incredibly flimsy towers, reaching up out of the ocean and soaring two or three miles into the atmosphere. At their upper levels they supported stacks of dully gleaming circular plates, translucent green spheres, and mazes of equipment as meaningless to him as a radar station would have been to ancient man.

The capsule was falling down the side of the structure,

at a distance of about a mile, and now he could see that all around its base, apparently floating on the surface of the sea, was a mass of vegetation forming a great raft of brilliant blue. Some of the plants climbed for several hundred feet up the latticework of the tower, as if struggling to reach the sun from the lightless ocean depths.

This burst of vegetation did not give any impression of neglect or decay; the great towers climbing through it were obviously quite unaffected by the efflorescence at their feet. On this reddish-yellow sea, the deep blue of the growing plants gave a startling vivid touch of color.

Now the capsule was only a few feet above the ocean, and Bowman could see that its surface had a curiously indeterminate texture. It was not as sharply defined as a liquid should be; for the first time, he began to realize that it might be some heavy gas.

Immediately under the capsule, it became concave, as if depressed by an invisible shield. The hole in the fluid—Bowman no longer thought of it as water—became deeper, and then closed over him.

Like a fly in amber, he was trapped in a bubble of crystalline transparency; and it was carrying him down into unknown depths.

The view was astonishing, especially to anyone accustomed to underwater exploration where the limit of visibility was never more than two hundred feet—and very seldom even near that. He could see for at least a mile, and was now certain that he was traveling through not a liquid, but a dense gas.

The "seabed" was just visible as a mottled dark blur far below; there were round patches of light glowing on it, ranged in regular lines right out to the misty horizon—like the lamps of cities, seen through a slight overcast. About half a mile away he could see the lower levels of those sky-piercing masts; they were entwined with gigantic roots, and there were clouds of small creatures swimming—or flying, or floating—among them. Though he knew that earthly terms were not applicable here, in his mind he had already labeled them as birds rather than fish; but they were too far away for him to see them clearly.

Then, swooping up toward him out of the depths, came something that was neither a fish nor a bird. It was a tubular object like the body of an early jet plane, with a gaping intake at the front and small fins or flukes at the rear. At first, Bowman thought it was a vehicle of some kind; then, when it was only a few yards away, he realized that it was an animal—driving itself through the water by powerful contractions of the flexible duct that ran the whole length of its body. It hovered just outside the window of the now almost motionless capsule; and then Bowman became aware that it had a rider.

For a moment he thought that the thing attached to it, about a third of the way back from the intake, was a large parasite. But then it suddenly took off, abandoning the tube-beast, and swam briskly toward the invisible bubble surrounding the capsule. Bowman had a perfect view of a beautifully streamlined, torpedo-shaped body, very much like one of the remora or suckerfish that attach themselves to sharks. The analogy was almost exact, for he could even see the set of suction pads that gave the creature a grip on its host.

Then he saw the four large, intelligent eyes, protruding from recesses in the side of the body—where, presumably, they retracted when the animal was moving at speed. There was a mind here, and it was contemplating him.

Presently the suckerfish began to move along the outer surface of the protective bubble, obviously examining the space pod. The riderless tube-beast remained hovering in midwater, pulsing gently from time to time. After a few minutes its master rejoined it, and the pair swiftly shot off into the distance. At the same moment the capsule began to sink again; it was hard to believe that this was a coincidence, and Bowman wondered if the suckerfish were the rulers of this semi-submarine world. But he had seen no trace of any limbs—and without organs of manipulation, it was surely impossible to develop a technology.

The seabed was now coming clearly into sight, and below he saw what looked like phosphorescent palm trees—but he quickly realized the utter folly of trying to judge this place in terms of Earth. Though the objects did look very much like palms, they were certainly nothing of the sort. They had thin, tubular stems about twenty feet high, and these ended in clusters of feathery fronds which beat the fluid around them continually, perhaps in search of food. Some of the creatures must have sensed him as he passed overhead, for they strained upward in a vain effort to reach the capsule.

The plantation of the luminous tube-beasts stretched for miles down a gentle slope, which ended abruptly in an almost vertical cliff. As the capsule passed over the rim of the plateau, and began to descend down the face of the cliff, Bowman saw that it was festooned with a network of creepers. These formed an intricate tangle that writhed continually, like some monstrous, multi-armed starfish; and sometimes it moved aside to reveal deep caves within which glowed unwavering, meaningless patches of luminescence.

Thousands of feet later, the cliff terminated in a level plain, only dimly illuminated by the light trickling down from far above. It was obviously cultivated, for it was divided up into huge squares and rectangles, tinted different shades of red and brown in this submarine twilight.

The first plants that he was able to examine at close quarters looked like tripods growing from the seabed; they had three black stems or roots that merged into a single trunk about ten feet from the ground. This continued upward for another five or six feet, and ended in a large inverted bowl. There were thousands of these tripods, ranging out to the misty horizon.

Bowman flew over them at a low altitude for several miles before he saw that this strange field had equally strange farmers. Tripods that seemed to belong to the same species, but were colored a pale, fleshy white, were creeping very slowly along the stationary ranks. Not until he had passed several of them was Bowman able to see how they moved.

Their root-legs were dug firmly into the ground; they would pull up one, slide it forward a few feet with slow-motion deliberation, then dig it in again before moving another. He judged that their speed was not more than a mile an hour; but for plants—if they *were* plants—that was very good going. . . .

Every so often a white tripod would lean toward a stationary one, and the two bells would meet in a kind of floral kiss or vegetable copulation. And then, after a pause of a few seconds, an extraordinary thing would happen.

The bell of the fixed plant would snap off its stem, and go swimming away like an animated parasol—while the rest of the creature collapsed on the seabed. He saw at least a dozen of the liberated bells go pulsing off into the distance, and noticed that they all swam in exactly the same direction—straight along the ranks of their "parents" until they had disappeared from sight.

And then there were miles of a kind of nondescript orange moss, which had one astonishing property. Like the tube-plants he had met earlier, it sensed his presence—and it reacted with luminosity. For as the capsule raced across this submarine tundra, a phosphorescent, V-shaped wake spread out below it, slowly fading away about a hundred yards astern.

Then, far ahead, he saw a band of milky white, flickering and dancing across the sensitive moss. He guessed that something had disturbed it, and he quickly saw that his guess was right.

A glowing red blanket, which from a distance looked like a sheet of lava, was crawling over the moss. It was only about fifty feet wide, but it was advancing on a front at least a mile broad, and it left a ribbon of bare, brown soil behind it. For it was not merely crawling but *eating* its way forward, consuming the moss in its progress.

Yet its victory was a hollow one, for as it flowed forward it too was being eaten, at such a rate that its width remained roughly constant. All along its trailing edge, clinging to it like giant leeches, were transparent slugs as large as a man; the whole network of their internal organs could be seen, pulsing and throbbing as they feasted.

And who or what eats the slugs? Bowman wondered. He did not learn the answer to this question before the subtly disquieting scene had passed behind him.

Now he had come to the edge of the farmlands, as he still mentally called them for want of a better word, and a range of rocky hills was appearing ahead. They seemed to have been carved out of multicolored strata by some natural erosive force which had left great caves and archways, hundreds of feet high. From the darkness of one cave stretched a bundle of black, whiplike tendrils or tentacles, lying motionless on a sandy seabed that had been recently disturbed, as if a broom had swept over it. It was hard not to connect those tendrils with the scrabblings in the sand, but though Bowman kept a careful watch on them as long as they were in sight, they never stirred.

The capsule was moving parallel to these hills when, for the first time, Bowman became aware of an unmistakable sound from the world outside his protective cocoon. It was a distant roar like a hurricane or a waterfall, and it grew louder minute by minute. And presently his eyes, a little tired of reds and browns and blacks, rested thankfully on a thin column of brilliant white light stretching vertically into the somber sky.

It was like an extremely narrow searchlight, and apparently originated from a point high up in the hills. Though its color reminded him of the world he knew, he looked at it with some alarm; for it was the first time he had ever seen a light that roared.

37

COSMOPOLIS

The brilliant hairline of incandescence emerged from a great metal web, supported on three spires of rock several hundred feet high. All around it was a vast cyclonic disturbance; Bowman felt that he was watching a stationary tornado, and from uncomfortably close at hand.

The tapering funnel of the tornado reared up out of sight through the miles of ocean above his head, and he was certain that it extended all the way into space. Some immense power was holding back the millions of tons of fluid around that fiercely radiant beam; but for what purpose, Bowman could only speculate.

The capsule sped on past the eroded hills, and the fury of the submarine tornado died away. He was moving at a great speed across an empty desert that was crisscrossed with faint white lines, meandering in all directions like the tracks of snails. There was no sign of the creatures who had made them.

He could no longer guess at his depth beneath the surface of this strange sea. The last rays of the sun had faded out miles above him, yet there was light all around. Overhead, living comets drifted through the ocean-atmosphere, sometimes flashing on and off like electric signs; and once a great swarm of shining spirals, of all sizes and traveling in exactly parallel lines, went spinning past.

But now the light ahead was growing minute by minute; and presently he could see that, beyond any doubt, he was at last approaching a city.

It was brilliantly illuminated by red artificial suns suspended in the sky, stretching out of sight along the horizon in either direction. In their slanting rays he saw a panorama as strange and wonderful as New York City would have seemed to Neanderthal Man.

There were no streets, only great buildings set in a widely spaced grid, on a plain made of some substance the color of deep ruby, sparkling with occasional flashes of light. Some of the structures were hemispherical domes, some resembled giant beehives, others were like overturned ships with their keels drawn upward into slender pinnacles. Though many were plain and angular, being based on a few simple elements, others were as complex as Gothic cathedrals or Cambodian temples; indeed, there was one group of buildings that reminded Bowman, very slightly, of Angkor Wat.

He first glimpsed the inhabitants from about a thousand yards away, as he was entering the outskirts of the city. There was a group of half a dozen, moving from one building to another, across the wide avenue that separated the structures. Though he could not yet judge their size accurately, he could see that they had two arms and legs, and walked upright. But even from a distance the head seemed most peculiar, and the method of locomotion was also odd. The creatures moved with a slow, fluid grace—almost as if forcing themselves through a heavy liquid. Compared with these beings, humans were jerky puppets.

It was soon obvious to Bowman that the city had no *surface* transportation; all its vehicles moved inside a narrow sandwich of space about fifty feet thick, and a hundred feet from the ground. He could see dozens of them, of many shapes and sizes, darting to and fro between the great towers, and he wondered how they managed to avoid collisions.

Then he noticed barely visible lines of light forming a colored network that extended right into the city, and radiated far beyond it. Some lines were scarlet, some blue, and they hung in the air like a grid of glowing wires. They were obviously not solid, for he could see objects through them.

Yet along those immaterial threads, either powered or controlled by them, the traffic of the city moved with unhesitating swiftness. The most common vehicles were small spheres, carrying one or two passengers; they looked like soap bubbles being driven by a gale, for they were perfectly transparent except for an opaque section of floor. There were two seats facing forward, and a small tapering column that presumably housed the controls. That was all; but Bowman knew that the nations of Earth would gladly pay billions for the secrets that must be concealed within them.

There were also considerably larger, oval-shaped vehicles that carried up to twenty passengers, as well as others which seemed used only for freight. Along one of the shining threads, hanging from it like raindrops on a spider's web but traveling at a good hundred miles an hour, shot a succession of spheres that contained nothing but reddish liquid. They raced past Bowman at perfectly regular intervals, heading out of sight into the city ahead of him.

He had already moved through the first line of buildings before he had a close view of the city's inhabitants. The capsule was traveling, at a height of about three hundred feet, past a great fluted cone, scalloped with little balconies. And on one of these, his first extraterrestrial was standing in full view.

Bowman's initial impression was of a tall, extremely elongated human being, wearing a shining metallic costume. As he came nearer, he saw that this was only partly correct. The creature was more than eight feet tall, but it was quite unclothed.

That shining metal was its skin, which appeared to be as flexible as chain mail—or the scales of a snake, though the overall impression was not in the least reptilian. The head was utterly inhuman; it had two huge, faceted eyes, and a small, curled-up trunk of proboscis where the nose should have been. Though there was no hair, feathery structures grew where one would have expected to find the ears, and Bowman decided that these were sense organs of some kind.

He was passing within fifty feet of the creature, and despite the abnormal and curiously detached psychological state in which he had been ever since leaving Jupiter, he felt a sudden uprush of excitement, wonder—and sheer personal pride. He was the first of all men to look upon an intelligent extraterrestrial; that was an honor of which he could never be robbed. And he was not, as some of the more pessimistic exobiologists had predicted, either shocked or nauseated. Though this creature was certainly very strange, it was not horrible. Indeed, like all living things, it had its own internal logic and beauty; even at rest, it gave an impression of power and grace.

He had already passed the balcony when it occurred to him that the alien's behavior was rather odd. Even in a cosmopolis like this, it could not be every day that an outworlder went flying beneath your window, and Bowman assumed that he was the very first human being that anyone on this planet had ever seen. Yet the creature had ignored him completely.

He glanced back in time to see that he had *not* been ignored. This alien (no, *he* was the alien here) had dropped its pose of indifference, and was now looking directly at him. Moreover, it was holding a small metallic rod rather like a lorgnette against one eye. At first Bowman thought that the device was some optical aid; then he decided that he was having his photograph—or its equivalent—taken.

The creature lowered the instrument and ducked out of sight as the capsule sped away. Bowman was utterly unable to read its expression, and for the first time he realized how much training and experience was needed before one could interpret the emotions even of another human being; to read the thoughts of an alien from its attitude might be forever impossible.

The long-awaited First Contact had come and gone in a way which seemed both anticlimactic and rather mysterious; yet it was possible, Bowman reflected, that for these creatures this was a wild and tumultuous greeting.

When he had traveled farther into the city, he became quite sure that everyone was aware of his presence and that he was being studiously ignored. In the center of one avenue, for example, there was a small crowd gathered around a vertical sheet like a billboard or an illuminated sign. The board was covered with moving patterns and symbols, which were being studied with great attention; Bowman wondered whether they were conveying news, selling detergent, quoting interstellar rates of exchange, or announcing the departure of bubble-vehicles to distant spots.

Whatever the information, he would not have thought it more exciting than the passage of a stranger from space only a hundred feet overhead—yet the spectators ignored him. But as he sailed by, Bowman continued to watch them in the capsule's rear-view mirror, and saw that many of them were taking peeps at him over their shoulders. So they *were* mildly interested; even so, there were still quite a number who never bothered to look, but continued to stare intently at the patterns on the board.

He was now traveling directly down one of the wide avenues; ahead of him, the strange, humped buildings marched away into the distance until they blurred into the rosy mists of the horizon. Many were set with luminous panels so that they glowed like multicolored jewels. Others were covered with unbelievably intricate carvings or etchings, and Bowman could not help contrasting them with the stark glass-and-metal boxes of his own world. The architects of this planet, it seemed, built for the ages; the city appeared to be complete and finished, for nowhere was there any sign of construction or demolition. At first this surprised him; then he remembered that all terrestrial cities had been built by ephemeral, exploding societies, and he must now be observing a culture of a wholly different type.

Another proof of that lay in the spaciousness of the city; there was none of the hideous urban overcrowding so universal on Earth. That also was not surprising, for any really long-lived civilization had to have complete population control. It must have been thousands of years since these creatures had stabilized their society, and decided that it was better for a million to live in comfort than for ten million to starve in squalor. This was a lesson that his own world had been slow to learn.

Sometimes he observed, as in a distorting mirror, obvious reflections of terrestrial life. Though there were no traffic jams, frustrated motorists, or harried pedestrians, he did see one stationary line of patient citizens waiting to enter a large domed structure. He wondered if they were first-nighters, bargain hunters, or enthusiasts for some wholly incomprehensible cause; it gave him a certain satisfaction to know that, even in the most advanced society, it was still sometimes necessary to wait in line.

And once he passed over what seemed to be a nursery school or a children's playground. He looked down at it with intense interest, for until now all the creatures he had seen in the streets had been adults; for the first time, it struck him as odd he had seen not a single specimen of their young.

But here they were, dozens of them—playing just like human children in a small park on the roof of a low, oval building. It was a charming, almost pastoral scene; there was a grove of trees that might have come from Earth, a plant like a gigantic orchid that obviously did not, a tiny lake with a fountain in its center, some mysterious machines that were being operated by small, intent figures— and a pair of grown-ups watching from a distance.

The children were all exactly the same size; Bowman judged them to be about five feet high. They looked as if they had been manufactured in an identical bath, and he wondered how these creatures reproduced. Despite their lack of any clothes except obviously functional harness that supported pouches, pockets, and occasional pieces of equipment, Bowman had seen no sign of sexual differentiation—or even of sex. Here was another of the thousands of questions he must file away, in the hope of one day finding the answer.

The children's reaction to his presence was wholly different from the adults'. As soon as the capsule passed over their playground, they at once abandoned their activities and stared up at him with obvious interest and excitement. Several pointed and waved; and one seemed to be aiming something like a small gun.

Bowman looked at this device uneasily. It reminded him of the toy "ray guns" he had played with as a child—and in a super-civilization like this, a toy might be capable of almost anything. . . .

He flinched as the trigger was pulled, for it suddenly occurred to him that he might be regarded as expendable as a rabbit, to a boy given his first air rifle. But all that happened was that a shining silver vortex ring emerged from the gun, shot swiftly toward the capsule, and bounced off it harmlessly, still expanding.

There was a considerable commotion in the playground. The two adults advanced rapidly on the young marksman, who was promptly deprived of his toy.

A little later he passed close to a shopping center—or so, for want of a better name, he supposed it to be. It was a huge, irregular structure with dozens of setback floors, and at least fifty of the luminous sky-tracks led into it at various levels. Along these tracks moved a steady flow of the transparent spheres and ovoids, carrying goods of various kinds. It was strange to see, hurrying through the air, perfectly recognizable articles of furniture like tables and chairs—followed by utterly weird pieces of machinery, or tanks of glowing colored gas.

And nothing seemed to go into the building; objects only came out of it. Nor were there any customers, though that was not so surprising; even on backward Earth, most shopping was now done by TV.

The cameos he glimpsed, in his swift passage through the City, confused as much as enlightened him. Many of the buildings had large transparent areas, and through these he caught brief, tantalizing views of their inhabitants. Once he saw a large group of them standing around a circular trough, full of redly fuming liquid, sipping it through their flexible trunks. *That* was understandable enough; but what was the heavy green mist that formed a complete blanket over the lower half of the room?

And there was one building inside which gravity seemed to have gone mad. He could see planes of glittering material, like faintly shining glass, intersecting at all angles. Figures were walking between or along these planes, with a total disregard for the conventions of "up" and "down." Some were moving straight upward, some at forty-five degrees to the horizontal; and often they would switch nonchalantly through a right angle as their private gravity field tilted and a wall became a floor. Even to an astronaut who had spent much of his career in weightless conditions, the sight was very disturbing.

There was one completely transparent dome beneath which some kind of demonstration, or game, or artistic performance was in progress. A small circular arena was surrounded by a rather thin crowd of a few hundred spectators, seated in swiveling chairs. What they were looking at was a dazzling—and, to Bowman, eye-wrenching —exhibition of shapes and colors, as if a mad geometrician was displaying his wares.

Apparently solid figures appeared, merged into each other, changed their perspective, receded to infinity while still remaining at the same spot. Sometimes there were maddening glimpses of what might almost have been another dimension; sometimes surfaces which seemed to be convex suddenly became concave. Once or twice the spectators became very agitated, waving their slender arms in excitement, for no reason that Bowman could see.

The character of the city was changing; the buildings were becoming smaller and more widely spaced. But ahead of him, still several miles away and partly shrouded in the eternal light haze, was one enormous structure, by far the largest he had seen. From a central dome and spire radiated four main wings separated by four smaller ones, so that the plan of the building roughly resembled a compass rose or a gigantic starfish. It was, Bowman estimated, at least a mile across at the base; and he was traveling straight toward it.

Then his eye was distracted by another strange sight. The capsule was moving over what appeared to be a broad sheet of shining metal—but no metal, unless it was molten, was corrugated with ripples that traveled back and forth across its surface. He seemed to be flying over a lake of mercury.

The ripples were produced by small, turtle-shaped machines that moved with slow deliberation over the shining surface; they left behind them broad, corrugated tracks that took several seconds to fade away. And then a huge bulge appeared in the center of the lake, as a thing like a submarine—or a whale?—emerged, and sank back again into the depths.

Beyond the lake was, at last, something wholly understandable. That great reddish-bronze torpedo could only be a spaceship; so, probably, were the shining crystal spheres and ovoids parked beside it. Small surface vehicles were scurrying to and fro, tiny figures were walking around, and there was even an observation tower surmounted by strange devices and bearing a flashing light. Everywhere and everywhen, Bowman decided, spaceports and airports look much the same; but the fact that these people operated *their* ships inside city limits showed how far their technology was ahead of Earth's.

Even while he was passing, one of the crystal spheres began to ascend, as effortlessly and as silently as a balloon. It rose straight upward, at a perfectly constant speed, until it was lost in the darkness of the sky. Bowman's thoughts traveled with it, and for a few moments he was almost overwhelmed by a devastating nostalgia for Earth.

It swiftly passed, for now he had something else to think about. That gigantic star-shaped building was looming up ahead.

38

SCRUTINY

Now the capsule was climbing again, and the central tower was looming above him, like a mountain piercing the clouds. And it was a very strange mountain, for it seemed made of glass or crystal, shot through with myriads of dark lines and threads, along many of which moved tiny nodes of light—some slowly, some at dazzling speed.

As a swallow may glide into its nest high up among the spires and buttresses of some great cathedral, so the capsule merged into the central tower. What from a distance had seemed merely a detail of the intricate ornamentation expanded until it was a circular tunnel, about ten feet in diameter. It was a fairly close fit, but the capsule raced along it with unchecked speed, and for the first time Bowman noticed a blue line of light glimmering faintly in the air before him, presumably acting as his guide. The tunnel was driven through some translucent material, so that it seemed to Bowman that he was hurtling into the heart of an iceberg—if one could imagine an iceberg that coruscated not with blues and greens, but with pale reds and golds. He could glimpse other shapes moving around him in all directions, vertically and horizontally, apparently in adjoining tunnels, but it was impossible to see them clearly.

Then he burst out into a large cavity blown like a bubble in the ice. It was a roughly hemispherical chamber about a hundred yards across, with walls of constantly changing curvature, so that they were sometimes concave, sometimes convex. He was moving along a transparent plane about fifty feet above the floor, and there were other equally transparent planes above and below him.

Some were stationary, some mobile, carrying with them

curious small structures and enigmatic pieces of machinery. The spectacle was confusing, yet orderly; and it was here, separated from him by the sliding crystal floors, that Bowman saw his first wholly non-humanoid intelligences.

Overhead, moving in a closely packed formation, were six squat cones, supported on dozens of tiny, tubelike legs. They looked rather like sea anemones walking on their tentacles, and Bowman could observe no signs of any sense organs. Around the middle of each cone was a white belt that seemed to be made of fur, and bore metal plates covered with angular hieroglyphics.

The capsule whisked past several of the snake-scaled humanoids, who this time turned to look at him with unconcealed interest. Then Bowman noticed, about two floors below, a most impressive creature like a giant praying mantis, hung with jewel-like ornaments or equipment, that went striding swiftly away, apparently quite oblivious to its surroundings. Its metallic limbs gleamed with the rainbow iridescence of a diffraction grating; Bowman had never seen anything so gorgeous, except for some of the tropical fish of coral reefs.

He passed quite close to one thing that could have been a robot, or a compound machine-organism, or perhaps a living animal made of metal. It looked like an elegant silvery crab, supported on four jointed legs, each of which terminated in a small, fat wheel; presumably the creature could walk or roll, whichever was more convenient. There was an ovoid body, into which various limbs were now retracted, and the whole was surmounted by a polyhedral head, each facet of which bore a deep-set lens.

There was one most disturbing entity on which he seemed unable to focus clearly. It was a gently pulsing golden flame, in the heart of which shone three intense and unwavering stars, like a triad of ruby eyes; unless Bowman's senses misled him completely, the thing kept disappearing and reappearing at intervals of a few yards, leaving behind it a ghostly afterimage which took a few seconds to fade away. He could not help wondering if he was looking at some being who existed, at least partly, in another dimension of space or time; there was certainly no remaining doubt that this city was the meeting place of many worlds.

There were even some beings who were apparently vegetable. They did not move under their own power, but were supported in little tubs or pans, filled with a glistening, muddy substance out of which their tubular bodies sprouted. At first glance, they looked rather like weeping willows, and their thin yellow tendrils trembled continually as if with ague. They moved in a blaze of light, from a ring of brilliant lamps arranged around them, so that whenever they traveled, they carried with them their own private suns.

Then he was through the great vaulted chamber and moving along another tunnel, this time a very short one. It ended in a low-ceilinged room, the roof of which appeared to be supported by six metal pillars arranged in a circle. The capsule glided between them, and settled down very gently on the floor, at the exact center of the circle.

So this, thought Bowman with a controlled but mounting excitement, is the end of the line. Someone—or something—had been to fantastic trouble to bring him here; and for what purpose? In a few minutes, he would know.

Almost at once he had the sensation of being watched; it was so powerful, so undeniable, that he twisted around and looked over his shoulder. But there was nothing here except the blankly shining pillars; he could not even see any sign of the tunnel through which he had come. The wall surrounding him was seamless and unbroken; there was no entrance, and no way out.

Then, like a fog creeping through a forest, something invaded his mind, and he knew himself in the presence of overwhelming intellectual power. Beneath that dispassionate scrutiny, he felt neither fear nor hope; all emotion had been leached away.

Out of the past, forgotten memories came flooding back, as if he was flicking through the pages of a snapshot album. He could see and hear and smell scenes from his childhood, in apparently total recall. Faces he did not even recognize flashed before him, as all the casual acquaintances and experiences of a lifetime went racing past, so swiftly now that he made no attempt to identify them. His whole life was unreeling, like a tape recorder playing back at hundreds of times normal speed.

Suddenly, like an illuminated glass model, he saw *Discovery*—in fantastic detail, with all its veins and arteries of electrical wiring, fuel lines, air and hydraulic systems, control circuits. Some parts were sharp and clear, others fuzzy and blurred. These, he presently realized, were the areas with which he was not familiar; he could see nothing that he did not know. It was as if, for some unfathomable reason, he had set himself the task of men-

tally picturing the ship—and had succeeded in doing so to
an extent altogether beyond his normal abilities. But that
again might be an illusion; perhaps he only *thought* he was
doing this—

And then came something that could not possibly be
real. He was no longer inside the pod—or even inside his
clothes. He was standing outside it, naked, looking
through the window at his own frozen image at the controls.

Nor was that all. Though he could not alter the direction of his gaze, he knew that he was completely transfixed
with a luminous, three-dimensional grid—a close-packed
mesh of thin horizontal and vertical lines. For a moment he
felt like a suspect in a police precinct, standing in front of
a measuring chart. Then the impression passed as swiftly
as it had come, and he was back inside the pod.

At the same instant, the vehicle was lifted off the floor,
and carried silently out of the chamber, away from the
ring of metal pillars. Once again it was swept along
luminous corridors, once again Bowman saw the alien
shapes coming and going in the passageways of the great
hive around him—though now they no longer seemed so
strange. Then, before he had realized what was happening, he had shot out of the building and was rising vertically through the glowing submarine twilight. He caught
one brief glimpse of the city through which he had
passed; then it was lost in the mists below him as he was
carried back toward the sky.

39

SKYROCK

The empty ocean rolled on beneath him, unmarked by ships or islands. Once or twice Bowman saw underwater shapes that might have been tightly packed schools of fish, or single marine beasts of appalling size; but nowhere was there any sign that this world held a civilization. He waited patiently, still under the influence of the strange euphoria that had gripped him when he left Jupiter V: he felt no hunger or fatigue, merely a vast and childlike wonder, and a readiness to accept anything that might come.

What came next was a long, low cloud—the first that Bowman had seen in this planet's pure and empty sky. Then, as it rose clear of the horizon, he realized that it was not cloud at all. Though its edges were irregular, they were sharply defined; it was also tinted with greens and browns and blacks, while here and there a few points sparkled like glass in the now almost level rays of the sun. And it seemed to be balanced at its center, like a one-legged table, on a single slim blue-green column rising from the sea.

It was some time before Bowman, dazed with wonders, realized that everything he now saw was perfectly familiar—but impossibly located. That low cloud was an island, its edges showing somber hues of earth and rock and stone. He absorbed this fact thankfully; later, he might start to worry about the minor problem that it was hanging motionless in the sky, linked to the sea beneath only by the dubious support of an eternally descending waterfall.

As he drew nearer, the details of the floating land became sharper; he could see that much of it was covered

218

with vegetation, above which metallic towers and white-domed buildings projected at infrequent intervals. There was a range of low hills near the center; from one of them a thin plume of vapor spiraled gently up into the almost cloudless sky.

At the same moment, Bowman became aware of two other facts. One was that the central waterfall—as he had tentatively labeled it—showed no signs of movement. Though it seemed to be made of water, that water was motionless; it was a frozen column of liquid, two or three miles in height; and it merged without a splash into the unruffled sea.

The second fact was that the flying land was not alone; it was surrounded by dozens of small satellites, hovering equally fixed in the sky. No—not *quite* fixed; some were drifting very slowly in different directions, like ships making their way through a crowded harbor. And presently Bowman could see that they appeared small only because of their overwhelming background; for he was heading directly toward one, and it began to fill his sky.

The thing was a huge rock, or an uprooted mountain, about a mile long and a thousand feet in thickness. Its flattened upper portion was elaborately landscaped into terraces and lawns and pools and little groves of exotic trees, with here and there wide open spaces in which stood enigmatic shapes that might have been statues, or motionless living creatures, or brooding machines. In one place a river flowed to the edge of the rock—yet refrained from leaping out into space toward the ocean miles below. Instead, it continued down and *under* the rough, craggy surface, as if glued to it by some force more powerful than gravity.

And some such force must certainly be operating here—for all these millions of tons of rock were hanging unsupported in the sky. This microcosm of a world was poised between sea and space, one member of an archipelago of aerial islands.

There was sky above and below it, and a gentle wind was disturbing the branches of the strange trees, yet this flying rock seemed as firmly anchored in the empty air as if it rested upon some great mountain peak. And the pod was descending toward it.

It came to rest on a large, perfectly smooth lawn about a hundred feet square, surrounded by trees with foliage consisting of flat, circular plates, piled one above the other. The lawn was colored a bright green that at first sight seemed to be that of grass, but was really due to tiny plants like multi-leaved clover.

It was some time, however, before Bowman noticed such details, for he had eyes only for the other vehicle lying on this flat clearing among the trees. Iridescent, apparently made of metal, it was a smooth projectile flaring to a point at either end. There were no windows, no sign of a door, no hint of any method of propulsion—only a few symmetrical bulges equally spaced around one end of the hull. Yet even in repose, it appeared ready to hurl itself at the stars; as Bowman gazed at it, he found to his surprise that his sense of wonder was not yet wholly satiated. There was a tingling in his blood as he stared at this symbol of power and speed, so close at hand. It was separated from him by only fifty feet of space; but by how many centuries of time?

Then his heart almost missed a beat; for he saw that there were people watching him from the shadow of the strange trees.

He did not hesitate to call them people, though by the standards of Earth they would have seemed incredibly alien. But already, his standards were not those of Earth; he had seen too much, and realized by now that only a few times in the whole history of the Universe could the fall of the genetic dice have produced a duplicate of Man. The suspicion was rapidly growing in his mind—or had something put it there?—that he had been sent to this place because these creatures were as close an approximation as could readily be found to *Homo sapiens,* both in appearance and in culture.

There were five of them, and because he had no sense of scale it was some time before he realized that they were extremely tall—perhaps eight or nine feet high. Their bodies were quite slender, and roughly human in proportion, but he could not even guess at the details of their anatomy, because from the neck down they were completely covered by a network of phosphorescent threads that glittered and sparkled like a field of stars.

Even the fact that they possessed necks was not something that could be taken for granted; Bowman remembered the discussions he had heard about the advantages of fixed heads with omnidirectional vision. These creatures, however, followed the human pattern in having only two eyes, set in very large, elliptical sockets that sloped downward from where the nose should have been.

But here was no sign of a nose; even more astonishing, there was no mouth. Apart from those two rather beautiful eyes, placed far apart on a slightly oval head whose long axis was not vertical, but horizontal, the face was quite featureless.

The general impression conveyed by the five entities, for all their weirdness, was not unattractive. The lovely golden-bronze color of the skin—if it was skin—helped to make them acceptable to human eyes. Bowman had been prepared for far worse—indeed, he had already seen it. He was sure that he would have no difficulty in adapting to these creatures, and perhaps becoming so accustomed to them that after a while the sight of another human being would be a shock.

Now what? he asked himself. Shall I wait for them to move, or are they waiting for me? They certainly seemed in no hurry, and might have been statues for all the activity they had shown so far.

Suddenly, there was a curious disturbance around the tallest of the five hominids. The glittering substance covering its left shoulder became humped and puckered; presently Bowman realized that some small, living creature was resting there. After a few ripples, the thing launched itself into the air, waving and fluttering like a tiny flying carpet, or a handkerchief blown before a breeze. It changed color as it flew; when it started, it was indistinguishable from the glittering phosphorescence on which it had been lying, but within seconds it became a gorgeous tapestry of reds and golds. Though it appeared too small, and moved too erratically, to be an intelligent being, it seemed to know where it was going, and presently it fluttered down onto the plastic dome of the capsule. Even at this close range, as he watched it crawling on the other side of his window, Bowman could not classify it in any branch of the known animal kningdom; it was merely an undulating sheet of color.

He continued to wait, and presently something strange happened to the capsule. The instruments on the little control board went suddenly crazy, the external manipulators flexed themselves as if testing their strength, and there was even a brief burst of power from the jets. It was as if a ghost had entered the machine, tested its operation, and, satisfied that it had discovered all that there was to know, abandoned it like a worn-out toy. But before it went, it operated one last circuit.

The little flying carpet must have known what was coming, for it abruptly took off and fluttered a few feet away. Seconds later, the emergency hatch blew out, and for the first time Bowman heard the sounds of this alien world.

Perhaps even the familiar noises of Earth would have seemed unreal, and hard to recognize, after his months in the artificial universe of *Discovery*. But there was one sound that no man could ever forget, as long as he lived; it was the distant murmur of the sea—the eternal dialog between mind and wave.

It came from all around him—from the ocean that was two or three miles below, and which covered all this strange planet. That ocean, Bowman realized, must be very shallow; even if there was no dry land, there must be many reefs almost breaking the surface, to produce that endless susurration. If he closed his eyes, he could imagine that he was standing beside one of the far-off seas of Earth.

That was not the only sound, though it was the most prominent. There was also the faint sighing of the wind through the alien trees—and, from time to time, a trio of descending bell-like notes. It came from somewhere in the depths of the little wood that covered so much of this flying island; though it was strikingly like the call of a bird, it seemed to have altogether too much power behind it for an avian origin.

Bowman sniffed cautiously at the air. He felt certain that these creatures would not have exposed him to their atmosphere unless they knew that he could breathe it. To his surprise, he could detect no change whatsoever; the air that flowed into his lungs was all too familiar. He could recognize the capsule's entire spectrum of odors from ozone through oil to sweat and pine-scented disinfectant.

Then he realized that he was still surrounded by an almost invisible envelope, like the one that had protected him on his journey. He wondered if it would permit him to leave the capsule; he had been offered the invitation, and was only too glad to accept it, after all these hours in his cramped little world. He unstrapped himself, climbed out of the pod, and stretched his limbs with relief, while the tiny flying carpet fluttered overhead, circling around and around with obvious excitement.

Gravity seemed absolutely normal. He walked once

around the capsule, getting the stiffness out of his limbs and enjoying this now almost forgotten mode of locomotion; the last time he had walked on an ordinary horizontal surface was a year ago, and unknown trillions of miles away. He felt like an invalid who had just been allowed out of bed after a long illness—reveling in his regained powers, but careful not to overexert them.

The faintly glimmering envelope, permeable to sounds but not to air, remained always a few feet away, changing its shape to accommodate him. It was as if he were inside a giant soap bubble, whose surface he could never quite reach, or even precisely locate. Presumably this was part of the decontamination procedure, and he wondered if he was a greater danger to this world than it was to him.

He looked questioningly toward the creatures still standing under the trees; and then, for the first time, one of them moved. It made a simple and unmistakable gesture, with the slowness of a dream; and Bowman realized that his time scale was not the same as theirs. Or perhaps they did not feel the need for haste; perhaps they had eternity at their command.

The tallest of the five hominids raised its right arm, and the network of glowing threads fell away to reveal a supple golden tube that divided in a rosette of eight symmetrically arranged tendrils, about a foot in length. It was exactly as if the creature's arm terminated in a sea anemone, and Bowman recalled, rather wryly, the arguments he had heard on Earth proving the universality of the hand—or something very much like it. In one of those moments of insight that come when one is confronted with the obvious, he realized where those arguments had gone hopelessly astray.

The human hand was a superb piece of engineering—but it was compromise. It was still designed to deal with heavy loads, to apply forces and pressures—to do mechanical work. Yet more and more, what was needed was precision and delicacy. Even for Man, the time of breaking branches and chipping flints had long since passed; the time of touching buttons and stroking keyboards had come.

Here, then, was the end of the hand's evolution. As he looked at those slim tendrils, Bowman was acutely conscious of his own stubby, clumsy fingers, and found himself involuntarily trying to conceal them by clenching his fist.

Then he realized that the creature was pointing, and he

turned his head in the direction that it indicated. To his alarm and surprise, it seemed to be ordering him off the island—asking him to step over the edge of this floating rock, to fall down to the endless ocean miles below.

As if to reinforce this command, the little flying carpet was fluttering ahead of him, leading the way to the brink of the abyss. It was all very strange, but he still could not believe that any harm was intended to him. He followed his chromatic guide to the edge of the island, and peered cautiously over the side.

Before and below him was a curving rocky slope, rapidly becoming as steep as the roof of a house, then plunging completely out of sight. Down its face, and starting from a point only a few yards away from his feet, was a wide road of smooth gray material, following the curve of the rock until it too disappeared from view. It had an unmistakable impression of freshness, as if it had just been cut in the flanks of this aerial world.

Was this some kind of ordeal or test? Bowman asked himself. But that seemed altogether too naive and primitive a concept for a place like this. Then he remembered that he was in the presence of creatures who had mastered gravity; perhaps this downward-plunging road was not what it seemed.

He took a few gingerly steps along it, and the flying carpet fluttered encouragingly ahead. While he kept his eyes fixed on the pavement, he felt quite secure; so he took a dozen more paces.

He *knew* that the road was curving downward, ever more and more steeply; yet his senses told him that it was still quite horizontal. But when he risked a glance backward along the way he had come, the path in that direction was unmistakably downhill. There was no question of it; gravity tilted as he walked around this little world; wherever he was, the pavement beneath him was always horizontal.

He looked ahead—and was almost overcome by vertigo. For now it was the planet above which he was floating that had become crazy; as he walked down towards it, the ocean was a 45-degree slope running up the sky. With a great effort of will he ignored the illusion. After all, he was used to such things in space; Earth had looked like this, when he had been in close orbit.

But there was a fundamental difference. Then he had been weightless—there was *no* direction of gravity. Here there was gravity, and it defied common sense.

He fixed his eyes on a point only a few yards ahead, and kept walking toward it. Now the trees and terraces on the upper part of the island had vanished completely, hidden by the curve of rock. Because he was looking at the ground, he almost ran into the building that barred his path.

It seemed as new as the road, which led directly to a rectangular green door just the right size to admit a man. Apart from this entrance, the side turned toward him was quite featureless, some thirty feet wide and fifteen high. And beyond it, a now absolutely vertical wall of water running up and down the sky, was the face of the ocean.

Somehow, he now found this easier to accept. Horizontal *or* vertical seas were all right; only the intermediate ones were hard on the nerves. But he did not wish to linger in this strange place for long, standing like a fly on a sheer wall of rock. His brain told him that the powers and forces operating here were not likely to experience any sudden failure; a civilization would hardly build homes in the sky unless it felt utterly secure. His emotions, however, were still those of the primitive jungle ape, afraid that the branch to which he was clinging would snap.

His race had not yet made infallible machines; therefore, he could not really believe in their existence. The building ahead offered mental security, for it would shut out the view of that impossible sky.

At the door itself, he paused for a moment, wondering if there was anything that he had left in the capsule, up on the summit of the island. No, there was nothing there that would help; indeed, all the resources of Earth could not aid him here, if the powers of this world were bent on his destruction. He hesitated no longer, but walked steadfastly toward the green door; and it opened silently as he approached.

[*In the next version (Chapters 40 to 42) Kubrick and I were getting close to our goal. We were still involved in fascinating, though dramatically irrelevant—not to say unfilmable—descriptions of extraterrestrial worlds. But we had begun to realize exactly what it was Bowman must meet, at the end of his journey. . . .*]

40

OCEANA

Not long afterward, he saw his first city. For some time the color of the ocean had been changing to a lighter hue, as if it was sloping up toward a continental shelf; and presently he was able to pick out markings on the seabed—including faint reticulations that might have been submerged highways. He thought he could see traffic moving along some of them.

Then the land humped up out of the sea in a great circle about ten miles across, exactly like a Pacific atoll. The ring of land was encrusted with brightly colored buildings, none of them very large or tall, and spaced at wide intervals. From a distance the ring-city looked disappointingly ordinary, and there was nothing to tell that it was made by a race other than man. Apart from a few very slim towers supporting wide, circular disks at a considerable height above the ground, there were none of the architectural fantasies that Bowman had half expected. Then he realized that there were only a limited number of sensible ways of enclosing space, which were the same throughout the universe; and there were very few designs, sensible or otherwise, that some enterprising architect had not already tried out on Earth.

However, the city had one strange characteristic: many of the buildings ran straight down into the sea, as if they had been built for amphibious creatures. There were no vehicles or aircraft, and Bowman was much too far away to glimpse any of the inhabitants.

But he did see one piquant detail before the circular island passed out of sight. The central lagoon was dotted with small moving objects which, even from this great distance, were quite unmistakable. The last thing that Bowman had ever expected to find on a world of such transcendental science was a sailboat; and the friendly, reassuring sight of all that wholly useless activity filled his heart with warmth.

The sun, still framed within the arches of the rings, continued to sink; now it had almost reached the horizon. Fleeing from it, *Discovery* had come to the very edge of day—and, it appeared, to the edge of the sea, for the line dividing water from sky was no longer a smooth, unbroken curve. It was splintered into dozens of sawtoothed peaks, as if a range of mountains was rising above the curve of the planet.

Yet these were no mountains, though they soared straight out of the sea to altitudes higher than the Himalayas. They were too regular and too symmetrical, and their leaping towers and buttresses showed a total disregard for the structural laws that natural objects must obey. They marched on either side to north and to south, continuing out of sight as if they would meet again at the antipodes.

It was a spectacle to steal away the breath, and as he looked at those approaching peaks, already touched with the hues of night, Bowman thought how strange it was that he had reached the first continental landmass at the precise moment of sunset. Then he remembered another odd coincidence—that the circular forest of the sky-planets had been at the exact center of the planet's illuminated disk, directly beneath the sun.

Then the truth exploded suddenly in his mind. Ages ago this world had lost its rotation, and had come to rest with the same face always turned toward the double star around which it revolved. Now dawn and sunset stood together for eternity on the same unchanging meridian; along it these great peaks were the boundary markers between night and day, and forever faced the sun.

Discovery had descended below the level of the highest peaks, and was traveling, quite slowly, parallel to them at a distance of several miles. No two of the artificial mountains were identical in design; some were plain and angular, being constructed from a few simple elements, while others were incredibly complex, like Gothic cathedrals or Cambodian temples magnified fifty or a hundred times. There was no indication of age; they could have been built yesterday, or a million years ago. Nor was there any hint of their purpose, or indication that they were occupied.

They might have been cities, or machines, or monuments, or tombs—or merely the follies of some omnipotent architect. They did nothing but stand and face that eternal dawn.

Now he could see, around the base of one of those approaching peaks, a glittering, crystalline fringe, as if intersecting sheets of glass were rising out of the ocean. *Discovery* was descending toward it; and Bowman saw that, at last, he was entering a city.

That word was misleading, but he could think of no better one. His first impression was of emptiness and space; there were no packed, scurrying throngs of anxious commuters, no crowded roads and sidewalks. It was some time, indeed, before he could see any sign of life or movement at all.

The ship was passing between vertical planes of some metallic substance that seemed to change its texture with the angle of view. At one moment it would be as flat and featureless as polished steel; then it would become flooded with iridescent, rainbow colors, behaving like a giant diffraction grating. Some areas were transparent; and through these, Bowman first glimpsed one of the city's inhabitants.

Ironically, yet not surprisingly, it was looking at him. Even on this world, thought Bowman, it could not be a common event for a two-hundred-foot-long alien space vehicle to go drifting past your window. . . .

The thing was either a robot, or a compound machine-organism; it looked like an elegant metal crab, supported on four jointed legs. Each of those legs terminated in a small, fat wheel; presumably the creature could walk or roll, whichever was more convenient. There was an ovoid body, into which various limbs were now retracted, and the whole was surmounted by a polyhedral head, each facet of which bore a deep-set lens.

The body never moved, but the head rotated steadily to follow him as he passed by. Bowman tried to look into the room behind the creature, but he could see only a moving patchwork quilt of soft, pastel colors—whether a work of art, or a scientific experiment, he could not guess.

A little later he saw another of these metal entities, but in quite a different environment. It was in the center of a small circular auditorium or amphitheater, which was flooded with some greenish foam to a depth of two or three feet. Rising out of the foam were little trees, like weeping willows or aspens, whose long, delicate leaves trembled continually, as if afflicted with ague. At the highest point of each stem was something that closely resembled an orchid; but it was an orchid with tiny, staring eyes, and fine tendrils that kept twisting and twining like nervous fingers. It was impossible to avoid the conclusion that these were intelligent plants, talking to each other—or to the robot—in some complex sign language.

Discovery was now drifting between walls of glass or metal that rose straight out of the sea, and immediately ahead was a fountain or waterspout that rose to a height of at least two hundred feet and then fell back into a huge circular moat that surrounded it like a halo. From this moat transparent tubes ran off in several directions, and as he approached, Bowman saw that this was not merely a piece of ornamental hydraulics; it was part of a sea-to-air transportation system.

Every few minutes there would be a flicker of darkness in the ascending column, and something like a large fish would splash into the moat, then go shooting off along one of the radiating tubes. Bowman was not surprised when he recognized the intelligent suckerfish he had seen among the roots of the skyplants, but there were also a few creatures remarkably like dolphins and seals. All seemed to know exactly where they were going; and once, a pair of the dolphinoids, apparently out of pure exuberance, leaped straight out of the moat and back into the sea. At the end of the two-hundred-foot dive, their gleaming bodies entered the water simultaneously with scarcely a splash.

This city seemed to have been designed for common use by creatures of the sea and the land—yet so far, he had seen nothing even remotely resembling a human being. Was it possible that, despite all the arguments of the exobiologists, the hominid shape was actually quite rare in the universe—perhaps even unique?

A few minutes later, he had the answer to that question.

41

INTO THE NIGHT LAND

The creature standing on the balcony below which the ship was now moving possessed two arms, two legs, a vertical torso supporting an ovoid head, and two eyes; almost all the main ingredients of the human body were there, and in approximately the right places. Yet the total result was completely alien, and for the first time Bowman realized how many variations were possible on the basic human design. The biologists had told him this, but he had never really believed it.

The thing was only about five feet tall, and was very stocky, as if it came from a planet with a high gravity. Two large eyes, protected by bony ridges, were set on almost opposite sides of the head. But there was nothing that could be called a face; he could see no sign of mouth, nostrils, or ears. How did the thing manage to eat and breathe? It appeared to be a living creature; presumably it had some kind of metabolism.

Then Bowman looked more carefully at the two small, dark patches which he had assumed were nipples—and he realized how dangerous it was to jump to conclusions about extra terrestrials. *These* were the nostrils, sensibly located at the nearest point to the lungs. There was no doubt of it; the two small pits were opening and closing with a slow, regular rhythm.

But where was the mouth? For a moment, still conditioned by his human prejudices, Bowman searched in vain. Then he remembered the lesson of the nostrils, asked himself where a competent efficiency expert would put the mouth, and had his answer.

The creature was wearing a somewhat elaborate dress that covered the body up to about a foot below the neck;

it hung by straps from a metal collar, and looked rather comically like a giant kilt, complete with sporran in the region of the navel—not that Bowman now imagined for a moment that the creature had a navel.

That "sporran" was really a kind of movable curtain or screen; and beneath it, Bowman was quite sure, would be the mouth, handily placed at the entrance to the stomach. He decided that he would not care to be invited to dinner by these entities, but he had to admit that their alimentary arrangements were more efficient than his. They would doubtless be revolted by his all-purpose eating-speaking-breathing organ, permanently exposed to public view.

He wondered how the creature communicated with its kind; perhaps it did not rely on sound at all. Then he remembered that many animals on earth had no visible organs of sound production or detection, and that the absence of external ears proved nothing.

The creature had been watching him as the ship passed beneath its balcony, and at the moment of closest approach it did something completely human. It reached into one of the pockets of its dress, brought out a small metallic box, and raised it to its eyes. It held it there for a few seconds, then put it away again; and Bowman realized that he had had his photograph taken by a collector of biological curiosities.

The ship was now moving slowly through the outskirts of the city, obviously according to some prearranged plan. Was he being shown to its people, or were they being shown to him? His arrival had certainly attracted little attention; he thought of all the crowds that would have gathered on Earth if an alien spaceship had landed. However, it was obvious that this planet was inhabited— or visited—by intelligent creatures of many races; it was also possible that they were too polite to stare at strangers.

He was wrong on that count, as he soon discovered. Skirting the edge of a large, circular courtyard or patio, he noticed his first crowd. It was a sparse one, containing not more than a hundred entities of at least six basic types. Besides the two varieties he had already seen, there were tall, slender creatures of almost human form, but with blank, egglike heads absolutely devoid of features. There were also squat cones, supported on dozens of tiny, tubelike legs; and there was one impressive thing like a giant praying mantis.

They were all looking (though how the apparently eyeless eggheads managed this was more than Bowman could imagine) at a large bubble hanging in midair at the center of the patio; and in that bubble was—at last—the image of a perfectly normal human face. For a few seconds he looked at it with all the relief of a lost traveler meeting a fellow countryman in a far land; then, with a jarring psychic shock, he realized how totally disoriented he had become.

The face was his own; he had failed to recognize himself.

The mouth inside the bubble fell slackly; then Bowman pulled himself together. You've been on TV before, he told himself wryly; this is no time to get camera fright. (But where the devil was the camera?) Then the scale of the picture changed, so that he could see the whole interior of the cabin. The invisible eye retreated, until it seemed that a scale model of *Discovery* was floating there before the intent little group of spectators. Bowman wondered how long they had been looking at him, and how much they had already seen.

Then the ship moved on, and he lost sight of his audience, though he remained highly conscious of it. He did not see himself again.

The feeling of confident well-being that had gripped him was beginning to wear off; he had seen too much, too swiftly, and was becoming punchdrunk with sensations. One fact that added to the mental strain was something that he had never anticipated; he simply had no words for many of the things he was seeing, and this made it impossible for him to marshal his thoughts and to put his experiences in order. He had to make up labels as he went along, but he knew that they were only temporary, perhaps even misleading. Some of the creatures he had hastily classed as hominid might well be less human than the robots (if they *were* robots). And on this world, there might no longer be any real distinction between intelligences housed in machines, and those that occupied bodies of flesh and blood.

The passing scenes began to blur in his mind, and on several occasions he blanked out for unknown periods of time. For once he found himself sinking down a huge vertical shaft surrounded by water, and had no idea how he had got here. At first he thought that the water was held back by a cylindrical wall of glass or transparent plastic—but then one of the porpoise creatures came shooting straight through the barrier, into the column of air down which *Discovery* was slowly falling.

The dolphinoid drifted across the well, keeping level with the ship and obviously inspecting it closely. It reached the other side, merged without resistance into the wall of water, and shot off effortlessly with a flurry of flukes.

Not only the laws of matter but the law of gravity seemed to have been repealed in this strange place. Bowman could see many other tunnels heading off into the distance through the incredibly clear water; some were vertical, some horizontal—and the inhabitants of the city were moving along them both with a total disregard for the conventions of "up" and "down." It was not a question of the weightlessness with which he was familiar in space; judging by the way they were standing, the creatures in these tunnels had normal weight, and appeared completely at ease. Where one tunnel had intersected another in the vertical plane, they would switch nonchalantly through a right angle as the gravity field tilted and a wall became a floor.

It was a very disconcerting sight; but doubtless an escalator would have appeared just as unsettling to a Neanderthal Man.

The well down which he was sinking was perhaps five hundred feet deep, and ended in one of the underwater patios of this amphibious city. He could see, fading away into the blue distance, lines of open structures which he could only describe as roofless—and largely wall-less—buildings. The creatures he had called suckerfish were swimming in and out of these submarine apartments; most of them were moving under their own power, but a few were operating small torpedolike machines. Bowman had never imagined that he would one day see fish riding scooters; and even when he contemplated this thought, it still didn't seem funny.

The suckerfish were very inquisitive; they gathered around in scores, peering into the ship, and they spiraled up with him when *Discovery* started to rise again, past that vista of radiating tunnels.

The hole in the water widened as it approached the surface; he seemed to be emerging from a kind of stationary whirlpool in the center of a small lake. There were smaller whirlpools orbiting around it, like planets around the sun, and Bowman wondered if they were part of a mobile, liquid sculpture. He could not imagine what other purpose they fulfilled.

And then he was flying over what must have been a

residential area, for beneath him were roads that rolled briskly along like moving belts, between wide-spaced buildings no two of which were of the same design—or even, as he presently realized, built to the same scale. Some would not have looked out of place in a housing estate on Earth, but there were others that resembled small chemical processing plants and were presumably occupied by creatures with peculiar domestic requirements. Some were made for giants; others for beings who could hardly be larger than pygmies. And there was one wide, flat pancake of a building whose roof was not more than two feet from the ground. . . .

As Bowman passed over this suburban area—though, in reality, the whole city was a giant suburb—he caught tantalizing glimpses of the life it housed. It was obvious that, to some of its inhabitants, privacy meant absolutely nothing; their homes were as transparent as goldfish bowls. Once he looked into a room where three iridescent beetles, as large as a man, were standing around a bowl of redly fuming liquid, sipping it through flexible trunks or proboscises. In another, dozens of things like giant grubs were busily weaving a web around a cocoon that must have been ten feet long, and vibrated slightly from time to time.

And he saw more of the intelligent plants, standing in troughs of green mud, and swaying ecstatically as they absorbed the rays from a brightly shining globe. Even as he watched, one of the creatures seemed to explode in a cloud of mist, which resolved itself into tiny white parachutes. As they drifted slowly to the ground, Bowman realized that he had witnessed birth and death, but not as humans knew either.

Now the city, with all its meaningless wonders, its mind-wracking vistas, and its fantastic inhabitants, was falling behind him; he could relax once more with the spectacle of those calm, magnificent peaks, gilded by the faintly aureate glow of the eternal dawn. *Discovery* was moving past them at a considerable speed, racing along the edge of night.

The sky ahead was changing; there was a mist spreading across the horizon, thickening into a great river of cloud. It seemed to form somewhere out in the darkness, and then to flow toward the line of day. Quite abruptly, it plunged downward, in an immense and silent cataract flanked by two of the mountain towers—a slow-moving Niagara, five miles high and fifty miles across. The illusion of falling water was almost perfect; but this avalanche of mist slid down the sky with a dreamlike lethargy, and merged without a splash into the unruffled sea.

The mountain-towers dropped behind him, and the last light of the sun faded from the sky. (How many millions of years, he wondered, since it had shone upon this land?) But the white rainbow of the rings, and two large crescent moons, provided plenty of cold illumination; he could see clear to the horizon, and it seemed that he was flying over a vast snowfield rather than a sea of clouds. He had once orbited across the Antarctic under a full moon, only a hundred miles up; it required little effort to imagine that he was back there, waiting to exchange greetings with Mirny or McMurdo. . . .

He passed one mountain, and that a very strange one. It jutted up above the clouds like a giant iceberg—though no structure of ice could possibly be so tall, or so transparent. He could see far into its interior, which was laced with veins of some dark material; though he could not be certain, it seemed that some of these veins pulsed slowly, giving him the impression that he was looking into a gigantic anatomical model. Or perhaps it was not a model, but the real thing, whatever that might be; but this was a thought on which he did not care to dwell.

Then there was only the level sea of cloud—and, just once, a great glowing patch like the lights of a city hidden by the overcast. Presently it too fell astern, and he was alone under the arches of the rings, and the utterly alien stars.

He had now almost completed one half-circuit of this world, and was nearing the center of the nightside. It was easy to tell this, for the great bite taken out of the rings by the eclipsing shadow of the planet was now exactly overhead; he was as far from the forest of the sky plants as he could travel, while still remaining on this world. If he continued on this course, he would be heading back into the day.

Something was eclipsing the stars—something utterly black, rising swiftly up the sky. For an instant he thought it was a mountain, lying directly in his path; but no natural substance could soak up light as did this column of Stygian darkness. He caught only the faintest gleam from the mingled rays of the two moons, glancing upon fluted, cylindrical walls like polished ebony; and even as *Discovery* hurtled into the thing, beyond all possibility of avoidance, a long-forgotten line of poetry surged up from the depths of his memory. He found himself repeating desperately, like an incantation to ward off disaster: "Childe Harold to the Dark Tower came."

Then the Dark Tower was upon him, and his only regret was that he had seen so much and learned so little.

42

SECOND LESSON

There was no impact and no sound, but the stars and the
clouds were gone. Instead, the ship was moving through
an infinite lattice of softly glowing lights—a misty, three-
dimensional grid which appeared to have neither beginning nor end. For a moment *Discovery* seemed to coast
foward on its own momentum; then it began to fall.

Faster and faster, the arrays of light went flickering by,
as *Discovery* plunged downward at ever-accelerating
speed. Without astonishment—for he was now beyond
such an emotion—Bowman saw that the nodes of luminescence were passing *through* the solid walls of the ship as
they raced upward; indeed, he could see them streaming
through his own body.

Now he was falling through the grid so swiftly that the
individual knots of light could no longer be seen; they
were merely pulsations in the lines that went flickering
vertically past. He must have descended for miles; by this
time, surely, he was far below the surface of the planet—
if he was moving through real space at all.

Suddenly, the shining lattice was gone; he was falling
toward darkness, out of a dully glowing sky. And on that
darkness, the ship came at last to rest.

It was a place without horizons, or any sense of scale.
A hundred feet or a hundred miles above his head was a
flat, endless plane, very much like the surface of the red
dwarf star from which he had emerged into this solar system. It was cherry red, and little nodules of brighter
luminescence appeared at random, wandered around for
a while like living things, and then faded out into the
glowing background. If Bowman had possessed a trace of
superstition, he could easily have imagined that this was the

roof of Hell. There was no mark to show how he had passed through it, to enter this underworld.

He waited, on an infinite black plain, beneath an infinite glowing sky. And presently, for the first time in all his travels, he heard a sound.

It was a gentle throbbing, like the beating of a drum, that grew louder and more insistent second by second. He did not attempt to fight its compulsion, but let its hypnotic rhythm take over control of his mind.

And now, light was appearing in the aching darkness of the plain. First there was a single star, that moved swiftly to trace out a line; then the line moved, to make a horizontal square; then the square lifted, leaving its presence where it had passed, until the ghost of a crystal cube hung before Bowman's eyes.

The drumming became louder, more complex. Now there were rhythms moving against each other, like clashing waves on the surface of a stormy sea. And the crystal cube began to glow.

First it lost its transparency and became suffused with a pale mist, within which moved tantalizing, ill-defined phantoms. They coalesced into bars of light and shadow, then formed intermeshed, spoked patterns that began to rotate.

Now the turning wheels of light merged together, and their spokes fused into luminous bars that slowly receded into the distance. They split into pairs, and the resulting sets of lines started to oscillate across each other, continually changing their angle of intersection. Fantastic, fleeting geometrical patterns flickered in and out of existence as the glowing grids meshed and unmeshed; and the hominid watched from its metal cave—wide-eyed, slack jawed, and wholly receptive.

The dancing *moiré* patterns suddenly faded, and the rhythm sank to a barely audible, almost subsonic, pulsing throb. The cube was empty again; but only for a moment.

The first lesson having been moderately successful, the second was about to begin.

EPILOGUE

And so at last, after many adventures, Odysseus returned home, transformed by the experiences he had undergone. . . .

What lies beyond the end of 2001, when the Star Child waits, "marshaling his thoughts and brooding over his still untested powers," I do not know. Many readers have interpreted the final paragraph to mean that he destroyed Earth, perhaps in order to create a new Heaven. This idea never occurred to me; it seems clear that he triggered the orbiting nuclear bombs *harmlessly*, because "he preferred a cleaner sky."

But now, I am not so sure. When Odysseus returned to Ithaca, and identified himself in the banqueting hall by stringing the great bow that he alone could wield, he slew the parasitical suitors who for years had been wasting his estate.

We have wasted and defiled our own estate, the beautiful planet Earth. Why should we expect any mercy from a returning Star Child? He might judge all of us as ruthlessly as Odysseus judged Leiodes, whose "head fell rolling in the dust while he was yet speaking"—and despite his timeless, ineffectual plea, "I tried to stop the others." Few indeed of us would have a better answer, if we had to face judgment from the stars. And such a *Dies Irae* may be closer than we dream; for consider these facts.

It is now some twenty years since our first superpowered radars began announcing to the Universe that a technological culture has arisen on Earth. By this time, therefore, those signals will have passed stars twenty light-years away, and they will still be detectable when they have traveled much greater distances.

How many civilizations already know of our existence? How many feel concerned—and are prepared to take some action? One can only guess.

Yet we know that the electronic birthcries of our culture have already reached at least a hundred suns, all the way out to giant Vega. By the year 2001, there will have been ample time for many replies, from many directions.

And there will have been time for more than that. Despite assertions to the contrary, from scientists who should have learned better by now, an advanced technology should be able to build ships capable of reaching at least a quarter of the speed of light. By the turn of the millennium, therefore, emissaries could be arriving from Alpha Centauri, Sirius, Procyon. . . .

And so I repeat the words I wrote in 1948:
I do not think we will have to wait for long.

Colombo
December 31, 1970

About the Author

Arthur C. Clarke, the son of a farmer, was born in Somerset in 1917. During the Second World War he became a specialist in radar, and afterward studied at London University, taking a B.Sc. in Physics in 1948. From 1949 to 1951 he was Assistant Editor of *Science Abstracts*. He has written several serious works on space, but is best known for his science fiction, which is among the best of its kind. For a number of years he was chairman of the British Interplanetary Society, and he was also a Fellow of the Royal Astronomical Society.

EXPEDITION
TO EARTH

Arthur C. Clarke

SIDGWICK & JACKSON/LONDON

First published in 1954
Reprinted 1968, 1976
Copyright © 1968 by Arthur C. Clarke
Published in this edition in 1976 by Sidgwick and Jackson Limited
Reprinted February 1980

Printed in Great Britain by
Hunt Barnard Printing Ltd., Aylesbury, Bucks.
for Sidgwick and Jackson Limited,
1 Tavistock Chambers, Bloomsbury Way, London WC1A 2SG

ISBN 0 283 98623 9

SECOND DAWN

'Here they come,' said Eris, rising to his forefeet and turning to look down the long valley. For a moment the pain and bitterness had left his thoughts, so that even Jeryl, whose mind was more closely tuned to his than to any other, could scarcely detect it. There was even an undertone of softness that recalled poignantly the Eris she had known in the days before the War – the old Eris who now seemed almost as remote and as lost as if he were lying with all the others out there on the plain.

A dark tide was flowing up the valley, advancing with a curious, hesitant motion, making odd pauses and little bounds forward. It was flanked with gold – the thin line of the Atheleni guards, so terrifyingly few compared with the black mass of the prisoners. But they were enough : indeed, they were only needed to guide that aimless river on its faltering way. Yet at the sight of so many thousands of the enemy, Jeryl found herself trembling and instinctively moved towards her mate, silver pelt resting against gold. Eris gave no sign that he had understood or even noticed the action.

The fear vanished as Jeryl saw how slowly the dark flood was moving forwards. She had been told what to expect, but the reality was even worse than she had imagined. As the prisoners came nearer, all the hate and bitterness ebbed from her mind, to be replaced by a sick compassion. No one of her race need ever more fear the aimless, idiot horde that was being shepherded through the pass into the valley it would never leave again.

The guards were doing little more than urge the prisoners on with meaningless but encouraging cries, like nurses calling to infants too young to sense their thoughts. Strain as she might, Jeryl could detect no vestige of reason in any of these thousands of minds passing so near at hand. That brought home to her, more vividly than could anything else, the magnitude of the victory – and of the defeat. Her mind was sensitive enough to detect the first faint thoughts of children, hovering on the verge of consciousness. The defeated enemy had become not even children, but babies with the bodies of adults.

The tide was passing within a few feet of them now. For the first time, Jeryl realized how much larger than her own people the Mithraneans were, and how beautifully the light of the twin suns gleamed on the dark satin of their bodies. Once a magnificent specimen, towering a full head above Eris, broke loose from the main body and came blundering towards them, halting a few paces away. Then it crouched down like a lost and frightened child, the splendid head moving uncertainly from side to side as if seeking it knew not what. For a moment the great, empty eyes fell full upon Jeryl's face. She was as beautiful, she knew, to the Mithraneans as to her own race – but there was no flicker of emotion on the blank features, and no pause in the aimless movement of the questing head. Then an exasperated guard drove the prisoner back to his fellows.

'Come away,' Jeryl pleaded. 'I don't want to see any more. Why did you ever bring me here?' The last thought was heavy with reproach.

Eris began to move away over the grassy slopes in great bounds that she could not hope to match, but as he went his mind threw its message back to hers. His thoughts were still gentle, though the pain beneath them was too deep to be concealed.

'I wanted everyone – even you – to see what we had to do to win the War. Then, perhaps, we will have no more in our lifetimes.'

He was waiting for her on the brow of the hill, undistressed by the mad violence of his climb. The stream of prisoners was now too far below for them to see the details of its painful progress. Jeryl crouched down beside Eris and began to browse on the sparse vegetation that had been exiled from the fertile valley. She was slowly beginning to recover from the shock.

'But what will happen to them?' she asked presently, still haunted by the memory of that splendid, mindless giant going into a captivity it could never understand.

'They can be taught how to eat,' said Eris. 'There is food in the valley for half a year, and then we'll move them on. It will be a heavy strain on our own resources, but we're under a moral obligation – and we've put it in the peace treaty.'

'They can never be cured?'

'No. Their minds have been totally destroyed. They'll be like this until they die.'

There was a long silence. Jeryl let her gaze wander across the hills, falling in gentle undulations to the edge of the ocean. She could just make out, beyond a gap in the hills, the distant line of blue that marked the sea – the mysterious, impassable sea. Its blue would soon be deepening into darkness, for the fierce white sun was setting and presently there would only be the red disk – hundreds of times larger but giving far less light – of its pale companion.

'I suppose we had to do it,' Jeryl said at last. She was thinking almost to herself, but she let enough of her thoughts escape for Eris to overhear.

'You've seen them,' he answered briefly. 'They were bigger and stronger than we. Though we outnumbered them, it was stalemate : in the end, I think they would have won. By doing what we did, we saved thousands from death – or mutilation.'

The bitterness came back into his thoughts, and Jeryl dared not look at him. He had screened the depths of his mind, but she knew that he was thinking of the shattered ivory stump upon his forehead. The War had been fought, except at the very end, with two weapons only – the razor-sharp hooves of the little, almost useless forepaws, and the unicornlike horns. With one of these Eris could never fight again, and from the loss stemmed much of the embittered harshness that sometimes made him hurt even those who loved him.

Eris was waiting for someone, though who it was Jeryl could not guess. She knew better than to interrupt his thoughts while he was in his present mood, and so remained silently beside him, her shadow merging with his as it stretched far along the hill-top.

Jeryl and Eris came of a race which, in Nature's lottery, had been luckier than most – and yet had missed one of the greatest prizes of all. They had powerful bodies and powerful minds, and they lived in a world which was both temperate and fertile. By human standards, they would have seemed strange but by no means repulsive. Their sleek, fur-covered bodies tapered to a single giant rear limb that could send them leaping over the ground in thirty-foot bounds. The two forelimbs were much smaller, and served merely for support and steadying. They ended in pointed hooves that could be deadly in combat, but had no other useful purpose.

Both the Atheleni and their cousins, the Mithraneans, possessed mental powers that had enabled them to develop a very advanced mathematics and philosophy : but over the physical world they had no control at all. Houses, tools, clothes – indeed, artifacts of any kind – were utterly unknown to them. To races which possessed hands, tentacles or other means of manipulation, their culture would have seemed incredibly limited : yet such is the adaptability of the mind, and the power of the commonplace, that they seldom realized their handicaps and could imagine no other way of life. It was natural to wander in great herds over the fertile plains, pausing where food was plentiful and moving on again when it was exhausted. This nomadic life had given them enough leisure for philosophy and even for certain arts. Their telepathic powers had not yet robbed them of their voices and they had developed a complex vocal music and an even more complex choreography. But they took the greatest pride of all in the range of their thoughts : for thousands of generations they had sent their minds roving through the misty infinities of metaphysics. Of *physics*, and indeed of all the sciences of matter, they knew nothing – not even that they existed.

'Someone's coming,' said Jeryl suddenly. 'Who is it?'

Eris did not bother to look, but there was a sense of strain in his reply.

'It's Aretenon. I agreed to meet him here.'

'I'm so glad. You were such good friends once – it upset me when you quarrelled.'

Eris pawed fretfully at the turf, as he did when he was embarrassed or annoyed.

'I lost my temper with him when he left me during the fifth battle of the Plain. Of course I didn't know then why he had to go.'

Jeryl's eyes widened in sudden amazement and understanding.

'You mean – he had something to do with the Madness, and the way the War ended?'

'Yes. There were very few people who knew more about the mind than he did. I don't know what part he played, but it must have been an important one. I don't suppose he'll ever be able to tell us much about it.'

Still a considerable distance below them, Aretenon was zigzagging up the hillside in great leaps. A little later he had reached them and instinctively bent his head to touch horns with Eris in the universal gesture of greeting. Then he stopped, horribly embarrassed, and there was an awkward pause until Jeryl came to the rescue with some conventional remarks.

When Eris spoke, Jeryl was relieved to sense his obvious pleasure at meeting his friend once again, for the first time since their angry parting at the height of the War. It had been longer still since her last meeting with Aretenon, and she was surprised to see how much he had changed. He was considerably younger than Eris – but no one would have guessed it now. Some of his once-golden pelt was turning black with age, and with a flash of his old humour Eris re-

marked that soon no one would be able to tell him from a
Mithranean.

Aretenon smiled.

'That would have been useful in the last few weeks. I've
just come through their country, helping to round up the
Wanderers. We weren't very popular, as you might expect.
If they'd known who I was, I don't suppose I'd have got
back alive – armistice or no armistice.'

'You weren't actually in charge of the Madness, were
you?' asked Jeryl, unable to control her curiosity.

She had a momentary impression of thick, defensive mists
forming around Aretenon's mind, shielding all his thoughts
from the outer world. Then the reply came, curiously
muffled, and with a sense of distance that was very rare in
telepathic-contact.

'No : I wasn't in supreme charge. But there were only
two others between myself and – the top.'

'Of course,' said Eris, rather petulantly, 'I'm only an
ordinary soldier and don't understand these things. But I'd
like to know just how you did it. Naturally,' he added,
'neither Jeryl nor myself would talk to anyone else.'

Again that veil seemed to descend over Aretenon's
thoughts. Then it lifted, ever so slightly.

'There's very little I'm allowed to tell. As you know, Eris,
I was always interested in the mind and its workings. Do you
remember the games we used to play, when I tried to un-
cover your thoughts, and you did your best to stop me? And
how I sometimes made you carry out acts against your will?'

'I still think,' said Eris, 'that you couldn't have done that
to a stranger, and that I was really unconsciously co-
operating.'

'That was true then – but it isn't any longer. The proof
lies down there in the valley.' He gestured towards the last
stragglers who were being rounded up by the guards. The
dark tide had almost passed, and soon the entrance to the
valley would be closed.

'When I grew older,' continued Aretenon, 'I spent more

and more of my time probing into the ways of the mind, and trying to discover why some of us can share our thoughts so easily, while others can never do so but must remain always isolated and alone, forced to communicate by sounds or gestures. And I became fascinated by those rare minds that are completely deranged, so that those who possess them seem less than children.

'I had to abandon these studies when the War began. Then, as you know, they called for me one day during the fifth battle. Even now, I'm not quite sure who was responsible for that. I was taken to a place a long way from here, where I found a little group of thinkers many of whom I already knew.

'The plan was simple – and tremendous. From the dawn of our race we've known that two or three minds, linked together, could be used to control another mind, *if it was willing*, in the way that I used to control you. We've employed this power for healing since ancient times. Now we planned to use it for destruction.

'There were two main difficulties. One was bound up with that curious limitation of our normal telepathic powers – the fact that, except in rare cases, we can only have contact over a distance *with someone we already know*, and can communicate with strangers only when we are actually in their presence.

'The second, and greater problem, was that the massed power of many minds would be needed, and never before had it been possible to link together more than two or three. How we succeeded is our main secret : like all things, it seems easy now it has been done. And once we had started, it was simpler than we had expected. Two minds are more than twice as powerful as one, and three are much more than thrice as powerful as a single will. The exact mathematical relationship is an interesting one. You know how very rapidly the number of ways a group of objects may be arranged increases with the size of the group ? Well, a similar relationship holds in this case.

'So in the end we had our Composite Mind. At first it was unstable, and we could hold it together only for a few seconds. It's still a tremendous strain on our mental resources, and even now we can only do it for – well, for long enough.

'All these experiments, of course, were carried out in great secrecy. If we could do this, so could the Mithraneans, for their minds are as good as ours. We had a number of their prisoners, and we used them as subjects.'

For a moment the veil that hid Aretenon's inner thoughts seemed to tremble and dissolve : then he regained control.

'That was the worst part. It was bad enough to send madness into a far land, but it was infinitely worse when you could watch with your own eyes the effects of what you did.

'When we had perfected our technique, we made the first long-distance test. Our victim was someone so well known to one of our prisoners – whose mind we had taken over – that we could identify him completely and thus the distance between us was no objection. The experiment worked, but of course no one suspected that we were responsible.

'We did not operate again until we were certain that our attack would be so overwhelming that it would end the War. From the minds of our prisoners we had identified about a score of Mithraneans – their friends and kindred – in such detail that we could pick them out and destroy them. As each mind fell beneath our attack, it gave up to us the knowledge of others, and so our power increased. We could have done far more damage than we did, for we took only the males.'

'Was that,' said Jeryl bitterly, 'so very merciful?'

'Perhaps not : but it should be remembered to our credit. We stopped as soon as the enemy sued for peace, and as we alone knew what had happened, we went into their country to undo what damage we could. It was little enough.'

There was a long silence. The valley was deserted now, and the white sun had set. A cold wind was blowing over the hills, passing, where none could follow it, out across the empty and untravelled sea. Then Eris spoke, his thoughts almost whispering in Aretenon's mind.

'You did not come to tell me this, did you? There is something more.' It was a statement rather than a query.

'Yes,' replied Aretenon. 'I have a message for you — one that will surprise you a good deal. It's from Therodimus.'

'Therodimus! I thought —'

'You thought he was dead, or worse still, a traitor. He's neither, although he's lived in enemy territory for the last twenty years. The Mithraneans treated him as we did, and gave him everything he needed. They recognized his mind for what it was, and even during the War no one touched him. Now he wants to see you again.'

Whatever emotions Eris was feeling at this news of his old teacher, he gave no sign of them. Perhaps he was recalling his youth, remembering now that Therodimus had played a greater part in the shaping of his mind than any other single influence. But his thoughts were barred to Aretenon and even to Jeryl.

'What's he been doing all this time?' Eris asked at length. 'And why does he want to see me now?'

'It's a long and complicated story,' said Aretenon, 'but Therodimus has made a discovery quite as remarkable as ours, and one that may have even greater consequences.'

'Discovery? What sort of discovery?'

Aretenon paused, looking thoughtfully along the valley. The guards were returning, leaving behind only the few who would be needed to deal with any wandering prisoners.

'You know as much of our history as I do, Eris,' he began. 'It took, we believe, something like a million generations for us to reach our present level of development — and that's a tremendous length of time! Almost all the progress we've made has been due to our telepathic powers : without them we'd be little different from all those other animals that show such puzzling resemblances to us. We're very proud of our philosophy and our mathematics, of our music and dancing — but have you ever thought, Eris, that there might be other lines of cultural development which we've never even dreamed of? *That there might be other forces in the Universe beside mental ones?*'

'I don't know what you mean,' said Eris flatly.

'It's hard to explain, and I won't try – except to say this. Do you realize just how pitiably feeble is our control over the external world, and how useless these limbs of ours really are? No – you can't, for you won't have seen what I have. But perhaps this will make you understand.'

The pattern of Eretenon's thoughts modulated suddenly into a minor key.

'I remember once coming upon a bank of beautiful and curiously complicated flowers. I wanted to see what they were like inside, so I tried to open one, steadying it between my hooves and picking it apart with my teeth. I tried again and again – and failed. In the end, half mad with rage, I trampled all those flowers into the dirt.'

Jeryl could detect the perplexity in Eris's mind, but she could see that he was interested and curious to know more.

'I have had that sort of feeling, too,' he admitted. 'But what can one do about it? And after all, is it really important? There are a good many things in this universe which are not exactly as we should like them.'

Aretenon smiled.

'That's true enough. But Therodimus has found how to do something about it. Will you come and see him?'

'It must be a long journey.'

'About twenty days from here, and we have to go across a river.'

Jeryl felt Eris give a little shudder. The Atheleni hated water, for the excellent and sufficient reason that they were too heavily boned to swim, and promptly drowned if they fell into it.

'It's in enemy territory : they won't like me.'

'They respect you, and it might be a good idea for you to go – a friendly gesture, as it were.'

'But I'm wanted here.'

'You can take my word that nothing you do here is as important as the message Therodimus has for you – and for the whole world.'

Eris veiled his thoughts for a moment, then uncovered them briefly.

'I'll think about it,' he said.

It was surprising how little Aretenon managed to say on the many days of the journey. From time to time Eris would challenge the defences of his mind with half-playful thrusts, but always they were parried with an effortless skill. About the ultimate weapon that had ended the War he would say nothing, but Eris knew that those who had wielded it had not yet disbanded and were still at their secret hiding-place. Yet though he would not talk about the past, Aretenon often spoke of the future, and with the urgent anxiety of one who had helped to shape it and was not sure if he had acted aright. Like many others of his race, he was haunted by what he had done, and the sense of guilt sometimes overwhelmed him. Often he made remarks which puzzled Eris at the time, but which he was to remember more and more vividly in the years ahead.

'We've come to a turning-point in our history, Eris. The powers we've uncovered will soon be shared by the Mithraneans, and another war will mean destruction for us both. All my life I've worked to increase our knowledge of the mind, but now I wonder if I've brought something into the world that is too powerful, and too dangerous for us to handle. Yet it's too late, now, to retrace our footsteps : sooner or later our culture was bound to come to this point, and to discover what we have found.

'It's a terrible dilemma : and there's only one solution. We cannot go back, and if we go forward we may meet disaster. So we must change the very nature of our civilization, and break completely with the million generations behind us. You can't imagine how that could be done : nor could I, until I met Therodimus and he told me of his dream.

2

'The mind is a wonderful thing, Eris – but by itself it is helpless in the universe of matter. We know now how to multiply the power of our brains by an enormous factor : we can solve, perhaps, the great problems of mathematics that have baffled us for ages. But neither our unaided minds, nor the group-mind we've now created, can alter in the slightest the one fact that all through history has brought us and the Mithraneans into conflict – the fact that the food supply is fixed, and our populations are not.'

Jeryl would watch them, taking little part in their thoughts, as they argued these matters. Most of their discussions took place while they were browsing, for like all active ruminants they had to spend a considerable part of each day searching for food. Fortunately the land through which they were passing was extremely fertile – indeed, its fertility had been one of the causes of the War. Eris, Jeryl was glad to see, was becoming something of his old self again. The feeling of frustrated bitterness that had filled his mind for so many months had not lifted, but it was no longer as all-pervading as it had been.

They left the open plain on the twenty-second day of their journey. For a long time they had been travelling through Mithranean territory, but those few of their ex-enemies they had seen had been inquisitive rather than hostile. Now the grasslands were coming to an end, and the forest with all its primeval terrors lay ahead.

'Only one carnivore lives in this region,' Aretenon re-assured them, 'and it's no match for the three of us. We'll be past the trees in a day and a night.'

'A night – in the forest !' gasped Jeryl, half-petrified with terror at the very thought.

Aretenon was obviously a little ashamed of himself.

'I didn't like to mention it before,' he apologized, 'but there's really no danger. I've done it by myself, several times. After all, none of the great flesh-eaters of ancient times still exists – and it won't be really dark, even in the woods. The red sun will still be up.'

Jeryl was still trembling slightly. She came of a race which, for thousands of generations, had lived on the high hills and the open plains, relying on speed to escape from danger. The thought of going among trees – and in the dim red twilight while the primary sun was down – filled her with panic. And of the three of them, only Aretenon possessed a horn with which to fight. (It was nothing like so long or sharp, thought Jeryl, as Eris's had been.)

She was still not at all happy even when they had spent a completely uneventful day moving through the woods. The only animals they saw were tiny, long-tailed creatures that ran up and down the tree-trunks with amazing speed, gibbering with anger as the intruders passed. It was entertaining to watch them, but Jeryl did not think that the forest would be quite so amusing in the night.

Her fears were well founded. When the fierce white sun passed below the trees, and the crimson shadows of the red giant lay everywhere, a change seemed to come over the world. A sudden silence swept across the forest – a silence abruptly broken by a very distant wail towards which the three of them turned instinctively, ancestral warnings shrieking in their minds.

'What was that?' gasped Jeryl.

Aretenon was breathing swiftly, but his reply was calm enough.

'Never mind,' he said. 'It was a long way off. I don't know what it was.'

They took turns to keep guard, and the long night wore slowly away. From time to time Jeryl would awaken from troubled dreams into the nightmare reality of the strange, distorted trees gathered threateningly around her. Once, when she was on guard, she heard the sound of a heavy body moving through the woods very far away – but it came no nearer and she did not disturb the others. So at last the longed-for brilliance of the white sun began to flood the sky, and the day had come again.

Aretenon, Jeryl thought, was probably more relieved than

he pretended to be. He was almost boyish as he frisked around in the morning sunlight, snatching an occasional mouthful of foliage from an overhanging branch.

'We've only half a day to go now,' he said cheerfully. 'We'll be out of the forest by noon.'

There was a mischievous undertone to his thoughts that puzzled Jeryl. It seemed as if Aretenon was keeping still another secret from them, and Jeryl wondered what further obstacles they would have to overcome. By mid-day she knew, for their way was barred by a great river flowing slowly past them as if in no haste to meet the sea.

Eris looked at it with some annoyance, measuring it with a practised eye.

'It's much too deep to ford here. We'll have to go a long way upstream before we can cross.'

Aretenon smiled.

'On the contrary,' he said cheerfully, 'we're going *downstream*.'

Eris and Jeryl looked at him in amazement.

'Are you mad?' Eris cried.

'You'll soon see. We've not far to go now – you've come all this way, so you might as well trust me for the rest of the journey.'

The river slowly widened and deepened. If it had been impassable before, it was doubly so now. Sometimes, Eris knew, one came upon a stream across which a tree had fallen, so that one could walk over the trunk – though it was a risky thing to do. But this river was the width of many trees, and was growing no narrower.

'We're nearly there,' said Aretenon at last. 'I recognize the place. Someone should be coming out of those woods at any moment.' He gestured with his horn to the trees on the far side of the river, and almost as he did so three figures came bounding out on to the bank. Two of them, Jeryl saw, were Atheleni : the third was a Mithranean.

They were now nearing a great tree, standing by the water's edge, but Jeryl had paid little attention : she was too interested in the figures on the distant bank, wondering what they were going to do next. So when Eris's amazement exploded like a thunderclap in the depths of her own mind, she was too confused for a moment to realize its cause. Then she turned towards the tree, and saw what Eris had seen.

To some minds and some races, few things could have been more natural or more commonplace than a thick rope tied round a tree-trunk, and floating out across the water of a river to another tree on the far bank. Yet it filled both Jeryl and Eris with the terror of the unknown, and for one awful moment Jeryl thought that a gigantic snake was emerging from the water. Then she saw that it was not alive, but her fear remained. For it was the first artificial object that she had ever seen.

'Don't worry about *what* it is, or how it was put there,' counselled Aretenon. 'It's going to carry you across, and that's all that matters for the moment. Look – there's someone coming over now !'

One of the figures on the far bank had lowered itself into the water, and was working its way with its forelimbs along the rope. As it came nearer – it was the Mithranean, and a female – Jeryl saw that it was carrying a second and much smaller rope looped round the upper part of its body.

With the skill of long practice, the stranger made her way across the floating cable, and emerged dripping from the river. She seemed to know Aretenon, but Jeryl could not intercept their thoughts.

'I can go across without any help,' said Aretenon, 'but I'll show you the easy way.'

He slipped the loop over his shoulders, and, dropping into the water, hooked his forelimbs over the fixed cable. A moment later he was being dragged across at a great speed by the two others on the far bank, where, after much trepidation, Eris and Jeryl presently joined him.

It was not the sort of bridge one would expect from a race which could quite easily have dealt with the mathematics of a reinforced concrete arch – if the possibility of such an object had ever occurred to it. But it served its purpose, and once it had been made, they could use it readily enough.

Once it had been made. But – who had made it?

When their dripping guides had rejoined them, Aretenon gave his friends a warning.

'I'm afraid you're going to have a good many shocks while you're here. You'll see some very strange sights, but when you understand them, they'll cease to puzzle you in the slightest. In fact, you will soon come to take them for granted.'

One of the strangers, whose thoughts neither Eris nor Jeryl could intercept, was giving him a message.

'Therodimus is waiting for us,' said Aretenon. 'He's very anxious to see you.'

'I've been trying to contact him,' complained Eris, 'but I've not succeeded.'

Aretenon seemed a little troubled.

'You'll find he's changed,' he said. 'After all, you've not seen each other for many years. It may be some time before you can make full contact again.'

Their road was a winding one through the forest, and from time to time curiously narrow paths branched off in various directions. Therodimus, thought Eris, must have changed indeed for him to have taken up permanent residence among trees. Presently the track opened out into a large, semi-circular clearing with a low white cliff lying along its diameter. At the foot of the cliff were several dark holes of varying sizes – obviously the openings of caves.

It was the first time that either Eris or Jeryl had ever entered a cave, and they did not greatly look forward to the experience. They were relieved when Aretenon told them to wait just outside the opening, and went on alone towards the puzzling yellow light that glowed in the depths. A moment later, dim memories began to pulse in Eris's mind, and he knew that his old teacher was coming, even though he could no longer fully share his thoughts.

Something stirred in the gloom, and then Therodimus came out into the sunlight. At the sight of him, Jeryl screamed once and buried her head in Eris's mane, but Eris stood firm, though he was trembling as he had never done before battle. For Therodimus blazed with a magnificence that none of his race had ever known since history began. Around his neck hung a band of glittering objects that caught and refracted the sunlight in a myriad colours, while covering his body was a sheet of some thick, many-hued material that rustled softly as he walked. And his horn was no longer the yellow of ivory : some magic had changed it to the most wonderful purple that Jeryl had ever seen.

Therodimus stood motionless for a moment, savouring their amazement to the full. Then his rich laugh echoed in their minds, and he reared up on his hind limb. The coloured garment fell whispering to the ground, and at a toss of his head the glittering necklace arched like a rainbow into a corner of the cave. But the purple horn remained unchanged.

It seemed to Eris that he stood at the brink of a great chasm, with Therodimus beckoning him on the far side. Their thoughts struggled to form a bridge, but could make no contact. Between them was the gulf of half a lifetime and many battles, of a myriad unshared experiences – Therodimus's years in this strange land, his own mating with Jeryl and the memory of their lost children. Though they stood face to face, a few feet only between them, their thoughts could never meet again.

Then Aretenon, with all the power and authority of his unsurpassed skill, did something to his mind that Eris was never quite able to recall. He only knew that the years seemed to have rolled back, that he was once more the eager, anxious pupil – and that he could speak to Therodimus again.

It was strange to sleep underground, but less unpleasant than spending the night amid the unknown terrors of the forest. As she watched the crimson shadows deepening beyond the entrance to the little cave, Jeryl tried to collect her scattered thoughts. She had understood only a small part of what had passed between Eris and Therodimus, but she knew that something incredible was taking place. The evidence of her eyes was enough to prove that: today she had seen things for which there were no words in her language.

She had heard things, too. As they had passed one of the cave-mouths, there had come from it a rhythmic 'whirring' sound, unlike that made by any animal she knew. It had continued steadily without pause or break as long as she could hear it, and even now its unhurried rhythm had not left her mind. Aretenon, she believed, had also noticed it, though without any surprise: Eris had been so engrossed with Therodimus.

The old philosopher had told them very little, preferring, as he said, to show them his empire when they had had a good night's rest. Nearly all their talk had been concerned with the events of their own land during the last few years, and Jeryl found it somewhat boring. Only one thing had interested her, and she had eyes for little else. That was the wonderful chain of coloured crystals that Therodimus had worn around his neck. What it was, or how it had been created, she could not imagine: but she coveted it. As she fell asleep, she found herself thinking idly, but more than half-seriously, of the sensation it would cause if she returned to her people with such a marvel gleaming against her own pelt. It would look so much better there than upon old Therodimus.

Aretenon and Therodimus met them at the cave soon after dawn. The philosopher had discarded his regalia — which he had obviously worn only to impress his guests — and his horn had returned to its normal yellow. That was one thing Jeryl thought she could understand, for she had come across fruits whose juices could cause colour changes.

Therodimus settled himself at the mouth of the cave. He began his narration without any preliminaries, and Eris

guessed that he must have told it many times before to
earlier visitors.

'I came to this place, Eris, about five years after leaving
our country. As you know, I was always interested in strange
lands, and from the Mithraneans I'd heard rumours that in-
trigued me very much. How I traced them to their source is
a long story that doesn't matter now. I crossed the river
far upstream one summer, when the water was very low.
There's only one place where it can be done, and then only
in the driest years. Higher still the river loses itself in the
mountains, and I don't think there's any way through them.
So this is virtually an island — almost completely cut off
from Mithranean territory.

'It's an island, but it's not uninhabited. The people who
live here are called the Phileni, and they have a very remarkable culture — one entirely different from our own.
Some of the products of that culture you've already seen.

'As you know, there are many different races on our
world, and quite a few of them have some sort of intelligence. But there is a great gulf between us and all other
creatures. As far as we know, we are the only beings capable
of abstract thought and complex logical processes.

'The Phileni are a much younger race than ours, and they
are intermediate between us and the other animals. They've
lived here on this rather large island for several thousand
generations — but their rate of development has been many,
many times swifter than ours. They neither possess nor
understand our telepathic powers, but they have something
else which we may well envy — something which is responsible for the whole of their civilization and its incredibly
rapid progress.'

Therodimus paused, then rose slowly to his feet.

'Follow me,' he said. 'I'll take you to see the Phileni.'

He led them back to the caves from which they had come
the night before, pausing at the entrance from which Jeryl
had heard that strange, rhythmic whirring. It was clearer
and louder now, and she saw Eris start as though he had

noticed it for the first time. Then Therodimus uttered a high-pitched whistle, and at once the whirring slackened, falling octave by octave until it had ebbed into silence. A moment later something came towards them out of the semi-gloom.

It was a little creature, scarcely half their height, and it did not hop, but walked upon two jointed limbs that seemed very thin and feeble. Its large spherical head was dominated by three huge eyes, set far apart and capable of independent movement. With the best will in the world, Jeryl did not think it was very attractive.

Then Therodimus uttered another whistle, and the creature raised its forelimbs towards them.

'Look closely,' said Therodimus, very gently, 'and you will see the answer to many of your questions.'

For the first time, Jeryl saw that the creature's forelimbs did not end in hooves, or indeed after the fashion of any animal with which she was acquainted. Instead, they divided into at least a dozen thin, flexible tentacles and two hooked claws.

'Go towards it, Jeryl,' commanded Therodimus. 'It has something for you.'

Hesitantly, Jeryl moved forward. She noticed that the creature's body was crossed with bands of dark material, to which were attached unidentifiable objects. It dropped a forelimb to one of these, and a cover opened to reveal a cavity inside which something glittered. Then the little tentacles were clutching that marvellous crystal necklace, and with a movement so swift and dexterous that Jeryl could scarcely follow it, the Phileni moved forward and clasped it round her neck.

Therodimus brushed aside her confusion and gratitude, but his shrewd old mind was well pleased. Jeryl would be his ally now in whatever he planned to do. But Eris's emotions might not be so easily swayed, and in this matter mere logic was not enough. His old pupil had changed so much, had been so deeply wounded by the past, that Therodimus could not be certain of success. Yet he had a plan that could turn even these difficulties to his advantage.

He gave another whistle, and the Phileni made a curious waving gesture with its hands and disappeared into the cave. A moment later that strange whirring ascended once more from the silence, but Jeryl's curiosity was now quite over-shadowed by her delight in her new possession.

'We'll go through the woods,' said Therodimus, 'to the nearest settlement — it's only a little way from here. The Phileni don't live in the open, as we do. In fact, they differ from us in almost every conceivable way. I'm even afraid,' he added ruefully, 'that they're much better natured than we are, and I believe that one day they'll be more intelli-gent. But first of all, let me tell you what I've learned about them, so that you can understand what I'm planning to do.'

The mental evolution of any race is conditioned, even dominated, by physical factors which that race almost in-variably takes for granted as part of the natural order of things. The wonderfully sensitive hands of the Phileni had enabled them to find by experiment and trial facts which had taken the planet's only other intelligent species a thousand times as long to discover by pure deduction. Quite early in their history, the Phileni had invented simple tools. From these they had proceeded to fabrics, pottery, and the use of fire. When Therodimus had discovered them, they had already invented the lathe and the potter's wheel, and were about to move into their first Metal Age — with all that that implied.

On the purely intellectual plane, their progress had been less rapid. They were clever and skilful, but they had a dis-like of abstract thought and their mathematics was purely empirical. They knew, for example, that a triangle with sides in the ratio three-four-five was right-angled, but had not suspected that this was only a special case of a much more general law. Their knowledge was full of such yawn-ing gaps, which, despite the help of Therodimus and his several score disciples, they seemed in no great hurry to fill.

Therodimus they worshipped as a god, and for two whole generations of their short-lived race they had obeyed him in everything, giving him all the products of their skill that he needed, and making at his suggestion the new tools and devices that had occurred to him. The partnership had been incredibly fertile, for it was as if both races had suddenly been released from their shackles. Great manual skill and great intellectual powers had fused in a fruitful union prob-ably unique in all the universe – and progress that would normally have taken millennia had been achieved in less than a decade.

As Aretenon had promised them, though Eris and Jeryl saw many marvels, they came across nothing that they could not understand once they had watched the little Phileni craftsmen at work and had seen with what magic their hands shaped natural materials into lovely or useful forms. Even their tiny towns and primitive farms soon lost their wonder and became part of the accepted order of things.

Therodimus let them look their fill, until they had seen every aspect of this strangely sophisticated Stone Age cul-ture. Because they knew no differently, they found nothing incongruous in the sight of a Phileni potter – who could scarcely count beyond ten – shaping a series of complex algebraic surfaces under the guidance of a young Mith-ranean mathematician. Like all his race, Eris possessed tremendous powers of mental visualization, but he realized how much easier geometry would be if one could actually *see* the shapes one was considering. From this beginning (though he could not guess it) would one day evolve the idea of a written language.

Jeryl was fascinated above all things by the sight of the little Phileni women weaving fabrics upon their primitive looms. She could sit for hours watching the flying shuttles and wishing that she could use them. Once one had seen it done, it seemed so simple and obvious – and so utterly beyond the powers of the clumsy, useless limbs of her own people.

They grew very fond of the Phileni, who seemed eager to please and were pathetically proud of all their manual skills. In these new and novel surroundings, meeting fresh wonders every day, Eris seemed to be recovering from some of the scars which the War had left upon his mind. Jeryl knew, however, that there was still much damage to be undone. Sometimes, before he could hide them, she would come across raw, angry wounds in the depths of Eris's mind, and she feared that many of them – like the broken stump of his horn – would never heal. Eris had hated the War, and the manner of its ending still oppressed him. Beyond this, Jeryl knew, he was haunted by the fear that it might come again.

These troubles she often discussed with Therodimus, of whom she had now grown very fond. She still did not fully understand why he had brought them here, or what he and his followers were planning to do. Therodimus was in no hurry to explain his actions, for he wished Jeryl and Eris to draw their own conclusions as far as possible. But at last, five days after their arrival, he called them to his cave.

'You've now seen,' he began, 'most of the things we have to show you here. You know what the Phileni can do, and perhaps you have thought how much our own lives will be enriched once we can use the products of their skill. That was my first thought when I came here, all those years ago.

'It was an obvious and rather naïve idea, but it led to a much greater one. As I grew to know the Phileni, and found how swiftly their minds had advanced in so short a time, I realized what a fearful disadvantage our own race had always laboured under. I began to wonder how much further forward *we* would have been had we the Phileni's control over the physical world. It is not a question of mere convenience, or the ability to make beautiful things like that necklace of yours, Jeryl, but something much more profound. It is the difference between ignorance and knowledge, between weakness and power.

'We have developed our minds, and our minds alone, until we can go no further. As Aretenon has told you, we have now come to a danger that threatens our entire race. We are under the shadow of the irresistible weapon against which there can be no defence.

'The solution is, quite literally, in the hands of the Phileni. We must use their skills to reshape our world, and so remove the cause of all our wars. We must go back to the beginning and re-lay the foundations of our culture. It won't be *our* culture alone, though, for we shall share it with the Phileni. They will be the hands – we the brains. Oh, I have dreamed of the world that may come, ages ahead, when even the marvels you see around you now will be considered childish toys! But not many are philosophers, and I need an argument more substantial than dreams. That final argument I believe I may have found, though I cannot yet be certain.

'I have asked you here, Eris, partly because I wanted to renew our old friendship, and partly because your word will now have far greater influence than mine. You are a hero among your own people, and the Mithraneans also will listen to you. I want you to return, taking with you some of the Phileni and their products. Show them to your people, and ask them to send their young men here to help us with our work.'

There was a pause during which Jeryl could gather no hints of Eris's thoughts. Then he replied hesitantly :

'But I still don't understand. These things that the Phileni make are very pretty, and some of them may be useful to us. But how can they change us as profoundly as you seem to think?'

Therodimus sighed. Eris could not see past the present into the future that was yet to be. He had not caught, as Therodimus had done, the promise that lay beyond the busy hands and tools of the Phileni – the first faint possibilities of the Machine. Perhaps he would never understand : but he could still be convinced.

Veiling his deeper thoughts, Therodimus continued :

'Perhaps some of these things are toys, Eris – but they may be more powerful than you think. Jeryl, I know, would be loath to part with hers ... and perhaps I can find one that would convince you.'

Eris was sceptical, and Jeryl could see that he was in one of his darker moods.

'I doubt it very much,' he said.

'Well, I can try.' Therodimus gave a whistle, and one of the Phileni came running up. There was a short exchange of conversation.

'Would you come with me, Eris? It will take some time.'

Eris followed him, the others, at Therodimus's request, remaining behind. They left the large cave and went towards the row of smaller ones which the Phileni used for their various trades.

The strange whirring was sounding loudly in Eris's ears, but for a moment he could not see its cause, the light of the crude oil lamps being too faint for his eyes. Then he made out one of the Phileni bending over a wooden table upon which something was spinning rapidly, driven by a belt from a treadle operated by another of the little creatures. He had seen the potters using a similar device, but this was different. It was shaping wood, not clay, and the potter's fingers had been replaced by a sharp metal blade from which long, thin shavings were curling out in fascinating spirals. With their huge eyes the Phileni, who disliked full sunlight, could see perfectly in the gloom, but it was some time before Eris could discover just what was happening. Then, suddenly, he understood.

'Aretenon,' said Jeryl when the others had left them, 'why should the Phileni do all these things for us? Surely they're quite happy as they are?'

The question, Aretenon thought, was typical of Jeryl and would never have been asked by Eris.

'They will do anything that Therodimus says,' he answered, 'but even apart from that there's so much we can

give them as well. When we turn our minds to their problems, we can see how to solve them in ways that would never
have occurred to them. They're very eager to learn, and
already we must have advanced their culture by hundreds
of generations. Also, they're physically very feeble. Although
we don't possess their dexterity, our strength makes possible
tasks they could never attempt.'

They had wandered to the edge of the river, and stood for
a moment watching the unhurried waters moving down to
the sea. Then Jeryl turned to go upstream, but Aretenon
stopped her.

'Therodimus doesn't want us to go that way, yet,' he
explained. 'It's just another of his little secrets. He never
likes to reveal his plans until they're ready.'

Slightly piqued, and distinctly curious, Jeryl obediently
turned back. She would, of course, come this way again as
soon as there was no one else about.

It was very peaceful here in the warm sunlight, among
the pools of heat trapped by the trees. Jeryl had almost
lost her fear of the forest, though she knew she would never
be quite happy there.

Aretenon seemed very abstracted, and Jeryl knew that he
wished to say something and was marshalling his thoughts.
Presently he began to speak, with the freedom that is only
possible between two people who are fond of each other but
have no emotional ties.

'It is very hard, Jeryl,' he began, 'to turn one's back on
the work of a lifetime. Once I had hoped that the great new
forces we have discovered could be safely used, but now I
know that it is impossible, at least for many ages. Therodimus was right – we can go no further with our minds alone.
Our culture has been hopelessly one-sided, though through
no fault of ours. We cannot solve the fundamental problem
of peace and war without a command over the physical
world such as the Phileni possess – and which we hope to
borrow from them.

'Perhaps there will be other great adventures here for

our minds, to make us forget what we will have to abandon. We shall be able to learn something from Nature at last. What is the difference between fire and water, between wood and stone? What are the suns, and what are those millions of faint lights we see in the sky when both the suns are down? Perhaps the answers to all these questions may lie at the end of the new road along which we must travel.'

He paused.

'New knowledge – new wisdom – in realms we have never dreamed of before. It may lure us away from the dangers we have encountered : for certainly nothing we can learn from Nature will ever be as great a threat as the peril we have uncovered in our own minds.'

The flow of Aretenon's thoughts was suddenly interrupted. Then he said : 'I think Eris wants to see you.'

Jeryl wondered why Eris had not sent the message to her : she wondered, too, at the undertone of amusement – or was it something else? – in Aretenon's mind.

There was no sign of Eris as they approached the caves, but he was waiting for them and came bounding out into the sunlight before they could reach the entrance. Then Jeryl gave an involuntary cry, and retreated a pace or two as her mate came towards her.

For Eris was whole again. Gone was the shattered stump on his forehead : it had been replaced by a new, gleaming horn no less splendid than the one he had lost.

In a belated gesture of greeting, Eris touched horns with Aretenon. Then he was gone into the forest in great joyous leaps – but not before his mind had met Jeryl's as it had seldom done since the days before the War.

'Let him go,' said Therodimus softly. 'He would rather be alone. When he returns I think you will find him – different.' He gave a little laugh. 'The Phileni are clever, are they not? Now, perhaps, Eris will be more appreciative of their "toys".'

'I know I am impatient,' said Therodimus, 'but I am old now, and I want to see the changes begin in my own life-

time. That is why I am starting so many schemes in the hope
that some at least will succeed. But this is the one, above all,
in which I have put most faith.'

For a moment he lost himself in his thoughts. Not one in
a hundred of his own race could fully share his dream. Even
Eris, though he now believed in it, did so with his heart
rather than his mind. Perhaps Aretenon – the brilliant and
subtle Aretenon, so desperately anxious to neutralize the
powers he had brought into the world – might have glimpsed
the reality. But his was of all minds the most impenetrable,
save when he wished otherwise.

'You know as well as I do,' continued Therodimus, as
they walked upstream, 'that our wars have only one cause –
Food. We and the Mithraneans are trapped on this continent of ours with its limited resources, which we can do
nothing to increase. Ahead of us we have always the nightmare of starvation, and for all our vaunted intelligence there
has been nothing we can do about it. Oh yes, we have
scraped some laborious irrigation ditches with our fore-
hooves, but how slight their help has been!

'The Phileni have discovered how to grow crops that increase the fertility of the ground manyfold. I believe that
we can do the same – once we have adapted their tools for
our own use. That is our first and most important task, but
it is not the one on which I have set my heart. The final
solution to our problem, Eris, *must be the discovery of new,
virgin lands into which our people can migrate.*'

He smiled at the other's amazement.

'No, don't think I'm mad. Such lands do exist, I'm sure of
it. Once I stood at the edge of the ocean and watched a great
flight of birds coming inland from far out at sea. I have seen
them flying outwards, too, so purposefully that I was certain
they were going to some other country. And I have followed
them with my thoughts.'

'Even if your theory is true, as it probably is,' said Eris,
'what use is it to us?' He gestured to the river flowing beside
them. 'We drown in the water, and you cannot build a rope

to support us —' His thoughts suddenly faded out into a jumbled chaos of ideas.

Therodimus smiled.

'So you have guessed what I hope to do. Well, now you can see if you are right.'

They had come to a level stretch of bank, upon which a group of the Phileni were busily at work, under the super-vision of some of Therodimus's assistants. Lying at the water's edge was a strange object which, Eris realized, was made of many tree-trunks joined together by ropes.

They watched in fascination as the orderly tumult reached its climax. There was a great pulling and pushing, and the raft moved ponderously into the water with a mighty splash. The spray had scarcely ceased to fall when a young Mithranean leaped from the bank and began to dance gleefully upon the logs, which were now tugging at the moorings as if eager to break away and follow the river down to the sea. A moment later he had been joined by others, rejoicing in their mastery of a new element. The little Phileni, unable to make the leap, stood watching patiently on the bank while their masters enjoyed them-selves.

There was an exhilaration about the scene that no one could fail to miss, though perhaps few of those present realized that they were at a turning-point in history. Only Therodimus stood a little apart from the rest, lost in his own thoughts. This primitive raft, he knew, was merely a begin-ning. It must be tested upon the river, then along the shores of the ocean. The work would take years, and he was never likely to see the first voyagers returning from those fabulous lands whose existence was still no more than a guess. But what had been begun, others would finish.

Overhead, a flight of birds was passing across the forest, Therodimus watched them go, envying their freedom to move at will over land and sea. He had begun the conquest of the water for his race, but that the skies might one day be theirs also was beyond even his imagination.

Aretenon, Jeryl and the rest of the expedition had already crossed the river when Eris said good-bye to Therodimus. This time they had done so without a drop of water touching their bodies, for the raft had come downstream and was performing valuable duties as a ferry. A new and much improved model was already under construction, as it was painfully obvious that the prototype was not exactly seaworthy. These initial difficulties would be quickly overcome by designers who, even if they were forced to work with Stone Age tools, could handle with ease the mathematics of metacentres, buoyancies and advanced hydrodynamics.

'Your task won't be a simple one,' said Therodimus, 'for you cannot show your people all the things you have seen here. At first you must be content to sow the seed, to arouse interest and curiosity – particularly among the young, who will come here to learn more. Perhaps you will meet opposition : I expect so. But every time you return to us, we shall have new things to show you and to strengthen your arguments.'

They touched horns : then Eris was gone, taking with him the knowledge that was to change the world – so slowly at first, then ever more swiftly. Once the barriers were down, once the Mithraneans and the Atheleni had been given the simple tools which they could fasten to their forelimbs and use unaided, progress would be swift. But for the present they must rely on the Phileni for everything : and there were so few of them.

Therodimus was well content. Only in one respect was he disappointed, for he had hoped that Eris, who had always been his favourite, might also be his successor. The Eris who was now returning to his own people was no longer self-obsessed or embittered, for he had a mission and hope for the future. But he lacked the keen, far-ranging vision that was needed here : it would be Aretenon who must continue what he had begun. Still, that could not be helped, and there was no need yet to think of such matters. Therodimus was very old, but he knew that he would be meeting Eris many times again here by the river at the entrance to his land.

The ferry was gone now, and though he had expected it, Eris stopped amazed at the great span of the bridge, swaying slightly in the breeze. Its execution did not quite match its design – a good deal of mathematics had gone into its parabolic suspension – but it was still the first great engineering feat in history. Constructed though it was entirely of wood and rope, it forecast the shape of the metal giants to come.

Eris paused in mid-stream. He could see smoke rising from the shipyards facing the ocean, and thought he could just glimpse the masts of some of the new vessels that were being built for coastal trade. It was hard to believe that when he had first crossed this river he had been dragged over dangling from a rope.

Aretenon was waiting for them on the far bank. He moved rather slowly now, but his eyes were still bright with the old, eager intelligence. He greeted Eris warmly.

'I'm glad you could come now. You're just in time.'

That, Eris knew, could mean only one thing.

'The ships are back?'

'Almost : they were sighted an hour ago, out on the horizon. They should be here at any moment, and then we shall know the truth at last, after all these years. If only —'

His thoughts faded out, but Eris could continue them. They had come to the great pyramid of stones beneath which Therodimus lay – Therodimus, whose brain was behind everything they saw, but who could never learn now if his most cherished dream was true or not.

There was a storm coming up from the ocean, and they hurried along the new road that skirted the river's edge. Small boats of a kind that Eris had not seen before went past them occasionally, operated by Atheleni or Mithraneans with wooden paddles strapped to their forelimbs. It always gave Eris great pleasure to see such new conquests, such new liberations of his people from their age-old chains. Yet sometimes they reminded him of children who had suddenly

been let loose into a wonderful new world, full of exciting
and interesting things that must be done, whether they were
likely to be useful or not. However, anything that promised
to make his race into better sailors was more than useful. In
the last decade Eris had discovered that pure intelligence
was sometimes not enough : there were skills that could not
be acquired by any amount of mental effort. Though this
people had largely overcome their fear of water, they were
still quite incompetent on the ocean, and the Phileni had
therefore become the first navigators of the world.

Jeryl looked nervously around her as the first peal of
thunder came rolling in from the sea. She was still wearing
the necklace that Therodimus had given her so long ago :
but it was by no means the only ornament she carried now.

'I hope the ships will be safe,' she said anxiously.

'There's not much wind, and they will have ridden out
much worse storms than this,' Aretenon reassured her, as
they entered his cave. Eris and Jeryl looked round with eager
interest to see what new wonders the Phileni had made during their absence : but if there were any they had, as usual,
been hidden away until Aretenon was ready to show them.
He was still rather childishly fond of such little surprises and
mysteries.

There was an air of absentmindedness about the meeting
that would have puzzled an onlooker ignorant of its cause.
As Eris talked of all the changes in the outer world, of the
success of the new Phileni settlements, and of the steady
growth of agriculture among his people, Aretenon listened
with only half his mind. His thoughts, and those of his
friends, were far out at sea, meeting the oncoming ships
which might be bringing the greatest news their world had
ever received.

As Eris finished his report, Aretenon rose to his feet and
began to move restlessly around the chamber.

'You have done better than we dared to hope at the beginning. At least there has been no war for a generation, and
our food supply is ahead of the population for the first time

in history – thanks to our new agricultural techniques.'

Aretenon glanced at the furnishings of his chamber, recalling with an effort the fact that in his own youth almost everything he saw would have appeared impossible or even meaningless to him. Not even the simplest of tools had existed then, at least in the knowledge of his people. Now there were ships and bridges and houses – and these were only the beginning.

'I am well satisfied,' he said. 'We have, as we planned, diverted the whole stream of our culture, turning it away from the dangers that lay ahead. The powers that made the Madness possible will soon be forgotten : only a handful of us still know of them, and we will take our secrets with us. Perhaps when our descendants rediscover them they will be wise enough to use them properly. But we have uncovered so many new wonders that it may be a thousand generations before we turn again to look into our own minds and to tamper with the forces locked within them.'

The mouth of the cave was illuminated by a sudden flash of lightning. The storm was coming nearer, though it was still some miles away. Rain was beginning to fall in large, angry drops from the leaden sky.

'While we're waiting for the ships,' said Aretenon rather abruptly, 'come into the next cave and see some of the new things we have to show you since your last visit.'

It was a strange collection. Side by side on the same bench were tools and inventions which in other cultures had been separated by thousands of years of time. The Stone Age was past : bronze and iron had come, and already the first crude scientific instruments had been built for experiments that were driving back the frontiers of the unknown. A primitive retort spoke of the beginnings of chemistry, and by its side were the first lenses the world had seen – waiting to reveal the unsuspected universes of the infinitely small and the infinitely great.

The storm was upon them as Aretenon's description of these new wonders drew to its close. From time to time he had glanced nervously at the mouth of the cave, as if await-ing a messenger from the harbour, but they had remained undisturbed save by the occasional crash of thunder.

'I've shown you everything of importance,' he said, 'but here's something that may amuse you while we're waiting. As I said, we've sent expeditions everywhere to collect and classify all the rocks they can, in the hope of finding useful minerals. One of them brought back this.'

He extinguished the lights and the cave became com-pletely dark.

'It will be some time before your eyes grow sensitive enough to see it,' Aretenon warned. 'Just look over there in that corner.'

Eris strained his eyes into the darkness. At first he could see nothing : then, slowly, a glimmering blue light became faintly visible. It was so vague and diffuse that he could not focus his eyes upon it, and he automatically moved forward.

'I shouldn't go too near,' advised Aretenon. 'It seems to be a perfectly ordinary mineral, but the Phileni who found it and carried it here got some very strange burns from handl-ing it. Yet it's quite cold to the touch. One day we'll learn its secret : but I don't suppose it's anything at all important.'

A vast curtain of sheet lightning split the sky, and for a moment the reflected glare lit up the cave, pinning weird shadows against the walls. At the same moment one of the Phileni staggered into the entrance and called something to Aretenon in its thin, reedy voice. He gave a great shout of triumph, as one of his ancestors might have done on some ancient battle-field : then his thoughts came crashing into Eris's mind.

'Land! They've found land — a whole new continent waiting for us!'

Eris felt the sense of triumph and victory well up within him like water bursting from a spring. Clear ahead now into the future lay the new, the glorious road along which their children would travel, mastering the world and all its secrets as they went. The vision of Therodimus was at last sharp and brilliant before his eyes.

He felt for the mind of Jeryl, so that she could share his
joy – and found that it was closed to him. Leaning toward
her in the darkness, he could sense that she was still staring
into the depths of the cave, as if she had never heard the
wonderful news, and could not tear her eyes away from that
enigmatic glow.

Out of the night came the roar of the belated thunder as
it raced across the sky. Eris felt Jeryl tremble beside him, and
sent out his thoughts to comfort her.

'Don't let the thunder frighten you,' he said gently. 'What
is there to fear now?'

'I do not know,' replied Jeryl. 'I am frightened – but not
of the thunder. Oh, Eris, it is a wonderful thing we have
done, and I wish Therodimus could be here to see it. But
where will it lead in the end – this new road of ours?'

Out of the past, the words that Aretenon had once spoken
had risen up to haunt her. She remembered their walk by
the river, long ago, when he had talked of his hopes and had
said : 'Certainly nothing we can learn from Nature will ever
be as great a threat as the peril we have encountered in our
own minds.' Now the words seemed to mock her and to cast
a shadow over the golden future : but why, she could not say.

Alone, perhaps, of all the races in the Universe, her
people had reached the second cross-roads – and had never
passed the first. Now they must go along the road that they
had missed, and must face the challenge at its end – the
challenge from which, this time, they could not escape.

In the darkness, the faint glow of dying atoms burned
unwavering in the rock. It would still be burning there,
scarcely dimmed, when Jeryl and Eris had been dust for
centuries. It would be only a little fainter when the civilization they were building had at last unlocked its secrets.

'IF I FORGET THEE, OH EARTH...'

WHEN Marvin was ten years old, his father took him through the long, echoing corridors that led up through Administration and Power, until at last they came to the uppermost levels of all and were among the swiftly growing vegetation of the Farmlands. Marvin liked it here : it was fun watching the great, slender plants creeping with almost visible eagerness towards the sunlight as it filtered down through the plastic domes to meet them. The smell of life was everywhere, awakening inexpressible longings in his heart : no longer was he breathing the dry, cool air of the residential levels, purged of all smells but the faint tang of ozone. He wished he could stay here for a little while, but Father would not let him. They went onwards until they had reached the entrance to the Observatory, which he had never visited : but they did not stop, and Marvin knew with a sense of rising excitement that there could be only one goal left. For the first time in his life, he was going Outside.

There were a dozen of the surface vehicles, with their wide balloon tyres and pressurized cabins, in the great servicing chamber. His father must have been expected, for they were led at once to the little scout car waiting by the huge circular door of the airlock. Tense with expectancy, Marvin settled himself down in the cramped cabin while his father started the motor and checked the controls. The inner door of the lock slid open and then closed behind them : he heard the roar of the great air-pumps fade slowly away as the pressure dropped to zero. Then the 'Vacuum' sign flashed on, the outer door parted, and before Marvin lay the land which he had never yet entered.

He had seen it in photographs, of course : he had watched it imaged on television screens a hundred times. But now it was lying all around him, burning beneath the fierce sun that crawled so slowly across the jet-black sky. He stared into the west, away from the blinding splendour of the sun — and there were the stars, as he had been told but had never quite believed. He gazed at them for a long time, marvelling that anything could be so bright and yet so tiny. They were intense unscintillating points, and suddenly he remembered a rhyme he had once read in one of his father's books :

> Twinkle, twinkle, little star,
> How I wonder what you are.

Well, he knew what the stars were. Whoever asked that question must have been very stupid. And what did they mean by 'twinkle'? You could see at a glance that all the stars shone with the same steady, unwavering light. He abandoned the puzzle and turned his attention to the landscape around him.

They were racing across a level plain at almost a hundred miles an hour, the great balloon tyres sending up little spurts of dust behind them. There was no sign of the Colony : in the few minutes while he had been gazing at the stars, its domes and radio towers had fallen below the horizon. Yet there were other indications of man's presence, for about a mile ahead Marvin could see the curiously shaped structures clustering round the head of a mine. Now and then a puff of vapour would emerge from a squat smoke-stack and would instantly disperse.

They were past the mine in a moment : Father was driving with a reckless and exhilarating skill as if — it was a strange thought to come into a child's mind — he was trying to escape from something. In a few minutes they had reached the edge of the plateau on which the Colony had been built. The ground fell sharply away beneath them in a dizzying slope whose lower stretches were lost in shadow. Ahead, as far as the eye could reach, was a jumbled wasteland of craters, mountain ranges, and ravines. The crests of the mountains, catching the low sun, burned like islands of fire in a sea of darkness : and above them the stars still shone as steadfastly as ever.

There could be no way forward – yet there was. Marvin clenched his fists as the car edged over the slope and started the long descent. Then he saw the barely visible track leading down the mountainside, and relaxed a little. Other men, it seemed, had gone this way before.

Night fell with a shocking abruptness as they crossed the shadow line and the sun dropped below the crest of the plateau. The twin searchlights sprang into life, casting blue-white bands on the rocks ahead, so that there was scarcely need to check their speed. For hours they drove through valleys and past the feet of mountains whose peaks seemed to comb the stars, and sometimes they emerged for a moment into the sunlight as they climbed over higher ground.

And now on the right was a wrinkled, dusty plain, and on the left, its ramparts and terraces rising mile after mile into the sky, was a wall of mountains that marched into the distance until its peaks sank from sight below the rim of the world. There was no sign that men had ever explored this land, but once they passed the skeleton of a crashed rocket, and beside it a stone cairn surmounted by a metal cross.

It seemed to Marvin that the mountains stretched on forever : but at last, many hours later, the range ended in a towering, precipitous headland that rose steeply from a cluster of little hills. They drove down into a shallow valley that curved in a great arc towards the far side of the mountains : and as they did so, Marvin slowly realized that something very strange was happening in the land ahead.

The sun was now low behind the hills on the right : the valley before them should be in total darkness. Yet it was awash with a cold white radiance that came spilling over the crags beneath which they were driving. Then, suddenly, they were out in the open plain, and the source of the light lay before them in all its glory.

It was very quiet in the little cabin now that the motors had stopped. The only sound was the faint whisper of the oxygen feed and an occasional metallic crepitation as the outer walls of the vehicle radiated away their heat. For no warmth at all came from the great silver crescent that floated low above the far horizon and flooded all this land with pearly light. It was so brilliant that minutes passed before Marvin could accept its challenge and look steadfastly into its glare, but at last he could discern the outlines of continents, the hazy border of the atmosphere, and the white islands of cloud. And even at this distance, he could see the glitter of sunlight on the polar ice.

It was beautiful, and it called to his heart across the abyss of space. There in that shining crescent were all the wonders that he had never known – the hues of sunset skies, the moaning of the sea on pebbled shores, the patter of falling rain, the unhurried benison of snow. These and a thousand others should have been his rightful heritage, but he knew them only from the books and ancient records, and the thought filled him with the anguish of exile.

Why could they not return? It seemed so peaceful beneath those lines of marching cloud. Then Marvin, his eyes no longer blinded by the glare, saw that the portion of the disk that should have been in darkness was gleaming faintly with an evil phosphorescence : and he remembered. He was looking upon the funeral pyre of a world – upon the radioactive aftermath of Armageddon. Across a quarter of a million miles of space, the glow of dying atoms was still visible, a perennial reminder of the ruined past. It would be centuries yet before that deadly glow died from the rocks and life could return again to fill that silent, empty world.

And now Father began to speak, telling Marvin the story which until this moment had meant no more to him than the fairy-tales he had heard in childhood. There were many things he could not understand : it was impossible for him to picture the glowing, multi-coloured pattern of life on the planet he had never seen. Nor could he comprehend the forces that had destroyed it in the end, leaving the Colony, preserved by its isolation, as the sole survivor. Yet he could share the agony of those final days, when the Colony had learned at last that never again would the supply ships come flaming down through the stars with gifts from home. One by one the radio stations had ceased to call: on the shadowed globe the lights of the cities had dimmed and died, and they were alone at last, as no men had ever been alone before, carrying in their hands the future of the race.

Then had followed the years of despair, and the long-drawn battle for survival in this fierce and hostile world. That battle had been won, though barely : this little oasis of life was safe against the worst that Nature could do. But unless there was a goal, a future towards which it could work, the Colony would lose the will to live and neither machines nor skill nor science could save it then.

So, at last, Marvin understood the purpose of this pilgrimage. He would never walk beside the rivers of that lost and legendary world, or listen to the thunder raging above its softly rounded hills. Yet one day – how far ahead? – his children's children would return to claim their heritage. The winds and the rains would scour the poisons from the burning lands and carry them to the sea, and in the depths of the sea they would waste their venom until they could harm no living things. Then the great ships that were still waiting here on the silent, dusty plains could lift once more into space, along the road that led to home.

That was the dream : and one day, Marvin knew with a sudden flash of insight, he would pass it on to his own son, here at this same spot with the mountains behind him and the silver light from the sky streaming into his face.

He did not look back as they began the homeward journey. He could not bear to see the cold glory of the crescent Earth fade from the rocks around him, as he went to rejoin his people in their long exile.

BREAKING STRAIN

GRANT was writing up the Star Queen's log when he heard the cabin door opening behind him. He didn't bother to look round – it was hardly necessary, for there was only one other man aboard the ship. But when nothing happened, and when McNeil neither spoke nor came into the room, the long silence finally roused Grant's curiosity and he swung the seat round in its gimbals.

McNeil was just standing in the doorway, looking as if he had seen a ghost. The trite metaphor flashed into Grant's mind instantly. He did not know for a moment how near the truth it was. In a sense McNeil *had* seen a ghost – the most terrifying of all ghosts – his own.

'What's the matter?' said Grant angrily. 'You sick or something?'

The engineer shook his head. Grant noticed the little beads of sweat that broke away from his forehead and went glittering across the room on their perfectly straight trajectories. His throat muscles moved, but for a while no sound came. It looked as if he were going to cry.

'We're done for,' he whispered at last. 'Oxygen reserve's gone.'

Then he did cry. He looked like a flabby doll, slowly collapsing on itself. He couldn't fall for there was no gravity, so he just folded up in mid-air.

Grant said nothing. Quite unconsciously he rammed his smouldering cigarette into the ash-tray, grinding it viciously until the last tiny spark had died. Already the air seemed to be thickening around him as the oldest terror of the space-ways gripped him by the throat.

He slowly loosed the elastic straps, which, while he was seated, gave some illusion of weight and with an automatic skill launched himself towards the doorway. McNeil did not offer to follow. Even making every allowance for the shock he had undergone, Grant felt he was behaving very badly. He gave the engineer an angry cuff as he passed and told him to snap out of it.

The hold was a large hemispherical room with a thick central column which carried the controls and cabling to the other half of the dumb-bell-shaped spaceship a hundred metres away. It was packed with crates and boxes arranged in a surrealistic three-dimensional array that made very few concessions to gravity.

But even if the cargo had suddenly vanished Grant would scarcely have noticed. He had eyes only for the big oxygen-tank, taller than himself, which was bolted against the wall near the inner door of the airlock.

It was just as he had last seen it, gleaming with aluminium paint, and the metal sides still held the faint touch of cold-ness that gave the only hint of their contents. All the piping seemed in perfect condition. There was no sign of anything wrong apart from one minor detail. The needle of the con-tents gauge lay mutely against the zero stop.

Grant gazed at that silent symbol as a man in ancient London returning home one evening at the time of the Plague might have stared at a rough cross newly scrawled upon his door. Then he banged half a dozen times on the glass in the futile hope that the needle had stuck — though he never really doubted its message. News that is sufficiently bad somehow carries its own guarantee of truth. Only good reports need confirmation.

When Grant got back to the control-room, McNeil was himself again. A glance at the opened medicine chest showed the reason for the engineer's rapid recovery. He even essayed a faint attempt at humour.

'It was a meteor,' he said. 'They tell us a ship this size should get hit once a century. We seem to have jumped the gun with ninety-five years still to go.'

'But what about the alarms? The air pressure's normal

– how could we have been holed?'

'We weren't,' McNeil replied. 'You know how the oxygen circulates night-side through the refrigerating coils to keep it liquid? The meteor must have smashed them and the stuff simply boiled away.'

Grant was silent, collecting his thoughts. What had happened was serious – deadly serious – but it need not be fatal. After all, the voyage was more than three-quarters over.

'Surely the regenerator can keep the air breathable, even if it does get pretty thick?' he asked hopefully.

McNeil shook his head. 'I've not worked it out in detail, but I know the answer. When the carbon dioxide is broken down and the free oxygen gets cycled back, there's a loss of about ten per cent. That's why we have to carry a reserve.'

'The spacesuits!' cried Grant in sudden excitement. 'What about their tanks?'

He had spoken without thinking, and the immediate realization of his mistake left him feeling worse than before.

'We can't keep oxygen in them – it would boil off in a few days. There's enough compressed gas there for about thirty minutes – merely long enough for you to get to the main tank in an emergency.'

'There must be a way out – even if we have to jettison cargo and run for it. Let's stop guessing and work out exactly where we are.'

Grant was as much angry as frightened. He was angry with McNeil for breaking down. He was angry with the designers of the ship for not having seen this God-knew-how-many-million-to-one chance. The deadline might be a couple of weeks away and a lot could happen before then. The thought helped for a moment to keep his fears at arm's length.

This was an emergency, beyond a doubt, but it was one of those peculiarly protracted emergencies that seem to happen only in space. There was plenty of time to think – perhaps too much time.

Grant strapped himself in the pilot's seat and pulled out a writing-pad.

'Let's get the facts right,' he said with artificial calmness. 'We've got the air that's still circulating in the ship and we lose ten per cent of the oxygen every time it goes through the regenerator. Chuck me over the Manual, will you? I never remember how many cubic metres we use a day.'

In saying that the *Star Queen* might expect to be hit by a meteor once every century, McNeil had grossly but unavoidably over-simplified the problem. For the answer depended on so many factors that three generations of statisticians had done little but lay down rules so vague that the insurance companies still shivered with apprehension when the great meteor showers went sweeping like a gale through the orbits of the inner worlds.

Everything depends, of course, on what one means by the word meteor. Each lump of cosmic slag that reaches the surface of the Earth has a million smaller brethren who perish utterly in the no-man's-land where the atmosphere has not quite ended and space has yet to begin – that ghostly region where the weird Aurora sometimes walks by night.

These are the familiar shooting stars, seldom larger than a pin's head, and these in turn are outnumbered a million-fold again by particles too small to leave any visible trace of their dying as they drift down from the sky. All of them, the countless specks of dust, the rare boulders and even the wandering mountains that Earth encounters perhaps once every million years – all of them are meteors.

For the purposes of space-flight, a meteor is only of interest if, on penetrating the hull of a ship, it leaves a hole large enough to be dangerous. This is a matter of relative speeds as well as size. Tables have been prepared showing approximate collision times for various parts of the Solar System – and for various sizes of meteors down to masses of a few milligrams.

That which had struck the *Star Queen* was a giant, being

nearly a centimetre across and weighing all of ten grams. According to the tables the waiting time for collision with such a monster was of the order of ten to the ninth days – say three million years. The virtual certainty that such an occurrence would not happen again in the course of human history gave Grant and McNeil very little consolation.

However, things might have been worse. The *Star Queen* was 115 days on her orbit and had only thirty still to go. She was travelling, as did all freighters, on the long tangential ellipse kissing the orbits of Earth and Venus on opposite sides of the Sun. The fast liners could cut across from planet to planet at three times her speed – and ten times her fuel consumption – but she must plod along her predetermined track like a street-car, taking 145 days, more or less, for each journey.

Anything more unlike the early-twentieth-century idea of a spaceship than the *Star Queen* would be hard to imagine. She consisted of two spheres, one fifty and the other twenty metres in diameter, joined by a cylinder about a hundred metres long. The whole structure looked like a matchstick-and-plasticine model of a hydrogen atom. Crew, cargo and controls were in the larger sphere, while the smaller one held the atomic motors and was – to put it mildly – out of bounds to living matter.

The *Star Queen* had been built in space and could never have lifted herself even from the surface of the Moon. Under full power her ion drive could produce an acceleration of a twentieth of a gravity, which in an hour would give her all the velocity she needed to change from a satellite of the Earth to one of Venus.

Hauling cargo up from the planets was the job of the powerful little chemical rockets. In a month the tugs would be climbing up from Venus to meet her, but the *Star Queen* would not be stopping for there would be no one at the controls. She would continue blindly on her orbit, speeding past Venus at miles per second – and five months later she would be back at the orbit of the Earth, though Earth herself would then be far away.

It is surprising how long it takes to do a simple addition when your life depends on the answer. Grant ran down the short column of figures half a dozen times before he finally gave up hope that the total would change. Then he sat doodling nervously on the white plastic of the pilot's desk.

'With all possible economies,' he said, 'we can last about twenty days. That means we'll be ten days out of Venus when —' His voice trailed off into silence.

Ten days didn't sound much – but it might just as well have been ten years. Grant thought sardonically of all the hack adventure writers who had used just this situation in their stories and radio serials. In these circumstances, according to the carbon-copy experts – few of whom had ever gone beyond the Moon – there were three things that could happen.

The proper solution – which had become almost a cliché – was to turn the ship into a glorified greenhouse or a hydroponics farm and let photosynthesis do the rest. Alternatively one could perform prodigies of chemical or atom engineering – explained in tedious technical detail – and build an oxygen-manufacturing plant which would not only save your life – and of course the heroine's – but would also make you the owner of fabulously valuable patents. The third or *deus ex machina* solution was the arrival of a convenient spaceship which happened to be matching your course and velocity exactly.

But that was fiction and things were different in real life. Although the first idea was sound in theory there wasn't even a packet of grass-seed aboard the *Star Queen*. As for feats of inventive engineering, two men – however brilliant and however desperate – were not likely to improve in a few days on the work of scores of great industrial research organizations over a full century.

The spaceship that 'happened to be passing' was, almost

by definition, impossible. Even if other freighters had been coasting on the same elliptic path – and Grant knew there were none – then by the very laws that governed their movements they would always keep their original separations. It was not quite impossible that a liner, racing on its hyperbolic orbit, might pass within a few hundred thousand kilometres of them – but at a speed so great that it would be as inaccessible as Pluto.

'If we threw out the cargo,' said McNeil at last, 'would we have a chance of changing our orbit?'

Grant shook his head.

'I'd hoped so,' he replied, 'but it won't work. We could reach Venus in a week if we wished – but we'd have no fuel for braking and nothing from the planet could catch us as we went past.'

'Not even a liner?'

'According to *Lloyd's Register* Venus has only a couple of freighters at the moment. In any case it would be a practically impossible manoeuvre. Even if it could match our speed, how would the rescue ship get back? It would need about fifty kilometres a second for the whole job!'

'If we can't figure a way out,' said McNeil, 'maybe someone on Venus can. We'd better talk to them.'

'I'm going to,' Grant replied, 'as soon as I've decided what to say. Go and get the transmitter aligned, will you?'

He watched McNeil as he floated out of the room. The engineer was probably going to give trouble in the days that lay ahead. Until now they had got on well enough – like most stout men McNeil was good-natured and easygoing. But now Grant realized that he lacked fibre. He had become too flabby – physically and mentally – through living too long in space.

A buzzer sounded on the transmitter switchboard. The parabolic mirror out on the hull was aimed at the gleaming arc-lamp of Venus, only ten million kilometres away and moving on an almost parallel path. The three-millimetre waves from the ship's transmitter would make the trip in little more than half a minute. There was bitterness in the knowledge that they were only thirty seconds from safety.

The automatic monitor on Venus gave its impersonal *Go ahead* signal and Grant began to talk steadily and, he hoped, quite dispassionately. He gave a careful analysis of the situation and ended with a request for advice. His fears concerning McNeil he left unspoken. For one thing he knew that the engineer would be monitoring him at the transmitter.

As yet no one on Venus would have heard the message, even though the transmitter time lag was over. It would still be coiled up in the recorder spools, but in a few minutes an unsuspecting signals officer would arrive to play it over.

He would have no idea of the bomb-shell that was about to burst, triggering trains of sympathetic ripples on all the inhabited worlds as television and news-sheet took up the refrain. An accident in space has a dramatic quality that crowds all other items from the headlines.

Until now Grant had been too preoccupied with his own safety to give much thought to the cargo in his charge. A sea-captain of ancient times, whose first thought was for his ship, might have been shocked by this attitude. Grant, however, had reason on his side.

The *Star Queen* could never founder, could never run upon uncharted rocks or pass silently, as many ships have passed, for ever from the knowledge of man. She was safe, whatever might befall her crew. If she was undisturbed she would continue to retrace her orbit with such precision that men might set their calendars by her for centuries to come.

The cargo, Grant suddenly remembered, was insured for over twenty million dollars. There were not many goods valuable enough to be shipped from world to world and most of the crates in the hold were worth more than their weight – or rather their mass – in gold. Perhaps some items might be useful in this emergency and Grant went to the safe to find the loading schedule.

He was sorting the thin, tough sheets when McNeil came

back into the cabin.

'I've been reducing the air pressure,' he said. 'The hull shows some leaks that wouldn't have mattered in the usual way.'

Grant nodded absently as he passed a bundle of sheets over to McNeil.

'Here's our loading schedule. I suggest we both run through it in case there's anything in the cargo that may help.'

If it did nothing else, he might have added, it would at least give them something to occupy their minds.

As he ran down the long columns of numbered items – a complete cross-section of interplanetary commerce – Grant found himself wondering what lay behind these inanimate symbols. *Item 347 – 1 book – 4 kilos gross.*

He whistled as he noticed that it was a starred item, insured for a hundred thousand dollars, and he suddenly remembered hearing on the radio that the Hesperian Museum had just bought a first edition *Seven Pillars of Wisdom.*

A few sheets later was a very contrasting item, *Miscellaneous books – 25 kilos – no intrinsic value.*

It had cost a small fortune to ship those books to Venus, yet they were of 'no intrinsic value'. Grant let his imagination loose on the problem. Perhaps someone who was leaving Earth for ever was taking with him to a new world his most cherished treasures – the dozen or so volumes that above all others had most shaped his mind.

Item 564 – 12 reels film.

That, of course, would be the Neronian super-epic, *While Rome Burns*, which had left Earth just one jump ahead of the censor. Venus was waiting for it with considerable impatience.

Medical supplies – 50 kilos. Case of cigars – 1 kilo. Precision instruments – 75 kilos. So the list went on. Each item was something rare or something which the industry and science of a younger civilization could not yet produce.

The cargo was sharply divided into two classes – blatant luxury or sheer necessity. There was little in between. And there was nothing, nothing at all, which gave Grant the slightest hope. He did not see how it could have been otherwise, but that did not prevent him from feeling a quite unreasonable disappointment.

The reply from Venus, when it came at last, took nearly an hour to run through the recorder. It was a questionnaire so detailed that Grant wondered morosely if he'd live long enough to answer it. Most of the queries were technical ones concerning the ship. The experts on two planets were pooling their brains in the attempt to save the *Star Queen* and her cargo.

'Well, what do you think of it?' Grant asked McNeil when the other had finished running through the message. He was watching the engineer carefully for any further sign of strain.

There was a long pause before McNeil spoke. Then he shrugged his shoulders and his first words were an echo of Grant's own thoughts.

'It will certainly keep us busy. I won't be able to do all these tests in under a day. I can see what they're driving at most of the time, but some of the questions are just crazy.

Grant had suspected that, but said nothing as the other continued.

'Rate of hull leakage – that's sensible enough, but why should anyone want to know the efficiency of our radiation screening? I think they're trying to keep up our morale by pretending they have some bright ideas – or else they want to keep us too busy to worry.'

Grant was relieved and yet annoyed by McNeil's calmness – relieved because he had been afraid of another scene and annoyed because McNeil was not fitting at all neatly into the mental category he had prepared for him. Was that first momentary lapse typical of the man or might it have happened to anyone?

Grant, to whom the world was very much a place for

blacks and whites, felt angry at being unable to decide whether McNeil was cowardly or courageous. That he might be both was a possibility that never occurred to him.

There is a timelessness about space-flight that is unmatched by any other experience of man. Even on the Moon there are shadows that creep sluggishly from crag to crag as the sun makes his slow march across the sky. Earthwards there is always the great clock of the spinning globe, marking the hours with continents for hands. But on a long voyage in a gyro-stabilized ship the same patterns of sunlight lie unmoving on wall or floor as the chronometer ticks off its meaningless hours and days.

Grant and McNeil had long since learned to regulate their lives accordingly. In deep space they moved and thought with a leisureliness that would vanish quickly enough when a voyage was nearing its end and the time for braking manœuvres had arrived. Though they were now under sentence of death they continued along the well-worn grooves of habit.

Every day Grant carefully wrote up the log, checked the ship's position and carried out his various routine duties. McNeil was also behaving normally as far as could be told, though Grant suspected that some of the technical maintenance was being carried out with a very light hand.

It was now three days since the meteor had struck. For the last twenty-four hours Earth and Venus had been in conference and Grant wondered when he would hear the result of their deliberations. He did not believe that even the finest technical brains in the Solar System could save them now, but it was hard to abandon hope when everything still seemed so normal and the air was still clean and fresh.

On the fourth day Venus spoke again. Shorn of its technicalities, the message was nothing more nor less than a funeral oration. Grant and McNeil had been written off, but they were given elaborate instructions concerning the safety of the cargo.

Back on Earth the astronomers were computing all the possible rescue orbits that might make contact with the *Star Queen* in the next few years. There was even a chance that she might be reached from Earth six or seven months later, when she was back at aphelion, but the manœuvre could only be carried out by a fast liner with no payload and would cost a fortune in fuel.

McNeil vanished soon after this message came through. At first Grant was a little relieved. If McNeil chose to look after himself that was his own affair. Besides there were various letters to write – though the last-will-and-testament business could come later.

It was McNeil's turn to prepare the 'evening' meal, a duty he enjoyed for he took good care of his stomach. When the usual sounds from the galley were not forthcoming Grant went in search of his crew.

He found McNeil lying in his bunk, very much at peace with the Universe. Hanging in the air beside him was a large metal crate which had been roughly forced open. Grant had no need to examine it closely to guess its contents. A glance at McNeil was enough.

'It's a dirty shame,' said the engineer without a trace of embarrassment, 'to suck this stuff up through a tube. Can't you put on some "g" so that we can drink it properly?'

Grant stared at him with angry contempt, but McNeil returned his gaze unabashed.

'Oh, don't be a sourpuss! Have some yourself – what does it matter now?'

He pushed across a bottle and Grant fielded it deftly as it floated by. It was a fabulously valuable wine – he remembered the consignment now – and the contents of that small crate must be worth thousands.

'I don't think there's any need,' said Grant severely, 'to behave like a pig – even in these circumstances.'

McNeil wasn't drunk yet. He had only reached the brightly lit anteroom of intoxication and not lost all contact with the drab outer world.

'I am prepared,' he said with great solemnity, 'to listen to any good argument against my present course of action – a course which seems eminently sensible to me. But you'd better convince me quickly while I'm still amenable to reason.'

He pressed the plastic bulb again and a purple jet shot into his mouth.

'Apart from the fact that you're stealing Company property which will certainly be salvaged sooner or later – you can hardly stay drunk for several weeks.'

'That,' said McNeil thoughtfully, 'remains to be seen.'

'I don't think so,' retorted Grant. Bracing himself against the wall he gave the crate a vicious shove that sent it flying through the open doorway.

As he dived after it and slammed the door he heard McNeil shout, 'Well, of all the dirty tricks !'

It would take the engineer some time – particularly in his present condition – to unbuckle himself and follow. Grant steered the crate back to the hold and locked the door. As there was never any need to lock the hold when the ship was in space McNeil wouldn't have a key for it himself and Grant could hide the duplicate that was kept in the control cabin.

McNeil was singing when, some time later, Grant went back past his room. He still had a couple of bottles for company and was shouting :

> 'We don't care *where* the oxygen goes
> If it doesn't get into the wine ...'

Grant, whose education had been severely technical, couldn't place the quotation. As he paused to listen he suddenly found himself shaken by an emotion which, to do him justice, he did not for a moment recognize.

It passed as swiftly as it had come, leaving him sick and trembling. For the first time, he realized that his dislike of McNeil was slowly turning to hatred.

It is a fundamental rule of space-flight that, for sound psychological reasons, the minimum crew on a long journey shall consist of not less than three men.

But rules are made to be broken and the *Star Queen*'s owners had obtained full authority from the Board of Space Control and the insurance companies when the freighter set off for Venus without her regular captain.

At the last moment he had been taken ill and there was no replacement. Since the planets are disinclined to wait upon man and his affairs, if she did not sail on time she would not sail at all.

Millions of dollars were involved – so she sailed. Grant and McNeil were both highly capable men and they had no objection at all to earning double their normal pay for very little extra work. Despite fundamental differences in temperament, they got on well enough in ordinary circumstances. It was nobody's fault that circumstances were now very far from ordinary.

Three days without food, it is said, is long enough to remove most of the subtle differences between a civilized man and a savage. Grant and McNeil were still in no physical discomfort. But their imaginations had been only too active and they now had more in common with two hungry Pacific Islanders in a lost canoe than either would have cared to admit.

For there was one aspect of the situation, and that the most important of all, which had never been mentioned. When the last figures on Grant's writing-pad had been checked and rechecked, the calculation was still not quite complete. Instantly each man had made the one further step, each had arrived simultaneously at the same unspoken result.

It was terribly simple – a macabre parody of those problems in first-year arithmetic that begin, 'If six men take two days to assemble five helicopters, how long . . .'

The oxygen would last *two* men for about twenty days, and Venus was thirty days away. One did not have to be a calculating prodigy to see at once that one man, and one man only, might yet live to walk the metal streets of Port Hesperus.

The acknowledged deadline was twenty days ahead, but the unmentioned one was only ten days off. Until that time there would still be enough air for two men—and thereafter for one man only for the rest of the voyage. To a sufficiently detached observer the situation would have been very entertaining.

It was obvious that the conspiracy of silence could not last much longer. But it is not easy, even at the best of times, for two people to decide amicably which one of them shall commit suicide. It is still more difficult when they are no longer on speaking terms.

Grant wished to be perfectly fair. Therefore the only thing to do was to wait until McNeil sobered up and then to put the question to him frankly. He could think best at his desk, so he went to the control cabin and strapped himself down in the pilot's chair.

For a while he stared thoughtfully into nothingness. It would be better, he decided, to broach the matter by correspondence, especially while diplomatic relations were in their present state. He clipped a sheet of note-paper on the writing-pad and began, 'Dear McNeil —' Then he tore it out and started again, 'McNeil —'

It took him the best part of three hours and even then he wasn't wholly satisfied. There were some things it was so darned difficult to put down on paper. But at last he managed to finish.

He sealed the letter and locked it away in his safe. It could wait for a day or two.

Few of the waiting millions on Earth and Venus could have had any idea of the tensions that were slowly building up aboard the *Star Queen*. For days press and radio had been full of fantastic rescue schemes. On three worlds there was hardly any other topic of conversation. But only the faintest echo of the planet-wide tumult reached the two men who were its cause.

At any time the station on Venus could speak to the *Star*

Queen, but there was so little that could be said. One could not with any decency give words of encouragement to men in the condemned cell, even when there was some slight uncertainty about the actual date of execution.

So Venus contented itself with a few routine messages every day and blocked the steady stream of exhortations and newspaper offers that came pouring in from Earth. As a result private radio companies on Earth made frantic attempts to contact the *Star Queen* directly. They failed, simply because it never occurred to Grant and McNeil to focus their receiver anywhere except on Venus, now so tantalizingly near at hand.

There had been an embarrassing interlude when McNeil emerged from his cabin, but though relations were not particularly cordial, life aboard the *Star Queen* continued much as before.

Grant spent most of his waking hours in the pilot's position, calculating approach manoeuvres and writing interminable letters to his wife. He could have spoken to her had he wished, but the thought of all those millions of waiting ears had prevented him from doing so. Interplanetary speech circuits were supposed to be private – but too many people would be interested in this one.

In a couple of days, Grant assured himself, he would hand his letter to McNeil and they could decide what was to be done. Such a delay would also give McNeil a chance of raising the subject himself. That he might have other reasons for his hesitation was something Grant's conscious mind still refused to admit.

He often wondered how McNeil was spending his time. The engineer had a large library of microfilm books, for he read widely and his range of interests was unusual. His favourite book, Grant knew, was *Jurgen*, and perhaps even now he was trying to forget his doom by losing himself in its strange magic. Others of McNeil's books were less respectable and not a few were of the class curiously described as 'curious'.

The truth of the matter was that McNeil was far too subtle and complicated a personality for Grant to understand. He was a hedonist and enjoyed the pleasures of life all the more for being cut off from them for months at a time. But he was by no means the moral weakling that the unimaginative and somewhat puritanical Grant had supposed.

It was true that he had collapsed completely under the initial shock and that his behaviour over the wine was – by Grant's standards – reprehensible. But McNeil had had his breakdown and had recovered. Therein lay the difference between him and the hard but brittle Grant.

Though the normal routine of duties had been resumed by tacit consent, it did little to reduce the sense of strain. Grant and McNeil avoided each other as far as possible except when mealtimes brought them together. When they did meet, they behaved with an exaggerated politeness as if each were striving to be perfectly normal – and inexplicably failing.

Grant had hoped that McNeil would himself broach the subject of suicide, thus sparing him a very awkward duty. When the engineer stubbornly refused to do anything of the sort it added to Grant's resentment and contempt. To make matters worse he was now suffering from nightmares and sleeping very badly.

The nightmare was always the same. When he was a child it had often happened that at bedtime he had been reading a story far too exciting to be left until morning. To avoid detection he had continued reading under the bedclothes by flashlight, curled up in a snug white-walled cocoon. Every ten minutes or so the air had become too stifling to breathe and his emergence into the delicious cool air had been a major part of the fun.

Now, thirty years later, these innocent childhood hours returned to haunt him. He was dreaming that he could not escape from the suffocating sheets while the air was steadily and remorselessly thickening around him.

He had intended to give McNeil the letter after two days, yet somehow he put it off again. This procrastination was very unlike Grant, but he managed to persuade himself that it was a perfectly reasonable thing to do.

He was giving McNeil a chance to redeem himself – to prove that he wasn't a coward by raising the matter himself. That McNeil might be waiting for him to do exactly the same thing somehow never occurred to Grant.

The all-too-literal deadline was only five days off when, for the first time, Grant's mind brushed lightly against the thought of murder. He had been sitting after the 'evening' meal trying to relax as McNeil clattered around in the galley with, he considered, quite unnecessary noise.

What use, he asked himself, was the engineer to the world? He had no responsibilities and no family – no one would be any the worse off for his death. Grant, on the other hand, had a wife and three children of whom he was moderately fond, though for some obscure reason they responded with little more than dutiful affection.

Any impartial judge would have no difficulty in deciding which of them should survive. If McNeil had a spark of decency in him he would have come to the same conclusion already. Since he appeared to have done nothing of the sort he had forfeited all further claims to consideration.

Such was the elemental logic of Grant's subconscious mind, which had arrived at its answer days before but had only now succeeded in attracting the attention for which it had been clamouring. To Grant's credit he at once rejected the thought with horror.

He was an upright and honourable person with a very strict code of behaviour. Even the vagrant homicidal impulses of what is misleadingly called 'normal' man had seldom ruffled his mind. But in the days – the very few days – left to him, they would come more and more often.

The air had now become noticeably fouler. Though there was still no real difficulty in breathing, it was a constant reminder of what lay ahead, and Grant found that it was keeping him from sleep. This was not pure loss, as it helped to break the power of his nightmares, but he was becoming physically run down.

His nerve was also rapidly deteriorating, a state of affairs accentuated by the fact that McNeil seemed to be behaving with unexpected and annoying calmness. Grant realized that he had come to the stage when it would be dangerous to delay the showdown any longer.

McNeil was in his room as usual when Grant went up to the control cabin to collect the letter he had locked away in the safe – it seemed a lifetime ago. He wondered if he need add anything more to it. Then he realized that this was only another excuse for delay. Resolutely he made his way towards McNeil's cabin.

A single neutron begins the chain-reaction that in an instant can destroy a million lives and the toil of generations. Equally insignificant and unimportant are the trigger-events which can sometimes change a man's course of action and so alter the whole pattern of his future.

Nothing could have been more trivial than that which made Grant pause in the corridor outside McNeil's room. In the ordinary way he would not even have noticed it. It was the smell of smoke – tobacco smoke.

The thought that the sybaritic engineer had so little self-control that he was squandering the last precious litres of oxygen in such a manner filled Grant with blinding fury. He stood for a moment quite paralysed with the intensity of his emotion.

Then slowly he crumpled the letter in his hand. The thought which had first been an unwelcomed intruder, then a casual speculation, was at last fully accepted. McNeil had had his chance and had proved, by his unbelievable selfishness, unworthy of it. Very well – he should die.

The speed with which Grant had arrived at this conclusion would not have deceived the most amateurish of psychologists. It was relief as much as hatred that drove him away from McNeil's room. He had wanted to convince himself that there would be no need to do the honourable thing, to suggest some game of chance that would give them each an equal probability of life.

This was the excuse he needed, and he had seized upon it to salve his conscience. For though he might plan and even carry out a murder, Grant was the sort of person who would have to do it according to his own particular moral code.

As it happened he was – not for the first time – badly misjudging McNeil. The engineer was a heavy smoker and tobacco was quite essential to his mental well-being even in normal circumstances. How much more essential it was now, Grant, who only smoked occasionally and without much enjoyment, could never have appreciated.

McNeil had satisfied himself by careful calculation that four cigarettes a day would make no measurable difference whatsoever to the ship's oxygen endurance whereas they would make all the difference in the world to his own nerves and hence indirectly to Grant's.

But it was no use explaining this to Grant. So he had smoked in private and with a self-control he found agreeably, almost voluptuously, surprising. It was sheer bad luck that Grant had detected one of the day's four cigarettes.

For a man who had only at that moment talked himself into murder, Grant's actions were remarkably methodical. Without hesitation, he hurried back to the control room and opened the medicine chest with its neatly labelled compartments, designed for almost every emergency that could occur in space.

Even the ultimate emergency had been considered, for there behind its retaining elastic bands was the tiny bottle he had been seeking, the image of which through all these days had been lying hidden far down in the unknown depths of his mind. It wore a white label carrying a skull-and-cross-bones, and beneath them the words: *Approx. one-half gramme will cause painless and almost instantaneous death.*

The poison was painless and instantaneous – that was

good. But even more important was a fact unmentioned on the label. It was also tasteless.

The contrast between the meals prepared by Grant and those organized with considerable skill and care by McNeil was striking. Anyone who was fond of food and who spent a good deal of his life in space usually learned the art of cooking in self-defence. McNeil had done this long ago.

To Grant, on the other hand, eating was one of those necessary but annoying jobs which had to be got through as quickly as possible. His cooking reflected this opinion. McNeil had ceased to grumble about it, but he would have been very interested in the trouble Grant was taking over this particular meal.

If he noticed any increasing nervousness on Grant's part as the meal progressed, he said nothing. They ate almost in silence but that was not unusual for they had long since exhausted most of the possibilities of light conversation. When the last dishes – deep bowls with inturned rims to prevent the contents drifting out – had been cleared away, Grant went into the galley to prepare the coffee.

He took rather a long time, for at the last moment something quite maddening and quite ridiculous happened. He suddenly recalled one of the film classics of the last century in which the fabulous Charlie Chaplin tried to poison an unwanted wife – and then accidentally changed the glasses.

No memory could have been more unwelcome, for it left him shaken with a gust of silent hysteria. Poe's *Imp of the Perverse*, that demon who delights in defying the careful canons of self-preservation, was at work and it was a good minute before Grant could regain his self-control.

He was sure that, outwardly at least, he was quite calm as he carried in the two plastic containers and their drinking-tubes. There was no danger of confusing them, for the engineer's had the letters MAC painted boldly across it.

At the thought Grant nearly relapsed into those psychopathic giggles again, but just managed to regain control with the sombre reflection that his nerves must be in even worse condition than he had imagined.

He watched, fascinated, though without appearing to do so, as McNeil toyed with his cup. The engineer seemed in no great hurry and was staring moodily into space. Then he put his lips to the drinking tube and sipped.

A moment later he spluttered slightly – and an icy hand seemed to seize Grant's heart and hold it tight. Then McNeil turned to him and said evenly, 'You've made it properly for once. It's quite hot.'

Slowly, Grant's heart resumed its interrupted work. He did not trust himself to speak, but managed a noncommittal nod. McNeil parked the cup carefully in the air, a few inches away from his face.

He seemed very thoughtful, as if weighing his words for some important remark. Grant cursed himself for having made the drink so hot – that was just the sort of detail that hanged murderers. If McNeil waited much longer he would probably betray himself through nervousness.

'I suppose,' said McNeil in a quietly conversational sort of way, 'it has occurred to you that there's still enough air to last one of us to Venus.'

Grant forced his jangling nerves under control and tore his eyes away from that hypnotic cup. His throat seemed very dry as he answered, 'It – it had crossed my mind.'

McNeil touched his cup, found it still too hot and continued thoughtfully, 'Then wouldn't it be more sensible if one of us decided to walk out of the airlock, say – or to take some of the poison in there?' He jerked his thumb towards the medicine chest, just visible from where they were sitting.

Grant nodded.

'The only trouble, of course,' added the engineer, 'is to decide which of us is to be the unlucky one. I suppose it would have to be by picking a card or in some other quite arbitrary way.'

Grant stared at McNeil with a fascination that almost outweighed his mounting nervousness. He had never believed that the engineer could discuss the subject so calmly. Grant was sure he suspected nothing. Obviously McNeil's thoughts had been running on parallel lines to his own and it was scarcely even a coincidence that he had chosen this time, of all times, to raise the matter.

McNeil was watching him intently, as if judging his reactions.

'You're right,' Grant heard himself say. 'We must talk it over.'

'Yes,' said McNeil quite impassively. 'We must.' Then he reached for his cup again, put the drinking-tube to his lips and sucked slowly.

Grant could not wait until he had finished. To his surprise the relief he had been expecting did not come. He even felt a stab of regret, though it was not quite remorse. It was a little late to think of it now, but he suddenly remembered that he would be alone in the *Star Queen*, haunted by his thoughts, for more than three weeks before rescue came.

He did not wish to see McNeil die, and he felt rather sick. Without another glance at his victim he launched himself towards the exit.

Immovably fixed, the fierce sun and the unwinking stars looked down upon the *Star Queen*, which seemed as motionless as they. There was no way of telling that the tiny dumbbell of the ship had now almost reached her maximum speed and that millions of horse-power were chained within the smaller sphere waiting the moment of its release. There was no way of telling, indeed, that she carried any life at all.

An airlock on the night-side of the ship slowly opened, letting a blaze of light escape from the interior. The brilliant circle looked very strange hanging there in the darkness. Then it was abruptly eclipsed as two figures floated out of the ship.

One was much bulkier than the other, and for a rather important reason – it was wearing a spacesuit. Now there are some forms of apparel that may be worn or discarded as the fancy pleases with no other ill effects than a possible loss of social prestige. But spacesuits are not among them.

Something not easy to follow was happening in the darkness. Then the smaller figure began to move, slowly at first but with rapidly mounting speed. It swept out of the shadow of the ship into the full blast of the Sun, and now one could see that strapped to its back was a small gas-cylinder from which a fine mist was jetting to vanish almost instantly into space.

It was a crude but effective rocket. There was no danger that the ship's minute gravitational pull would drag the body back to it again.

Rotating slightly, the corpse dwindled against the stars and vanished from sight in less than a minute. Quite motionless, the figure in the airlock watched it go. Then the outer door swung shut, the circle of brilliance vanished and only the pale Earthlight still glinted on the shadowed wall of the ship.

Nothing else whatsoever happened for twenty-three days.

The captain of the *Hercules* turned to his mate with a sigh of relief.

'I was afraid he couldn't do it. It must have been a colossal job to break his orbit single-handed – and with the air as thick as it must be by now. How soon can we get to him?'

'It will take about an hour. He's still got quite a bit of eccentricity but we can correct that.'

'Good. Signal the *Leviathan* and *Titan* that we can make contact and ask them to take off, will you? But I wouldn't drop any tips to your news-commentator friends until we're safely locked.'

The mate had the grace to blush. 'I don't intend to,' he said in a slightly hurt voice as he pecked delicately at the keys of his calculator. The answer that flashed instantly on the screen seemed to displease him.

'We'd better board and bring the *Queen* down to circular speed ourselves before we call the other tugs,' he said, 'otherwise we'll be wasting a lot of fuel. She's still got a velocity of nearly a kilometre a second.'

'Good idea – tell *Leviathan* and *Titan* to stand by but not to blast until we give them the new orbit.'

While the message was on its way down through the unbroken cloudbanks that covered half the sky below, the mate remarked thoughtfully, 'I wonder what he's feeling like now?'

'I can tell you. He's so pleased to be alive that he doesn't give a hoot about anything else.'

'Still, I'm not sure I'd like to have left my shipmate in space so that I could get home.'

'It's not the sort of thing that anyone would like to do. But you heard the broadcast – they'd talked it over calmly and the loser went out of the airlock. It was the only sensible way.'

'Sensible, perhaps – but it's pretty horrible to let someone else sacrifice himself in such a cold-blooded way so that you can live.'

'Don't be a ruddy sentimentalist. I'll bet that if it happened to us you'd push me out before I could even say my prayers.'

'Unless you did it to me first. Still, I don't think it's ever likely to happen to the *Hercules*. Five days out of port's the longest we've ever been, isn't it? Talk about the romance of the spaceways !'

The captain didn't reply. He was peering into the eyepiece of the navigating telescope, for the *Star Queen* should now be within optical range. There was a long pause while he adjusted the vernier controls. Then he gave a little sigh of satisfaction.

'There she is – about nine-fifty kilometres away. Tell the crew to stand by – and send a message to cheer him up. Say we'll be there in thirty minutes even if it isn't quite true.'

Slowly the thousand-metre nylon ropes yielded beneath the strain as they absorbed the relative momentum of the ships, then slackened again as the *Star Queen* and the *Her-*

cules rebounded towards each other. The electric winches began to turn and, like a spider crawling up its thread, the *Hercules* drew alongside the freighter.

Men in spacesuits sweated with heavy reaction units — tricky work, this — until the airlocks had registered and could be coupled together. The outer doors slid aside and the air in the locks mingled, fresh with the foul. As the mate of the *Hercules* waited, oxygen cylinder in hand, he wondered what condition the survivor would be in. Then the *Star Queen's* inner door slid open.

For a moment, the two men stood looking at each other across the short corridor that now connected the two air-locks. The mate was surprised and a little disappointed to find that he felt no particular sense of drama.

So much had happened to make this moment possible that its actual achievement was almost an anticlimax even in the instant when it was slipping into the past. He wished — for he was an incurable romantic — that he could think of something memorable to say, some 'Doctor Livingstone, I presume?' phrase that would pass into history.

But all he actually said was, 'Well, McNeil, I'm pleased to see you.'

Though he was considerably thinner and somewhat haggard, McNeil had stood the ordeal well. He breathed gratefully the blast of raw oxygen and rejected the idea that he might like to lie down and sleep. As he explained, he had done very little but sleep for the last week to conserve air. The first mate looked relieved. He had been afraid he might have to wait for the story.

The cargo was being trans-shipped and the other two tugs were climbing up from the great blinding crescent of Venus while McNeil retraced the events of the last few weeks and the mate made surreptitious notes.

He spoke quite calmly and impersonally, as if he were relating some adventure that had happened to another person, or indeed had never happened at all. Which was, of course, to some extent the case, though it would be unfair to suggest that McNeil was telling any lies.

He invented nothing, but he omitted a good deal. He had had three weeks in which to prepare his narrative and he did not think it had any flaws —

Grant had already reached the door when McNeil called softly after him, 'What's the hurry? I thought we had something to discuss.'

Grant grabbed at the doorway to halt his headlong flight. He turned slowly and stared unbelievingly at the engineer. McNeil should be already dead — but he was sitting quite comfortably, looking at him with a most peculiar expression.

'Sit down,' he said sharply — and in that moment it suddenly seemed that all authority had passed to him. Grant did so, quite without volition. Something had gone wrong, though what it was he could not imagine.

The silence in the control-room seemed to last for ages. Then McNeil said rather sadly, 'I'd hoped better of you, Grant.'

At last Grant found his voice, though he could barely recognize it.

'What do you mean?' he whispered.

'What do you think I mean?' replied McNeil, with what seemed no more than a mild irritation. 'This little attempt of yours to poison me, of course.'

Grant's tottering world collapsed at last, but he no longer cared greatly one way or the other. McNeil began to examine his beautifully kept fingernails with some attention.

'As a matter of interest,' he said, in the way that one might ask the time, 'when did you decide to kill me?'

The sense of unreality was so overwhelming that Grant felt he was acting a part, that this had nothing to do with real life at all.

'Only this morning,' he said, and believed it.

'Hmm,' remarked McNeil, obviously without much conviction. He rose to his feet and moved over to the medicine chest. Grant's eyes followed him as he fumbled in the compartment and came back with the little poison bottle. It still appeared to be full. Grant had been careful about that.

'I suppose I should get pretty mad about this whole business,' McNeil continued conversationally, holding the bottle between thumb and forefinger. 'But somehow I'm not. Maybe it's because I never had many illusions about human nature. And, of course, I saw it coming a long time ago.'

Only the last phrase really reached Grant's conciousness.

'You – saw it coming?'

'Heavens, yes! You're too transparent to make a good criminal, I'm afraid. And now that your little plot's failed it leaves us both in an embarrassing position, doesn't it?'

To this masterly understatement there seemed no possible reply.

'By rights,' continued the engineer thoughtfully, 'I should now work myself up into a temper, call Venus Central, and denounce you to the authorities. But it would be a rather pointless thing to do, and I've never been much good at losing my temper anyway. Of course, you'll say that's because I'm too lazy – but I don't think so.'

He gave Grant a twisted smile.

'Oh, I know what you think about me – you've got me neatly classified in that orderly mind of yours, haven't you? I'm soft and self-indulgent, I haven't any moral courage – or any morals for that matter – and I don't give a damn for anyone but myself. Well, I'm not denying it. Maybe it's ninety per cent true. But the odd ten per cent is mighty important, Grant!'

Grant felt in no condition to indulge in psychological analysis, and this seemed hardly the time for anything of the sort. Besides, he was still obsessed with the problem of his failure and the mystery of McNeil's continued existence. McNeil, who knew this perfectly well, seemed in no hurry to satisfy his curiosity.

'Well, what do you intend to do now?' Grant asked, anxious to get it over.

'I would like,' said McNeil calmly, 'to carry on our discussion where it was interrupted by the coffee.'

'You don't mean —'

'But I do. Just as if nothing had happened.'

'That doesn't make sense. You've got something up your sleeve!' cried Grant.

McNeil sighed. He put down the poison bottle and looked firmly at Grant.

'*You're* in no position to accuse me of plotting anything. To repeat my earlier remarks, I am suggesting that we decide which one of us shall take poison — only we don't want any more unilateral decisions. Also' — he picked up the bottle again — 'it will be the real thing this time. The stuff in here merely leaves a bad taste in the mouth.'

A light was beginning to dawn in Grant's mind. 'You changed the poison!'

'Naturally. You may think you're a good actor, Grant, but frankly — from the stalls — I thought the performance stank. I could tell you were plotting something, probably before you knew it yourself. In the last few days I've deloused the ship pretty thoroughly. Thinking of all the ways you might have done me in was quite amusing and helped to pass the time. The poison was so obvious that it was the first thing I fixed. But I rather overdid the danger signals and nearly gave myself away when I took the first sip. Salt doesn't go at all well with coffee.'

He gave that wry grin again. 'Also, I'd hoped for something more subtle. So far I've found fifteen infallible ways of murdering anyone aboard a spaceship. But I don't propose to describe them now.'

This was fantastic, Grant thought. He was being treated, not like a criminal, but like a rather stupid schoolboy who hadn't done his homework properly.

'Yet you're still willing,' said Grant unbelievingly, 'to start all over again? And you'd take the poison yourself if you lost?'

McNeil was silent for a long time. Then he began slowly, 'I can see that you still don't believe me. It doesn't fit at all

nicely into your tidy little picture, does it? But perhaps I
can make you understand. It's really quite simple.

'I've enjoyed life, Grant, without many scruples or regrets
– but the better part of it's over now and I don't cling to
what's left as desperately as you might imagine. Yet while I
am alive I'm rather particular about some things.

'It may surprise you to know that I've got any ideals at
all. But I have, Grant – I've always tried to act like a
civilized rational being. I've not always succeeded. When
I've failed I've tried to redeem myself.'

He paused, and when he resumed it was as though he, and
not Grant, was on the defensive. 'I've never exactly liked
you, Grant, but I've often admired you and that's why I'm
sorry it's come to this. I admired you most of all the day the
ship was holed.'

For the first time, McNeil seemed to have some difficulty
in choosing his words. When he spoke again he avoided
Grant's eyes.

'I didn't behave too well then. Something happened that
I thought was impossible. I've always been quite sure that
I'd never lose my nerve but – well – it was so sudden it
knocked me over.'

He attempted to hide his embarrassment by humour. 'The
same sort of thing happened on my very first trip. I was sure
I'd never be spacesick – and as a result I was much worse
than if I had not been over-confident. But I got over it then
– and again this time. It was one of the biggest surprises of
my life, Grant, when I saw that you of all people were
beginning to crack.

'Oh, yes – the business of wines! I can see you're thinking about that. Well, that's one thing I *don't* regret. I said
I've always tried to act like a civilized man – and a civilized
man should always know when to get drunk. But perhaps
you wouldn't understand.'

Oddly enough, that was just what Grant was beginning
to do. He had caught his first real glimpse of McNeil's intricate and tortuous personality and realized how utterly he

had misjudged him. No – misjudged was not the right word. In many ways his judgement had been correct. But it had only touched the surface – he had never suspected the depths that lay beneath.

In a moment of insight that had never come before, and from the nature of things could never come again, Grant understood the reasons behind McNeil's action. This was nothing so simple as a coward trying to reinstate himself in the eyes of the world, for no one need ever know what happened aboard the *Star Queen*.

In any case, McNeil probably cared nothing for the world's opinion, thanks to the sleek self-sufficiency that had so often annoyed Grant. But that very self-sufficiency meant that at all costs he must preserve his own good opinion of himself. Without it life would not be worth living – and McNeil had never accepted life save on his own terms.

The engineer was watching him intently and must have guessed that Grant was coming near the truth, for he suddenly changed his tone as though he was sorry he had revealed so much of his character.

'Don't think I get a quixotic pleasure from turning the other cheek,' he said. 'Just consider it from the point of view of pure logic. After all, we've got to come to *some* agreement.

'Has it occurred to you that if only one of us survives without a covering message from the other, he'll have a very uncomfortable time explaining just what happened?'

In his blind fury, Grant had completely forgotten this. But he did not believe it bulked at all important in McNeil's own thoughts.

'Yes,' he said, 'I suppose you're right.'

He felt far better now. All the hate drained out of him and he was at peace. The truth was known and he had accepted it. That it was so different from what he had imagined did not seem to matter now.

'Well, let's get it over,' he said unemotionally. 'There's a new pack of cards lying around somewhere.'

'I think we'd better speak to Venus first – both of us,' replied McNeil, with peculiar emphasis. 'We want a complete agreement on record in case anyone asks awkward questions later.'

Grant nodded absently. He did not mind very much now one way or the other. He even smiled, ten minutes later, as he drew his card from the pack and laid it, face upwards, beside McNeil's.

'So that's the whole story, is it?' said the first mate, wondering how soon he could decently get to the transmitter.

'Yes,' said McNeil evenly, 'that's all there was to it.'

The mate bit his pencil, trying to frame the next question. 'And I suppose Grant took it all quite calmly?'

The captain gave him a glare, which he avoided, and McNeil looked at him coldly as if he could see through the sensation-mongering headlines ranged behind. He got to his feet and moved over to the observation port.

'You heard his broadcast, didn't you? Wasn't that calm enough?'

The mate sighed. It still seemed hard to believe that in such circumstances two men could have behaved in so reasonable, so unemotional a manner. He could have pictured all sorts of dramatic possibilities – sudden outbursts of insanity, even attempts at murder. Yet according to McNeil nothing at all had happened. It was too bad.

McNeil was speaking again, as if to himself. 'Yes, Grant behaved very well – very well indeed. It was a great pity —'

Then he seemed to lose himself in the ever-fresh, incomparable glory of the approaching planet. Not far beneath, and coming closer by kilometres every second, the snow-white crescent arms of Venus spanned more than half the sky. Down there were life and warmth and civilization – and air.

The future, which not long ago had seemed contracted to a point, had opened out again into all its unknown possibilities and wonders. But behind him McNeil could sense the

eyes of his rescuers, probing, questioning – yes, and con-
demning too.

All his life he would hear whispers. Voices would be saying behind his back, 'Isn't that the man who —?'

He did not care. For once in his life at least, he had done
something of which he could feel unashamed. Perhaps one
day his own pitiless self-analysis would strip bare the motives
behind his actions, would whisper in his ear. 'Altruism?
Don't be a fool! You did it to bolster up your own good
opinion of yourself – so much more important than anyone
else's!'

But the perverse maddening voices, which all his life had
made nothing seem worth while, were silent for the moment
and he felt content. He had reached the calm at the centre
of the hurricane. While it lasted he would enjoy it to the full.

EXPEDITION TO EARTH

N<small>O ONE</small> could remember when the tribe had begun its long journey: the land of great rolling plains that had been its first home was now no more than a half-forgotten dream. For many years Shann and his people had been fleeing through a country of low hills and sparkling lakes, and now the mountains lay ahead. This summer they must cross them to the southern lands, and there was little time to lose.

The white terror that had come down from the poles, grinding continents to dust and freezing the very air before it, was less than a day's march behind. Shann wondered if the glaciers could climb the mountains ahead, and within his heart he dared to kindle a little flame of hope. They might prove a barrier against which even the remorseless ice would batter in vain. In the southern lands of which the legends spoke, his people might find refuge at last.

It took many weeks to discover a pass through which the tribe and its animals could travel. When midsummer came, they had camped in a lonely valley where the air was thin and the stars shone with a brilliance none had ever seen before. The summer was waning when Shann took his two sons and went ahead to explore the way. For three days they climbed, and for three nights slept as best they could on the freezing rocks. And on the fourth morning there was nothing ahead but a gentle rise to a cairn of grey stones built by other travellers, centuries ago.

Shann felt himself trembling, and not with cold, as they walked towards the little pyramid of stones. His sons had fallen behind; no one spoke, for too much was at stake. In a little while they would know if all their hopes had been betrayed.

To east and west, the wall of mountains curved away as if embracing the land beneath. Below lay endless miles of undulating plain, with a great river swinging across it in tremendous loops. It was fertile land; one in which the tribe could raise its crops knowing that there would be no need to flee before the harvest came.

Then Shann lifted his eyes to the south, and saw the doom of all his hopes. For there, at the edge of the world, glimmered that deadly light he had seen so often to the north – the glint of ice below the horizon.

There was no way forward. Through all the years of flight, the glaciers from the south had been advancing to meet them. Soon they would be crushed beneath the moving walls of ice —

The southern glaciers did not reach the mountains until a generation later. In that last summer, the sons of Shann carried the sacred treasures of the tribe to the lonely cairn overlooking the plain. The ice that had once gleamed below the horizon was now almost at their feet; by the spring it would be splintering against the mountain walls.

No one understood the treasures, now : they were from a past too distant for the understanding of any man alive. Their origins were lost in the mists that surrounded the Golden Age, and how they had come at last into the possession of this wandering tribe was a story that now never would be told. For it was the story of a civilization that had passed beyond recall.

Once, all these pitiful relics had been treasured for some good reason and now they had become sacred, though their meaning had long been lost. The print in the old books had faded centuries ago, though much of the lettering was still readable – if there had been any to read it. But many generations had passed since anyone had had a use for a set of seven-figure logarithms, an atlas of the world, and the score of Sibelius's Seventh Symphony printed, according to the flyleaf, by H. K. Chu & Sons at the City of Pekin in the year A D 2021.

The old books were placed reverently in the little crypt that had been made to receive them. There followed a motley collection of fragments : gold and platinum coins, a broken telephoto lens, a watch, a cold-light lamp, a microphone, the cutter from an electric shaver, some midget radio valves – the flotsam that had been left behind when the great tide of civilization ebbed for ever. All these were carefully stowed away in their resting-place. Then came three more relics, the most sacred of all because the least understood.

The first was a strangely shaped piece of metal, showing the coloration of intense heat. It was, in its way, the most pathetic of all these symbols from the past, for it told of Man's greatest achievement and of the future he might have known. The mahogany stand on which it was mounted bore a silver plate with the inscription :

Auxiliary igniter from starboard jet of spaceship
Morning Star, Earth–Moon, A D 1985

Next followed another miracle of the ancient science : a sphere of transparent plastic with oddly shaped pieces of metal embedded in it. At its centre was a tiny capsule of synthetic radio-element, surrounded by the converting screens that shifted its radiation far down the spectrum. As long as the material remained active, the sphere would be a tiny radio transmitter broadcasting power in all directions. Only a few of these spheres had ever been made; they had been designed as perpetual beacons to mark the orbits of the Asteroids. But Man had never reached the Asteroids, and the beacons had never been used.

Last of all was a flat circular tin, very wide in comparison to its depth. It was heavily sealed, and rattled when it was shaken. The tribal lore predicted that disaster would follow if it were ever opened, and no one knew that it held one of the great works of art of nearly a thousand years before.

The work was finished. The two men rolled the stones back into place and slowly began to descend the mountainside. Even at the last, Man had given some thought to the future and had tried to preserve something for posterity.

That winter, the great waves of ice began their first assault on the mountains, attacking from north and south. The foothills were overwhelmed in the first onslaught, and the glaciers ground them into dust. But the mountains stood firm, and when the summer came the ice retreated for a while.

So, winter after winter, the battle continued, and the roar of the avalanches, the grinding of rock and the explosions of splintered ice filled the air with tumult. No war of Man's had been fiercer nor had engulfed the globe more completely than this. Until at last the tidal waves of ice began to subside and to creep slowly down the flanks of the mountains they had never quite subdued; though the valleys and passes were still firmly in their grip. It was stalemate : the glaciers had met their match.

But their defeat was too late to be of any use to Man.

So the centuries passed; and presently there happened something that must occur once at least in the history of every world in the Universe, no matter how remote and lonely it may be —

The ship from Venus came five thousand years too late, but its crew knew nothing of this. While still many millions of miles away, the telescopes had seen the great shroud of ice that made Earth the most brilliant object in the sky next to the Sun itself. Here and there the dazzling sheet was marred by black specks that revealed the presence of almost buried mountains. That was all. The rolling oceans, the plains and forests, the deserts and lakes – all that had been the world of Man was sealed beneath the ice, perhaps for

The ship closed into Earth and established an orbit less than a thousand miles distant. For five days it circled the planet while cameras recorded all that was left to view and a hundred instruments gathered information that would give the Venusian scientists many years of work. An actual landing was not intended; there seemed little purpose in it. But on the sixth day the picture changed. A panoramic

monitor, driven to the limit of its amplification, detected the
dying radiation of the five-thousand-years-old beacon.
Through all the centuries it had been sending out its signals,
with ever-failing strength as its radioactive heart steadily
weakened.

The monitor locked on the beacon frequency. In the
control-room, a bell clamoured for attention. A little later,
the Venusian ship broke free from its orbit and slanted
down towards Earth – towards a range of mountains that
still towered proudly above the ice, and to a cairn of grey
stones that the years had scarcely touched.

The great disk of the Sun blazed fiercely in a sky no
longer veiled with mist, for the clouds that had once hidden
Venus had now completely gone. Whatever force had caused
the change in the Sun's radiation had doomed one civilization but given birth to another. Less than five thousand
years before, the half-savage people of Venus had seen Sun
and stars for the first time. Just as the science of Earth had
begun with astronomy, so had that of Venus, and on the
warm, rich world that Man had never seen, progress had
been incredibly rapid.

Perhaps the Venusians had been lucky. They never knew
the Dark Age that held Man enchained for a thousand years;
they missed the long detour into chemistry and mechanics,
but came at once to the more fundamental laws of radiation
physics. In the time that Man had taken to progress from
the Pyramids to the rocket-propelled spaceship, the Venusians had passed from the discovery of agriculture to anti-
gravity itself – the ultimate secret that Man had never
learned.

The warm ocean that still bore most of the young planet's
life rolled its breakers languidly against the sandy shore.
So new was this continent that the very sands were coarse
and gritty : there had not yet been time enough for the sea
to wear them smooth. The scientists lay half in the water,
their beautiful reptilian bodies gleaming in the sunlight. The

greatest minds of Venus had gathered on this shore from all the islands of the planet. What they were going to hear they did not yet know, except that it concerned the Third World and the mysterious race that had peopled it before the coming of the ice.

The Historian was standing on the land, for the instruments he wished to use had no love of water. By his side was a large machine which attracted many curious glances from his colleagues. It was clearly concerned with optics, for a lens system projected from it towards a screen of white material a dozen yards away.

The Historian began to speak. Briefly he recapitulated what little had been discovered concerning the Third Planet and its people. He mentioned the centuries of fruitless research that had failed to interpret a single word of the writings of Earth. The planet had been inhabited by a race of great technical ability; that at least was proved by the few pieces of machinery that had been found in the cairn upon the mountain.

'We do not know why so advanced a civilization came to an end. Almost certainly, it had sufficient knowledge to survive an Ice Age. There must have been some other factor of which we know nothing. Possibly disease or racial degeneration may have been responsible. It has even been suggested that the tribal conflicts endemic to our own species in prehistoric times may have continued on the Third Planet after the coming of technology. Some philosophers maintain that knowledge of machinery does not necessarily imply a high degree of civilization, and it is theoretically possible to have wars in a society possessing mechanical power, flight, and even radio. Such a conception is very alien to our thoughts, but we must admit its possibility. It would certainly account for the downfall of the lost race.

'It has always been assumed that we should never know anything of the physical form of the creatures who lived on Planet Three. For centuries our artists have been depicting scenes from the history of the dead world, peopling it with

all manner of fantastic beings. Most of these creations have
resembled us more or less closely, though it has often been
pointed out that because we are reptiles it does not follow
that all intelligent life must necessarily be reptilian. We now
know the answer to one of the most baffling problems of
history. At last, after five hundred years of research, we have
discovered the exact form and nature of the ruling life on
the Third Planet.'

There was a murmur of astonishment from the assembled
scientists. Some were so taken aback that they disappeared
for a while into the comfort of the ocean, as all Venusians
were apt to do in moments of stress. The Historian waited
until his colleagues re-emerged into the element they so disliked. He himself was quite comfortable, thanks to tiny
sprays that were continually playing over his body. With
their help he could live on land for many hours before having to return to the ocean.

The excitement slowly subsided, and the lecturer continued.

'One of the most puzzling of the objects found on Planet
Three was a flat metal container holding a great length of
transparent plastic material, perforated at the edges and
wound tightly into a spool. This transparent tape at first
seemed quite featureless, but an examination with the new
sub-electronic microscope has shown that this is not the case.
Along the surface of the material, invisible to our eyes but
perfectly clear under the correct radiation, are literally
thousands of tiny pictures. It is believed that they were im-
printed on the material by some chemical means, and have
faded with the passage of time.

'These pictures apparently form a record of life as it was
on the Third Planet at the height of its civilization. They
are not independent; consecutive pictures are almost identical, differing only in the detail of movement. The purpose
of such a record is obvious : it is only necessary to project
the scenes in rapid succession to give an illusion of continuous movement. We have made a machine to do this, and

I have here an exact reproduction of the picture sequence.

'The scenes you are now going to witness take us back many thousands of years to the great days of our sister planet. They show a very complex civilization, many of whose activities we can only dimly understand. Life seems to have been very violent and energetic, and much that you will see is quite baffling.

'It is clear that the Third Planet was inhabited by a number of different species, none of them reptilian. That is a blow to our pride, but the conclusion is inescapable. The dominant type of life appears to have been a two-armed biped. It walked upright and covered its body with some flexible material, possibly for protection against the cold, since even before the Ice Age the planet was at a much lower temperature than our own world.

'But I will not try your patience any further. You will now see the record of which I have been speaking.'

A brilliant light flashed from the projector. There was a gentle whirring, and on the screen appeared hundreds of strange beings moving rather jerkily to and fro. The picture expanded to embrace one of the creatures, and the scientists could see that the Historian's description had been correct. The creature possessed two eyes, set rather closely together, but the other facial adornments were a little obscure. There was a large orifice in the lower portion of the head that was continually opening and closing; possibly it had something to do with the creature's breathing.

The scientists watched spellbound as the strange beings became involved in a series of fantastic adventures. There was an incredibly violent conflict with another, slightly different, creature. It seemed certain that they must both be killed – but no; when it was all over neither seemed any the worse. Then came a furious drive over miles of country in a four-wheeled mechanical device which was capable of extraordinary feats of locomotion. The ride ended in a city packed with other vehicles moving in all directions at breathtaking speeds. No one was surprised to see two of the machines meet head-on, with devastating results.

After that, events became even more complicated. It was now quite obvious that it would take many years of research to analyse and understand all that was happening. It was also clear that the record was a work of art, somewhat stylized, rather than an exact reproduction of life as it actually had been on the Third Planet.

Most of the scientists felt themselves completely dazed when the sequence of pictures came to an end. There was a final flurry of motion, in which the creature that had been the centre of interest became involved in some tremendous but incomprehensible catastrophe. The picture contracted to a circle, centred on the creature's head. The last scene of all was an expanded view of its face, obviously expressing some powerful emotion, but whether it was rage, grief, defiance, resignation or some other feeling could not be guessed.

The picture vanished. For a moment some lettering appeared on the screen; then it was all over.

For several minutes there was complete silence, save for the lapping of the waves on the sand. The scientists were too stunned to speak. The fleeting glimpse of Earth's civilization had had a shattering effect on their minds. Then little groups began to start talking together, first in whispers and then more loudly as the implications of what they had seen became clearer. Presently the Historian called for attention and addressed the meeting again.

'We are now planning,' he began, 'a vast programme of research to extract all available knowledge from the record. Thousands of copies are being made for distribution to all workers. You will appreciate the problems involved; the psychologists in particular have an immense task confronting them. But I do not doubt that we shall succeed. In another generation, who can say what we may not have learned of this wonderful race? Before we leave, let us look again at our remote cousins, whose wisdom may have surpassed our own but of whom so little has survived.'

Once more the final picture flashed on the screen, motionless this time, for the projector had been stopped. With something like awe, the scientists gazed at the still figure from the past, while in turn the little biped stared back at them with its characteristic expression of arrogant bad temper.

For the rest of Time it would symbolize the human race. The psychologists of Venus would analyse its actions and watch its every movement until they could reconstruct its mind. Thousands of books would be written about it. Intricate philosophies would be contrived to account for its behaviour. But all this labour, all this research, would be utterly in vain.

Perhaps the proud and lonely figure on the screen was smiling sardonically at the scientists who were starting on their age-long, fruitless quest. Its secret would be safe as long as the Universe endured, for no one now would ever read the lost language of Earth. Millions of times in the ages to come those last few words would flash across the screen, and none could ever guess their meaning :

A Walt Disney Production.

SUPERIORITY

In making this statement – which I do of my own free will – I wish to make it perfectly clear that I am not in any way trying to gain sympathy, nor do I expect any mitigation of whatever sentence the Court may pronounce. I am writing this in an attempt to refute some of the lying reports published in the papers I have been allowed to see, and broadcast over the prison radio. These have given an entirely false picture of the true cause of our defeat, and as the leader of my race's armed forces at the cessation of hostilities I feel it my duty to protest against such libels upon those who served under me.

I also hope that this statement may explain the reasons for the application I have twice made to the Court, and will now induce it to grant a favour for which I can see no possible grounds of refusal.

The ultimate cause of our failure was a simple one: despite all statements to the contrary, it was not due to lack of bravery on the part of our men, or to any fault of the Fleet's. We were defeated by one thing only – by the inferior science of our enemies. I repeat – by the *inferior* science of our enemies.

When the war opened we had no doubts of our ultimate victory. The combined fleets of our allies greatly exceeded in number and armament those which the enemy could muster against us, and in almost all branches of military science we were their superiors. We were sure that we could maintain this superiority. Our belief proved, alas, to be only too well founded.

At the opening of the war our main weapons were the long-range homing torpedo, dirigible ball-lightning and the various modifications of the Klydon beam. Every unit of the Fleet was equipped with these and though the enemy pos-

sessed similar weapons their installations were generally of
lesser power. Moreover, we had behind us a far greater military Research Organization, and with this initial advantage
we could not possibly lose.

The campaign proceeded according to plan until the
Battle of the Five Suns. We won this, of course, but the opposition proved stronger than we had expected. It was realized
that victory might be more difficult, and more delayed, than
had first been imagined. A conference of supreme commanders was therefore called to discuss our future strategy.

Present for the first time at one of our war conferences was
Professor-General Norden, the new chief of the Research
Staff, who had just been appointed to fill the gap left by the
death of Malvar, our greatest scientist. Malvar's leadership
had been responsible, more than any other single factor, for
the efficiency and power of our weapons. His loss was a very
serious blow, but no one doubted the brilliance of his successor – though many of us disputed the wisdom of appoint-
ing a theoretical scientist to fill a post of such vital importance. But we had been overruled.

I can well remember the impression Norden made at that
conference. The military advisers were worried, and as usual
turned to the scientists for help. Would it be possible to improve our existing weapons, they asked, so that our present
advantage could be increased still further?

Norden's reply was quite unexpected. Malvar had often
been asked such a question – and he had always done what
we requested.

'Frankly, gentlemen,' said Norden, 'I doubt it. Our existing weapons have practically reached finality. I don't wish
to criticize my predecessor, or the excellent work done by the
Research Staff in the last few generations, but do you realize
that there has been no basic change in armaments for over a
century? It is, I am afraid, the result of a tradition that has
become conservative. For too long, the Research Staff has
devoted itself to perfecting old weapons instead of developing new ones. It is fortunate for us that our opponents have

been no wiser : we cannot assume that this will always be so.'

Norden's words left an uncomfortable impression, as he had no doubt intended. He quickly pressed home the attack.

'What we want now are *new* weapons – weapons totally different from any that have been employed before. Such weapons can be made : it will take time, of course, but since assuming charge I have replaced some of the older scientists by young men and have directed research into several unexplored fields which show great promise. I believe, in fact, that a revolution in warfare may soon be upon us.'

We were sceptical. There was a bombastic tone in Norden's voice that made us suspicious of his claims. We did not know, then, that he never promised anything that he had not already perfected in the laboratory. *In the laboratory* – that was the operative phrase.

Norden proved his case less than a month later, when he demonstrated the Sphere of Annihilation, which produced complete disintegration of matter over a radius of several hundred metres. We were intoxicated by the power of the new weapon, and were quite prepared to overlook one fundamental defect – the fact that it *was* a sphere and hence destroyed its rather complicated generating equipment at the instant of formation. This meant, of course, that it could not be used on warships but only on guided missiles, and a great programme was started to convert all homing torpedoes to carry the new weapon. For the time being all further offensives were suspended.

We realize now that this was our first mistake. I still think that it was a natural one, for it seemed to us then that all our existing weapons had become obsolete overnight, and we already regarded them almost as primitive survivals. What we did not appreciate was the magnitude of the task we were attempting and the length of time it would take to get the revolutionary super-weapon into battle. Nothing like this had happened for a hundred years and we had no previous experience to guide us.

The conversion problem proved far more difficult than

anticipated. A new class of torpedo had to be designed, as the standard model was too small. This meant in turn that only the larger ships could launch the weapon, but we were prepared to accept this penalty. After six months, the heavy units of the Fleet were being equipped with the Sphere. Training manoeuvres and tests had shown that it was operating satisfactorily and we were ready to take it into action. Norden was already being hailed as the architect of victory, and had half-promised even more spectacular weapons.

Then two things happened. One of our battleships disappeared completely on a training flight, and an investigation showed that under certain conditions the ship's long-range radar could trigger the Sphere immediately it had been launched. The modification needed to overcome this defect was trivial, but it caused a delay of another month and was the source of much bad feeling between the naval staff and the scientists. We were ready for action again – when Norden announced that the radius of effectiveness of the Sphere had now been increased by ten, thus multiplying by a thousand the chances of destroying an enemy ship.

So the modifications started all over again, but everyone agreed that the delay would be worth it. Meanwhile, however, the enemy had been emboldened by the absence of further attacks and had made an unexpected onslaught. Our ships were short of torpedoes, since none had been coming from the factories, and were forced to retire. So we lost the systems of Kyrane and Floranus, and the planetary fortress of Rhamsandron.

It was an annoying but not a serious blow, for the recaptured systems had been unfriendly and difficult to administer. We had no doubt that we could restore the position in the near future, as soon as the new weapon became operational.

These hopes were only partially fulfilled. When we renewed our offensive, we had to do so with fewer of the Spheres of Annihilation than had been planned, and this was one reason for our limited success. The other reason was more serious.

While we had been equipping as many of our ships as we could with the irresistible weapon, the enemy had been building feverishly. His ships were of the old pattern, with the old weapons – but they outnumbered ours. When we went into action, we found that the numbers ranged against us were often 100 per cent greater than expected, causing target confusion among the automatic weapons and resulting in higher losses than anticipated. The enemy losses were higher still, for once a Sphere had reached its objective, destruction was certain, but the balance had not swung as far in our favour as we had hoped.

Moreover, while the main fleets had been engaged, the enemy had launched a daring attack on the lightly held systems of Eriston, Duranus, Carmanidor and Pharanidon – recapturing them all. We were thus faced with a threat only fifty light-years from our home planets.

There was much recrimination at the next meeting of the supreme commanders. Most of the complaints were addressed to Norden – Grand Admiral Taxaris in particular maintaining that thanks to our admittedly irresistible weapon we were now considerably worse off than before. We should, he claimed, have continued to build conventional ships, thus preventing the loss of our numerical superiority.

Norden was equally angry and called the naval staff ungrateful bunglers. But I could tell that he was worried – as indeed we all were – by the unexpected turn of events. He hinted that there might be a speedy way of remedying the situation. We now know that Research had been working on the Battle Analyser for many years, but at the time it came as a revelation to us and perhaps we were too easily swept off our feet. Norden's argument, also, was seductively convincing. What did it matter, he said, if the enemy had twice as many ships as we – if the efficiency of ours could be doubled or even trebled? For decades the limiting factor in warfare had been not mechanical but biological – it had become more and more difficult for any single mind, or group of minds, to cope with the rapidly changing complexities of battle in three-dimensional space. Norden's mathematicians had analysed some of the classic engagements of the past, and had shown that even when we had been victorious we had often operated our units at much less than half of their theoretical efficiency.

The Battle Analyser would change all this by replacing operations staff by electronic calculators. The idea was not new in theory, but until now it had been no more than a Utopian dream. Many of us found it difficult to believe that it was still anything but a dream : after we had run through several very complex dummy battles, however, we were convinced.

It was decided to install the Analyser in four of our heaviest ships, so that each of the main fleets could be equipped with one. At this stage, the trouble began – though we did not know it until later.

The Analyser contained just short of a million vacuum tubes and needed a team of five hundred technicians to maintain and operate it. It was quite impossible to accommodate the extra staff aboard a battleship, so each of the four units had to be accompanied by a converted liner to carry the technicians not on duty. Installation was also a very slow and tedious business, but by gigantic efforts it was completed in six months.

Then, to our dismay, we were confronted by another crisis. Nearly five thousand highly skilled men had been selected to service the Analysers and had been given an intensive course at the Technical Training Schools. At the end of seven months, 10 per cent of them had had nervous breakdowns and only 40 per cent had qualified.

Once again, everyone started to blame everyone else. Norden, of course, said that the Research Staff could not be held responsible, and so incurred the enmity of the Personnel and Training Commands. It was finally decided that the only thing to do was to use two instead of four Analysers and to bring the others into action as soon as men could be trained. There was little time to lose, for the enemy was still on the offensive and his morale was rising.

The first Analyser fleet was ordered to recapture the system of Eriston. On the way, by one of the hazards of war, the liner carrying the technicians was struck by a roving mine. A warship would have survived, but the liner with its irreplaceable cargo was totally destroyed. So the operation had to be abandoned.

The other expedition was, at first, more successful. There was no doubt at all that the Analyser fulfilled its designers' claims, and the enemy was heavily defeated in the first engagements. He withdrew, leaving us in possession of Saphran, Leucon and Hexanerax. But his Intelligence Staff must have noted the change in our tactics and the inexplicable presence of a liner in the heart of our battle-fleet. It must have noted, also, that our first fleet had been accompanied by a similar ship – and had withdrawn when it had been destroyed.

In the next engagement, the enemy used his superior numbers to launch an overwhelming attack on the Analyser ship and its unarmed consort. The attack was made without regard to losses – both ships were, of course, very heavily protected – and it succeeded. The result was the virtual decapitation of the fleet, since an effectual transfer to the old operational methods proved impossible. We disengaged under heavy fire, and so lost all our gains and also the systems of Lorymia, Ismarnus, Beronis, Alphanidon and Sideneus.

At this stage, Grand Admiral Taxaris expressed his disapproval of Norden by committing suicide, and I assumed supreme command.

The situation was now both serious and infuriating. With stubborn conservatism and complete lack of imagination, the enemy continued to advance with his old-fashioned and inefficient but now vastly more numerous ships. It was galling to realize that if we had only continued building, without seeking new weapons, we would have been in a far more advantageous position. There were many acrimonious conferences at which Norden defended the scientists while every-one else blamed them for all that had happened. The difficulty was that Norden had proved every one of his claims; he had a perfect excuse for all the disasters that had occurred. And we could not now turn back – the search for an irresistible weapon must go on. At first it had been a luxury that would shorten the war. Now it was a necessity if we were to end it victoriously.

We were on the defensive, and so was Norden. He was more than ever determined to re-establish his prestige and that of the Research Staff. But we had been twice disap-pointed, and would not make the same mistake again. No doubt Norden's twenty thousand scientists would produce many further weapons : we would remain unimpressed.

We were wrong. The final weapon was something so fan-tastic that even now it seems difficult to believe that it ever existed. Its innocent, non-committal name – the Exponential Field – gave no hint of its real potentialities. Some of Nor-den's mathematicians had discovered it during a piece of entirely theoretical research into the properties of space, and to everyone's great surprise their results were found to be physically realizable.

It seems very difficult to explain the operation of the Field to the layman. According to the technical description, it 'produces an exponential condition of space, so that a finite distance in normal, linear space may become infinite in pseudo-space'. Norden gave an analogy which some of us found useful. It was as if one took a flat disk of rubber – representing a region of normal space – and then pulled its centre out to infinity. The circumference of the disk would be unaltered – but its 'diameter' would be infinite. That was the sort of thing the generator of the Field did to the space around it.

As an example, suppose that a ship carrying the generator was surrounded by a ring of hostile machines. If it switched on the Field, *each* of the enemy ships would think that it – and the ships on the far side of the circle – had suddenly receded into nothingness. Yet the circumference of the circle would be the same as before : only the journey to the centre would be of infinite duration, for as one proceeded, distances would appear to become greater and greater as the 'scale' of space altered.

It was a nightmare condition, but a very useful one. Nothing could reach a ship carrying the Field : it might be englobed by an enemy fleet yet would be as inaccessible as if it were at the other side of the Universe. Against this, of course, it could not fight back without switching off the Field, but this still left it at a very great advantage, not only in defence but in offence. For a ship fitted with the Field could approach an enemy fleet undetected and suddenly appear in its midst.

This time there seemed to be no flaws in the new weapon. Needless to say, we looked for all the possible objections before we committed ourselves again. Fortunately the equipment was fairly simple and did not require a large operating staff. After much debate, we decided to rush it into production, for we realized that time was running short and the war was going against us. We had now lost almost the whole of our initial gains and the enemy forces had made several raids into our own Solar System.

We managed to hold off the enemy while the Fleet was re-equipped and the new battle techniques were worked out. To use the Field operationally it was necessary to locate an enemy formation, set a course that would intercept it, and then switch on the generator for the calculated period of time. On releasing the Field again – if the calculations had been accurate – one would be in the enemy's midst and could do great damage during the resulting confusion, retreating by the same route when necessary.

The first trial manoeuvres proved satisfactory and the equipment seemed quite reliable. Numerous mock attacks were made and the crews became accustomed to the new technique. I was on one of the test flights and can vividly remember my impressions as the Field was switched on. The ships around us seemed to dwindle as if on the surface of an

expanding bubble : in an instant they had vanished completely. So had the stars – but presently we could see that
the Galaxy was still visible as a faint band of light around the
ship. The virtual radius of our pseudo-space was not really
infinite, but some hundred thousand light-years, and so the
distance to the farthest stars of our system had not been
greatly increased – though the nearest had of course totally
disappeared.

These training manoeuvres, however, had to be cancelled
before they were complete owing to a whole flock of minor
technical troubles in various pieces of equipment, notably
the communications circuits. These were annoying, but not
important, though it was thought best to return to Base to
clear them up.

At that moment the enemy made what was obviously
intended to be a decisive attack against the fortress planet
of Iton at the limits of our Solar System. The Fleet had to
go into battle before repairs could be made.

The enemy must have believed that we had mastered the
secret of invisibility – as in a sense we had. Our ships
appeared suddenly out of nowhere and inflicted tremendous
damage – for a while. And then something quite baffling
and inexplicable happened.

I was in command of the flag-ship *Hircania* when the
trouble started. We had been operating as independent units,
each against assigned objectives. Our detectors observed an
enemy formation at medium range and the navigating offi-
cers measured its distance with great accuracy. We set course
and switched on the generator.

The Exponential Field was released at the moment when
we should have been passing through the centre of the
enemy group. To our consternation, we emerged into normal
space at a distance of many hundred miles – and when we
found the enemy, he had already found us. We retreated,
and tried again. This time we were so far away from the
enemy that he located us first.

Obviously, something was seriously wrong. We broke

communicator silence and tried to contact the other ships of the Fleet to see if they had experienced the same trouble. Once again we failed – and this time the failure was beyond all reason, for the communication equipment appeared to be working perfectly. We could only assume, fantastic though it seemed, that the rest of the Fleet had been destroyed.

I do not wish to describe the scenes when the scattered units of the Fleet struggled back to Base. Our casualties had actually been negligible, but the ships were completely de-moralized. Almost all had lost touch with each other and had found that their ranging equipment showed inexplic-able errors. It was obvious that the Exponential Field was the cause of the troubles, despite the fact that they were only apparent when it was switched off.

The explanation came too late to do us any good, and Norden's final discomfiture was small consolation for the virtual loss of the war. As I have explained, the Field genera-tors produced a radial distortion of space, distances appear-ing greater and greater as one approached the centre of the artificial pseudo-space. When the field was switched off, conditions returned to normal.

But not quite. It was never possible to restore the initial state *exactly*. Switching the Field on and off was equivalent to an elongation and contraction of the ship carrying the generator, but there was an hysteresis effect, as it were, and the initial condition was never quite reproducible, owing to all the thousands of electrical changes and movements of mass aboard the ship while the Field was on. These asym-metries and distortions were cumulative, and though they seldom amounted to more than a fraction of one per cent, that was quite enough. It meant that the precision ranging equipment and the tuned circuits in the communication apparatus were thrown completely out of adjustment. Any single ship could never detect the change – only when it compared its equipment with that of another vessel, or tried to communicate with it, could it tell what had happened.

It is impossible to describe the resultant chaos. Not a single component of one ship could be expected with certainty to work aboard another. The very nuts and bolts were no longer interchangeable, and the supply position became quite impossible. Given time, we might even have overcome these difficulties, but the enemy ships were already attacking in thousands with weapons which now seemed centuries behind those that we had invented. Our magnificent Fleet, crippled by our own science, fought on as best it could until it was overwhelmed and forced to surrender. The ships fitted with the Field were still invulnerable, but as fighting units they were almost helpless. Every time they switched on their generators to escape from enemy attack, the permanent distortion of their equipment increased. In a month, it was all over.

This is the true story of our defeat, which I give without prejudice to my defence before this Court. I make it, as I have said, to counteract the libels that have been circulating against the men who fought under me, and to show where the true blame for our misfortunes lay.

Finally, my request, which as the Court will now realize I make in no frivolous manner and which I hope will therefore be granted.

The Court will be aware that the conditions under which we are housed and the constant surveillance to which we are subjected night and day are somewhat distressing. Yet I am not complaining of this : nor do I complain of the fact that shortage of accommodation has made it necessary to house us in pairs.

But I cannot be held responsible for my future actions if I am compelled any longer to share my cell with Professor Norden, late Chief of the Research Staff of my armed forces.

NEMESIS

ALREADY the mountains were trembling with the thunder that only man can make. But here the war seemed very far away, for the full moon hung over the ageless Himalayas and the furies of the battle were still hidden below the edge of the world. Not for long would they so remain. The Master knew that the last remnants of his fleet were being hurled from the sky as the circle of death closed in upon his stronghold.

In a few hours at the most, the Master and his dreams of empire would have vanished into the maelstrom of the past. Nations would still curse his name, but they would no longer fear it. Later, even the hatred would be gone and he would mean no more to the world than Hitler or Napoleon or Genghis Khan. Like them he would be a blurred figure far down the infinite corridor of time, dwindling towards oblivion. For a little while his name would dwell in the uncertain land between history and fable; then the world would think of him no more. He would be one with the nameless legions who had died to work his will.

Far to the south, a mountain suddenly edged with violet flame. Ages later, the balcony on which the Master stood shuddered beneath the impact of the ground-wave racing through the rocks below. Later still, the air brought the echo of a mammoth concussion. Surely they could not be so close already! The Master hoped it was no more than a stray torpedo that had swept through the contracting battle line. If it were not, time was even shorter than he feared.

The Chief of Staff walked out from the shadows and joined him by the rail. The Marshal's hard face – the second most hated in all the world – was lined and beaded with sweat. He had not slept for days and his once gaudy uniform hung limply upon him. Yet his eyes, though unutterably weary, were still resolute even in defeat. He stood in silence, awaiting his last orders. Nothing else was left for him to do.

Thirty miles away, the eternal snow-plume of Everest flamed a lurid red, reflecting the glare of some colossal fire below the horizon. Still the Master neither moved nor gave any sign. Not until a salvo of torpedoes passed high over-head with a demon wail did he at last turn and, with one backward glance at the world he would see no more, descend into the depths.

The lift dropped a thousand feet and the sound of battle died away. As he stepped out of the shaft, the Master paused for a moment to press a hidden switch. The Marshal even smiled when he heard the crash of falling rock far above, and knew that both pursuit and escape were equally impossible.

As of old, the handful of generals sprang to their feet when the Master entered the room. He ran his eyes round the table. They were all there; even at the last there had been no traitors. He walked to his accustomed place in silence, steeling himself for the last and the hardest speech he would ever have to make. Burning into his soul he could feel the eyes of the men he had led to ruin. Behind and be-yond them he could see the squadrons, the divisions, the armies whose blood was on his hands. And more terrible still were the silent spectres of the nations that now could never be born.

At last he began to speak. The hypnosis of his voice was as powerful as ever, and after a few words he became once more the perfect, implacable machine whose destiny was destruction.

'This, gentlemen, is the last of all our meetings. There are no more plans to make, no more maps to study. Somewhere above our heads the fleet we built with such pride and care is fighting to the end. In a few minutes, not one of all those thousands of machines will be left in the sky.

'I know that for all of us here surrender is unthinkable, even if it were possible, so in this room you will shortly have to die. You have served our cause well and deserved better, but it was not to be. Yet I do not wish you to think that we have wholly failed. In the past, as you saw many times, my plans were always ready for anything that might arise, no matter how improbable. You should not, therefore, be surprised to learn that I was prepared even for defeat.'

Still the same superb orator, he paused for effect, noting with satisfaction the ripple of interest, the sudden alertness on the tired faces of his listeners.

'My secret is safe enough with you,' he continued, 'for the enemy will never find this place. The entrance is already blocked by hundreds of feet of rock.'

Still there was no movement. Only the Director of Propaganda turned suddenly white, and swiftly recovered -- but not swiftly enough to escape the Master's eye. The Master smiled inwardly at this belated confirmation of an old doubt. It mattered little now; true and false, they would all die together. All but one.

'Two years ago,' he went on, 'when we lost the battle of Antarctica, I knew that we could no longer be certain of victory. So I made my preparations for this day. The enemy has already sworn to kill me. I could not remain in hiding anywhere on the earth, still less hope to rebuild our fortunes. But there is another way, though a desperate one.

'Five years ago, one of our scientists perfected the technique of suspended animation. He found that by relatively simple means all life processes could be arrested for an indefinite period. I am going to use this discovery to escape from the present into a future which will have forgotten me. There I can begin the struggle again, not without the help of certain devices that might yet have won this war had we been granted more time.

'Good-bye, gentlemen. And once again, my thanks for your help and my regrets at your ill fortune.'

He saluted, turned on his heels, and was gone. The metal door thudded decisively behind him. There was a frozen silence; then the Director of Propaganda rushed to the exit, only to recoil with a startled cry. The steel door was already too hot to touch. It had been welded immovably into the wall.

The Minister for War was the first to draw his automatic.

The Master was in no great hurry, now. On leaving the council room he had thrown the secret switch of the welding circuit. The same action had opened a panel in the wall of the corridor, revealing a small circular passage sloping steadily upwards. He began to walk slowly along it.

Every few hundred feet the tunnel angled sharply, though still continuing the upward climb. At each turning the Master stopped to throw a switch, and there was the thunder of falling rock as a section of corridor collapsed.

Five times the passageway changed its course before it ended in a spherical, metal-walled room. Multiple doors closed softly on rubber seatings, and the last section of tunnel crashed behind. The Master would not be disturbed by his enemies, nor by his friends.

He looked swiftly round the room to satisfy himself that all was ready. Then he walked to a simple control-board and threw, one after another, a set of peculiarly massive switches. They had to carry little current – but they had been built to last. So had everything in that strange room. Even the walls were made of metals far less ephemeral than steel.

Pumps started to whine, drawing the air from the chamber and replacing it with sterile nitrogen. Moving more swiftly now, the Master went to the padded couch and lay down. He thought he could feel himself bathed by the bacteria-destroying rays from the lamps above his head, but that of course was fancy. From a recess beneath the couch he drew a hypodermic and injected a milky fluid into his arm. Then he relaxed and waited.

It was already very cold. Soon the refrigerators would bring the temperature down far below freezing, and would hold it there for many hours. Then it would rise to normal, but by that time the process would be completed, all bacteria would be dead and the Master could sleep, unchanged, for ever.

He had planned to wait a hundred years. More than that he dared not delay, for when he awoke he would have to master all the changes in science and society that the passing years had wrought. Even a century might have altered the face of civilization beyond his understanding, but that was a risk he would have to take. Less than a century would not be safe, for the world would still be full of bitter memories.

Sealed in a vacuum beneath the couch were three electronic counters operated by thermocouples hundreds of feet above on the eastern face of the mountain where no snow could ever cling. Every day the rising sun would operate them and the counters would add one unit to their store. So the coming of dawn would be noted in the darkness where the Master slept.

When any one of the counters reached the total of thirty-six thousand, a switch would close and oxygen would flow back into the chamber. The temperature would rise, and the automatic hypodermic strapped to the Master's arm would inject the calculated amount of fluid. He would awaken, and only the counters would tell him that the century had really passed. Then all he need do would be to press the button which would blast away the mountainside and give him free passage to the outer world.

Everything had been considered. There could be no failure. All the machinery had been triplicated and was as perfect as science could contrive.

The Master's last thought as consciousness ebbed was not of his past life, nor of the mother whose hopes he had betrayed. Unbidden and unwelcome, there came into his mind the words of an ancient poet :

'To sleep, perchance to dream —'

No, he would not, dared not dream. He would only sleep. Sleep — sleep —

Twenty miles away, the battle was coming to its end. Not a dozen of the Master's ships were left, fighting hopelessly against overwhelming fire. The action would have ended long ago had the attackers not been ordered to risk no ships in unnecessary adventures. The decision was to be left to the long-range artillery. So the great destroyers, the airborne battleships of this age, lay with their fighter screens in the shelter of the mountains, pouring salvo after salvo into the doomed formations.

Aboard the flagship, a young Hindu gunnery officer set vernier dials with infinite accuracy and gently pressed a pedal with his foot. There was the faintest of shocks as the dirigible torpedoes left their cradles and hurled themselves at the enemy. The young Indian sat waiting tensely as the chronometer ticked off the seconds. This, he thought, was probably the last salvo he would fire. Somehow he felt none of the elation he had expected; indeed, he was surprised to discover a kind of impersonal sympathy for his doomed opponents, whose lives were now ebbing with every passing second.

Far away a sphere of violet fire blossomed above the mountains, among the darting specks that were the enemy ships. The gunner leaned forward tensely and counted. One – two – three – four – five times came that peculiar explosion. Then the sky cleared. The struggling specks were gone.

In his log, the gunner noted briefly : '0124 hrs. Salvo No. 12 fired. Five torps exploded among enemy ships, which were totally destroyed. One torp failed to detonate.'

He signed the entry with a flourish and laid down his pen. For a while he sat staring at the log's familiar brown cover, with the cigarette-burns at the edges and the inevitable stained rings where cups and glasses had been carelessly set down. Idly he thumbed through the leaves, noting once again the handwriting of his many predecessors. And as he had done so often before, he turned to a familiar page where a man who had once been his friend had begun to sign his name but had never lived to complete it.

With a sigh, he closed the book and locked it away. The war was over.

Far away among the mountains, the torpedo that had failed to explode was still gaining speed under the drive of its rockets. Now it was a scarcely visible line of light, racing between the walls of a lonely valley. Already the snows that had been disturbed by the scream of its passage were beginning to rumble down the mountain slopes.

There was no escape from the valley : it was blocked by a sheer wall a thousand feet high. Here the torpedo that had missed its mark found a greater one. The Master's tomb was too deep in the mountain even to be shaken by the explosion, but the hundreds of tons of falling rock swept away three tiny instruments and their connections, and a future that might have been went with them into oblivion. The first rays of the rising sun would still fall on the shattered faces of the mountain, but the counters that were waiting for the thirty-six-thousandth dawn would still be waiting when dawns and sunsets were no more.

In the silence of the tomb that was not quite a tomb, the Master knew nothing of this, and his face was more peaceful than it had any right to be. So the century passed, as he had planned. It is not likely that, for all his evil genius and the secrets he had buried with him, the Master could have conquered the civilization that had come to flower since that final battle above the roof of the world. No one can say, unless it is indeed true that time has many branches and that all imaginable universes lie side by side, merging one into the other. Perhaps in some of those other worlds the Master might have triumphed. But in the one we know he slumbered on, until the century was far behind – very far indeed.

After what by some standards would have been a little while, the earth's crust decided that it had borne the weight of the Himalayas for long enough. Slowly the mountains dropped, tilting the southern plains of India towards the sky. And presently the plateau of Ceylon was the highest point on the surface of the globe, and the ocean above

Everest was five and a half miles deep. Yet the Master's slumber was still dreamless and undisturbed.

Slowly, patiently, the silt drifted down through the towering ocean heights on to the wreck of tne Himalayas. The blanket that would one day be chalk began to thicken at the rate of an inch or two every century. If one had returned some time later one might have found that the sea-bed was no longer five miles down, or even four, or three. Then the land tilted again, and a mighty range of limestone mountains towered where once had been the oceans of Tibet. But the Master knew nothing of this, nor was his sleep troubled when it happened again – and again – and yet again.

Now the rain and the rivers were washing away the chalk and carrying it out to the strange new oceans, and the surface was moving down towards the hidden tomb. Slowly the miles of rock were winnowed away until at last the sphere which housed the Master's body returned to the light of day – though to a day much longer, and much dimmer, than it had been when the Master closed his eyes.

Little did the Master dream of the races that had flowered and died since that early morning of the world when he went to his long sleep. Very far away was that morning now, and the shadows were lengthening to the east : the sun was dying and the world was very old. But still the children of Adam ruled its seas and skies, and filled with their tears and laughter the plains and the valleys and the woods that were older than the shifting hills.

The Master's dreamless sleep was more than half ended when Trevindor the Philosopher was born, between the fall of the Ninety-seventh Dynasty and the rise of the Fifth Galactic Empire. He was born on a world very far from Earth, for few were the men who ever set foot on the ancient home of their race, now so distant from the throbbing heart of the Universe.

They brought Trevindor to Earth when his brief clash with the Empire had come to its inevitable end. Here he was tried by the men whose ideals he had challenged, and here it was that they pondered long over the manner of his fate. The case was unique. The gentle, philosophic culture that now ruled the Galaxy had never before met with opposition, even on the level of pure intellect, and the polite but implacable conflict of wills had left it severely shaken. It was typical of the Council's members that, when a decision had proved impossible, they appealed to Trevindor himself for help.

In the whitely gleaming Hall of Justice, that had not been entered for nigh on a million years, Trevindor stood proudly facing the men who had proved stronger than he. In silence he listened to their request; then he paused in reflection. His judges waited patiently until he spoke.

'You suggest that I should promise not to defy you again,' he began, 'but I shall make no promise that I may be unable to keep. Our views are too divergent and sooner or later we should clash again.

'There was a time when your choice would have been easy. You could have exiled me, or put me to death. But today – where among all the worlds of the Universe is there one planet where you could hide me if I did not choose to stay? Remember, I have many disciples scattered the length and breadth of the Galaxy.

'There remains the other alternative. I shall bear you no malice if you revive the ancient custom of execution to meet my case.'

There was a murmur of annoyance from the Council, and the President replied sharply, his colour heightening, 'That remark is in somewhat questionable taste. We asked for serious suggestions, not reminders – even if intended humorously – of the barbaric customs of our remote ancestors.'

Trevindor accepted the rebuke with a bow. 'I was merely mentioning all the possibilities. There are two others that have occurred to me. It would be a simple matter to change my mind pattern to your way of thinking so that no future disagreement can arise.'

'We have already considered that. We were forced to reject it, attractive though it is, for the destruction of your personality would be equivalent to murder. There are only fifteen more powerful intellects than yours in the Universe, and we have no right to tamper with it. And your final suggestion?'

'Though you cannot exile me in space, there is still one alternative. The river of Time stretches ahead of us as far as our thoughts can go. Send me down that stream to an age when you are certain this civilization will have passed. That I know you can do with the aid of the Roston time-field.'

There was a long pause. In silence the members of the Council were passing their decisions to the complex analysis machine which would weigh them one against the other and arrive at the verdict. At length the President spoke.

'It is agreed. We will send you to an age when the Sun is still warm enough for life to exist on the Earth, but so remote that any trace of our civilization is unlikely to survive. We will also provide you with everything necessary for your safety and reasonable comfort. You may leave us now. We will call for you again when all arrangements have been .made.'

Trevindor bowed, and left the marble hall. No guards followed him. There was nowhere he could flee, even if he wished, in this Universe which the great Galactic liners could span in a single day.

For the first and last time, Trevindor stood on the shore of what had once been the Pacific, listening to the wind sighing through the leaves of what had once been palms. The few stars of the nearly empty region of space through which the Sun was now passing shone with a steady light through the dry air of the ageing world. Trevindor wondered bleakly if they would still be shining when he looked again upon the sky, in a future so distant that the Sun itself would be sinking to its death.

There was a tinkle from the tiny communicator band upon his wrist. So, the time had come. He turned his back

upon the ocean and walked resolutely to meet his fate. Before he had gone a dozen steps the time-field had seized him
and his thoughts froze in an instant that would remain unchanged while the oceans shrank and vanished; the Galactic
Empire passed away, and the great star-clusters crumbled
into nothingness.

But, to Trevindor, no time elapsed at all. He only knew
that at one step there had been moist sand beneath his feet,
and at the next hard-baked rock, cracked by heat and
drought. The palms had vanished, the murmur of the sea
was stilled. It needed only a glance to show that even the
memory of the sea had long since faded from this parched
and dying world. To the far horizon, a great desert of red
sandstone stretched unbroken and unrelieved by any growing thing. Overhead, the orange disk of a strangely altered
sun glowered from a sky so black that many stars were
clearly visible.

Yet, it seemed, there was still life on this ancient world.
To the north – if that were still the north – the sombre light
glinted upon some metallic structure. It was a few hundred
yards away, and as Trevindor started to walk towards it he
was conscious of a curious lightness, as if gravity itself had
weakened.

He had not gone far before he saw that he was approaching a low metal building which seemed to have been set
down on the plain rather than constructed there, for it was
at a slight angle to the horizontal. Trevindor wondered at
his incredible good fortune at finding civilization so easily.
Another dozen steps, and he realized that not chance but
design had so conveniently placed this building here, and
that it was as much a stranger to this world as he himself.
There was no hope at all that anyone would come to meet
him as he walked towards it.

The metal plaque above the door added little to what he
had already surmised. Still new and untarnished as if it had
just been engraved – as indeed, in a sense, it had – the lettering brought a message at once of hope and of bitterness.

To Trevindor, the greetings of the Council.

This building, which we have sent after you through the time-field, will supply all your needs for an indefinite period.

We do not know if civilization will still exist in the age in which you find yourself. Man may now be extinct, since the chromosome K Star K will have become dominant and the race may have mutated into something no longer human. That is for you to discover.

You are now in the twilight of the Earth and it is our hope that you are not alone. But if it is your destiny to be the last living creature on this once lovely world, remember that the choice was yours. Farewell.

Twice Trevindor read the message, recognizing with an ache the closing words which could only have been written by his friend, the poet Cintillarne. An overwhelming sense of loneliness and isolation came flooding into his soul. He sat down upon a shelf of rock and buried his face in his hands.

A long time later, he arose to enter the building. He felt more than grateful to the long-dead Council which had treated him so chivalrously. The technical achievement of sending an entire building through time was one he had believed beyond the resources of his age. A sudden thought struck him and he glanced again at the engraved lettering, noticing for the first time the date it bore. It was five thousand years later than the time when he had faced his peers in the Hall of Justice. Fifty centuries had passed before his judges could redeem their promise to a man as good as dead. Whatever the faults of the Council, its integrity was of an order beyond the comprehension of an earlier age.

Many days passed before Trevindor left the building again. Nothing had been overlooked: even his beloved thought records were there. He could continue to study the nature of reality and to construct philosophies until the end of the Universe, barren though that occupation would be if his were the only mind left on Earth. There was little danger, he thought wryly, that his speculations concerning the

8

purpose of human existence would once again bring him into conflict with society.

Not until he had investigated the building thoroughly did Trevindor turn his attention once more to the outer world. The supreme problem was that of contacting civilization, should such still exist. He had been provided with a powerful receiver, and for hours he wandered up and down the spectrum in the hope of discovering a station. The far-off crackle of static came from the instrument and once there was a burst of what might have been speech in a tongue that was certainly not human. But nothing else rewarded his search. The ether, which had been man's faithful servant for so many ages, was silent at last.

The little automatic flyer was Trevindor's sole remaining hope. He had what was left of eternity before him, and Earth was a small planet. In a few years, at the most, he could have explored it all.

So the months passed while the exile began his methodical exploration of the world, returning ever and again to his home in the desert of red sandstone. Everywhere he found the same picture of desolation and ruin. How long ago the seas had vanished he could not even guess, but in their dying they had left endless wastes of salt, encrusting both plains and mountains with a blanket of dirty grey. Trevindor felt glad that he had not been born on Earth and so had never known it in the glory of its youth. Stranger though he was, the loneliness and desolation of the world chilled his heart; had he lived here before, its sadness would have been unbearable.

Thousands of square miles of desert passed beneath Trevindor's fleeting ship as he searched the world from pole to pole. Only once did he find any sign that Earth had ever known civilization. In a deep valley near the equator he discovered the ruins of a small city of strange white stone and stranger architecture. The buildings were perfectly preserved though half-buried by the drifting sand, and for a moment Trevindor felt a surge of sombre joy at the know-

ledge that man had, after all, left some traces of his handiwork on the world that had been his first home.

The emotion was short-lived. The buildings were stranger
than Trevindor had realized, for no man could ever have
entered them. Their only openings were wide, horizontal
slots close to the ground; there were no windows of any
kind. Trevindor's mind reeled as he tried to imagine the
creatures that must have occupied them. In spite of his
growing loneliness, he felt glad that the dwellers in this
inhuman city had passed away so long before his time. He
did not linger here, for the bitter night was almost upon him
and the valley filled him with an oppression that was not
entirely rational.

And once, he actually discovered life. He was cruising
over the bed of one of the lost oceans when a flash of colour
caught his eye. Upon a knoll which the drifting sand had
not yet buried was a thin, wiry covering of grass. That was
all, but the sight brought tears to his eyes. He grounded the
machine and stepped out, treading warily lest he destroy
even one of the struggling blades. Tenderly he ran his hands
over the threadbare carpet which was all the life that Earth
now knew. Before he left, he sprinkled the spot with as much
water as he could spare. It was a futile gesture, but one
which he felt happier at having made.

The search was now nearly completed. Trevindor had
long ago given up all hope, but his indomitable spirit still
drove him on across the face of the world. He could not rest
until he had proved what as yet he only feared. And so it
was that he came at last to the Master's tomb as it lay
gleaming dully in the sunlight from which it had been
banished for so long.

The Master's mind awoke before his body. As he lay
powerless, unable to lift his eyelids, memory came flooding
back. The hundred years were safely behind him. His
gamble, the most desperate that any man had ever made,
had succeeded! An immense weariness came over him and

for a while consciousness faded once more.

Presently the mists cleared again and he felt stronger, though still too weak to move. He lay in the darkness gathering his strength together. What sort of a world, he wondered, would he find when he stepped forth from the mountainside into the light of day? Would he be able to put his plans into —? *What was that?* A spasm of sheer terror shook the very foundations of his mind. Something was moving beside him, here in the tomb where nothing should be stirring but himself.

Then, calm and clear, a thought rang serenely through his mind and quelled in an instant the fears that had threatened to overturn it.

'Do not be alarmed. I have come to help you. You are safe, and everything will be well.'

The Master was too stunned to make any reply, but his subconscious must have formulated some sort of answer, for the thought came again.

'That is good. I am Trevindor, like yourself an exile in this world. Do not move, but tell me how you came here and what is your race, for I have seen none like it.'

And now fear and caution were creeping back into the Master's mind. What manner of creature was this that could read his thoughts, and what was it doing in his secret sphere? Again that clear, cold thought echoed through his brain like the tolling of a bell.

'Once more I tell you that you have nothing to fear. Why are you alarmed because I can see into your mind? Surely there is nothing strange about that.'

'Nothing strange!' cried the Master. 'What are you, for God's sake?'

'A man like yourself. But your race must be primitive indeed if the reading of thoughts is strange to you.'

A terrible suspicion began to dawn in the Master's brain. The answer came even before he consciously framed the question.

'You have slept infinitely longer than a hundred years.

The world you knew has ceased to be for longer than you can imagine.'

The Master heard no more. Once again the darkness swept over him and he sank down into blissful unconsciousness.

In silence Trevindor stood beside the couch on which the Master lay. He was filled with an elation which for the moment outweighed any disappointment he might feel. At least, he would no longer have to face the future alone. All the terror of the Earth's loneliness, that was weighing so heavily upon his soul, had vanished in a moment. *No longer alone* . . . no longer alone! Dominating all else, the thought hammered through his brain.

The Master was beginning to stir once more, and into Trevindor's mind crept broken fragments of thought. Pictures of the world the Master had known began to form in the watcher's brain. At first Trevindor could make nothing of them then, suddenly, the jumbled shards fell into place and all was clear. A wave of horror swept over him at the appalling vista of nation battling against nation, of cities flaming to destruction and men dying in agony. What kind of world was this? Could man have sunk so low from the peaceful age Trevindor had known? There had been legends, from times incredibly remote, of such things in the early dawn of Earth's history, but man had left them with his childhood. Surely they could never have returned!

The broken thoughts were more vivid now, and even more horrible. It was truly a nightmare age from which this other exile had come – no wonder that he had fled from it!

Suddenly the truth began to dawn in the mind of Trevindor as, sick at heart, he watched the ghastly patterns passing through the Master's brain. This was no exile seeking refuge from an age of horror. This was the very creator of that age, who had embarked on the river of time with one purpose alone – to spread contagion down to later years.

Passions that Trevindor had never imagined began to

parade themselves before his eyes: ambition, the lust for power, cruelty, intolerance, hatred. He tried to close his mind, but found he had lost the power to do so. Unchecked, the evil stream flowed on, polluting every level of consciousness. With a cry of anguish, Trevindor rushed out into the desert and broke the chains binding him to that evil mind.

It was night, and very still, for the Earth was now too weary even for winds to blow. The darkness hid everything, but Trevindor knew that it could not hide the thoughts of that other mind with which he must now share the world. Once he had been alone, and he had imagined nothing more dreadful. But now he knew that there were things more fearful even than solitude.

The stillness of the night, and the glory of the stars that had once been his friends, brought calm to the soul of Trevindor. Slowly he turned and retraced his footsteps, walking heavily, for he was about to perform a deed that no man of his kind had ever done before.

The Master was standing when Trevindor re-entered the sphere. Perhaps some hint of the other's purpose must have dawned upon his mind, for he was very pale and trembled with a weakness that was more than physical. Steadfastly, Trevindor forced himself to look once more into the Master's brain. His mind recoiled at the chaos of conflicting emotions, now shot through with the sickening flashes of fear. Out of the maelstrom one coherent thought came quavering.

'What are you going to do? Why do you look at me like that?'

Trevindor made no reply, holding his mind aloof from contamination while he marshalled his resolution and his strength.

The tumult in the Master's mind was rising to a crescendo. For a moment his mounting terror brought something akin to pity to the gentle spirit of Trevindor, and his will faltered. But then there came again the picture of those ruined and burning cities, and his indecision vanished. With

all the power of his superhuman intellect, backed by thousands of centuries of mental evolution, he struck at the man
before him. Into the Master's mind, obliterating all else,
flooded the single thought of – death.

For a moment the Master stood motionless, his eyes
staring wildly before him. His breath froze as his lungs
ceased their work; in his veins the pulsing blood, which had
been stilled for so long, now congealed for ever. Without a
sound, the Master toppled and lay still.

Very slowly Trevindor turned and walked out into the
night. Like a shroud the silence and loneliness of the world
descended upon him. The sand, thwarted so long, began to
drift through the open portals of the Master's tomb.

HIDE-AND-SEEK

WE WERE walking back through the woods when King-man saw the grey squirrel. Our bag was a small but varied one – three grouse, four rabbits (one, I am sorry to say, an infant in arms) and a couple of pigeons. And contrary to certain dark forecasts, both the dogs were still alive.

The squirrel saw us at the same moment. It knew that it was marked for immediate execution as a result of the damage it had done to the trees on the estate, and perhaps it had lost close relatives to Kingman's gun. In three leaps it had reached the base of the nearest tree, and vanished behind it in a flicker of grey. We saw its face once more, appearing for a moment round the edge of its shield a dozen feet from the ground : but though we waited, with guns levelled hopefully at various branches, we never saw it again.

Kingman was very thoughtful as we walked back across the lawn to the magnificent old house. He said nothing as we handed our victims to the cook – who received them without much enthusiasm – and only emerged from his reverie when we were sitting in the smoking-room and he remembered his duties as a host.

'That tree-rat,' he said suddenly – he always called them 'tree-rats', on the grounds that people were too sentimental to shoot the dear little squirrels – 'it reminded me of a very peculiar experience that happened shortly before I retired. Very shortly indeed, in fact.'

'I thought it would,' said Carson dryly. I gave him a glare: he'd been in the Navy and had heard Kingman's stories before but they were still new to me.

'Of course,' Kingman remarked, slightly nettled, 'if you'd rather I didn't —'

'Do go on,' I said hastily. 'You've made me curious. What

connection there can possibly be between a grey squirrel and the Second Jovian War I can't imagine.'

Kingman seemed mollified.

'I think I'd better change some names,' he said thoughtfully, 'but I won't alter the places. The story begins about a million kilometres sunwards of Mars —'

K.15 was a military intelligence operative. It gave him considerable pain when unimaginative people called him a spy but at the moment he had much more substantial grounds for complaint. For some days now a fast cruiser had been coming up astern, and though it was flattering to have the undivided attention of such a fine ship and so many highly trained men, it was an honour that K.15 would willingly have forgone.

What made the situation doubly annoying was the fact that his friends would be meeting him off Mars in about twelve hours, aboard a ship quite capable of dealing with a mere cruiser – from which you will gather that K.15 was a person of some importance. Unfortunately, the most optimistic calculation showed that the pursuers would be within accurate gun range in six hours. In some six hours five minutes, therefore, K.15 was likely to occupy an extensive and still expanding volume of space. There might just be time for him to land on Mars, but that would be one of the worst things he could do. It would certainly annoy the aggressively neutral Martians, and the political complications would be frightful. Moreover, if his friends *had* to come down to the planet to rescue him, it would cost them more than ten kilometres a second in fuel – most of their operational reserve.

He had only one advantage, and that a very dubious one. The commander of the cruiser might guess that he was heading for a rendezvous, but he would not know how close it was nor how large was the ship that was coming to meet him. If he could keep alive for only twelve hours, he would be safe. The 'if' was a somewhat considerable one.

K.15 looked moodily at his charts, wondering if it was worth while to burn the rest of his fuel in a final dash. But a dash to where? He would be completely helpless then, and the pursuing ship might still have enough in her tanks to catch him as he flashed outwards into the empty darkness, beyond all hope of rescue – passing his friends as they came sunwards at a relative speed so great that they could do nothing to save him.

With some people, the shorter the expectation of life, the more sluggish are the mental processes. They seem hypnotized by the approach of death, so resigned to their fate that they do nothing to avoid it. K.15, on the other hand, found that his mind worked better in such a desperate emergency. It began to work now as it had seldom done before.

Commander Smith – the name will do as well as any other – of the cruiser *Doradus* was not unduly surprised when K.15 began to decelerate. He had half-expected the spy to land on Mars, on the principle that internment was better than annihilation, but when the plotting-room brought the news that the little scout ship was heading for Phobos, he felt completely baffled. The inner moon was nothing but a jumble of rock some twenty kilometres across, and not even the economical Martians had ever found any use for it. K.15 must be pretty desperate if he thought it was going to be of any greater value to him.

The tiny scout had almost come to rest when the radar operator lost it against the mass of Phobos. During the braking manoeuvre, K.15 had squandered most of his lead and the *Doradus* was now only minutes away – though she was now beginning to decelerate lest she overrun him. The cruiser was scarcely three thousand kilometres from Phobos when she came to a complete halt : of K.15's ship there was still no sign. It should be easily visible in the telescopes, but it was probably on the far side of the little moon.

It reappeared only a few minutes later, travelling under full thrust on a course directly away from the Sun. It was accelerating at almost five gravities – and it had broken its radio silence. An automatic recorder was broadcasting over and over again this interesting message :

'I have landed on Phobos and am being attacked by a Z-class cruiser. Think I can hold out until you come, but hurry.'

The message wasn't even in code, and it left Commander Smith a sorely puzzled man. The assumption that K.15 was still aboard the ship and that the whole thing was a ruse was just a little too naïve. But it might be a double-bluff : the message had obviously been left in plain language so that he would receive it and be duly confused. He could afford neither the time nor the fuel to chase the scout if K.15 really had landed. It was clear that reinforcements were on the way and the sooner he left the vicinity the better. The phrase 'Think I can hold out until you come' might be a piece of sheer impertinence, or it might mean that help was very near indeed.

Then K.15's ship stopped blasting. It had obviously exhausted its fuel, and was doing a little better than six kilometres a second away from the Sun. K.15 *must* have landed, for his ship was now speeding helplessly out of the Solar System. Commander Smith didn't like the message it was broadcasting, and guessed that it was running into the track of an approaching warship at some indefinite distance, but there was nothing to be done about that. The *Doradus* began to move towards Phobos, anxious to waste no time.

On the face of it, Commander Smith seemed the master of the situation. His ship was armed with a dozen heavy guided missiles and two turrets of electromagnetic guns. Against him was one man in a spacesuit, trapped on a moon only twenty kilometres across. It was not until Commander Smith had his first good look at Phobos, from a distance of less than a hundred kilometres, that he began to realize that, after all, K.15 might have a few cards up his sleeve.

To say that Phobos has a diameter of twenty kilometres, as the astronomy books invariably do, is highly misleading.

The word 'diameter' implies a degree of symmetry which Phobos most certainly lacks. Like those other lumps of cosmic slag, the Asteroids, it is a shapeless mass of rock floating in space with, of course, no hint of an atmosphere and not much more gravity. It turns on its axis once every seven hours thirty-nine minutes, thus keeping the same face always to Mars – which is so close that appreciably less than half the planet is visible, the Poles being below the curve of the horizon. Beyond this, there is very little more to be said about Phobos.

K.15 had no time to enjoy the beauty of the crescent world filling the sky above him. He had thrown all the equipment he could carry out of the airlock, set the controls, and jumped. As the little ship went flaming out towards the stars he watched it go with feelings he did not care to analyse. He had burned his boats with a vengeance, and he could only hope that the oncoming battleship would intercept the radio message as the empty vessel went racing by into nothingness. There was also a faint possibility that the enemy cruiser might go in pursuit but that was rather too much to hope for.

He turned to examine his new home. The only light was the ochre radiance of Mars, since the Sun was below the horizon, but that was quite sufficient for his purpose and he could see very well. He stood in the centre of an irregular plain about two kilometres across, surrounded by low hills over which he could leap rather easily if he wished. There was a story he remembered reading long ago about a man who had accidentally jumped off Phobos : that wasn't quite possible – though it was on Deimos – as the escape velocity was still about ten metres a second. But unless he was careful, he might easily find himself at such a height that it would take hours to fall back to the surface – and that would be fatal. For K.15's plan was a simple one : he must remain as close to the surface of Phobos as possible – *and diametrically opposite the cruiser*. The *Doradus* could then fire all her armament against the twenty kilometres of rock, and he wouldn't even feel the concussion. There were only two serious dangers, and one of these did not worry him greatly.

To the layman, knowing nothing of the finer details of astronautics, the plan would have seemed quite suicidal. The *Doradus* was armed with the latest in ultra-scientific weapons : moreover, the twenty kilometres which separated her from her prey represented less than a second's flight at maximum speed. But Commander Smith knew better, and was already feeling rather unhappy. He realized, only too well, that of all the machines of transport man has ever invented, a cruiser of space is far and away the least manoeuvrable. It was a simple fact that K.15 could make half a dozen circuits of his little world while her commander was persuading the *Doradus* to do even one.

There is no need to go into technical details, but those who are still unconvinced might like to consider these elementary facts. A rocket-driven spaceship can, obviously, only accelerate along its major axis – that is, 'forwards'. Any deviation from a straight course demands a physical turning of the ship, so that the motors can blast in another direction. Everyone knows that this is done by internal gyros or tangential steering jets : but very few people know just how long this simple manoeuvre takes. The average cruiser, fully fuelled, has a mass of two or three thousand tons, which does not make for rapid footwork. But things are even worse than this, for it is not the mass, but the moment of inertia that matters here – and since a cruiser is a long, thin object, its moment of inertia is slightly colossal. The sad fact remains (though it is seldom mentioned by astronautical engineers) that it takes a good ten minutes to rotate a spaceship through 180 degrees, with gyros of any reasonable size. Control jets are not much quicker, and in any case their use is restricted because the rotation they produce is permanent and they are liable to leave the ship spinning like a slow-motion pinwheel, to the annoyance of all inside.

In the ordinary way, these disadvantages are not very

grave. One has millions of kilometres and hundreds of hours in which to deal with such minor matters as a change in the ship's orientation. It is definitely against the rules to move in ten-kilometre-radius circles, and the commander of the *Doradus* felt distinctly aggrieved. K.15 wasn't playing fair.

At the same moment that resourceful individual was taking stock of the situation, which might very well have been worse. He had reached the hills in three jumps and felt less naked than he had out in the open plain. The food and equipment he had taken from the ship he had hidden where he hoped he could find it again, but as his suit could keep him alive for over a day that was the least of his worries. The small packet that was the cause of all the trouble was still with him, in one of those numerous hiding places a well-designed spacesuit affords.

There was an exhilarating loneliness about his mountain eyrie, even though he was not quite as lonely as he would have wished. For ever fixed in his sky, Mars was waning almost visibly as Phobos swept above the night side of the planet. He could just make out the lights of some of the Martian cities, gleaming pin-points marking the junctions of the invisible canals. All else was stars and silence and a line of jagged peaks so close it seemed he could almost touch them. Of the *Doradus* there was still no sign. She was presumably carrying out a careful telescopic examination of the sunlit side of Phobos.

Mars was a very useful clock : when it was half-full the Sun would rise and, very probably, so would the *Doradus*. But she might approach from some quite unexpected quarter : she might even – and this was the one real danger – she might even have landed a search party.

This was the first possibility that had occurred to Commander Smith when he saw just what he was up against. Then he realized that the surface area of Phobos was over a thousand square kilometres and that he could not spare more than ten men from his crew to make a search of that jumbled wilderness. Also, K.15 would certainly be armed.

Considering the weapons which the *Doradus* carried, this last objection might seem singularly pointless. It was very far from being so. In the ordinary course of business, side-arms and other portable weapons are as much use to a space-cruiser as are cutlasses and crossbows. The *Doradus* happened, quite by chance – and against regulations at that – to carry one automatic pistol and a hundred rounds of ammunition. Any search party would therefore consist of a group of unarmed men looking for a well-concealed and very desperate individual who could pick them off at his leisure. K.15 was breaking the rules again.

The terminator of Mars was now a perfectly straight line, and at almost the same moment the Sun came up, not so much like thunder as like a salvo of atomic bombs. K.15 adjusted the filters of his visor and decided to move. It was safer to stay out of the sunlight, not only because he was less likely to be detected in the shadow but also because his eyes would be much more sensitive there. He had only a pair of binoculars to help him, whereas the *Doradus* would carry an electronic telescope of twenty centimetres aperture at least.

It would be best, K.15 decided, to locate the cruiser if he could. It might be a rash thing to do, but he would feel much happier when he knew exactly where she was and could watch her movements. He could then keep just below the horizon, and the glare of the rockets would give him ample warning of any impending move. Cautiously launching himself along an almost horizontal trajectory, he began the circumnavigation of his world.

The narrowing crescent of Mars sank below the horizon until only one vast horn reared itself enigmatically against the stars. K.15 began to feel worried : there was still no sign of the *Doradus*. But this was hardly surprising, for she was painted black as night and might be a good hundred kilometres away in space. He stopped, wondering if he had done the right thing after all. Then he noticed that something quite large was eclipsing the stars almost vertically overhead, and was moving swiftly even as he watched. His heart stopped for a moment : then he was himself again, analysing the situation and trying to discover how he had made so disastrous a mistake.

It was some time before he realized that the black shadow slipping across the sky was not the cruiser at all, but something almost equally deadly. It was far smaller, and far nearer, than he had at first thought. The *Doradus* had sent her television-homing guided missiles to look for him.

This was the second danger he had feared, and there was nothing he could do about it except to remain as inconspicuous as possible. The *Doradus* now had many eyes searching for him, but these auxiliaries had very severe limitations. They had been built to look for sunlit spaceships against a background of stars, not to search for a man hiding in a dark jungle of rock. The definition of their television systems was low, and they could only see in the forward direction.

There were rather more men on the chess-board now, and the game was a little deadlier, but his was still the advantage.

The torpedo vanished in the night sky. As it was travelling on a nearly straight course in this low-gravitational field, it would soon be leaving Phobos behind, and K.15 waited for what he knew must happen. A few minutes later, he saw a brief stabbing of rocket exhausts and guessed that the projectile was swinging slowly back on its course. At almost the same moment he saw another flare away in the opposite quarter of the sky and wondered just how many of these infernal machines were in action. From what he knew of Z-class cruisers – which was a good deal more than he should – there were four missile control channels, and they were probably all in use.

He was suddenly struck by an idea so brilliant that he was quite sure it could not possibly work. The radio on his suit was a tunable one, covering an unusually wide band, and somewhere not far away the *Doradus* was pumping out power on everything from a thousand megacycles upwards.

He switched on the receiver and began to explore.

It came in quickly – the raucous whine of a pulse trans-mitter not far away. He was probably only picking up a sub-harmonic, but that was quite good enough. It D/F'ed sharply, and for the first time K.15 allowed himself to make long-range plans about the future. The *Doradus* had be-trayed herself : as long as she operated her missiles, he would know exactly where she was.

He moved cautiously forward towards the transmitter. To his surprise the signal faded, then increased sharply again. This puzzled him until he realized that he must be moving through a diffraction zone. Its width might have told him something useful if he had been a good enough physi-cist, but he could not imagine what.

The *Doradus* was hanging about five kilometres above the surface in full sunlight. Her 'non-reflecting' paint was over-due for renewal, and K.15 could see her clearly. As he was still in darkness, and the shadow line was moving away from him, he decided that he was as safe here as anywhere. He settled down comfortably so that he could just see the cruiser and waited, feeling fairly certain that none of the guided projectiles would come so near the ship. By now, he calcu-lated, the Commander of the *Doradus* must be getting pretty mad. He was perfectly correct.

After an hour, the cruiser began to heave herself round with all the grace of a bogged hippopotamus. K.15 guessed what was happening. Commander Smith was going to have a look at the antipodes, and was preparing for the perilous fifty-kilometre journey. He watched very carefully to see the orientation the ship was adopting, and when she came to rest again was relieved to see that she was almost broad-side on to him. Then, with a series of jerks that could not have been very enjoyable aboard, the cruiser began to move down to the horizon. K.15 followed her at a comfortable walking pace – if one could use the phrase – reflecting that this was a feat very few people had ever performed. He was particularly careful not to overtake her on one of his kilometre-long glides, and kept a close watch for any missiles that might be coming up astern.

It took the *Doradus* nearly an hour to cover the fifty kilometres. This, as K.15 amused himself by calculating, represented considerably less than a thousandth of her normal speed. Once, she found herself going off into space at a tangent, and rather than waste time turning end over end again fired off a salvo of shells to reduce speed. But she made it at last, and K.15 settled down for another vigil, wedged between two rocks where he could just see the cruiser and he was quite sure she could not see him. It occurred to him that by this time Commander Smith might have great doubts as to whether he really was on Phobos at all, and he felt like firing off a signal flare to reassure him. However, he resisted the temptation.

There would be little point in describing the events of the next ten hours, since they differed in no important detail from those that had gone before. The *Doradus* made three other moves, and K.15 stalked her with the care of the big-game hunter following the spoor of some elephantine beast. Once, when she would have led him out into full sunlight, he let her fall below the horizon until he could only just pick up her signals. But most of the time he kept her just visible, usually low down behind some convenient hill.

Once a torpedo exploded some kilometres away, and K.15 guessed that some exasperated operator had seen a shadow he did not like – or else that a technician had forgotten to switch off a proximity fuse. Otherwise nothing happened to enliven the proceedings : in fact the whole affair was becoming rather boring. He almost welcomed the sight of an occasional guided missile drifting inquisitively overhead, for he did not believe that they could see him if he remained motionless and in reasonable cover. If he could have stayed on the part of Phobos exactly opposite the cruiser he would have been safe even from these, he realized, since the ship would have no control there in the Moon's radio-shadow. But he could think of no reliable way in which he could be sure of staying in the safety zone if the cruiser moved again.

The end came very abruptly. There was a sudden blast of steering-jets, and the cruiser's main drive burst forth in all its power and splendour. In seconds the *Doradus* was shrinking sunwards, free at last, thankful to leave, even in defeat, this miserable lump of rock that had so annoyingly baulked her of her legitimate prey. K.15 knew what had happened, and a great sense of peace and relaxation swept over him. In the radar room of the cruiser, someone had seen an echo of disconcerting amplitude approaching with altogether excessive speed. K.15 now had only to switch on his suit beacon and to wait. He could even afford the luxury of a cigarette.

'Quite an interesting story,' I said, 'and I see now how it ties up with that squirrel. But it does raise one or two queries in my mind.'

'Indeed?' said Rupert Kingman politely.

I always like to get to the bottom of things, and I knew that my host had played a part in the Jovian War about which he seldom spoke. I decided to risk a long shot in the dark.

'May I ask how you happen to know so much about this unorthodox military engagement? It isn't possible, is it, that *you* were K.15?'

There was an odd sort of strangling noise from Carson. Then Kingman said, quite calmly : 'No, I wasn't.'

He got to his feet and went off towards the gun-room.

'If you'll excuse me a moment, I'm going to have another shot at that tree-rat. Maybe I'll get him this time.' Then he was gone.

Carson looked at me as if to say : 'This is another house you'll never be invited to again.' When our host was out of earshot he remarked in a coldly clinical voice :

'You've torn it. What did you have to say that for?'

'Well, it seemed a safe guess. How else could he have known all that?'

'As a matter of fact, I believe he met K.15 after the War: they must have had an interesting conversation together. But I thought you knew that Rupert was retired from the Service with only the rank of Lieutenant-Commander. The Court of Inquiry could never see his point of view. After all, it just wasn't reasonable that the Commander of the fastest ship in the Fleet couldn't catch a man in a spacesuit.'

ENCOUNTER IN THE DAWN

I T was in the last days of the Empire. The tiny ship was far from home, and almost a hundred light-years from the great parent vessel searching through the loosely packed stars at the rim of the Milky Way. But even here it could not escape from the shadow that lay across civilization : beneath that shadow, pausing ever and again in their work to wonder how their distant homes were faring, the scientists of the Galactic Survey still laboured at their never-ending task.

The ship held only three occupants, but between them they carried knowledge of many sciences, and the experience of half a lifetime in space. After the long inter-stellar night, the star ahead was warming their spirits as they dropped down towards its fires. A little more golden, a trifle more brilliant than the Sun that now seemed a legend of their childhood. They knew from past experience that the chance of locating planets here was more than ninety per cent, and for the moment they forgot all else in the excitement of discovery.

They found the first planet within minutes of coming to rest. It was a giant, of a familiar type, too cold for proto-plasmic life and probably possessing no stable surface. So they turned their search sunward, and presently were rewarded.

It was a world that made their hearts ache for home, a world where everything was hauntingly familiar, yet never quite the same. Two great land masses floated in blue-green seas, capped by ice at either pole. There were some desert regions, but the larger part of the planet was obviously fertile. Even from this distance, the signs of vegetation were unmistakably clear.

They gazed hungrily at the expanding landscape as they

fell down into the atmosphere, heading towards noon in the sub-tropics. The ship plummeted through cloudless skies towards a great river, checked its fall with a surge of sound-less power, and came to rest among the long grasses by the water's edge.

No one moved : there was nothing to be done until the automatic instruments had finished their work. Then a bell tinkled softly and the lights on the control board flashed in a pattern of meaningful chaos. Captain Altman rose to his feet with a sigh of relief.

'We're in luck,' he said. 'We can go outside without pro-tection, if the pathogenic tests are satisfactory. What did you make of the place as we came in, Bertrond?'

'Geologically stable – no active volcanoes, at least. I didn't see any trace of cities, but that proves nothing. If there's a civilization here, it may have passed that stage.'

'Or not reached it yet?'

Bertrond shrugged. 'Either's just as likely. It may take us some time to find out on a planet this size.'

'More time than we've got,' said Clindar, glancing at the communications panel that linked them to the mother ship and thence to the Galaxy's threatened heart. For a moment there was a gloomy silence. Then Clindar walked to the control board and pressed a pattern of keys with automatic skill.

With a slight jar, a section of the hull slid aside and the fourth member of the crew stepped out on to the new planet, flexing metal limbs and adjusting servo motors to the unaccustomed gravity. Inside the ship, a television screen glimmered into life, revealing a long vista of waving grasses, some trees in the middle distance, and a glimpse of the great river. Clindar punched a button, and the picture flowed steadily across the screen as the robot turned its head.

'Which way shall we go?' Clindar asked.

'Let's have a look at those trees,' Altman replied. 'If there's any animal life we'll find it there.'

'Look !' cried Bertrond. 'A bird !'

Clindar's fingers flew over the keyboard; the picture centred on the tiny speck that had suddenly appeared on the left of the screen, and expanded rapidly as the robot's telephoto lens came into action.

'You're right,' he said. 'Feathers – beak – well up the evolutionary ladder. This place looks promising. I'll start the camera.'

The swaying motion of the picture as the robot walked forward did not distract them : they had grown accustomed to it long ago. But they had never become reconciled to this exploration by proxy when all their impulses cried out to them to leave the ship, to run through the grass and to feel the wind blowing against their faces. Yet it was too great a risk to take, even on a world that seemed as fair as this. There was always a skull hidden behind Nature's most smiling face. Wild beasts, poisonous reptiles, quagmires – death could come to the unwary explorer in a thousand disguises. And worst of all were the invisible enemies, the bacteria and viruses against which the only defence might often be a thousand light-years away.

A robot could laugh at all these dangers and even if, as sometimes happened, it encountered a beast powerful enough to destroy it – well, machines could always be replaced.

They met nothing on the walk across the grasslands. If any small animals were disturbed by the robot's passage, they kept outside its field of vision. Clindar slowed the machine as it approached the trees, and the watchers in the spaceship flinched involuntarily at the branches that appeared to slash across their eyes. The picture dimmed for a moment before the controls readjusted themselves to the weaker illumination; then it came back to normal.

The forest was full of life. It lurked in the undergrowth, clambered among the branches, flew through the air. It fled chattering and gibbering through the trees as the robot advanced. And all the while the automatic cameras were recording the pictures that formed on the screen, gathering material for the biologists to analyse when the ship returned to base.

Clindar breathed a sigh of relief when the trees suddenly thinned. It was exhausting work, keeping the robot from smashing into obstacles as it moved through the forest, but on open ground it could take care of itself. Then the picture trembled as if beneath a hammer-blow, there was a grinding metallic thud, and the whole scene swept vertiginously upward as the robot toppled and fell.

'What's that?' cried Altman. 'Did you trip?'

'No,' said Clindar grimly, his fingers flying over the keyboard. 'Something attacked from the rear. I hope – ah – I've still got control.'

He brought the robot to a sitting position and swivelled its head. It did not take long to find the cause of the trouble. Standing a few feet away, and lashing its tail angrily, was a large quadruped with a most ferocious set of teeth. At the moment it was, fairly obviously, trying to decide whether to attack again.

Slowly, the robot rose to its feet, and as it did so the great beast crouched to spring. A smile flitted across Clindar's face : he knew how to deal with this situation. His thumb felt for the seldom-used key labelled 'Siren'.

The forest echoed with a hideous undulating scream from the robot's concealed speaker, and the machine advanced to meet its adversary, arms flailing in front of it. The startled beast almost fell over backward in its effort to turn, and in seconds was gone from sight.

'Now I suppose we'll have to wait a couple of hours until everything comes out of hiding again,' said Bertrond ruefully.

'I don't know much about animal psychology,' interjected Altman, 'but is it usual for them to attack something completely unfamiliar?'

'Some will attack anything that moves, but that's unusual. Normally they attack only for food, or if they've already been threatened. What are you driving at? Do you suggest that there are other robots on this planet?'

'Certainly not. But our carnivorous friend may have mistaken our machine for a more edible biped. Don't you think that this opening in the jungle is rather unnatural? It could easily be a path.'

'In that case,' said Clindar promptly, 'we'll follow it and find out. I'm tired of dodging trees, but I hope nothing jumps on us again : it's bad for my nerves.'

'You were right, Altman,' said Bertrond a little later. 'It's certainly a path. But that doesn't mean intelligence. After all, animals —'

He stopped in mid-sentence, and at the same instant Clindar brought the advancing robot to a halt. The path had suddenly opened out into a wide clearing, almost completely occupied by a village of flimsy huts. It was ringed by a wooden palisade, obviously defence against an enemy who at the moment presented no threat. For the gates were wide open, and beyond them the inhabitants were going peacefully about their ways.

For many minutes the three explorers stared in silence at the screen. Then Clindar shivered a little and remarked: 'It's uncanny. It might be our own planet, a hundred thousand years ago. I feel as if I've gone back in time.'

'There's nothing weird about it,' said the practical Altman. 'After all, we've discovered nearly a hundred planets with our type of life on them.'

'Yes,' retorted Clindar. 'A hundred in the whole Galaxy! I still think that it's strange it had to happen to us.'

'Well, it had to happen to *somebody*,' said Bertrond philosophically. 'Meanwhile, we must work out our contact procedure. If we send the robot into the village it will start a panic.'

'That,' said Altman, 'is a masterly understatement. What we'll have to do is catch a native by himself and prove that we're friendly. Hide the robot, Clindar — somewhere in the woods where it can watch the village without being spotted. We've a week's practical anthropology ahead of us !'

It was three days before the biological tests showed that it would be safe to leave the ship. Even then Bertrond insisted on going alone – alone, that is, if one ignored the substantial company of the robot. With such an ally he was not afraid of this planet's larger beasts, and his body's natural defences could take care of the micro-organisms, so, at least, the analysers had assured him : and considering the complexity of the problem, they made remarkably few mistakes.

He stayed outside for an hour, enjoying himself cautiously, while his companions watched with envy. It would be another three days before they could be quite certain that it was safe to follow Bertrond's example. Meanwhile, they kept busy enough watching the village through the lenses of the robot, and recording everything they could with the cameras. They had moved the spaceship at night so that it was hidden in the depths of the forest, for they did not wish to be discovered until they were ready.

And all the while the news from home grew worse. Though their remoteness here at the edge of the Universe deadened its impact, it lay heavily on their minds and sometimes overwhelmed them with a sense of futility. At any moment, they knew, the signal for recall might come as the Empire summoned up its last resources in its extremity. But until then they would continue their work as though pure knowledge were the only thing that mattered.

Seven days after landing, they were ready to make the experiment. They knew now what paths the villagers used when going hunting, and Bertrond chose one of the less frequented ways. Then he placed a chair firmly in the middle of the path and settled down to read a book.

It was not, of course, quite as simple as that: Bertrond had taken all imaginable precautions. Hidden in the undergrowth fifty yards away, the robot was watching through its telescopic lenses, and in its hand it held a small but deadly weapon. Controlling it from the spaceship, his fingers poised over the keyboard, Clindar waited to do what might be necessary.

That was the negative side of the plan : the positive side was more obvious. Lying at Bertrond's feet was the carcass of a small, horned animal which he hoped would be an acceptable gift to any hunter passing this way.

Two hours later the radio in his suit harness whispered a warning. Quite calmly, though the blood was pounding in his veins, Bertrond laid aside his book and looked down the trail. The savage was walking forward confidently enough, swinging a spear in his right hand. He paused for a moment when he saw Bertrond, then advanced more cautiously. He could tell that there was nothing to fear, for the stranger was slightly built and obviously unarmed.

When only twenty feet separated them, Bertrond gave a reassuring smile and rose slowly to his feet. He bent down, picked up the carcass, and carried it forward as an offering. The gesture would have been understood by any creature on any world, and it was understood here. The savage reached forward, took the animal, and threw it effortlessly over his shoulder. For an instant he stared into Bertrond's eyes with a fathomless expression; then he turned and walked back towards the village. Three times he glanced round to see if Bertrond was following, and each time Bertrond smiled and waved reassurance. The whole episode lasted little more than a minute. As the first contact between two races it was completely without drama, though not without dignity.

Bertrond did not move until the other had vanished from sight. Then he relaxed and spoke into his suit microphone.

'That was a pretty good beginning,' he said jubilantly. 'He wasn't in the least frightened, or even suspicious. I think he'll be back.'

'It still seems too good to be true,' said Altman's voice in his ear. 'I should have thought he'd have been either scared or hostile. Would *you* have accepted a lavish gift from a peculiar stranger with such little fuss?'

Bertrond was slowly walking back to the ship. The robot had now come out of cover and was keeping guard a few paces behind him.

'*I* wouldn't,' he replied, 'but I belong to a civilized community. Complete savages may react to strangers in many different ways, according to their past experience. Suppose this tribe has never had any enemies. That's quite possible on a large but sparsely populated planet. Then we may expect curiosity, but no fear at all.'

'If these people have no enemies,' put in Clindar, no longer fully occupied in controlling the robot, 'why have they got a stockade round the village?'

'I mean no *human* enemies,' replied Bertrond. 'If that's true, it simplifies our task immensely.'

'Do you think he'll come back?'

'Of course. If he's human as I think, curiosity and greed will make him return. In a couple of days we'll be bosom friends.'

Looked at dispassionately, it became a fantastic routine. Every morning the robot would go hunting under Clindar's direction, until it was now the deadliest killer in the jungle. Then Bertrond would wait until Yaan — which was the nearest they could get to his name — came striding confidently along the path. He came at the same time every day, and he always came alone. They wondered about this : did he wish to keep his great discovery to himself and thus get all the credit for his hunting prowess? If so, it showed unexpected foresight and cunning.

At first Yaan had departed at once with his prize, as if afraid that the donor of such a generous gift might change his mind. Soon, however, as Bertrond had hoped, he could be induced to stay for a while by simple conjuring tricks and a display of brightly coloured fabrics and crystals, in which he took a child-like delight. At last Bertrond was able to engage him in lengthy conversations, all of which were recorded as well as being filmed through the eyes of the hidden robot.

One day the philologists might be able to analyse this material; the best that Bertrond could do was to discover the meanings of a few simple verbs and nouns. This was made more difficult by the fact that Yaan not only used different words for the same thing, but sometimes the same word for different things.

Between these daily interviews, the ship travelled far, surveying the planet from the air and sometimes landing for more detailed examinations. Although several other human settlements were observed, Bertrond made no attempt to get in touch with them, for it was easy to see that they were all at much the same cultural level as Yaan's people.

It was, Bertrond often thought, a particularly bad joke on the part of Fate that one of the Galaxy's very few truly human races should have been discovered at this moment of time. Not long ago this would have been an event of supreme importance; now civilization was too hard-pressed to concern itself with these savage cousins waiting at the dawn of history.

Not until Bertrond was sure he had become part of Yaan's everyday life did he introduce him to the robot. He was showing Yaan the patterns in a kaleidoscope when Clindar brought the machine striding through the grass with its latest victim dangling across one metal arm. For the first time Yaan showed something akin to fear; but he relaxed at Bertrond's soothing words, though he continued to watch the advancing monster. It halted some distance away, and Bertrond walked forward to meet it. As he did so, the robot raised its arms and handed him the dead beast. He took it solemnly and carried it back to Yaan, staggering a little under the unaccustomed load.

Bertrond would have given a great deal to know just what Yaan was thinking as he accepted the gift. Was he trying to decide whether the robot was master or slave? Perhaps such conceptions as this were beyond his grasp : to him the robot might be merely another man, a hunter who was a friend of Bertrond.

Clindar's voice, slightly larger than life, came from the robot's speaker.

'It's astonishing how calmly he accepts us. Won't anything scare him?'

'You will keep judging him by your own standards,' replied Bertrond. 'Remember, his psychology is completely different, and much simpler. Now that he has confidence in me anything that I accept won't worry him.'

'I wonder if that will be true of all his race?' queried Altman. 'It's hardly safe to judge by a single specimen. I want to see what happens when we send the robot into the village.'

'Hello!' exclaimed Bertrond. '*That* surprised him. He's never met a person who could speak with two voices before.'

'Do you think he'll guess the truth when he meets us?' said Clindar.

'No. The robot will be pure magic to him – but it won't be any more wonderful than fire and lightning and all the other forces he must already take for granted.'

'Well, what's the next move?' asked Altman, a little impatiently. 'Are you going to bring him to the ship, or will you go into the village first?'

Bertrond hesitated. 'I'm anxious not to do too much too quickly. You know the accidents that have happened with strange races when that's been tried. I'll let him think this over and when we get back tomorrow I'll try to persuade him to take the robot back to the village.'

In the hidden ship, Clindar reactivated the robot and started it moving again. Like Altman, he was growing a little impatient of this excessive caution, but on all matters relating to alien life-forms Bertrond was the expert, and they had to obey his orders.

There were times now when he almost wished he were a robot himself, devoid of feelings or emotions, able to watch the fall of a leaf or the death agonies of a world with equal detachment —

The Sun was low when Yaan heard the great voice crying from the jungle. He recognized it at once, despite its inhuman volume : it was the voice of his friend calling him.

In the echoing silence, the life of the village came to a stop. Even the children ceased their play : the only sound was the thin cry of a baby frightened by the sudden silence.

All eyes were upon Yaan as he walked swiftly to his hut and grasped the spear that lay beside the entrance. The stockade would soon be closed against the prowlers of the night, but he did not hesitate as he stepped out into the lengthening shadows. He was passing through the gates when once again that mighty voice summoned him, and now it held a note of urgency that came clearly across all the barriers of language and culture.

The shining giant who spoke with many voices met him a little way from the village and beckoned him to follow. There was no sign of Bertrond. They walked for almost a mile before they saw him in the distance, standing not far from the river's edge and staring out across the dark, slowly moving waters.

He turned as Yaan approached, yet for a moment seemed unaware of his presence. Then he gave a gesture of dismissal to the shining one, who withdrew into the distance.

Yaan waited. He was patient and, though he could never have expressed it in words, contented. When he was with Bertrond he felt the first intimations of that selfless, utterly irrational devotion his race would not fully achieve for many ages.

It was a strange tableau. Here at the river's brink two men were standing. One was dressed in a closely fitting uniform equipped with tiny, intricate mechanisms. The other was wearing the skin of an animal and was carrying a flint-tipped spear. Ten thousand generations lay between them, ten thousand generations and an immeasurable gulf of space. Yet they were both human. As she must often do in eternity, Nature had repeated one of her basic patterns.

Presently Bertrond began to speak, walking to and fro in short, quick steps as he did so, and in his voice there was a trace of sadness.

'It's all over, Yaan, I'd hoped that with our knowledge

we could have brought you out of barbarism in a dozen generations but now you will have to fight your way up from the jungle alone, and it may take you a million years to do so. I'm sorry – there's so much we could have done. Even now I wanted to stay here, but Altman and Clindar talk of duty, and I suppose that they are right. There is little enough that we can do, but our world is calling and we must not forsake it.

'I wish you could understand me, Yaan. I wish you knew what I was saying. I'm leaving you these tools : some of them you will discover how to use, though as likely as not in a generation they'll be lost or forgotten. See how this blade cuts : it will be ages before your world can make its like. And guard this well : when you press the button – look ! If you use it sparingly, it will give you light for years, though sooner or later it will die. As for these other things – find what use for them you can.

'Here come the first stars, up there in the east. Do you ever look at the stars, Yaan? I wonder how long it will be before you have discovered what they are, and I wonder what will have happened to us by then. Those stars are our homes, Yaan, and we cannot save them. Many have died already, in explosions so vast that I can imagine them no more than you. In a hundred thousand of your years, the light of those funeral pyres will reach your world and set its peoples wondering. By then, perhaps, your race will be reaching for the stars. I wish I could warn you against the mistakes we made, and which now will cost us all that we have won.

'It is well for your people, Yaan, that your world is here at the frontier of the Universe. You may escape the doom that waits for us. One day, perhaps, your ships will go searching among the stars as we have done, and they may come upon the ruins of our worlds and wonder who we were. But they will never know that we met here by this river when your race was young.

'Here come my friends; they would give me no more

time. Good-bye, Yaan – use well the things I have left you. They are your world's greatest treasures.'

Something huge, something that glittered in the starlight, was sliding down from the sky. It did not reach the ground, but came to rest a little way above the surface, and in utter silence a rectangle of light opened in its side. The shining giant appeared out of the night and stepped through the golden door. Bertrond followed, pausing for a moment at the threshold to wave back at Yaan. Then the darkness closed behind him.

No more swiftly than smoke drifts upward from a fire, the ship lifted away. When it was so small that Yaan felt he could hold it in his hands, it seemed to blur into a long line of light slanting upward into the stars. From the empty sky a peal of thunder echoed over the sleeping land : and Yaan knew at last that the gods were gone and would never come again.

For a long time he stood by the gently moving waters, and into his soul there came a sense of loss he was never to forget and never to understand. Then, carefully and reverently, he collected together the gifts that Bertrond had left.

Under the stars, the lonely figure walked homeward across a nameless land. Behind him the river flowed softly to the sea, winding through the fertile plains on which, more than a thousand centuries ahead, Yaan's descendants would build the great city they were to call Babylon.

LOOPHOLE

From : President.
To : Secretary, Council of Scientists.

I have been informed that the inhabitants of Earth have succeeded in releasing atomic energy and have been making experiments with rocket propulsion. This is most serious. Let me have a full report immediately. And make it *brief* this time.

KK. IV.

From : Secretary, Council of Scientists.

To : President.

The facts are as follows. Some months ago our instruments detected intense neutron emission from Earth, but an analysis of radio programmes gave no explanation at the time. Three days ago a second emission occurred, and soon afterwards all radio transmissions from Earth announced that atomic bombs were in use in the current war. The translators have not completed their interpretation, but it appears that the bombs are of considerable power. Two have so far been used. Some details of their construction have been released, but the elements concerned have not yet been identified. A fuller report will be forwarded as soon as possible. For the moment all that is certain is that the inhabitants of Earth *have* liberated atomic power, so far only explosively.

Very little is known concerning rocket research on Earth. Our astronomers have been observing the planet carefully ever since radio emissions were detected a generation ago. It is certain that long-range rockets of some kind are in existence on Earth, for there have been numerous references to them in recent military broadcasts. However, no serious attempt has been made to reach interplanetary space. When the war ends, it is expected that the inhabitants of the planet may carry out research in this direction. We will pay very careful attention to their broadcasts and the astronomical watch will be rigorously enforced.

From what we have inferred of the planet's technology, it should require about twenty years before Earth develops atomic rockets capable of crossing space. In view of this, it would seem that the time has come to set up a base on the Moon, so that a close scrutiny can be kept on such experiments when they commence.

Trescon.

[Added in manuscript]

The war on Earth has now ended, apparently owing to the intervention of the atomic bomb. This will not affect the above arguments but it may mean that the inhabitants of Earth can devote themselves to pure research again more quickly than expected. Some broadcasts have already pointed out the application of atomic power to rocket propulsion.

T.

From : President.

To : Chief of Bureau of Extra-Planetary Security
        (C.B.E.P.S).

You have seen Trescon's minute.

Equip an expedition to the satellite of Earth immediately. It is to keep a close watch on the planet and to report at once if rocket experiments are in progress.

The greatest care must be taken to keep our presence on the Moon a secret. You are personally responsible for this. Report to me at yearly intervals, or more often if necessary.

K.K. IV.

From : President.

To : C.B.E.P.S.

Where is the report of Earth? ! !

K.K. IV.

From : C.B.E.P.S.

To : President.

The delay is regretted. It was caused by the breakdown of the ship carrying the report.

There have been no signs of rocket experimenting during the past year, and no reference to it in broadcasts from the planet.

Ranthe

From : C.B.E.P.S.

To : President.

You will have seen my yearly reports to your respected father on this subject. There have been no developments of interest for the past fifteen years, but the following message has just been received from our base on the Moon :

> Rocket projectile, apparently atomically propelled, left Earth's atmosphere today from nothern land-mass, travelling into space for one-quarter diameter of planet before returning under control.

Ranthe

From : President.

To : Chief of State.

Your comments, please.

K.K. V.

From : Chief of State.

To : President.

This means the end of our traditional policy.

The only hope of security lies in preventing the Terrestrials from making further advances in this direction. From what we know of them, this will require some overwhelming threat.

Since its high gravity makes it impossible for us to land on the planet, our sphere of action is restricted. The problem was discussed nearly a century ago by Anvar, and I agree with his conclusions. We must act *immediately* along those lines.

F. K. S.

From : President.

To : Secretary of State.

Inform the Council that an emergency meeting is convened for noon tomorrow.

K. K. V.

From : President.

To : C.B.E.P.S.

Twenty battleships should be sufficient to put Anvar's plan into operation. Fortunately there is no need to arm them – yet. Report progress of construction to me weekly.

K. K. V.

From : C.B.E.P.S.

To : President.

Nineteen ships are now completed. The twentieth is still delayed owing to hull failure and will not be ready for at least a month.

Ranthe

From : President.

To : C.B.E.P.S.

Nineteen will be sufficient. I will check the operational plan with you tomorrow. Is the draft of our broadcast ready yet?

K. K. V.

From : C.B.E.P.S.

To : President.

Draft herewith :

People of Earth !

We, the inhabitants of the planet you call Mars, have for

many years observed your experiments towards achieving interplanetary travel. *These experiments must cease.* Our study of your race has convinced us that you are not fitted to leave your planet in the present state of your civilization. The ships you now see floating above your cities are capable of destroying them utterly, and will do so unless you discontinue your attempts to cross space.

We have set up an observatory on your Moon and can immediately detect any violation of these orders. If you obey them, we will not interfere with you again. Otherwise, one of your cities will be destroyed every time we observe a rocket leaving the Earth's atmosphere.

By order of the President and Council of Mars.

Ranthe

From : President.

To : C.B.E.P.S.

I approve. The translation can go ahead.

I will not be sailing with the fleet, after all. Report to me in detail immediately on your return.

K.K. V.

From : C.B.E.P.S.

To : President.

I have the honour to report the successful completion of our mission. The voyage to Earth was uneventful : radio messages from the planet indicated that we were detected at a considerable distance and great excitement had been aroused before our arrival. The fleet was dispersed according to plan and I broadcast the ultimatum. We left immediately and no hostile weapons were brought to bear against us.

I will report in detail within two days.

Ranthe

From : Secretary, Council of Scientists.

To : President.

The psychologists have completed their report, which is attached herewith.

As might be expected, our demands at first infuriated this stubborn and high-spirited race. The shock to their pride must have been considerable, for they believed themselves to be the only intelligent beings in the Universe.

However, within a few weeks there was a rather unexpected change in the tone of their statements. They had begun to realize that we were intercepting all their radio transmissions, and some messages have been broadcast directly to us. They state that they have agreed to ban all rocket experiments, in accordance with our wishes. This is as unexpected as it is welcome. Even if they are trying to deceive us, we are perfectly safe now that we have established the second station just outside the atmosphere. They cannot possibly develop spaceships without our seeing them or detecting their tube radiation.

The watch on Earth will be continued rigorously, as instructed.

Trescon

From : C.B.E.P.S.

To : President.

Yes, it is quite true that there have been no further rocket experiments in the last ten years. We certainly did not expect Earth to capitulate so easily !

I agree that the existence of this race now constitutes a permanent threat to our civilization and we are making experiments along the lines you suggest. The problem is a difficult one, owing to the great size of the planet. Explosives would be out of the question, and a radioactive poison of some kind appears to offer the greatest hope of success.

Fortunately, we now have an indefinite time in which to complete this research, and I will report regularly.

Ranthe

[*End of Document*]

From : Lieutenant Commander Henry Forbes, Intelligence Branch, Special Space Corps.

To : Professor S. Maxton, Philological Department, University of Oxford.

Route : Transender II (via Schenectady).

The above papers, with others, were found in the ruins of what is believed to be the capital Martian city. (Mars Grid KL302895.) The frequent use of ideograph for 'Earth' suggests that they may be of special interest and it is hoped that they can be translated. Other papers will be following shortly.

H. Forbes, Lt./Cdr.

[*Added in manuscript*]

Dear Max,

Sorry I've had no time to contact you before. I'll be seeing you as soon as I get back to Earth.

Gosh ! Mars *is* in a mess ! Our Co-ordinates were dead accurate and the bombs materialized right over their cities, just as the Mount Wilson boys predicted.

We're sending a lot of stuff back through the two small machines, but until the big transmitter is materialized we're rather restricted, and, of course, none of us can return. So hurry up with it !

I'm glad we can get to work on rockets again. I may be old-fashioned, but being squirted through space at the speed of light doesn't appeal to me !

Yours in haste,

Henry

INHERITANCE

As DAVID said, when one falls on Africa from a height of two hundred and fifty kilometres, a broken ankle may be an anti-climax but is none the less painful. But what hurt him most, he pretended, was the way we had all rushed out into the desert to see what had happened to the A.20 and had not come near him until hours later.

'Be logical, David,' Jimmy Langford had protested. 'We knew that you were OK because the base 'copter radioed when it picked you up. But the A.20 might have been a complete write-off.'

'There's only one A.20,' I said, trying to be helpful, 'but rocket test-pilots are – well, if not two a penny, at any rate seven for sixpence.'

David glared back at us from beneath his bushy eyebrows and said something in Welsh.

'The Druid's curse,' Jimmy remarked to me. 'Any moment now you'll turn into a leek or a perspex model of Stonehenge.'

You see, we were still pretty lightheaded and it would not do to be serious for a while. Even David's iron nerve must have taken a terrific beating, yet somehow he seemed the calmest of us all. I could not understand it – then.

The A.20 had come down fifty kilometres from her launching-point. We had followed her by radar for the whole trajectory, so we knew her position to within a few metres – though we did not know at the time that David had landed ten kilometres farther east.

The first warning of disaster had come seventy seconds after take-off. The A.20 had reached fifty kilometres and was following the correct trajectory to within a few per cent. As far as the eye could tell, the luminous track on the radar screen had scarcely deviated from the pre-computed path.

David was doing two kilometres a second : not much, but the fastest any man had ever travelled up to then. And 'Goliath' was just about to be jettisoned.

The A.20 was a two-step rocket. It had to be, for it was using chemical fuels. The upper component, with its tiny cabin, its folded aerofoils and flaps, weighed just under twenty tons when fully fuelled. It was to be lifted by a lower two-hundred-ton booster which would take it up to fifty kilometres, after which it could carry on quite happily under its own power. The big fellow would then drop back to Earth by parachute : it would not weigh much when its fuel was burnt. Meanwhile the upper step would have built up enough speed to reach the six-hundred-kilometre level before falling back and going into a glide that would take David half-way round the world if he wished.

I do not remember who called the two rockets 'David' and 'Goliath' but the names caught on at once. Having two Davids around caused a lot of confusion, not all of it accidental.

Well, that was the theory, but as we watched the tiny green spot on the screen fall away from its calculated course, we knew that something had gone wrong. And we guessed what it was.

At fifty kilometres the spot should have divided in two. The brighter echo should have continued to rise as a free projectile, and then fallen back to Earth. But the other should have gone on, still accelerating, drawing swiftly away from the discarded booster.

There had been no separation. The empty 'Goliath' had refused to come free and was dragging 'David' back to Earth – helplessly, for 'David's' motors could not be used. Their exhausts were blocked by the machine beneath.

We saw all this in about ten seconds. We waited just long enough to calculate the new trajectory, and then we climbed into the 'copters and set off for the target area.

All we expected to find, of course, was a heap of magnesium looking as if a bulldozer had gone over it. We knew that 'Goliath' could not eject his parachute while 'David' was sitting on top of him, any more than 'David' could use his motors while 'Goliath' was clinging beneath. I remember wondering who was going to break the news to Mavis, and then realizing that she would be listening to the radio and would know all about it as soon as anyone.

We could scarcely believe our eyes when we found the two rockets still coupled together, lying almost undamaged beneath the big parachute. There was no sign of David, but a few minutes later Base called to say that he had been found. The plotters at Number Two Station had picked up the tiny echo from his parachute and sent a 'copter to collect him. He was in hospital twenty minutes later, but we stayed out in the desert for several hours checking over the machines and making arrangements to retrieve them.

When at last we got back to Base, we were pleased to see our best-hated science-reporters among the mob being held at bay. We waved aside their protests and sailed on into the ward.

The shock and the subsequent relief had left us all feeling rather irresponsible and perhaps childish. Only David seemed unaffected : the fact that he had just had one of the most miraculous escapes in human history had not made him turn a hair. He sat there in the bed pretending to be annoyed at our jibes until we had calmed down.

'Well,' said Jimmy at last, 'what went wrong?'

'That's for you to discover,' David replied. '"Goliath" went like a dream until fuel cut-off point. I waited then for the five-second pause before the explosive bolts detonated and the springs threw him clear, but nothing happened. So I punched the emergency release. The lights dimmed, but the kick I'd expected never came. I tried a couple more times but somehow I knew it was useless. I guessed that something had shorted in the detonator circuit and was earthing the power supply.

'Well, I did some rather rapid calculations from the flight charts and abacs in the cabin. At my present speed I'd continue to rise for another two hundred kilometres and would reach the peak of my trajectory in about three minutes. Then I'd start the two-hundred-and-fifty-kilometre fall and should make a nice hole in the desert four minutes later. All told, I seemed to have a good seven minutes of life left — ignoring air resistance, to use your favourite phrase. That might add a couple of minutes to my expectation of life.

'I knew that I couldn't get the big parachute out, and "David's" wings would be useless with the forty-ton mass of "Goliath" on its tail. I'd used up two of my seven minutes before I decided what to do.

'It's a good job I made you widen that airlock. Even so, it was a squeeze to get through it in my spacesuit. I tied the end of the safety rope to a locking lever and crawled along the hull until I reached the junction of the two steps.

'The parachute compartment couldn't be opened from the outside, but I'd taken the emergency axe from the pilot's cabin. It didn't take long to get through the magnesium skin : once it had been punctured I could almost tear it apart with my hands. A few seconds later I'd released the 'chute. The silk floated aimlessly around me : I had expected some trace of air resistance at this speed but there wasn't a sign of it. The canopy simply stayed where it was put. I could only hope that when we re-entered atmosphere it would spread itself without fouling the rocket.

'I thought I had a fairly good chance of getting away with it. The additional weight of "David" would increase the loading of the parachute by less than twenty per cent, but there was always the chance that the shrouds would chafe against the broken metal and be worn through before I could reach Earth. In addition the canopy would be distorted when it did open, owing to the unequal lengths of the chords. There was nothing I could do about that.

'When I'd finished, I looked about me for the first time. I couldn't see very well, for perspiration had misted over the glass of my suit. (Someone had better look into that : it can be dangerous.) I was still rising, though very slowly now. To the north-east I could see the whole of Sicily and some of the Italian mainland: farther south I could follow the Libyan coast as far as Benghazi. Spread out beneath me was all the land over which Alexander and Montgomery and Rommel had fought when I was a boy. It seemed rather surprising that anyone had ever made such a fuss about it.

'I didn't stay long: in three minutes I would be entering the atmosphere. I took a last look at the flaccid parachute, straightened some of the shrouds, and climbed back into the cabin. Then I jettisoned "David's" fuel – first the oxygen, and then, as soon as it had had time to disperse, the alcohol.

'That three minutes seemed an awfully long time. I was just over twenty-five kilometres high when I heard the first sound. It was a very high-pitched whistle, so faint that I could scarcely hear it. Glancing through the portholes, I saw that the parachute shrouds were becoming taut and the canopy was beginning to billow above me. At the same time I felt weight returning and knew that the rocket was beginning to decelerate.

'The calculation wasn't very encouraging. I'd fallen free for over two hundred kilometres and if I was to stop in time I'd need an *average* deceleration of ten gravities. The peaks might be twice that, but I'd stood fifteen g before now in a lesser cause. So I gave myself a double shot of dynocaine and uncaged the gimbals of my seat. I remember wondering whether I should let out "David's" little wings, and decided that it wouldn't help. Then I must have blacked out.

'When I came round again it was very hot, and I had normal weight. I felt very stiff and sore, and to make matters worse the cabin was oscillating violently. I struggled to the port and saw that the desert was uncomfortably close. The big parachute had done its work, but I thought that the impact was going to be rather too violent for comfort. So I jumped.

'From what you tell me I'd have done better to have stayed in the ship. But I don't suppose I can grumble.'

We sat in silence for a while. Then Jimmy remarked casually :

'The accelerometer shows that you touched twenty-one gravities on the way down. Only for three seconds, though. Most of the time it was between twelve and fifteen.'

David did not seem to hear and presently I said :

'Well, we can't hold the reporters off much longer. Do you feel like seeing them?'

David hesitated.

'No,' he answered. 'Not now.'

He read our faces and shook his head violently.

'No,' he said with emphasis, 'it's not that at all. I'd be willing to take off again right now. But I want to sit and think things over for a while.'

His voice sank, and when he spoke again it was to show the real David behind the perpetual mask of extroversion.

'You think I haven't any nerves,' he said, 'and that I take risks without bothering about the consequences. Well, that isn't quite true and I'd like you to know why. I've never told anyone this, not even Mavis.

'You know I'm not superstitious,' he began, a little apologetically, 'but most materialists have some secret reservations, even if they won't admit them.

'Many years ago I had a peculiarly vivid dream. By itself, it wouldn't have meant much, but later I discovered that two other men had put almost identical experiences on record. One you've probably read, for the man was J. W. Dunne.

'In his first book, *An Experiment with Time*, Dunne tells how he once dreamed that he was sitting at the controls of a curious flying-machine with swept-back wings, and years later the whole experience came true when he was testing his inherent stability airplane. Remembering my own dream, which I'd had *before* reading Dunne's book, this made a considerable impression on me. But the second incident I found even more striking.

'You've heard of Igor Sikorsky : he designed some of the first commercial long-distance flying boats – "Clippers", they were called. In his autobiography, *The Story of the Flying S*, he tells us how he had a dream very similar to Dunne's.

'He was walking along a corridor with doors opening on either side and electric lights glowing overhead. There was a slight vibration underfoot and somehow he knew that he was in a flying machine. Yet at that time there were no airplanes in the world, and few people believed there ever would be.

'Sikorsky's dream, like Dunne's, came true many years later. He was on the maiden flight of his first Clipper when he found himself walking along that familiar corridor.'

David laughed, a little self-consciously.

'You've probably guessed what my dream was about,' he continued. 'Remember, it would have made no permanent impression if I hadn't come across these parallel cases.

'I was in a small, bare room with no windows. There were two other men with me, and we were all wearing what I thought at the time were diving-suits. I had a curious control panel in front of me, with a circular screen built into it. There was a picture on the screen, but it didn't mean anything to me and I can't recall it now, though I've tried many times since. All I remember is turning to the other two men and saying : "Five minutes to go, boys" – though I'm not sure if those were the exact words. And then, of course, I woke up.

'That dream has haunted me ever since I became a test pilot. No – haunted isn't the right word. It's given me confidence that in the long run everything would be all right – at least until I'm in that cabin with those other two men. What happens after that I don't know. But now you understand why I felt quite safe when I brought down the A.20, and when I crashlanded the A.15 off Pantelleria.

'So now you know. You can laugh if you please: I sometimes do myself. But even if there's nothing in it, that dream's given my subconscious a boost that's been pretty useful.'

We didn't laugh, and presently Jimmy said :

'Those other men – did you recognize them?'

David looked doubtful.

'I've never made up my mind,' he answered. 'Remember, they were wearing spacesuits and I didn't see their faces clearly. But one of them looked rather like you, though he seemed a good deal older than you are now. I'm afraid you weren't there, Arthur. Sorry.'

'I'm glad to hear it,' I said. 'As I've told you before, I'll have to stay behind to explain what went wrong. I'm quite content to wait until the passenger service starts.'

Jimmy rose to his feet.

'OK, David,' he said, 'I'll deal with the gang outside. Get some sleep now – with or without dreams. And by the way, the A.20 will be ready again in a week. I think she'll be the last of the chemical rockets : they say the atomic drive's nearly ready for us.'

We never spoke of David's dream again, but I think it was often in our minds. Three months later he took the A.20 up to six hundred and eighty kilometres, a record which will never be broken by a machine of this type, because no one will ever build a chemical rocket again. David's uneventful landing in the Nile Valley marked the end of an epoch.

It was three years before the A.21 was ready. She looked very small compared with her giant predecessors, and it was hard to believe that she was the nearest thing to a spaceship man had yet built. This time the take-off was from sea-level, and the Atlas Mountains which had witnessed the start of our earlier shots were now merely the distant background to the scene.

By now both Jimmy and I had come to share David's

belief in his own destiny. I remember Jimmy's parting words as the airlock closed.

'It won't be long now, David, before we build that three-man ship.'

And I knew he was only half joking.

We saw the A.21 climb slowly into the sky in great, widening circles, unlike any rocket the world had ever known before. There was no need to worry about gravitational loss now that we had a built-in fuel supply, and David was not in a hurry. The machine was still travelling quite slowly when I lost sight of it and went into the plotting-room.

When I got there the signal was just fading from the screen, and the detonation reached me a little later. And that was the end of David and his dreams.

The next I recall of that period is flying down the Conway Valley in Jimmy's 'copter, with Snowdon gleaming far away on our right. We had never been to David's home before and were not looking forward to this visit. But it was the least we could do.

As the mountains drifted beneath us we talked about the suddenly darkened future and wondered what the next step would be. Apart from the shock of personal loss, we were beginning to realize how much of David's confidence we had come to share ourselves. And now that confidence had been shattered.

We wondered what Mavis would do, and discussed the boy's future. He must be fifteen now, though I had not seen him for several years and Jimmy had never met him at all. According to his father he was going to be an architect and already showed considerable promise.

Mavis was quite calm and collected, though she seemed much older than when I had last met her. For a while we talked about business matters and the disposal of David's estate. I had never been an executor before, but tried to pretend that I knew all about it.

We had just started to discuss the boy when we heard the front door open and he came into the house. Mavis

11

called to him and his footsteps came slowly along the passage. We could tell that he did not want to meet us, and his eyes were still red when he entered the room.

I had forgotten how much like his father he was, and I heard a little gasp from Jimmy.

'Hello, David,' I said.

But he did not look at me. He was staring at Jimmy, with that puzzled expression of a man who had seen someone before but cannot remember where.

And quite suddenly I knew that young David would never be an architect.

THE SENTINEL

THE next time you see the full Moon high in the south, look carefully at its right-hand edge and let your eye travel upwards along the curve of the disk. Round about two o'clock, you will notice a small, dark oval : anyone with normal eyesight can find it quite easily. It is the great walled plain, one of the finest on the Moon, known as the Mare Crisium – the Sea of Crises. Three hundred miles in diameter – and almost completely surrounded by a ring of magnificent mountains, it had never been explored until we entered it in the late summer of 1996.

Our expedition was a large one. We had two heavy freighters which had flown our supplies and equipment from the main lunar base in the Mare Serenitatis, five hundred miles away. There were also three small rockets which were intended for short-range transport over regions which our surface vehicles could not cross. Luckily, most of the Mare Crisium is very flat. There are none of the great crevasses so common and so dangerous elsewhere, and very few craters or mountains of any size. As far as we could tell, our powerful caterpillar tractors would have no difficulty in taking us wherever we wished.

I was geologist – or selenologist, if you want to be pedantic – in charge of the group exploring the southern region of the Mare. We had crossed a hundred miles of it in a week, skirting the foothills of the mountains along the shore of what was once the ancient sea, some thousand million years before. When life was beginning on Earth, it was already dying here. The waters were retreating down the flanks of those stupendous cliffs, retreating into the empty heart of the Moon. Over the land which we were crossing, the tideless ocean had once been half a mile deep and now the only trace of moisture was the hoar frost one could sometimes find in caves which the searing sunlight never penetrated.

We had begun our journey early in the slow lunar dawn, and still had almost a week of Earth-time before nightfall. Half a dozen times a day we would leave our vehicle and go outside in the spacesuits to hunt for interesting minerals, or to place markers for the guidance of future travellers. It was an uneventful routine. There is nothing hazardous or even particularly exciting about lunar exploration. We could live comfortably for a month in our pressurized tractors, and if we ran into trouble we could always radio for help and sit tight until one of the spaceships came to our rescue. When that happened there was always a frightful outcry about the waste of rocket fuel, so a tractor sent out an SOS only in a real emergency.

I said just now that there was nothing exciting about lunar exploration, but of course that is not true. One could never grow tired of those incredible mountains, so much more rugged than the gentle hills of Earth. We never knew, as we rounded the capes and promontories of that vanished sea, what new splendours would be revealed to us. The whole southern curve of the Mare Crisium is a vast delta where a score of rivers had once found their way into the ocean, fed perhaps by the torrential rains that must have lashed the mountains in the brief volcanic age when the moon was young. Each of these ancient valleys was an invitation, challenging us to climb into the unknown uplands beyond. But we had a hundred miles still to cover, and could only look longingly at the heights which others must scale.

We kept Earth-time aboard the tractor, and precisely at 22.00 hours the final radio message would be sent out to base and we could close down for the day. Outside, the rocks would still be burning beneath the almost vertical sun, but to us it was night until we awoke again eight hours later. Then one of us would prepare breakfast, there would be a great buzzing of electric shavers and someone would switch on the short-wave radio from Earth. Indeed, when the smell of frying bacon began to fill the cabin, it was sometimes hard to believe that we were not back on our own world – everything was so normal and homely, apart from the feeling of decreased weight and the unnatural slowness with which objects fell.

It was my turn to prepare breakfast in the corner of the main cabin that served as a galley. I can remember that moment quite vividly after all these years, for the radio had just played one of my favourite melodies, the old Welsh air, 'David of the White Rock'. Our driver was already outside in his spacesuit, inspecting our caterpillar treads. My assistant, Louis Garnett, was up forward in the control position, making some belated entries in yesterday's log.

As I stood by the frying-pan, waiting, like any terrestrial housewife, for the sausages to brown, I let my gaze wander idly over the mountain walls which covered the whole of the southern horizon, marching out of sight to the east and west below the curve of the Moon. They seemed only a mile or two from the tractor, but I knew that the nearest was twenty miles away. On the Moon, of course, there is no loss of detail with distance – none of that almost imperceptible haziness which softens and sometimes transfigures all far-off things on Earth.

Those mountains were ten thousand feet high, and they climbed steeply out of the plain as if ages ago some subterranean eruption had smashed them skywards through the molten crust. The base of even the nearest was hidden from sight by the steeply curving surface of the plain, for the Moon is a very little world, and from where I was standing the horizon was only two miles away.

I lifted my eyes towards the peaks which no man had ever climbed, the peaks which, before the coming of terrestrial life, had watched the retreating oceans sink sullenly into their graves, taking with them the hope and the morning promise of a world. The sunlight was beating against those ramparts with a glare that hurt the eyes, yet only a little way above them the stars were shining steadily in a sky blacker than a winter midnight on Earth.

I was turning away when my eye caught a metallic glitter high on the ridge of a great promontory thrusting out into the sea thirty miles to the west. It was a dimensionless point of light as if a star had been clawed from the sky by one of those cruel peaks, and I imagined that some smooth rock-surface was catching the sunlight and heliographing it straight into my eyes. Such things were not uncommon. When the Moon is in her second quarter, observers on Earth can sometimes see the great ranges in the Oceanus Procellarum burning with a blue-white iridescence as the sunlight flashes from their slopes and leaps again from world to world. But I was curious to know what kind of rock could be shining so brightly up there, and I climbed into the observation turret and swung our four-inch telescope round to the west.

I could see just enough to tantalize me. Clear and sharp in the field of vision, the mountain peaks seemed only half a mile away, but whatever was catching the sunlight was still too small to be resolved. Yet it seemed to have an elusive symmetry, and the summit upon which it rested was curiously flat. I stared for a long time at that glittering enigma, straining my eyes into space, until presently a smell of burning from the galley told me that our breakfast sausages had made their quarter-million-mile journey in vain.

All that morning we argued our way across the Mare Crisium while the western mountains reared higher in the sky. Even when we were out prospecting in the spacesuits, the discussion would continue over the radio. It was absolutely certain, my companions argued, that there had never been any form of intelligent life on the Moon. The only living things that had ever existed there were a few primitive plants and their slightly less degenerate ancestors. I knew that as well as anyone, but there are times when a scientist must not be afraid to make a fool of himself.

'Listen,' I said at last, 'I'm going up there, if only for my own peace of mind. That mountain's less than twelve thousand feet high – that's only two thousand under Earth gravity – and I can make the trip in twenty hours at the outside. I've always wanted to go up into those hills, anyway, and this gives me an excellent excuse.'

'If you don't break your neck,' said Garnett, 'you'll be the laughing-stock of the expedition when we get back to Base. That mountain will probably be called Wilson's Folly from now on.'

'I won't break my neck,' I said firmly. 'Who was the first man to climb Pico and Helicon?'

'But weren't you rather younger in those days?' asked Louis gently.

'That,' I said with great dignity, 'is as good a reason as any for going.'

We went to bed early that night, after driving the tractor to within half a mile of the promontory. Garnett was coming with me in the morning; he was a good climber, and had often been with me on such exploits before. Our driver was only too glad to be left in charge of the machine.

At first sight, those cliffs seemed completely unscalable, but to anyone with a good head for heights, climbing is easy on a world where all weights are only a sixth of their normal value. The real danger in lunar mountaineering lies in over-confidence; a six-hundred-foot drop on the Moon can kill you just as thoroughly as a hundred-foot fall on Earth.

We made our first halt on a wide ledge about four thousand feet above the plain. Climbing had not been very difficult but my limbs were stiff with the unaccustomed effort, and I was glad of the rest. We could still see the tractor as a tiny metal insect far down at the foot of the cliff, and we reported our progress to the driver before starting on the next ascent.

Hour by hour the horizon widened and more and more of the great plain came into sight. Now we could look for fifty miles out across the Mare, and could even see the peaks of the mountains on the opposite coast more than a hundred miles away. Few of the great lunar plains are as smooth as the Mare Crisium, and we could almost imagine that a sea of water and not of rock was lying there two miles below. Only a group of crater pits low down on the skyline spoiled the illusion.

Our goal was still invisible over the crest of the mountain and we were steering by maps, using the Earth as a guide. Almost due east of us, that great silver crescent hung low over the plain, already well into its first quarter. The Sun and the stars would make their slow march across the sky and would sink presently from sight, but Earth would always be there, never moving from her appointed place, waxing and waning as the years and seasons passed. In ten days' time she would be a blinding disk bathing these rocks with her midnight radiance, fifty-fold brighter than the full moon. But we must be out of the mountains long before night, or else we would remain among them for ever.

Inside our suits it was comfortably cool, for the refrigeration units were fighting the fierce Sun and carrying away the body-heat of our exertions. We seldom spoke to each other, except to pass climbing instructions and to discuss our best plan of ascent. I do not know what Garnett was thinking, probably that this was the craziest goose chase he had ever embarked upon. I more than half agreed with him, but the joy of climbing, the knowledge that no man had ever gone this way before and the exhilaration of the steadily widening landscape gave me all the reward I needed.

I do not think I was particularly excited when I saw in front of us the wall of rock I had first inspected through the telescope from thirty miles away. It would level off about fifty feet above our heads, and there on the plateau would be the thing that had lured me over these barren wastes. It was, almost certainly, nothing more than a boulder splintered ages ago by a falling meteor, and with its cleavage planes still fresh and bright in this incorruptible, unchanging silence.

There were no hand-holds on the rock face and we had to use a grapnel. My tired arms seemed to gain new strength as I swung the three-pronged metal anchor round my head and sent it sailing up towards the stars. The first time it broke loose and came falling slowly back when we pulled the rope. On the third attempt, the prongs gripped firmly and our combined weights could not shift it.

Garnett looked at me anxiously. I could tell that he wanted to go first, but I smiled back at him through the glass of my helmet and shook my head. Slowly, taking my time, I began the final ascent.

Even with my spacesuit, I weighed only forty pounds here, so I pulled myself up hand over hand without bothering to use my feet. At the rim I paused and waved to my companion, then I scrambled over the edge and stood upright, staring ahead of me.

You must understand that until this very moment I had been almost completely convinced that there could be nothing strange or unusual for me to find here. Almost, but not quite; it was that haunting doubt that had driven me forwards. Well, it was a doubt no longer, but the haunting had scarcely begun.

I was standing on a plateau perhaps a hundred feet across. It had once been smooth – too smooth to be natural – but falling meteors had pitted and scored its surface through immeasurable aeons. It had been levelled to support a glittering roughly pyramidal structure, twice as high as a man, that was set in the rock like a gigantic, many-faceted jewel.

Probably no emotion at all filled my mind in those first few seconds. Then I felt a great lifting of my heart, and a strange inexpressible joy. For I loved the Moon, and now I knew that the creeping moss of Aristarchus and Eratosthenes was not the only life she had brought forth in her youth. The old, discredited dream of the first explorers was true. There had, after all, been a lunar civilization – and I was the first to find it. That I had come perhaps a hundred million years too late did not distress me; it was enough to have come at all.

My mind was beginning to function normally, to analyse and to ask questions. Was this a building, a shrine – or something for which my language had no name? If a building, then why was it erected in so uniquely inaccessible a spot? I wondered if it might be a temple, and I could picture the adepts of some strange priesthood calling on their gods to preserve them as the life of the Moon ebbed with the dying oceans, and calling on their gods in vain.

I took a dozen steps forward to examine the thing more closely, but some sense of caution kept me from going too near. I knew a little of archaeology, and tried to guess the cultural level of the civilization that must have smoothed this mountain and raised the glittering mirror surfaces that still dazzled my eyes.

The Egyptians could have done it, I thought, if their workmen had possessed whatever strange materials these far more ancient architects had used. Because of the thing's smallness, it did not occur to me that I might be looking at the handiwork of a race more advanced than my own. The idea that the Moon had possessed intelligence at all was still almost too tremendous to grasp, and my pride would not let me take the final, humiliating plunge.

And then I noticed something that set the scalp crawling at the back of my neck – something so trivial and so innocent that many would never have noticed it at all. I have said that the plateau was scarred by meteors; it was also coated inches deep with the cosmic dust that is always filtering down upon the surface of any world where there are no winds to disturb it. Yet the dust and the meteor scratches ended quite abruptly in a wide circle enclosing the little pyramid, as though an invisible wall was protecting it from the ravages of time and the slow but ceaseless bombardment from space.

There was someone shouting in my earphones, and I realized that Garnett had been calling me for some time.

I walked unsteadily to the edge of the cliff and signalled him to join me, not trusting myself to speak. Then I went back towards that circle in the dust. I picked up a fragment of splintered rock and tossed it gently toward the shining enigma. If the pebble had vanished at that invisible barrier I should not have been surprised, but it seemed to hit a smooth, hemispherical surface and slide gently to the ground.

I knew then that I was looking at nothing that could be matched in the antiquity of my own race. This was not a building, but a machine, protecting itself with forces that had challenged Eternity. Those forces, whatever they might be, were still operating, and perhaps I had already come too close. I thought of all the radiations man had trapped and tamed in the past century. For all I knew, I might be as irrevocably doomed as if I had stepped into the deadly, silent aura of an unshielded atomic pile.

I remember turning then towards Garnett, who had joined me and was now standing motionless at my side. He seemed quite oblivious of me, so I did not disturb him but walked to the edge of the cliff in an effort to marshal my thoughts. There below me lay the Mare Crisium – Sea of Crises, indeed – strange and weird to most men, but reassuringly familiar to me. I lifted my eyes towards the crescent Earth, lying in her cradle of stars, and I wondered what her clouds had covered when these unknown builders had finished their work. Was it the steaming jungle of the Carboniferous, the bleak shoreline over which the first amphibians must crawl to conquer the land – or, earlier still, the long loneliness before the coming of life?

Do not ask me why I did not guess the truth sooner – the truth that seems so obvious now. In the first excitement of my discovery, I had assumed without question that this crystalline apparition had been built by some race belonging to the Moon's remote past, but suddenly, and with overwhelming force, the belief came to me that it was as alien to the Moon as I myself.

In twenty years we had found no trace of life but a few degenerate plants. No lunar civilization, whatever its doom, could have left but a single token of its existence.

I looked at the shining pyramid again, and the more remote it seemed from anything that had to do with the Moon. And suddenly I felt myself shaking with a foolish, hysterical laughter, brought on by excitement and over-exertion : for I had imagined that the little pyramid was speaking to me and was saying : 'Sorry, I'm a stranger here myself.'

It has taken us twenty years to crack that invisible shield and to reach the machine inside those crystal walls. What we could not understand, we broke at last with the savage might of atomic power and now I have seen the fragments of the lovely, glittering thing I found up there on the mountain.

They are meaningless. The mechanisms – if indeed they are mechanisms – of the pyramid belong to a technology that lies far beyond our horizon, perhaps to the technology of paraphysical forces.

The mystery haunts us all the more now that the other planets have been reached and we know that only Earth has ever been the home of intelligent life. Nor could any lost civilization of our own world have built that machine, for the thickness of the meteoric dust on the plateau has enabled us to measure its age. It was set there upon its mountain before life had emerged from the seas of Earth.

When our world was half its present age, *something* from the stars swept through the Solar System, left this token of its passage, and went again upon its way. Until we destroyed it, that machine was still fulfilling the purpose of its builders; and as to that purpose, here is my guess.

Nearly a hundred thousand million stars are turning in the circle of the Milky Way, and long ago other races on the worlds of other suns must have scaled and passed the heights that we have reached. Think of such civilizations, far back in time against the fading afterglow of Creation, masters of a universe so young that life as yet had come

only to a handful of worlds. Theirs would have been a loneliness we cannot imagine, the loneliness of gods looking out
across infinity and finding none to share their thoughts.

They must have searched the star-clusters as we have
searched the planets. Everywhere there would be worlds, but
they would be empty or peopled with crawling, mindless
things. Such was our own Earth, the smoke of the great
volcanoes still staining the skies, when that first ship of the
peoples of the dawn came sliding in from the abyss beyond
Pluto. It passed the frozen outer worlds, knowing that life
could play no part in their destinies. It came to rest among
the inner planets, warming themselves around the fire of
the Sun and waiting for their stories to begin.

Those wanderers must have looked on Earth, circling
safely in the narrow zone between fire and ice, and must
have guessed that it was the favourite of the Sun's children.
Here, in the distant future, would be intelligence; but there
were countless stars before them still, and they might never
come this way again.

So they left a sentinel, one of millions they have scattered
throughout the universe, watching over all worlds with the
promise of life. It was a beacon that down the ages has been
patiently signalling the fact that no one had discovered it.

Perhaps you understand now why that crystal pyramid
was set upon the Moon instead of on the Earth. Its builders
were not concerned with races still struggling up from
savagery. They would be interested in our civilization only
if we proved our fitness to survive – by crossing space and
so escaping from the Earth, our cradle. That is the challenge
that all intelligent races must meet, sooner or later. It is a
double challenge, for it depends in turn upon the conquest
of atomic energy and the last choice between life and
death.

Once we had passed that crisis, it was only a matter of
time before we found the pyramid and forced it open. Now
its signals have ceased, and those whose duty it is will be
turning their minds upon Earth. Perhaps they wish to help

our infant civilization. But they must be very, very old, and the old are often insanely jealous of the young.

I can never look now at the Milky Way without wondering from which of those banked clouds of stars the emissaries are coming. If you will pardon so commonplace a simile, we have broken the glass of the fire-alarm and have nothing to do but to wait.

I do not think we will have to wait for long.